BLACKJACK

BLACKJACK

LEE SINGER

FIVE STAR

An imprint of Thomson Gale, a part of The Thomson Corporation

THOMSON

GALE

Detroit • New York • San Francisco • New Haven, Conn. • Waterville, Maine • London

ALL RIGHTS RESERVED

Set in 11 pt. Plantin.

LIBRARY OF CONGRESS CATALOGING-IN-PUBLICATION DATA

Singer, Lee.
    Blackjack / Lee Singer. — 1st ed.
      p. cm.
    ISBN-13: 978-1-59414-597-1 (hardcover : alk. paper)
    ISBN-10: 1-59414-597-0 (hardcover : alk. paper)
    I. Title.
PS3619.I57244B57 2007
813'.6—dc22   2007008152

First Edition. First Printing: June 2007.

Published in 2007 in conjunction with Tekno Books and Ed Gorman.

Printed in the United States of America on permanent paper
10 9 8 7 6 5 4 3 2 1

For Paula

ACKNOWLEDGMENTS

The following people helped to carry and sometimes drag the author through this process:

Bette Golden Lamb and J. J. Lamb for a nudge at the right time and in the right direction; Mark Dahlby for being the best boss, sort of, that I never met; The Saturday Group for motivational feedback; Teresa Cambare for great mapmaking; and Don Gastwirth, for having faith.

OLYMPIA

NORTH

NEBRAS

SIERRA

ROCKYMOUNTAIN

REDWOOD

DESERT

TEXA

ALASKA

CALIFORNIA

HAWAII

COUNTRIES OF THE FORM

NEW ENGLAND

AND

ATLANTIS

LAKELAND

MIDDLE

BLUE
RIDGE

CAROLINA

DIXIE

FLORIDA

LOUISIANNE

MAP BY
cambare

ᴇʀ UNITED STATES 2066

CHAPTER 1
HUGGER MUGGER

I didn't have enough eyes to check out the horizon and my backside and the hills right and left, keeping a watch for bandits.

Iowa's rotten with them, especially along old Route 80. They often run in packs and tend to carry lots of stolen weapons. I had a car, money, guns, food, fuel cells, and a body. Female and not so old. Prime prey, or at least I looked that way.

Some of them just want money and don't care about the rest, a lot of them can be outsmarted; but I'd come too close to death a time or two. The last time I'd been careless enough to get waylaid I'd been lucky. The band of godders who stole my float-car and left me hiking over a mountain had been the kind who not only preached chastity for others, but practiced it as well.

In any case, even the milder sort could do enough damage to put a hole in my timeline, and there was a big job waiting out in Sierra and a possible short-term one on my way through Rocky. I kept my eyes open and my throttle ready to roar.

The gig in Northland had lasted just a few days. I was happy to be leaving, heading west toward home. Iowa in particular always felt more than normally foreign to me. So alien it made my skin itch, like the nasty August heat that stewed the green landscape even now, an hour after dawn, in heavy humidity. Strange accents, unpredictable people, unstable politics. The kind of craziness that meant well-paying work I couldn't turn down, but work that was always chancy. And sometimes left a long bad taste. Like this last job. Yet another new chief of the Northeast Iowa Quadrant, and he wanted me to spy on his sheriff. Should have been short and simple, but I'd ended up having to kill the sheriff before he got me. It turned out he was also the chief's brother, and the chief was not happy.

Messy and ugly. I don't like killing and I don't like blood. A handicap for a mercenary, but there it was. I'd be having nightmares for a while, dreams where the blood of that crooked sheriff was oozing from the eyes and ears and mouths of my parents. Once again, I'd be watching them die, night after night.

And of course, I hadn't gotten paid. So I was in a hurry to get to the next job and feeling itchier than ever about August in Iowa.

I cut south, to 92, figuring I'd follow it as far as it went, however far that was this month, and see how much trouble I could avoid. I was making reasonably good if bumpy time on that patchy mess of rubble when, just past an abandoned quarry, I saw a bowed figure, dressed completely in dirty green rags, limping along the side of the road.

A hugger. Like every other loony-group, huggers ran the gamut from peaceful dogmatic to moon-howling crazy. Unlike some, they tended not to be vicious, not so much these days anyway.

I passed him and looked back at him in the rearview. I didn't have to be on anyone's side to feel sorry for the bent old guy stumping along the road, slow, limping, way out there in the middle of nothing, his life tied up in a sack slung over his shoulder, his green rags flapping around him in the breeze of a coming thunderstorm.

I pulled over, tapped the horn, and waited.

I avoid causies, generally, but I liked the way the huggers wanted things to stay broken up. If you lived in a too-big nation, 3,000 miles away from a dying forest, they said, that forest just wasn't personal enough to matter. Smaller countries, they said, didn't make as much of a mess.

All of that was true, far as I was concerned.

There had been huggers before, during, and after the Poison. The most extreme huggers had been the first ones to hang toxies. But a few years into it, there were bodies hanging upside down from trees everywhere—toxies, terrorists, and innocent people that someone didn't like.

Gran said the whole world smelled like death.

That time's past. It didn't stink any more. There were still crazy people, but there weren't very many of them because there weren't very many people. There were some who called themselves huggers, and others who called themselves godders, and still others who said they were joiners and wanted the countries to grow again.

I'm not anything. Not a hugger, not a godder, and certainly not a joiner.

Joiner least of all. My work depends on things staying the way they are. Balkanized, Gran called it. Everything was easier to get to the top of, everybody had something close by to fight about, and local money paid to wade into the fracas could be traded elsewhere without too much trouble. And without caring too much about who won and who lost.

The hugger was nearing my car. I yelled at him: "Hey! Where you going?"

He caught up and smiled at me, his eyes crinkling to slits in his dirt-smudged no-color bearded face. Most of his teeth were gone.

"Going? Well, let's talk about it. About going." He leaned in the driver's side window, breathing stale garlic in my face, and began to shout a poem that sounded vaguely familiar, about taking the road less traveled by. Then he dumped some of the

13

contents of his sack into my lap. Food, rags, money . . . something that smelled bad. Okay. He was one of the crazy ones, spotty as a fever-dance. I opened the door and was busy tossing the mess onto the ground, so I didn't see the cars pull out of the quarry. Didn't know they were coming until I heard the nearby soft whir of their motors. Hadn't recovered from the hugger's assault on my ears, my nose, and my lap enough to pull away before they had me surrounded. Three cars. Four men, not counting the hugger.

A large blubbery hulk with a black beard, waving an ancient handgun, jumped out of the sand-colored car in front of me and swaggered up to the old hugger, who stepped aside, grinning.

"Shut it off, you." My mind was skittering all over the place and the adrenaline was nearly bubbling but I jabbed a thumb at the touch-key and the motor sighed to a stop. "That's a good girl. Now, we'll take your packs and your cell. And your money, of course."

"Of course." I began to reach for the gun I'd stuck under the seat.

He yanked open the car door, grabbing my arm. Too hard. "No, no, no, no reaching. Gimme your cash." He pointed at the wallet lying on the seat beside me.

I handed it over. This one held about a fifth of my money. I had three more stashed in the car, each with ID and health certificate. He took the bills out, looked at my ID, muttered, "Huh. Rica Marin. Citizen of Redwood. Big Deal."

"That's Marin," I said. "Accent on the second syllable."

"Who gives a shit." He slid the certificate out, stuck it in his pocket, and handed the wallet back, sneering. "Thought everyone out there owned a floater, so I hear."

"Not everyone," I said bitterly. Not anymore. I was hoping I'd earn enough on the next job or two to replace the one the

14

godders had jacked.

"Too bad. I could use one." The blackbeard reached in, felt around beside the seat, and pulled out the gun I'd been trying to get hold of. He grinned. Just an ordinary twenty-shot automatic, hardly state-of-the-art but a lot newer than the chunk of iron he was waving around. He jammed it into his pocket. That was okay. I had a few extra guns, too. He pointed at the button that unlocked the fuel cell. No good arguing; I punched it and slid it out of its slot under the dash. He grabbed it out of my hand and dropped it on the ground. I hit the switch that opened the back of the car. A couple of his scraggly-looking specimens began unloading the spare cell and hydropacks. The third, a skinny little man with greasy yellow hair, pulled two cans out of his car and began siphoning off my small supply of ethanol, insurance for the wide spaces where hydropacks could be hard to find, from the tank bolted to the floor. They'd probably drink half of it, I guessed, and convert some for power. But then I realized no one was bothering to unhook my alkie converter. So maybe they'd drink all of it. Too bad I hadn't filled up on wood alcohol instead. It would be a service to humanity to forget to tell them. And the thought of Blackbeard going blind or worse would have made me feel marginally better about my sore arm and aching ego.

Yellow-hair said something about the car, and Blackbeard shook his head. "Piece a shit. Not worth recutting the key." My little green '60 Electra was not a piece of shit. It could outrun the beer cans they were riding in. But I kept it looking bad so dummies like these guys wouldn't want it. Dented, paint-scraped, un-upholstered.

"What about the tires?"

"They're permies. We'll never get 'em off." They could if they really wanted to, but they weren't workers.

So far, so good. They weren't going to try to reprogram the

key and take Electra and they were too lazy to steal the permies. Up 'til now, no one had grabbed my boobs or stuck a knife in my ear lobe. No one was giggling insanely or drooling or groping himself or using me for target practice. I still had a car full of hidden weapons and cash. But spares and packs are harder to hide than wallets and guns, and they'd get them all. Could I appeal to Blackbeard's compassion?

"Come on," I said, watching the last of the packs hit the ground, "I'll be stuck out here on the road to nowhere." Could I reach the laser pistol stashed behind the passenger seat before he noticed? I let my hand wander in that direction.

Blackbeard shook his head. "Not my problem." He grabbed my wandering hand and twisted the wrist, reached back of the seat and pulled out the laser. He stared at it, his mouth hanging open to show a dozen rotted teeth.

"Where'd you get this, you some kind of chief?" He looked at me with a mixture of suspicion, awe, and hate.

"No. I had money for a while once."

He sneered and stuck the pistol in his waistband. "Where's your food?" So much for his compassion. I jabbed a thumb toward the insulated box under the back of my seat. I'd still have the dry-packs and water I'd stashed in the hollow bottom of the passenger seat.

Cells, packs, and the fresh apples I'd picked up the day before were now all sitting in the dirt; the greasy-haired runt was tossing booty into a sack. Blackbeard strutted around toward the back of the car. "Hugger!" He barked. "Take your share!" Damn hugger was a decoy. I should have guessed.

I closed my door, raising my hand uselessly and automatically toward the touch-key, dropping it back into my lap, staring at the hole where my fuel cell had been like I could make it reappear. I had one more weapon within reach, but I'd have to slide into the passenger seat to grab hold of it.

My left wrist was not working very well. I propped it in my lap and began to wiggle across the seat. Could I get to the gun, grab it, and shoot them all before any of them got me? Not much chance. Would it be smarter to assume these germs weren't planning to kill me? No, never assume. Especially, never assume that anyone ever plans anything.

The hugger was singing, dancing to his own tune. Dancing around the pile of booty and the runt picking it off the ground.

The song was a hundred years old at least. It was called . . . what was it . . . ? Oh, yes. "Imagine." "Imagine all the people . . ." something-something-something.

Blackbeard was squinting at me. He'd noticed that I'd moved to the other seat. I pretended I'd done it so I could talk to him better, leaning out the window.

"Can't you at least let me keep one spare?" I yelled at him. He snorted and stalked slowly back toward me. Maybe he was willing to negotiate, after all.

He wasn't. He grabbed my collar, pulled me half-outside through the window, and slammed his big pistol—not my sleek little laser—into the side of my head. A starburst of pain, but I didn't quite pass out, and weirdly, it occurred to me to be grateful that he'd hit a different part of my head than the car thieves in Rocky had. I felt a trickle of blood meander down my cheek. Damn. Blood again. Stomach turning, I reached up to touch the wound. Just an injury. Injuries heal.

He dropped me back onto my seat, his filthy hand closing around my throat. "I hate loudmouthed women." Then he laughed, showing those teeth again. "But I don't kill 'em, except when people pay me to."

That was nice to know.

"Even when they got red hair. I hate red hair."

I always liked to think of it as auburn, but I decided not to argue with him again. He still had hold of my throat; I reached for the last front-of-the-car pistol anyway.

"Too bad you're old and got red hair." He let go of my neck and walked away. I had my fingers on the gun but waited. If he came back, I'd shoot him.

They let the hugger take a spare cell and one hydropack—take them where? and did he have a weapon hidden somewhere in those green rags?—and loaded everything else into one of their cars and took off again, leaving the old crazy standing beside the road. Did they expect him to catch another fool that day? Not likely anyone else would come along. I hoped they rode out of the quarry and fed him once in a while. He was still singing. ". . . And no religion, too . . ."

Helluva headache. My throat hurt and my wrist burned. As the guffaws of the bandits receded, so did my pain and nausea; I tried to shrug it all off and turn my attention to the business at hand. Grabbing the gun, I pushed open the car door and stumbled, head pounding, to where the hugger stood, shoving his share of the booty into his bag. He had stopped singing, intent on his work, lips pursed. He glanced up at me.

"Nice new gun you've got there. Trade you back your stuff for a ride." His eyes shifted nervously between my gun and the quarry where his friends were no doubt already tossing back the hundred-proof.

"Give me the cell and put the pack in my car." He did as he was told. I slid the spare into the fuel-slot, while he dropped the hydropack in back and slammed the lid. Then he hoisted his foul-smelling sack over his shoulder and started to open the passenger side door.

"Take me to California. Dreamin'." This guy seemed to be celebrating the centennial of the Summer of Love—a year early.

"Not going that far, green-man," I lied, hoping he'd come up with a destination more like twenty-five miles into Nebraska.

"You have flowers in your hair." I didn't, but I was sure he saw some there. I waited. "Okay," he said finally, "Maybe another time." He turned and started walking toward the quarry, singing something about an American Pie.

CHAPTER 2
SO MUCH FOR LADY MACBETH

The summer landscape changed, gradually, from rolling green softness to hard, flat, far-horizoned prairie, from sheltered farms to stark brown ranches. I saw a lot of it through a gray scrim of heavy rain, navigating in black-cloud thunderstorms nearly all the way across Nebraska, wondering if I'd be seeing a funnel touching down any time soon. When I tapped into the netsys I kept under a flap of arm-rest upholstery, it three-beeped me, saying it was temporarily out of service. Which could mean anything from the next half hour to 500 miles from now or more.

By late afternoon, the rain was letting up, settling in to a steady dismal patter, but I was too tired to go any farther. My head had stopped bleeding but it still hurt, my eyes ached from the struggle to focus, my fingers had cramped so hard around the disk I could barely wiggle them. The brace I'd wrapped around my wrist itched.

Just west of the ruins of outer North Platte, I nearly missed a turquoise blue motel with cracked stucco and an almost-dead sign that said MO; I jammed on the brakes and U-ed back into its half-flooded empty parking lot.

The office was tiny and the mustard yellow paint was peeling off the front of the desk. Three taps on the bell brought a "Hang on!" from somewhere the other side of a faded red curtain. The woman who finally appeared, a skinny wrinkled sack with dyed red hair, didn't even look at the registration form after I filled it out with my name and car number and country of origin, and didn't ask for ID.

"You got any hydropacks?"

She shook her head. I wasn't surprised. "But my brother's got a still out back if you can run on that."

Might as well refill my alkie tank, just in case. "I could use some."

She opened a drawer and pulled out a big dusty, dented, ancient sys the size of my hand, punching a few buttons. I didn't hear a voice at the other end, but she yelled, "Carl! Customer!" She shoved the sys back into the drawer and told me he'd be right with me.

"Okay." That necessity dealt with, I added, "Any food?" I looked around the lobby. Not so much as a potato in sight.

"Got some soup left." She slouched off to the back room, returning with a screw-top mug of something that didn't smell too good. I took it anyway. As she handed it to me, our eyes met for the first time. There was anger and pain in hers, the look of a dog left tied up in the yard too long.

A door slammed and a male version of the motel clerk strolled out of the back room. He was wearing jeans that were brown and stiff with dirt and he hadn't shaved for a while. His hair was pulled back in a skimpy gray ponytail. From the look of his red nose, he'd indulged too much in his own product.

"You need some corn?" His teeth took up too much room in his small mouth and his protruding incisors turned the word "some" into a whistle.

He looked like the type who'd raise the price if he thought I was desperate. "Sure, if it's good enough."

"Pure sixty percent. Guaranteed." If he said sixty there was a hope of it being fifty, good enough to replace the barely adequate hundred-proof Blackbeard was probably busy throwing up.

"Okay. How much for a six-gallon tank?"

He squinted at me, his flat, pale blue eyes all but disappearing in the pouches around them. "Ten a gallon. That'll be sixty Lincolns."

"Make it forty-five."

He shrugged and jerked a thumb toward his sister. "Pay her." I handed over enough for the moonshine, the soup, and one night in the motel. She gave me a key. It was an actual metal key, rusty and pitted, must have been seventy years old or more. I slipped it into my pocket. Carl went back through the curtain again; in a few seconds, I heard something rattling around outside and went to look. He was pulling a big rolling tank up to the back of my car. I set my soup down out of the way and tapped the lock, watching while he screwed one end of a black hose into his tank, climbed in, started the siphon by sucking at the hose, spat onto my floor, and stuck the other end in my tank. When he finished, I checked the gauge. Full. I nodded. He made an odd, jerky half-bow and rolled his tank back around the side of the motel.

I slipped my sys out of the arm-rest slot and dropped it into my shirt pocket, retrieved my three remaining laser pistols and the charger from their hiding places, and grabbed the pack of necessaries from the back. Clean shirt, underwear, socks. Toothbrush, soap, comb. I shoved a bag of raisins and nuts from the passenger seat, along with the soup mug, into the outside pocket of the pack and slung it over my shoulder.

The kinks were slipping out of my muscles already and fatigue was easing into relief and a measure of cheer, despite the headache and the sore wrist. I wasn't proud that I'd killed a shoot-first-ask-questions-later sheriff or let a brain-rotted hugger wander back to his keepers, but I'd gotten out of Iowa alive one more time and was traveling west. That was worth a celebration. I stopped at the vender next to the ice machine and searched my wallet for more Nebraska paper. Wine? No, beer. I pushed the bills through the intake and poked at the LaCrosse button. A decent import from Northland. The can dropped into the catch-tray, bouncing hard and more than once before it settled.

I'd heard that someone up in Olympia, Seattle I think, was working on getting that dance bug out of the organic plastic. But then a lot of people were working on a lot of things. They were trying to put together a new web in Redwood, and I'd heard that someone way the hell out in Atlantis was working on it, too, but so far all we had was a ragged and rare mess of spotty egos spiking out of the West, nowhere near as far as Nebraska, and no matter how close I got to the East Coast I still couldn't get anything there except comlink email that didn't work half the places I traveled.

It took three tries to get the sticky lock open. The room had water stains on the ceiling but no drips that I could see. The bed was dry. The bathroom was spotted with mildew. A cheap fifty-year-old sys hung from the bedroom wall, a low-speed, unsecure clunker no better than a toy linked to TV, capsule player/recorder, and phone. I tapped its on-button. Dead. This motel could use a fixer. But then why would a fixer hang around here?

I set the bounced beer down to rest on the nightstand—I wanted it in me, not all over me—the food next to it, and my own sys beside that, and tapped the on-button hopefully.

"New Mail."

Hallelujah. Back in service. Most recent message:

An officious male voice said, "Rica Marin, by order of the . . ." The Iowa general was demanding that I appear in his offices by ten a.m. that day for questioning in the death of blah blah blah. Eight hours ago. Well gee whiz damn, I'd missed the appointment. If things stayed true to form he wouldn't be the Iowa general in a week, anyway.

As always, a message from Gran:

"Why does the mercenary cross the road? To get home, dummy. I miss you. See you after Sierra?"

I punched the talk-back:

"Yeah. Getting homesick for the fog."

She wouldn't expect more than that and there was no need to tell her about my day.

I damped the mike and shot the screen. The holo shimmied for a second and resolved, backdropped against the stains on the dirty beige wall. I needed to do some searching and I do that better with my eyes than my ears. Headers scrolled to the unread messages.

What I was looking for first was a message confirming a three-day gig in Rocky, a quick catch-a-bandit job for a local chief that I really wanted to do. He was offering a one-night acting undercover as Lady Macbeth at a Denver amphitheater that I knew attracted crowds of a hundred or more. A great gig. I'd always wanted to do The Lady.

No such luck. A short message from the chief.

"Godders wrecked the theater, bandits bribed my cops, I'm on my way to Desert. Phoenix I think. Maybe see you there some time."

So much for Lady Macbeth. Well, that just meant I'd get to Sierra and the Tahoe job sooner. I unscrewed the soup lid. Split pea. Sniffed close up. Not spoiled, anyway. I tasted it. Oniony, but probably not dangerous.

I realized suddenly that I hadn't let the Sierra chief know I was on my way. After a quick send to her, I scrolled to the earlier messages we'd lobbed back and forth. The case had grown vague in my mind.

It involved a group of people—a clan, really, mostly related—who Chief Graybel said the neighbors suspected of a conspiracy to grab some kind of power. They were accusing them of several different kinds of illegal activity: everything from skimming taxable profits to murdering the mayor of Tahoe to smuggling bootlegged vaccines to plotting secession from Sierra. Maybe even running antibiotic medicine shows to sucker the mountain people. They owned a casino called Blackjack, one of the two big ones left, and pieces of more little Tahoe shops than the chief could be sure of. Graybel said the matriarch, Judith Coleman, was very smart and very slippery. The cover job involved working in the restaurant but they were also looking for a singer and I might be able to negotiate a show a night in the lounge. Was I interested? That had been message one.

My answer: "Might? Negotiate? Send more data." I knew the pay would be good. Graybel was an old friend who never cut corners. But she was being awfully fuzzy about the rest. The answer had come back in a few hours. Blackjack needed a server in the restaurant. They always did. That didn't sound good. But they were opening a new lounge and were looking for a singer. The chief said she'd pass on the word that I could do both and she was sure I'd get a chance to audition. No promises about the lounge, but she'd gotten me a fake reference and had been willing to wait for me to finish the Iowa job, even spend a couple days in Rocky if that worked out; she offered me a bonus on completion, and we'd struck a deal.

By the time I'd finished the soup, dabbed some salve on my scabby head-bump, laid my stuff out on the dresser, checked the bed—nothing walking or crawling or hopping on the sheets—and opened my can of LaCrosse, the new mail icon was dancing through the air. First in line, the chief was responding.

"Good that you're coming, Rica. Go right to the casino and ask to talk to Judith Coleman. Your reference from Riverboat Queen's already there, waiting for you. It says you worked in the restaurant and sang in their lounge. Once you're in at Blackjack, the person you need to talk to first is Newt Scorsi.

The Scorsis own the other big casino. They're the accusers. Just keep in mind there's some kind of feud between the two families, so it's hard to tell what's really going on. Don't contact the local sheriff in Tahoe when you get there. He doesn't know about you and he may be tight with Coleman."

Fine with me. I'd had enough of local sheriffs for a while.

Sipping at the beer, I scrolled through the rest of the new headers. A couple of notes from friends. As usual, nothing from Sylvia. No answer to my last message. She was still hiding silently in her safe little house. Hiding from me down in that rash-spot village on the ass-end of Dixie, a million miles from anything.

I punched off and found a wall outlet that shot a spark at me but at least worked, plugged in my charger, and hooked the lasers up. No telling how much privacy I'd have on the job and I wouldn't stay undercover long if someone saw me charging a state-of-the-art laser.

I lay back on the lumpy bed. Nothing to do but think about where I was going.

A casino. Sounded like fun. The atmosphere, the sounds, the excitement. I'd done jobs in Sierra before and spent my share of time in the Tahoe casinos, but I'd never worked in one.

I finished the LaCrosse, unwrapped the wrist brace, and wiggled my hand. Much better. Back in the mildewed bathroom, I took a long cooling shower in rusty water, colder than my tears, singing a few torch songs for Sylvia. Including my own composition, "Every Day." I sang that one three times. "You're only memory and grief . . . I'll face the West and say good-bye . . ." But I knew I never really would. I wondered again if there was a difference between love and obsession, and whether it mattered if there was.

The rain stopped completely sometime during the night. I

woke up sweating in the silence, shreds of a dream forcing me out of bed to the light and the dresser mirror to make sure it was only sweat and not my life bleeding out of me. It took a while to fall back asleep and if I dreamed again I wasn't aware of it the next morning.

The motel offered stale rolls and weak tea, but it was good enough compared to what I had left: overspiced chicken jerky of doubtful safety and some hard grain bars that tasted like two-by-fours. I thanked the sagging woman, who never met my eyes again, and headed out in bright hot sunlight, west on 80, or, as they called it here, the Old Road.

I hadn't been driving an hour before I saw a big herd of wild cattle, must have been a thousand of them, raising the dust on the plain to the north. I was thinking, I'd hate to get in the middle of that. I heard once about a man driving through there when a plane flew overhead and spooked the cows. A freak kind of thing. I see a plane from time to time but they're about as common as bandits who can spell. Anyway, a traveler found the trampled wreckage a month later. Of the car and its driver. Hard to know whether stories like that are true, but I could certainly see it happening.

Gran had told me about how the cattle were turned loose in the Twenties when a steer was no longer worth the price of its feed. No people, no demand. And no people also meant they were safe, and multiplied, and it was said they'd soon compete with the growing herds of buffalo, covering the prairies like the waterfowl covered every pond and marsh. Food for the dog and wolf packs and the cats, calico to cougar.

All through Nebraska I saw one bus and maybe a half-dozen cars. A few people on foot, but I swallowed the impulse to help. I wasn't looking to fall into any more bandit traps.

I just couldn't imagine what things were like out there before the Poison. Cars all over this road. More cars than cattle. Buses, airplanes. People everywhere. They even had space ships. I'd heard rumors that there were one or two of those still around, hidden away by mythically rich people, used to hop continents. I doubted it.

Big countries, big money. Gran had lived with all of that. Big hatreds, too.

First it was terrorists blowing things up. They did that for years. Directed, organized, sent out of the Middle East and western Asia and the Far East, recruiting native-borns, too. Jihad. Right about the time that Holy War was getting a running start, scaring people to death, the other varieties of militant godders were getting stronger, feeding on fear, and viciousness did what it always does—got contagious. Jihadists on one side, the New Crusaders on the other. Bad laws. Riots. More fear, more murder, then came the bio- and chem-bombs. Cities. Water supplies. Food. The nuke-dirt hit in only a few places. Ohio and East Dixie. France. The Arabian Peninsula. Roaming vigilantes who were neither Jihadists nor Crusaders, only ordinary criminals. Far left thin-lips who wouldn't help a cop if he was trying to save their lives. Mobs of looters. Gran said it was hard to keep track, after a while, of who the terrorists really were. And the fact was, she said, that they just started the ball rolling down a hill already imploding with overpopulation and filth. Their kills were more deliberate than what the domestic toxies had been doing for decades, but the terrorists used whatever they could, including the poisons created in local factories, so it all came down to the same thing. Eventually, everything came down to dying.

It went on and on for years. By the end of the Twenties, when I was born, the world map, if anyone had tried to draw one, looked nothing like it had in the Teens. A few years into my life, nine-tenths of the people in the world were dead, including my parents. It didn't much matter whether all those people were gone because a terrorist exploded hyped-up dengue fever in the sky above a city or blew up a factory full of pesticide. Or because a mob set fire to a hospital full of carriers or attacked a price-gouging lab looking for vaccines and turned experimental "defensive" mutated botulism or plague loose. Or because a dirty bomb left nothing but irradiated death for miles around. Everybody was dying and it still hadn't stopped.

Memories of what the world was like before made Gran cry at the loss sometimes even now, and I would hold her and murmur and she would pat my hand, knowing I had flashes of baby memory that still left me shivering at night.

Despite the loss, Gran was glad enough to be alive. She was one of the last to escape when a mob of feverish, crazy, rash-covered carriers—they were calling them spotties by then—destroyed the county building where she'd been working, killing everyone they could find, even people who had no vaccines, no power, and no connection to either the black market or the labs. One of the rioters had brought a banner and hung it over the shrubs near the entrance. It said, "We Who Are About To Die Won't Go Alone!" She'd told me that story more than once.

Within sight of the Nebraska checkpoint into Rockymountain, a roar in the sky startled me. An airplane. Looked like a Gullwing Two, or maybe a four-seater. A rich man's ride. No cattle anywhere in sight, fortunately.

When I pulled up at the checkpoint, the tall blond border guard kept me waiting a full thirty seconds while he scowled at the plane that was getting by him unchecked and fast becoming a speck of tinsel in the west.

Annoyed by his futile rudeness, I snapped, "Maybe you should have shot him down." The guard turned his scowl toward me and demanded to see my health certificate, then demanded to know what I was doing so far from Redwood. By his accent, he was a native of Rocky. The edge of his speech was western, slow, drawling, full in the vowels. Rounder than the speech of the woman in Nebraska, fuller than the accents of the tight-lipped, sing-song Northland. I wouldn't be hearing "yah" anymore. I was well inside the land of "yup."

I told him I was traveling from one job to another. "I'm an actor. A singer." I handed over my Redwood Arts ID. The guard looked at the health certificate again, studied the ID, studied me. "I was working in Iowa." I hoped he wouldn't check on that part, but if he did, it wouldn't really matter much once he got tired of delaying and tormenting me. There was no extradition from Wyoming. "You can check with the chief—Graybel—in Truckee; she'll tell you I've got a legitimate job in Tahoe. I'm registered. And you saw my papers."

He snorted. "Why don't you stay in your own country?"

And why don't you go climb a tree, ape-man? "Performers travel."

"Yeah, I guess." He scowled.

I stood there, waiting for him to finish his posturing, wishing I could fly over his empty head in that Gullwing. Wishing I could afford one. He'd let me cross eventually. Rockymountain, Sierra, and Redwood had fairly friendly relations. Most of the time. At least this year, so far. When Rocky wasn't strutting too much.

Staring at me for a moment longer, he jerked a thumb in the general direction of the kiosk. I got out of the car and followed him.

"How much you got?"

I already had my wallet out, counting the rest of the scrip I'd gotten at the Eastern Nebraska border the day before. "Four hundred and sixty Lincolns."

"I'll need to take twenty percent for the exchange." Deadpan. Thieving bastard. But why bother to argue? Who would I complain to? I handed over the Lincolns and got their equivalent, minus twenty percent, in Rockie dollars.

The guard bowed slightly, mocking my justified suspicion.

"Thank you, welcome to Rockymountain, and have a nice trip."

I grunted back at him, got in the car and moved on across the border.

Driving went faster in Rocky. Fewer big holes in the pavement. A road crew was actually working outside Little Cheyenne, something I'd seen three or four times in fifteen years of travel. There were billboards, too, one every fifty or so miles now. They were all the same. A big color drawing of a mother, a father, and a baby, and four words: "For You—For Rocky." The Rocky president had ambition, people said. He was gathering power, pushing for population growth and talking about "securing the border." No one seemed to know exactly what all that might mean, but everyone outside of Rocky knew it didn't mean anything good. Stockholm had been working that "securing" line for years, busting through its borders on all sides. North Korea had hordes of twenty-year-olds grabbing chunks of South Manchuria, or so I'd heard. I wondered how big a horde was. How fast were they multiplying? How fast could Rocky grow?

I did sometimes wonder if fewer people were dying now. If they were, I didn't think it was because everyone had the vax; I knew that wasn't true. I'd heard it said that a lot of the hostels weren't full any more, and more of us seemed to be immune. But I didn't know how anyone could get real information out of a hostel, isolated and quarantined as they were, and that kind of thinking made me nervous. I would stick with the vax, keep getting it one way or another, thanks just the same.

A couple hours inside the border, I passed a ranch house that looked abandoned, glass missing from windows, porch roof collapsed, an old dusty car in the yard. But as I looked I saw that the place wasn't abandoned after all. A tall figure—man? woman?—stood in the yard, still, watching me. I looked back as I drove by, slowing, wondering if I should stop, and the person was turning, climbing over the porch debris and crawling back into the house through the open doorway.

In Little Cheyenne, I spotted a hydro station, bought a spare cell and all of their half-dozen packs, relieved that I wouldn't have to take a chance on Carl's corn this time around. A few more packs at Salt Lake and I'd have enough to take me all the way to Tahoe and more. The station store had bread, jam, real chicken on spits, and lettuce, beets, apples, and carrots. I bought a wheat loaf, apples, a chicken I'd eat for lunch and dinner, and a bag of carrots.

Electra couldn't do better than 100 easily, but I pushed myself to do a long day, driving two more hours beyond Salt Lake. I gave up just inside East Nevada, stopping at a half-demolished motel with no other guests. The next morning I'd cross the high desert. With luck and stamina, Sierra and then Tahoe that night, even taking my usual detour around Reno. Just one big trailer camp populated by killers and thieves. You could hear the screaming from a mile away.

But then I'd be there. A friendly border and a friendly currency exchange. I'd do better than twenty percent in Sierra. Damn Rockies.

CHAPTER 3
STARS AND STRIPES

Samm was dealing five-card stud at table two. When Jo walked up, a ten-high straight was taking the hand. The winner, a woman wearing a black jumpsuit with silver bugle beads around the cuffs, wasn't even smiling. Jo recognized her. Winning, losing, up, down, even, it didn't seem to matter. Her scarred face was frozen into inscrutability. A regular for the last couple of months. Jo had heard she was a fixer, maybe even that true rarity, a good one. Was it possible to get the elevator running again? And those sixty-year-old toilets on the third floor . . . The woman nodded to her. She nodded back.

"Come see me when you have some time," Jo said. "There may be work for you." The gambler smiled, the scar down her cheek a deep crease. Jo caught Samm's eye and he gave her a questioning look in return.

"Take a walk with me, Samm."

He nodded and turned toward the stocky, muscular dealer at the empty table three and raised his hand. "Zack!" Zack gave Samm a smile and a salute, stopped brushing lint off the green baize and took his place. Jo led Samm out the front door and into the warm night, the lights of Blackjack casino dimming and scattering the stars.

The people out on the strip glanced at the two of them, some with excited, glittering eyes, nudging each other, whispering, some with sidelong, sulky envy. Jo loved it. Loved the feeling of celebrity. The tourists looked at them and dreamed of living rich, of slot machines that always paid off. It was good for business and most of the locals were happy with that. Their leading citizens were stars and their town was an attraction. Of course like any attraction, it also drew those who were neither honest tourists nor job-holding locals, the ones whose thoughts were more primitive. The ones who made it dangerous to look rich and healthy.

She and Samm dressed and walked and probably—she smiled at the thought—even smelled like casino people. Jo with her bright blue brocade waistcoat, her velvet knickers, her sleek helmet of short dark brown and deep gold hair. Samm with his wide shoulders in the ruffled white shirt, his black vest, shiny boots, clever, exotic, angular olive-skinned face, and his well-brushed black and yellow hair.

A carefully cultivated glamour that made their status, their power, their wealth obvious. Outlanders and ordinary citizens tried to ape it sometimes, but it didn't work. They dyed their hair in stripes, but the stripes were never perfect. They bought expensive clothing but never looked comfortable, always a frayed edge, a tight seam somewhere. Some of the people at lesser casinos did okay, but nobody carried off the look like a Coleman, except for Samm, and if he wasn't blood, he was close enough.

Several locals nodded as they passed. Jo knew the nods were likely for Samm, a more public figure than she was and well-liked.

She touched his arm and got a warm smile in response. "Judith says you're getting restless."

"Restless? Yeah. I feel like we're never going to do anything but plan and bullshit."

She nodded. "You want war."

He didn't deny it. "We train and talk and train and talk . . . I'm tired of games and game plans. Pictures of war. My soldiers are tired of it, too. We need to do something real."

She shook her head, smiling. He caught the look and grunted, irritated. She wiped the smile away. He didn't need to be patronized, he needed to be accommodated. Samm was a born soldier, a sword that chafed in the sheath. His passion and daring didn't attract her any more, but she still loved him for it. He was a good man under all the swagger.

And beautiful. Those cheekbones. The dark almond eyes. Sometimes she couldn't help it, she remembered how they'd been, how long ago?—must be fifteen years now. Back when she was as restless and impulsive as he was. Like brother and sister, but not quite. Loving each other but feeling the discomfort of what almost amounted to incest. They were the same age, close since they were ten, lovers in their twenties. A long time ago.

He had never changed. He still played a rash game of poker; she observed and planned, loving the sly slow games of power and politics.

A shout behind them. Sam whirled around, took a step back. Just a man selling bread. She had begun to move forward again when a toothless bearded man dressed in filthy denim appeared out of the rubble across the street and jogged to the Blackjack side. She caught an angry, flushed look as his eyes flickered over the people around them and settled on her. He touched the knife at his hip, half-grinning. She glared back and touched hers. He swerved and disappeared inside a cheese shop. He'd find a pocket to pick tonight. The bandits and cutthroats who slithered in and out of the town knew the casino people carried no negotiable wealth except their clothing, but the bravest had been known to try kidnapping for ransom. The sheriff and his deputy and half-time help sometimes made a show of patrolling, but they weren't interested in risking their lives, not for anyone. Neither were most of the citizens. The cheaper life was, the more scared and selfish people were. One of those observations she'd tucked away early in life.

Samm caught up with her. He hadn't noticed the quick and silent exchange.

"We were talking," he said, "about war."

"We're not ready. Judith isn't ready. And war's not the goal. You know that." Jo's older sister was cautious, everything lined up and perfect before she'd take a step. Conquest, she always said, was like a rock rolling downhill. The right size, the right shape, the exact right course, and you get where you want to go. Any of those elements missing, you've got chaos, damned thing bumps around all over the place and stops halfway down.

Samm knew the plan. Consolidation was going to happen, it was inevitable, Sierra would get bigger. And the only way to be sure it grew in the right ways and for the right purpose was to be in charge of it. But Jo and Judith Coleman didn't want to do it with war. He knew that they saw the army as a distraction first, a deterrent second, and, only in extreme necessity, a cure. The real war was political, a war of spies and influence and social control. A slower way, possibly. But stronger in the end.

He knew that, and he agreed in principle. But . . . "You can't expect an army to sit around on its ass. They're getting hemorrhoids for Christ's sake."

She laughed. He grinned back at her.

"You need a day on the road, wear off some of that testosterone."

"Doing what?" He looked grudgingly hopeful.

"Sacramento. The first new vax batch is ready."

A lab down in Redwood, just outside of the old capital, had agreed to bootleg vaccine for them for a high price. It would do for now until they got something set up closer to home. If not in Tahoe itself then in Sierra, in their own country, and in their pockets.

He nodded, "Well, at least it's movement. Too bad I can't

take the troops with me." Jo could just see that. Fifty of them trotting down the western road. She grinned and he smiled back. "I'll go right away."

"Good. But don't go waving the stuff around in every tavern en route just so someone will try to take it away from you."

He laughed. "You know I never pick fights, Jo. I'll bring it home safe and sound."

If only she could send that aggressive energy to the Sierra Council. Or even to the local lame-duck Tahoe cabinet. But he had no interest in political office, which was a terrible shame with his looks and charisma. He would win any election, look and act and speak like the leader he was, charm the few citizens who believed votes counted as much as influence and money, and build a fire under the followers who would go along with any policy he endorsed. But he stuck stubbornly with his own passion, and even if the army was secondary in her plans, at best, he could put it together as no one else could. She wished she had three of him, and maybe an extra to take over for the dead Tahoe mayor. Poor bastard.

They walked around the corner and cut back through the Blackjack parking lot, half-filled with six-passenger buses and single- and double-passenger cars, the bright-colored plastic shining under the tall white lights.

He grabbed her hand. "Come with me."

There was that old heat again. He would never give up; it just wasn't in him.

"No, Samm. I've got a lot to do here."

He sighed, dropped her hand.

"I'll make sure your table's covered. Take off. Take care."

"Thanks. I'll be back by tomorrow afternoon."

"Take some time off. Carouse. I won't expect you until Thursday morning."

"Carouse?" He laughed. He gave her a quick cool kiss on the

cheek and turned toward the lot, heading for his own floater. Amazing. He didn't even have to go to his rooms to get a change of underwear. He was always ready.

Jo had been planning to send one of the cashiers on the mission. Someone not so conspicuous. She liked to keep Samm around, keep the triumvirate intact. But he needed to get away, sometimes. And although she always missed him, his occasional absence was also a relief.

She headed toward the building, slowly, reluctant for once to quit the evening air for the clangor of the casino. Was she getting tired? Was she the one who needed a road trip? Maybe she should have gone herself, just for the change of scene.

Her home shop stood like a bright dwarf among dead giants and burned rubble at the western end of the old strip. The old ones, Harvey's and Caesar's and Harrah's, had been built for a bigger tourist trade. They'd been built for a massive power grid, too. Those still standing were dark, left to crumble, the casinos closed. She wished she could either get them up and running again or just tear the damned things down like they'd tried to do in Vegas before they ran out of workers. People came to Tahoe for a good time; relics of the crowded past were too depressing.

Blackjack was wide and long and three stories high, bleeding light from every door and window, noise from every chink and crack. This had been a good season. Lots of people tossing their coins and bills into the slots, braving the tables, losing their money with the self-satisfaction of high rollers. And Judith always made sure there were plenty of winners, that Blackjack had the payoff rep, the word-of-mouth whisper.

Judith was wise and she was clever and that was why the Colemans owned Blackjack and pieces of the relics and of a couple much smaller independent casinos on the strip near Stateline. They had only one real competitor: Scorsi's Luck, opened thirty years before in a motel down past the old California line. She felt acid burn the back of her throat, felt her mouth twist in disgust. Scorsi.

Back to work.

She pushed open the rear door and strode through the bell-clanging and laughter, the shouts of the winners and the persistent, grim silence of the losers, back to Samm's poker table. The fixer was still winning.

She took the dealer aside and spoke softly. People might notice that Samm was gone on an errand but she didn't want to advertise it. He'd be vulnerable alone on the road. "Samm's off for a day or so, Zack. Table's yours. Put Emmy on for any shifts you can't cover until he gets back." The dealer nodded his orange and blue striped head, no questions, no comment. Just the way she liked it. Efficient. Perfect.

Judith's office was up on the mezzanine at the rear, next to Jo's smaller one. Jo had just touched the knob when the door jerked back and Judith's two kids came out, Lizzie pushing ahead of Drew, bumping into Jo.

"Watch it, kid," Jo growled.

At seventeen, the girl had passed through her sullen victim phase and now seemed to be caught up in a dominance game with her two-years-older brother. But not with her Aunt Jo. Lizzie mumbled an apology.

Jo waved it away, ruffled the girl's stripes, and stepped inside her sister's office.

Judith, holding a cup of that imported San Francisco black tea she liked so much, sat behind her six-foot desk, squeezed into her oversized and overstuffed green chair, looking like a beefsteak tomato sitting in its own leaves, big and round and powerful in her red dress.

"Want some tea?"

Jo shook her head. "Just wanted you to know Samm's gone

until tomorrow. Sent him to pick up the vax."

"Good. We'll have our treaty meeting when he gets back." Judith wanted the three of them to work out a phony "tactical peace treaty" with the Scorsi clan.

Jo laughed. "You think they're dumb enough to sign one?"

Judith chuckled, deep and warm. "Maybe. And if they are it'll throw them off balance for a while. Actually, it'll probably throw them off balance even if they don't fall for it."

"You do love your games."

"They're almost as good as yours."

Jo nodded. "Almost. By the way, Judith, I've got a fixer coming to see me. I hear she's good."

Judith looked pleased. "When?"

"When she has time."

They both laughed again. "Could be months," Judith said.

Jo shrugged. "Could be, but maybe not." She half-turned. "I'm going to talk to Waldo now. See you later."

"Good luck. You tell him from me I'm sick of losing the help because he's a lecher. Costs too damned much." She held up an index finger, scanning her desk. "Oh . . . wait, there was something . . ." She fanned a pile of papers like a poker hand and jabbed at one scribbled note with a blunt forefinger. "Yes. Riverboat Queen over on the Delta. Recommending someone who's heading this way in the next few days. They say she can wait tables and she can sing, too."

"Sounds good."

"We'll see." Judith yawned. "I'll let you check her out." She yawned again. "If there's nothing you need me for, I think I'll take a nap."

They'd both been up most of the night before talking business, trying to convince several good citizens to take on the newly vacated job of mayor. No one was interested; the last one's murder had made them nervous. Cowards. Of course, she and Judith had both considered running themselves but had ultimately vetoed that idea, at least for now. They needed to stay alive to move things where they wanted them to be, and as long as they didn't know who'd killed Madera, they didn't feel that they could or should take that kind of chance.

Jo assured her sister that there was nothing urgent Judith had to deal with personally, and trotted down the steps back into the main room. Some old guy had hit the jackpot on a nickel slot. He was hopping around like a puppy. Good. Good for business.

The dimly lit restaurant was beginning to fill up for dinner. Candles were burning on all the tables; the setups were in place. The server still on the job was moving pretty fast, but there'd be some unhappy diners that night.

Cousin Waldo was sitting in the kitchen under the big round pot rack that hung from the ceiling like a chandelier. He was playing Klondike on the wooden cutting board. Jo grabbed a chair and sat across from him. The two cooks were banging utensils, chopping vegetables, chattering to each other; steam rose from every pot and pan. The food smelled good, basil and rosemary and garlic, but the kitchen was hot and damp. She unbuttoned her vest.

"Waldo."

"Jo." He didn't look up. He knew what was coming. She thought about what she was going to say, studying the pink scalp that showed through the thin red and black hair on the top of his narrow head.

"Waldo, this has got to stop."

He looked up, then, his mouth set in a pout, his face flushed.

"I didn't do anything."

"Of course you did. We both know that. And we both know you'd be out of here if you weren't so good at your job." Meaning, if you weren't a Coleman and didn't know so much about the family.

"I put my hand on her shoulder, Jo!" Bullshit. The woman had been a good worker, and now she was gone, on her way to a job in Hangtown.

"Look, Waldo. We're going to hire a new server. Maybe another woman. And I want her to stay around long enough to pay off her costs. And that means you're going to keep your hands off her."

He shrugged, sighed, and looked sad. Poor misunderstood Waldo.

Tim, the senior waiter, now the only waiter, and Waldo's assistant manager, opened the door with his good hand and peeked in at them. The old man looked pale and tired.

"Waldo, I can't keep seating people and take care of my tables, too. It's too busy . . ." His words trailed off in a distracted little shrug.

Waldo swung his head around, "Well, maybe if you weren't such a damned sissy you could do the job. I'll be out there in a minute. Go back to work." Tim's face flushed, his eyes glittering with silent anger. The gray and black pompadour disappeared, the door closed.

Jo stared at her cousin. "You're an asshole, Waldo."

"Why, because he's got a withered arm? Crap. I've got a bad leg and I don't whine."

"The hell you don't."

Waldo glanced at his watch and stood up. "Okay. I better get out there now."

"Yes, you'd better. And if it gets any busier you're going to have to do more than manage and seat people." She knew he hated waiting tables and refused to do any bussing.

"Can I keep my tips, then?"

He was already overpaid. "No. Give them to Timmy. For calling him a sissy. For being a prick."

Waldo opened his mouth to object, closed it again, stood, and limped heavily to the door. Poor, overworked, underpaid, lame Waldo. How she wished there were a way to get rid of the silly son of a bitch.

CHAPTER 4
LIKE A FRIENDLY
BLUE MOON

"Nation of origin?"

"Redwood."

"Welcome, neighbor." She winked at me. Nothing like a tourist country for friendliness and more. "Let's see your papers." I handed them over. "Got any fruit in there?" The Sierra border guard leaned down, resting a tanned arm on the window frame, and glanced into the back of the car.

"No. Nothing." The dried stuff didn't count. Any bugs that had ever lived in those squashed bits of leather were fossils now and no danger to Sierra's precious orchards.

She took my word for it, straightened again, checked my ID and certs, yawned, smiled, and handed them back. "Currency?"

"Yes. A little." She opened my car door for me with a gallant flourish. I followed her to the blue and gold kiosk. Between the bandits and the Rocky currency exchange, I was low on cash.

The guard gave me an honest count in reals for my Rockies. We used reals in Redwood, too; the common currency was one of the strongest links in the Sierra-Redwood alliance. The name came from the Spanish word for "royal," but the pronunciation had changed when I was a kid to the English "real"—for the real thing. The real wasn't that much more stable than other countries' money, but Sierrans and Redwooders liked to believe it was.

I tucked the bills into my wallet and thanked the guard, who doffed her sky-blue cap and smiled back. Damn it was good to be in friendly country, among people who made sense, holding my own kind of money.

I suppose that some day, long after I quit being a merc and find another way to earn my vax, I might consider visiting a well-patrolled, close-to-home vacation village for pleasure. San Jose. San Francisco. Even Tahoe. But I'd been wandering for a living more than a decade and on the road with almost no breaks most of the past two years. Travel was exhaustion, hunger, loneliness, cold, heat, and deadly danger. I'd have loved to climb those peaks ahead of me and coast all the way home to sweet Redwood. But I couldn't do that yet. I had a job to do first, and money to make.

Just a short hop to Tahoe, now, from high desert to high Sierra, from tumbleweed to pine and Douglas fir and snowy peaks. I'd be getting there in time for dinner.

I flipped the toggle on the dashboard tune-slot and ejected the jazz capsule I'd been listening to, old stuff, re-recordings from the 1990s to 2020, uploading another I'd bought recently and hadn't yet opened. By a new group that was doing a revival of pop songs from the Teens. Right before the Poison. I'd never liked the stuff, but I'd heard it was going to be the next trend. Maybe they'd dug up some music I'd never heard. Maybe they had a slant on it that would show me I'd been wrong. I felt obligated to keep current with that kind of thing, anyway. Didn't want to be left behind if something really caught on. I couldn't afford to be.

After a hard five minutes, I decided that if this goop was the next trend, I was going to be out of style. Whiny and cynical and mean and stupid. Not even melodic—no, it didn't even have that.

I upped three of my favorites—older, newer, anything but Twenty-Teen—and was singing along with the last of them when the first signs for Tahoe started appearing at the side of the road.

I'd stopped at Blackjack for the night once, several years before, but I didn't remember much about it. The place was easy to find, just a half mile this side of Stateline. They'd kept the old street name for historical color, even though that state line hadn't existed for nearly fifty years. A few of the old clubs still rose smack against the line, the skyscraper face of a giddier time. Gran's youth. She'd probably played the slots at that one, braved the poker tables at the one across the street, spent the night with a lover somewhere in that burned-out stretch over there.

I parked in the quarter-full lot—they did a good business—and walked through the back door, strolling between the aisles of slots, past two poker games and a bank of three twenty-one tables, aiming for the sign that hung over the cashier's booth.

"I'm looking for the office."

The thin sixtyish woman studied me for a moment, her face blank. "Who did you want to see?"

I studied her in return. Her nameplate read "Willa". The gray stripes in her long straight hair were real, the dark ones solid with green dye. "Judith Coleman."

"What's your name?"

"Rica Marin. Here about a job."

"Lemme check."

She unclipped a sys from her shirt pocket, punched a couple of buttons, turned away, and mumbled something into the receiver. What could she possibly be saying, I wondered, that she didn't want me to hear? I guessed she was just another one of those people who either was suspicious and secretive all the time or made herself important by acting that way.

I turned, too, leaning back against the counter, and surveyed the room. No sign of a lounge anywhere, unless it was the dark room next to the restaurant, but it looked like there was a big enough crowd to support a show. At least one of the upper floors, I knew from that one visit, included guest rooms, and from the outside, all three floors had showed light.

Quite a few people were still wearing those crazy headstripes. Mostly dealers and other casino employees. Black stripes in light hair, light stripes in black. Maybe this time visiting, I'd give it a try. When in Tahoe . . . I'd look good with white stripes in my auburn hair. Or would black look better? But where was the lounge? I needed to see that.

"Go on up. Stairs over in that corner." I swung around to catch the gesture. "Up to the mezzanine. At the back. First door on the right." A lot of words, and good directions. She had decided I was okay. She was wrong. If she ever found that out it would give her one more reason to be suspicious.

The office door was open a few inches, but I rapped gently anyway.

"Come on in."

I pushed the door open all the way and found myself facing an enormous woman with striped gray-brown curls, sitting in a very large leaf-green chair behind an oversized wooden desk scattered with papers, some of them under glass paperweights. The front of the desk was edged with another two or maybe three dozen paperweights, all lined up like a wall around a fort, all of them snow globes. Little cabins in the snow. Snowmen. An igloo. A fairy princess, or maybe an angel. Yes, there were the little white folded-up angel wings. A tiny Blackjack casino with snow on the roof. She must have had that one specially made.

The woman was dressed in royal blue and wore lapis earrings that looked like small chandeliers and stretched the holes in her ears to half-inch slits.

"Rica Marin?"

I nodded. "Judith Coleman?"

"Sit down. Let's talk." Judith waved at a straight-backed wooden side chair with token cushions. I sat. She glanced at a handwritten note clipped to a single-sheet letter on the desk in front of her.

"So you heard we had an opening in the restaurant. Riverboat Queen says you're good." She tapped a thick, tapered finger on the letter. I would have loved to read it, but couldn't very well ask.

"I can do the job for you."

"It's not much of a job. Just serving."

Oh no, I wouldn't let her get away with that. "I heard you're also looking for a singer."

"Ah. Yes." She squinted at me. "You're a singer. That's right. So it says. What do you sing?"

"Anything you want. Torch songs, slow rock, blues, jazz . . ."

"The lounge is new. It isn't open yet. We need a server more." She hesitated. "For right now anyway. Until it opens. And I can't give you an exact date on that yet, I'm afraid."

"I can do both." I handed Judith a phony résumé, bumping my forearm against one of the paperweights on the edge of the desk. It didn't move. It seemed to be stuck.

Pushing the sheet of paper back at me across her wooden plateau, Judith smiled for the first time. She looked like a friendly blue moon. Against my will and better judgment, I liked her.

"Don't really care about a list of serving jobs or whatever you've done before. None of my business. The reference from the Riverboat Queen is enough. You go see Waldo in the restaurant; he'll put you to work, tell you what you need to know. I'll talk to my sister about an audition. She handles all that kind of thing. If you're good enough, you'll sing here, too."

"Is Waldo there now?"

Judith nodded. "Just look for the maitre d'. If you have to look too hard, he isn't doing his job." She chuckled at her own joke. Then she reached in her desk drawer and pulled out a new-looking plastic room key. "Here you go. For your room. Up on three. Part of the pay." That was a nice perk. "Now run along. Go see Waldo." With a wave and a grin, she dismissed me. I stood and began to leave—but couldn't resist a question.

Touching a finger to the paperweight I'd brushed against, a little winter scene with skaters, I asked, "Are these, uh, cemented to the desk?"

"For heavens sake, no!" Judith gripped the snowy scene and yanked. The globe came away with a pop. She showed me the bottom. "See? Suction cups. What good would a glued-down paperweight be?" She shook her head, implying that I was some kind of idiot.

The maitre d' was a pudgy man with a thick neck, heavy-looking legs and arms that he moved slowly, and black stripes in his straight, chin-length, dirty-blond hair. He was dressed in a plain blue suit with a short double-breasted jacket. I introduced myself.

"Well, I'm the man you want to see, all right. Waldo Coleman. Maitre d'." He seemed proud of both his name and his title. He nodded as if he were agreeing with himself about his job. "You say you've talked to Judith?"

"Just came from her office. She said you'd put me to work here in the restaurant."

"You bet." He grinned. His teeth were large and white. Despite the grin, his gray eyes stayed neutral and appraising. "Can you start now?" It was five o'clock. The place didn't look busy yet, but dinner time was fast approaching. Waldo was clearly eager for help.

An elderly server dressed in black, the only one I saw, hovered at a table nearby where two customers sat studying big menus. He was small, his shirt's overlong sleeves half-covering his hands.

"Is that what you want me to wear? I don't have a black shirt."

"White's fine. With black pants. Got some?"

"Yeah. In the car. I just got here half an hour ago. From the Delta." No harm in repeating the lie. "Haven't gone up to my room yet."

"Plenty of time for that later. Change in the ladies'. Just outside the door on the left."

I hadn't planned on starting work instantly, but I couldn't beg off by saying I'd been driving for ten hours. The Sacramento Delta, and the riverboat I'd supposedly worked for, were no more than a couple of hours away.

I told the grinning Waldo—well, at least he was cheerful—that I'd get the clothes, change, and be back inside twenty minutes.

Fifteen minutes later, dressed in white shirt, black pants, and soft, sturdy shoes, I began working the all-but-deserted five-table station at the back of the room.

The work wasn't hard. For the first couple of hours, until around eight, only three of my tables were occupied at any given time. Tim, the gray-haired senior waiter, said it would probably pick up later.

"Sometimes on weekends, it's really—well, you'll see. People come from all over. I had someone yesterday who said he came from Northern Redwood, up in Oregon, but I don't know if I believe that. People will tell you anything." He sighed, then patted my arm, just the way Gran does. I felt a rush of affection for him, and a touch of homesickness.

"I have to say I'm sure glad you're here. After the last one quit I like to worked myself to death, honey, let me tell you!"

I started to ask him why he or she had quit, but I couldn't

50

get a word in. Tim rattled on.

"Oh, my god, what am I thinking of? Here, I'll carry that."
He reached for the tureen I'd brought out of the kitchen.

"No, really, Tim, that's all right." I held tight to the hot soup.
He pulled his hands back, but shook his head. "You should
let me help."

"You've done enough, Tim." He'd helped me set up, made
sure the busboy took good care of my tables, told me about the
customers he knew, and generally had made a helpful pest of
himself. Sweet old guy. About Gran's age, too. I wondered if
they'd like each other.

"But you look so peaked, honey. First night on the job, I
understand how that can be." Peaked? A little tired, a little
hungry, but peaked? Did I look that bad? At that moment my
stomach growled loudly enough to startle Tim and remind me
that I'd had no dinner. I mentioned the problem to him. He
told me to sit down, take a fifteen-minute meal break, and he'd
bring me a sandwich.

"Then I'll just get right back to work," I promised.

"Well, okay, but I don't want to lose you." He glared toward
the kitchen. "Just be sure to stay away from Waldo, honey. Okay?
I'll put in that sandwich order for you now." He swept away to
the kitchen. Stay away from Waldo? What did that mean?

I was serving a half-drunk party of two at about eleven o'clock
when a pretty woman wearing knickers, black stockings, and a
ruffled shirt came in, caught Waldo lumbering between the
kitchen and the entry, and spoke to him. He nodded and
waved me over.

The woman watched me coolly as I walked across the room.
I had been stared at by much less interesting people, but I
wasn't intimidated by the scrutiny, I was intrigued by it. She
had nerve. Maybe even power. Pretty didn't half describe her.

She glanced at Waldo. "You can leave us now." He scowled and walked back to his station by the door, where a pair of customers was waiting to be seated. She turned back to me. "I'm Jo Coleman. Judith's sister." Ah. She did have power. Lots of it. And warm brown eyes. And a soft, deep voice. Not as deep as Judith's. Softer. "She tells me you're going to be working here." I nodded. "And that you want to sing for us, too."

"Yes, I do."

"Are you any good?" A challenging half smile. I smiled back, agreeably, with less challenge, allowing Jo to be alpha bitch.

"I'm very good." Our eyes locked for a second before I looked away. I could feel heat rising to my face.

"When is your shift over?"

"One o'clock."

"Fine. Meet me in the lounge." She waved her hand in the direction of the unlighted room I'd noticed earlier. "Sing something sad."

A slight nod, the smile only in the eyes now, and Jo walked out. This time, I was the one doing the watching, and I wondered if she knew it.

CHAPTER 5
RIGHT DOWN TO HER
VELVET KNICKERS

The restaurant salary was standard, which Chief Graybel had already mentioned and which meant it was low. But I discovered in the first few hours that the tips weren't bad, and it turned out that Blackjack was a very good employer, better than most. The free lodging brought the pay up to more than reasonable. Drew, the busboy, mentioned in passing that people who stayed past six weeks got benefits worth more than the pay—vaccines, certificates, and yearly boosters. Neither Judith nor Waldo had mentioned that. Stupidly, I'd never thought to ask about benefits at all. Someone really looking for work and expecting to stick around would have. Maybe I'd been so overwhelmed by Judith's snow globes, or by Judith herself, that I'd forgotten the drill. I'd have to do better. A distracted merc is a dead merc.

Timmy confirmed the vax.

"It's one of the things that's kept us working here." He sneered in the general direction of Waldo, who was seating a man and woman at one of Tim's busy tables. The place had first started filling up around eight, just as Timmy had predicted it would. And now, after eleven, people were coming in for a late supper. Timmy grabbed a couple of menus from the host station. "That and the free rooms. A suite because there's two of us."

He had now used the word "us" twice. "Us?"

"Me and my sweetie Fredo. You'll meet him later."

Well, he and Gran could still like each other. "I guess you and Waldo don't get along?"

He snorted and shook his head. "We get along. I do what he says and ignore his nasty self."

Tim went off, menus under his arm, before I could ask more. And although we spoke briefly on and off through the rest of my shift, I never got a chance to hear more about the "nasty self."

I had guessed the place probably closed at one, but when Timmy told me they stayed open through the night I thought it must be the most popular eating spot in Tahoe. Or pretty much anywhere.

"It's really busy all night?"

"No. We can get good crowds up 'til two or so but it's pretty darned dead by three. Judith wants to provide the service anyway. She's very smart, you know." I was beginning to see that. She kept the restaurant open all night for a dozen diners, but if those dozen diners were up all night gambling, and they gambled enough, the place more than paid for itself. Blackjack not only stayed in business, it built its rep as an old-style always-hot casino.

Fredo, it turned out, was my relief. Just before the end of my shift, when I was pushing hard to cover my filled tables, Timmy mentioned that he wished Waldo would let Fredo start after three a.m., when things were really quiet, because he had a tendency to fall asleep.

I thought that was funny, but only until I realized it was one o'clock. Then I got nervous. Had he fallen asleep before he even got to work that evening? By the time he tottered in, ten minutes late, I was tense with waiting, sure that Jo expected me to be exactly on time for our meeting in the lounge. And I had to pee.

"You're late," I snapped, handing him a plate I was carrying to table twelve.

He shook his head, dislodging the few hairs he'd combed across his nearly bald head. "Well, aren't we cranky?"

"Yes. We are."

He shook his head again. I could have sworn his big ears flopped, but that was probably just hallucination. I was exhausted. The long drive, the long evening, and a performance still to come.

"Sorry, princess." He seemed to mean it. Guilty, I mumbled and shrugged, and he smiled, taking my inarticulate response for the apology it was. He balanced table twelve's steak plate on his palm and set off slowly across the room.

Trying to gather my energy, I made a quick stop at the restroom and leaned for a moment against the sink, closing my eyes. I saw lightning in Nebraska, sunlight in Nevada, and long miles of road passing under the car. I felt my chin drop to my chest, shook off the half dreams, and splashed cold water on my face

I'd just have to keep my eyes open while I was singing.

The lounge was definitely under construction, but at least someone had turned on a light, a temporary-looking globe that dangled from a beam and washed out the shadows and contours. The room stank of fresh paint. Jo was sitting on the edge of the small stage at the far end of the room, drinking a glass of red wine. I walked toward her. She wasn't smiling. Two tall stepladders stood against a wall. One row of spotlights lay on the floor near them, wires trailing, another was attached near the ceiling to the left of the stage.

"Sorry I'm late, I—"

"Never mind." She waved a graceful hand at the stage. The steps to it were unfinished, missing the last two treads. I made the stretch. Jo moved to the back wall, flipped a switch, and the room was dark. She flipped another one and a single spotlight lasered through the darkness to blind and illuminate me. On the stage, in the spotlight, dressed in old black pants and a white shirt with beet stains on the sleeve, I felt underdressed even for a construction site.

"Sing, Rica."

Jo had said she wanted to hear a sad song. All evening, waiting tables, I'd leafed mentally through my repertoire. There were a few good new sad ones; I'd picked up a couple in Middle a year or so ago, in a village on the Mississippi. But the mid-Twentieth Century was enjoying a romantic revival these days, in Redwood and probably in Sierra, too. Jo might follow the fashions in music, as well as in clothing and hair, and somehow I didn't think she'd be inclined toward Twenty-Teen, so mid-Twentieth seemed right. I had settled first on "I'll Be Seeing You," rejected that as possibly too hopeful, and veered briefly toward "I'll Walk Alone," before I decided finally on the torchiest tragedy of all—"I Wish You Love." I'd heard Marlene Dietrich's version of that once on a remake of a very old disk. Dietrich was legend, a god of torch. The song bled tragedy.

Picturing Sylvia's sad good-bye face, tight with held-back tears, and breathing deeply to relax and call up reserves of energy and passion, I sang. By the time I got to the bridge— "my breaking heart and I agree"—I was deep into the song, knowing it was right, sure the performance would touch a chord in my audience of one if Jo had ever loved anyone at all and lost for whatever reason. My exhaustion didn't get in the way, it carried the message.

I sang into the darkness beyond the glare, and when the song was done, dropped my head, my arms, my shoulders in a spent bow that I hoped looked humble. And waited.

A second passed. I held my breath.

The sound of two hands clapping.

"Brava, Miss Rica. Brava." The spotlight went out, the ceiling globe came back on, Jo was walking toward the stage. She reached her hand up, helping me down.

"Lovely. Damned near broke my heart. I hope you're not really that sad."

"Well—"

"Never mind. The room will be finished, we think"—she emphasized the "think," raising one dark eyebrow to show that the workers were perhaps not as efficient as she might have wished—"in three days. Be ready to do an hour. We'll reschedule your restaurant shift around it. Does that suit you?"

If Jo, perfectly groomed right down to her velvet knickers, said an hour, I thought, she meant exactly an hour.

"Suits me fine. Thank you."

She glanced at the beet stains on my shirt. "Guess we'll wait until tomorrow to take a photo." She shot me a quick smile to soothe the sting of that. "I'll set it up. Probably around noon. Wear something gorgeous."

We talked about pay, and it wasn't bad. Another hundred reals a week. Adding it to the restaurant gig made a living wage.

"Are you vaxed?"

I thought about saying no, to conceal my income. But then she might have gotten nervous about my health. "Yes." She didn't show any reaction at all.

"Did anyone tell you?—if you stay here, we'll take care of your boosters."

"You're generous, Jo."

She grinned, showing a dimple in her left cheek, a dimple that seemed to be out of character somehow. I wasn't sure I liked it. Too cute, maybe. "Yes, I am. And so is Judith. You look tired. Go to bed. I'll let you know when and where on the photos. And when you'll be starting. Exactly."

We walked out of the lounge together, not speaking. With a

little salute, Jo turned off and headed toward the mezzanine and Judith's office. I was on my way to the back door, planning to grab what I could from my car in one trip, when I heard a commotion from the direction of the front of the casino. Yells, cries, metal crashing, glass shattering. Shots and the sssst of lasers! As I ran to the end of a row of slots to take a look, Timmy the headwaiter dashed by, shrieking, Fredo behind him, part of a crowd running for the back door, right toward me.

Behind them, two big ugly men, heads shaved, dressed in heavy black boots and jackets, one of them clutching a broken chair from the restaurant, the other waving a laser pistol, were shoving their way toward the wide aisle, where they joined a stream of a dozen more just like them crashing through the front door, knocking people down, pushing them aside, blasting holes in slot machines, roaring like hungry cougars. I stepped aside, out of the traffic, half-concealed behind a slot machine. What should I do, run with Timmy and the others?

Customers were dashing in all directions, screaming; some of them were bleeding. One man, apparently not in the mood to run, grabbed his beer bottle, broke it against the bar, raced between two rows of slots to the wide aisle and lunged for the invader with the chair, who brought it down hard on the brave customer's arm. He shrieked and dropped to the floor, but got up again and fled. I saw a middle-aged woman in a flowered dress half-sitting, half-lying against a poker table, holding her right wrist, eyes wide with shock; her shoulder looked wrong; dislocated, probably. I went to her, helped her to shelter behind the bar.

"Someone will come to take care of you," I said. She nodded and I turned and looked back at the melee, hoping I'd find a way to make good on that promise.

It wasn't going to happen any time soon. At least three of the marauders were armed with guns like mine: new and effective, capable of stunning or killing. One was waving a large blade-studded club wildly in sweeping, bloody arcs as wailing customers tried to run past him out the door, tried to huddle under tables or hide behind machines. Two of the bandits doubled back for the cashier's cage on the west wall, jumping the counter. Robbery? Was this whole thing about robbery? Two dealers jumped the counter after them, fighting beside the cashier.

What was I going to do? Wade in, start beating them off? I stood there, undecided, adrenaline firing my weary cells, afraid to show I could fight, even more afraid to show the new, very uncommon weapon I had tucked in my boot. I was supposed to be a waitress, a singer, not a soldier, a cop, a merc. I seemed to be out of the way of the path of destruction, but how much of this could I watch before I had to pull out my pistol and start burning holes through ugly shaved heads? And how would I explain that? Innocent people were getting hurt and I was crouched behind a bar like a victim. I was holding myself so tightly my neck cramped.

Shouts erupted from the back hallway, access to the stairs and elevator. A tall man with black and yellow striped hair came charging through, leading a gang of half-dressed men and women—all of them, I guessed, employees pulled from their beds to defend the turf—on a collision course with the invaders. He had a gun, I couldn't tell what kind, and some of the others were carrying knives and guns, too. The young busboy, Drew, was with them, racing into battle wielding a cleaver. When they passed, I stepped out into the aisle and grabbed Drew's shoulder.

"Who . . ." I started to ask.

Drew pulled away, glaring, his eyes wide with excitement and fear.

"Dunno! Bandits! Mercs!" he yelled back at me. Mercenaries? Could be. There were some who didn't rely on brainpower to do their jobs. Thugs. The kind who liked to say, "Merc don't stand for mercy."

But if they were more than just bandits, who did they work for? I might have been sent there to spy on the Colemans, but I hated standing by and watching their casino being attacked by guys who looked more like the enemy than they did. I couldn't stand it any more. I was just reaching into my boot for my laser when Jo, a laser pistol in her hand, raced down from the mezzanine, followed by a wild-eyed teenage girl who seemed to be unarmed except for what looked like one of Judith's paperweights clutched in her right hand.

Jo caught up with the tall man's group just as Drew, howling like a dog, threw himself onto a wildly shooting merc. The boy went down, still howling, the cleaver dropping from his hand, red blood spreading across his shirt.

CHAPTER 6
ABOUT TIME YOU GOT HERE

Jo was pointing her laser at the broad khaki backside of a retreating enemy but she forgot all about that target when a gut-piercing shriek spun her around, eyes searching desperately for the source of the cry. Lizzie, young Lizzie, still screaming, had dropped to her knees beside a black-clad body, reaching for a cleaver near it on the floor. A merc stood only a few feet away, taking aim at Lizzie.

Racing toward him, Jo stumbled over the leg of a broken stool as she fired, only grazing his thigh, but it was enough of a distraction to turn him toward her. Before either Jo or the merc could shoot again, Liz had flown at the invader and chopped him across the neck, dropping him in a wide spray of blood.

And the man on the floor—wait a minute. Drew! Dressed in his restaurant black. Jo lunged toward him through a red tunnel of rage. Shouts near the door cleared the haze and pulled her eyes back toward the battle, tearing her in two. Samm, fighting hand-to-hand with two mercs, one of them huge, bigger and heavier than her six-foot-three general. She forced a deep breath, swallowed her sickening fear for Drew, raced to clear-shot range and burned a hole in the giant's chest. By the time she turned again toward her niece and nephew, Lizzie was back at Drew's side, bloody footprints marking her trail from the dead merc back to her brother, and that new singer, Rica, was reaching down to Drew.

Yes! He was shaking his head. Moving.

Jo exhaled.

Alive, then.

He waved Rica away and began trying to get up on his own, blood dribbling down his arm. Maybe not hurt too badly after all.

Jo focused again on the sounds behind her, the hiss of a laser, the pop-pop-pop of an old pistol, a man screaming, something heavy crashing metallically into something else. Thick glass breaking. A merc ran past her with a big overfilled sack dribbling reals. She shot and winged him, but he kept on running. Damn! Pulled between what was left of the battle and a desire to touch Drew, speak to him, assure herself, she looked around, desperately, and noticed Waldo peeking out from behind a slot machine.

"Waldo! Go help Drew. Now!" Waldo came creeping out into the aisle, his eyes wide and fearful. Drew was on his feet, sagging in Rica's arms; Lizzie was watching him uncertainly, her outstretched hand shaking. "Get him upstairs!" Waldo picked Drew up and tried to hoist him across his wide shoulders.

"Put me down, you asshole!" Drew screamed, struggling out of Waldo's thick arms and falling to his knees with a grunt of pain. Rica was right there, taking his good arm, trying to help him to his feet.

Samm and the others were backing the mercs out the door. Not counting Drew, six people down that she could see: two customers, three mercs who were dead or unconscious, and over there, by the poker tables, a cashier, holding his bloody head and crying. The last merc out the door aimed at Jo, missed, and hit a poker slot slam in the screen.

The battle seemed to be over. Samm turned around, flushed, tense, eyes bright, scanning the casino; looking for someone more to attack. There was no one. They were gone, leaving a mess of blood and broken machinery behind them. His body relaxed, shoulders slumped. Jo caught his eye and he straight-ened up again, nodding in acknowledgment. Showing her he was ready to deal with the cleanup.

Always the soldier, just as she needed him to be. Because she certainly wasn't one. She'd done a lousy job of defending the casino. Too smug, too cerebral, she thought, to think she might ever have to actually engage in a fight. No dirty hands for her. Well, she could do a little better. She could at least keep up with target practice.

It was a lucky accident that Samm had returned from Sacramento in time for the battle. She hadn't expected him until the next morning. Then she had an unnerving thought: time. She'd been thinking there was time, that she could plan and prepare and work on her own timetable. Make her moves when her people were ready. But today the choice of when and where and how to fight had not been theirs. Bandits? She doubted it very much. Bandits weren't usually that clean, didn't usually wear shiny boots. Sure, they'd gone right for the money, but why not? No rule that mercs couldn't steal. If the Scorsis were behind this—and who else could it be?—it was a major escalation in their rivalry when the Colemans were trying to hold the line. And yet another thought: Had they known that Samm was on the road? Had they also not expected him back so soon?

"Drew!" Her sister's deep voice. There came Judith, cruising down the mezzanine stairs at low speed like one of those big old ships you could tour in San Francisco Bay for five reals. Jo went to meet her.

Lizzie had returned to the dead merc with the cleaver in his neck. Staring at him, she vomited suddenly into the wide pool of his blood. Drew was on his feet, Waldo dancing around him ineffectually. Rica, her hand light on Drew's good shoulder, was saying, "You really should let Waldo take you upstairs. You need to lie down and you need a doctor." Had Rica been there from the start of the battle? She hadn't seen her taking part in it, but it had all been over very quickly and she was new, after all. Probably confused by the mayhem and by who was fighting whom. And probably not a fighter. Not muscular, not particularly tall.

Jo reached Drew a moment ahead of Judith. She brushed hair out of the boy's eyes, touched his cheek. He raised his eyes to her. "Rica's right, Drew. The battle's over. Go upstairs. Go to bed." She glanced at Rica, who had backed away a couple of paces. "Thanks for helping him." Rica nodded.

Judith looked hard for a moment at Drew, then at Lizzie, and then glanced over the battlefield.

Samm and Monte, the head cashier, were searching the corpses of two mercs. Samm looked over toward Jo and Judith and shook his head. Nothing on the bodies that told them anything about the raid. No IOUs from Newt Scorsi, she thought wryly. A cleaner and a young change guy were carrying the cashier with the head injury, stepping over another merc's body where it lay in the shards of the shattered door. Willa was talking to an injured customer who was peeking around the end of the bar, probably reassuring her that Doc was on his way. Lizzie turned from the man she'd killed, bumped into a customer blindly dashing for the exit, and stumbled against Jo, who wrapped a supporting arm around her.

"It's okay, Lizzie. You saved my life, and Drew's." Jo knew it wasn't okay.

Judith and Waldo together were leading Drew toward the hallway. It wouldn't be easy getting him up to his room. Damn elevator. Where was Rica? Over there, helping Zack move a broken slot machine. Waldo turned and called out to Lizzie. Jo said softly, "Go upstairs now with your brother."

Lizzie shook her head. "Rather stay with you."

"All right." What else could she say to that?

"I've never killed anyone before."

"I know. You had to." Jo was twenty years older than Liz, and she'd never killed anyone. She'd never had to. She almost wished she'd been able to, today. No, not almost. She did wish it. Now Lizzie was carrying the burden for both of them.

The last of the ambulatory customers, a few with scrapes and bruises, some of them glancing at the shivering, staring, blood-spattered teenager, stepped gingerly around the dead and injured, through the breakage, and out onto the street, headed, undoubtedly, for safer shops. Probably Scorsi's.

Jo and the young girl had disappeared; the beautiful tall olive-skinned man was directing the cleanup. The woman with the dislocated shoulder was wearing a sling; someone had found her a chair.

The way the employees fell to, sweeping up debris, removing the dead, and tending the injured, I wondered for a moment if they were used to this kind of thing. The chief hadn't said the feud had turned to war. Maybe she didn't know, or didn't care. But the stunned looks on their faces and the scared, shocked conversational bits I picked up led me to believe this was all a surprise. A couple of people I recognized as cleaners were posturing and laughing together, but they were breathing hard, shaky, and damp with sweat. I heard speculation about both "bandits" and "mercs." I heard anger that anyone would do this to their casino and I saw a determination to make everything right and get the customers back in the doors.

I followed the lead of the others, righting some of the fallen machines, taking an offered broom. A young woman and a man were sweeping glass nearby, rehashing the attack. The woman said it started with a ruckus in the restaurant. I remembered hearing a lot of noise coming from that direction at the start.

Two raiders, she said, had run out of there and nearly collided with their pals coming in the front door.

"Must have been trying for a diversion," her large, bald friend said. "Get a fight going in the restaurant, come in, and take the place easy. What do you think, Emmy?"

The woman agreed. "Yes. But their timing was off or something."

Maybe just too eager to start the main event, I thought.

I helped Willa, who was trying to bandage a cut on a friend's arm. Her hands were shaking and she kept dropping the tape. She'd given me directions to Judith's office just that afternoon, but it seemed like days before. A man in a gold jumpsuit with white braid stood near the back door, staring, it seemed, at nothing.

Bending over to collect a mound of chips that had fallen off a blackjack table, I felt someone stick a hand in my hip pocket.

"Hey!" I grabbed the hand, swinging around, ready to bash the bastard.

"No, no—look in your pocket." He was whispering, peering around furtively. No one was looking at us. I let go of his hand. He was one of the change guys, dressed in change-guy red, a pale flabby man who managed to look soft and scrawny at the same time. His nameplate read "Bernard." He edged away again before I could say anything.

What he'd put in my pocket was a short and uncoded message from Newt Scorsi. A meeting time, directions to the place, and the words: "About time you got here. I was beginning to think I'd have to do it all myself." I had sent a coded message to him earlier that day, following instructions the chief had given me, asking for a meeting: "The showboat delivery has arrived, specify time and place."

Now I was thinking that I should have kept my arrival to myself for a couple days, done some observing first. The raid had surprised me. There was too much I didn't know. That was often the case when I started a job. The local chief would leave out some important bit of information, sometimes on purpose, sometimes through incompetence, usually through ignorance. The chief's story had been vague to start with, but I'd thought I had enough to go on—the complaining party said a powerful family was overstepping the law; find out what they're doing and how, so we can stop the hanky-panky. Suddenly I was dealing with something that looked more complicated, and uglier.

Shaved heads, shiny black boots—pretty spiffy for bandits. If they were mercs, were the Scorsis behind the foray? Why? In any case, it seemed unlikely the elaborate attack had been staged just to deliver a message to me.

I stuck the message back in my pocket.

Everything seemed to be under control and I wondered if anyone would notice if I went missing. I didn't even have to go to my car; I could fall on the bed in my clothes and worry about cleaning myself up and changing in the morning.

"Hey, Rica!" I turned at the sound of Waldo's whiny voice. "You're wanted in the restaurant."

Well, crap. More cleanup, probably.

But the restaurant had been pretty much set to rights already. A cleaner was sweeping up the last of the broken dishes. And there was Jo, sitting with the young girl and Waldo, who had just brought them cold drinks from the bar: something red over ice. He squeezed into the booth with them. The girl, I saw now, looked a little like Jo—her gold-brown hair striped with black—or was it the other way around?—blue-eyed, slender but not thin.

I approached the table. Jo looked up.

"I wanted to thank you again for your help back there. This is my niece, Lizzie."

"You're more than welcome." I turned to Lizzie. "Hi, Lizzie.

Are you Judith's daughter, then?" And I had heard Jo refer to Drew as Lizzie's brother. Drew had Judith's brown curls. Clan connections were falling into place.

The girl nodded. She was, pale, teary, but had recovered enough to give me a who-the-hell-are-you look.

So Judith had two teenagers. Dangerous country for kids.

I slid into the seat beside Waldo. "That was sure some awful scene—who were those guys, anyway?"

"Just bandits," Jo said coolly, making it clear that if she knew or guessed more, she wouldn't be telling me.

"I heard some talk that they tried to create a diversion in here first, but it didn't work out . . . ?"

Jo laughed and glanced at Waldo. "They did. But the minute they started yelling, Waldo ran out the door and everyone here pretty much followed." Waldo looked pouty. "Hard to keep a fight going when there's no one to fight with. So the bandits ran out after them."

No bravery on the one side and no patience on the other. What a mess.

At that moment, a potbellied middle-aged man in a white jumpsuit peeked in the door of the restaurant. When his eyes fixed on Jo, he walked our way. He was carrying a fat white valise with a red caduceus on the side. It wasn't too hard to figure out that he was the local doctor.

"Hi, George," Jo said. "Drew's up in his room."

"Everyone here okay?"

"Sure."

George glanced at me, but didn't stop for introductions.

"I'll be on my way up, then. Quinn's going to be fine, by the way, minor concussion I'd say." Probably the cashier I'd noticed. He'd had a head injury. "The customer with the broken arm and the woman with the dislocated shoulder are on their way to the clinic."

Jo nodded. She and Lizzie finished their drinks and stood. Jo smiled at me and said thanks one more time before walking toward the door with the doctor. Just before they stepped out into the casino, I heard Jo say, "Frank's on his way. Guess he was busy rousting a tourist." The doctor laughed, and Jo laughed with him.

Frank. I remembered the chief had said the sheriff's name was Frank Holstein.

Waldo still sat. He looked sidelong at me. "Probably no point in trying to find Fredo and Timmy. No one's going to come back here, not tonight anyway. I don't know when the cooks will get back, if ever. Of course if we have to—if someone does come in looking for a meal—can you cook?" He moved a little closer. Uh oh. With Jo and Lizzie gone, there was not a soul in the place except me and Waldo.

I slid out of the booth and stood. "No, I don't cook. Do you?" He pouted. He didn't like that. Would he talk about what had happened? Would he know anything to talk about? I didn't like being there with him but maybe I could learn something if I acted nicer to him. That wouldn't be easy.

I put on an earnest, interested, friendly face. "You've been here a long time, right?"

That relaxed him, made him feel like an expert of some sort. He nodded wisely.

"Tell me, Waldo, do you get bandits in here often?"

Waldo stood, too. "No. Not for years." He smiled, showing his big white teeth. "I saw you watching the fight."

I waited for him to make his point. I didn't like that smile. It was too familiar, this time. Even intimate.

"I have a bad leg. So I couldn't jump in. Kind of hard to just stand there and watch, but exciting, too."

The way he said the word "exciting" confirmed my suspicion. That and the drooly look on his face. And the oily maneuver that moved his body closer until it was just a few inches from mine.

"I don't find death exciting, Waldo."

He laughed, reached out and grabbed my waist.

No. Not even for information. I gripped his arm hard and cartwheeled him over my right thigh. He was even heavier than he looked. He landed hard on his back, screaming on impact, his foot catching a chair and tossing it to the floor.

"Hey!" The yell came from behind me. Timmy?

I whirled to see who the voice belonged to. Jo. She strode across the room and reached a hand down toward Waldo, helping him struggle to his feet. Uh oh. Had I tossed a family favorite? Even if he'd fled the restaurant at the first sight of trouble? Couldn't do the job if I got fired.

"Waldo, you stupid—How many times . . . ?" Jo turned to me. "I suppose he grabbed you?" I nodded. Good. She sounded disgusted.

"Just her hand!" Bullshit. Jo shook her head. She didn't believe him.

"But you won't do that any more, will you?" she snapped.

"No." I could barely hear him grunt the word. He was pouting again, like a nasty little kid.

"Because this one seems capable of hurting you, Waldo."

Waldo shrugged, gave me a last resentful look, and hobbled into the kitchen.

"You're okay, Rica?"

"Of course."

She nodded, appraising me. Looking deeper into my eyes than I liked.

"Well, I guess you can fight, after all."

CHAPTER 7
GOSSIP WITH STRANGERS

The worn royal blue drapes let pinpoints of daylight into the room, dusty beams brushing the scarred, white-painted bureau. The room was cleaner than most I'd slept in, clean enough to please Gran. The bed wasn't too lumpy, the walls were recently painted a soft cream, the tan carpet was worn but unstained. The clock worked. It was just before eleven. I'd slept hard. I was supposed to get my picture taken in an hour.

My sys told me there was new mail.

Not from Sylvia, of course. Still worn out from the day before, I revisited my crankiest fantasy. I was knocking on her door—no idea what it looked like—and when she appeared I said, "Now ignore me. Now tell me you still hate me for one little mistake with that whatever-his-name-was. Look me in the eye and say you'd rather stay here with whatever-this-guy's-name-is than travel with me."

I'd been replaying that scene for nearly ten years. Like some kind of stubborn rehearsal for a play that would probably never open because I was afraid, if I did go there and say those words, she'd actually do what I was daring her to do, tell me she hated me and wasn't going anywhere.

The only message was a new offer, from New Orleans, dealing with some kind of corruption—nothing new there—but it included the cover role of Maggie the Cat at a theater in the French Quarter. I'd seen the original with Elizabeth Taylor, restored but a lot the worse for use, and fallen in love with Tennessee Williams. And Paul Newman. And Elizabeth Taylor. Maggie. New Orleans music and food, too.

I answered: "Thanks for the offer. Sierra assignment queued first. I'll check back with you when it's winding down." The job could still be waiting, even if I took a side trip to visit Gran. That's one wild old city. Came back from a hurricane and flood way before the Poison and managed to rebuild before everything everywhere went to hell. Nearly two thousand people by last count. Greatest music on earth and lots to drink. But it wouldn't tempt a lot of freelancers. The streets were dark and violent and the people stuck to their own. The language was a problem, too. My own Loosianne was better than most, even though I couldn't seem to keep Redwood Spanish out of the French mix.

Shooting the screen, I punched a line to channel one, Redwood, or what I hoped would be Redwood, looking for any little piece of home. The holo shimmied for a second, a man's head resolved shakily. Fading in and out. Singing. Badly. I muted the sound, watching his face and hoping the screen would shift to the prettier sight of Webber Doe, sending out the hearsay of Doe's Data from San Francisco. No Webber Doe. Ten minutes of staring at jiggles and fades, no luck. During one fade, another guy appeared, in Tahoe, he said, and introduced his wife. She started playing the violin. Mercifully, she was interrupted by a flicker from the Coast, back to channel one, a vision of Webber Doe laughing and then she was gone. I gave up and shut down.

It was then that I noticed that the roomsys, mounted on the desk, was blinking at me. Imagine that, I thought, a roomsys that works—not that I'd use it for anything private. I had a message from Jo.

Her dusky voice told me to meet Monte, the head cashier, in his cage, at noon. He'd take my picture. I realized that I was disappointed that Jo wouldn't be doing it, and that irritated me.

I wasn't in Tahoe for that kind of fun, certainly not with someone I was spying on.

The bloodstained glass-sequined working clothes I'd been wearing during the raid were soaking in the bathroom sink. The blood was coming out but the bits of broken glass were hanging on. I might just have to buy new black pants.

I'd managed to make it to my car the night before and get some of my things. I'd hesitated about my sys. A new-from-Redwood coin-sized personal sys would be harder to explain away than a new weapon, if someone decided to check out my room. They were hard to get, wildly expensive, and nobody owned one who wasn't either rich enough to buy it as a toy or doing something that required secrecy and flash-distance communication. In the end I stuck it in a money-pocket flap I'd sewn into a pair of pants, and hauled those pants and maybe a third of my clothes, along with personal odds and ends, to the elevator. Which, it turned out, didn't work. So, at least an hour after the last of my adrenaline had leaked away, I'd had to drag my sacks of stuff up the stairs to the third floor.

I'd taken the time to find my snoop-sniffer before I fell asleep and run a scan on the room. No bugs that I could find. But I still wouldn't trust the roomsys.

My meeting with Scorsi wasn't until three that afternoon. I had enough time to sit through the photo session, change clothes, and do a little scouting around town. Research. Background. Gossip with strangers. Catch the local threads and tie them together. Read some back issues of the local newspaper.

I took a long shower and laid out three outfits. A floor-length dark blue dress with long tight sleeves and a low-cut neckline; a white one that came to mid-calf and had loose, gauzy sleeves and real sequins on the bodice; and flowing pants and blouse made of forest green silk that had actually come to San Francisco on a boat from China. I didn't much like the white one and wasn't in the mood for the blue, so I chose the green. It set off my hair.

By the time I'd dressed and put on just enough makeup to create an effect for the picture, I had ten minutes to meet Monte.

Even if there had been time for breakfast, I couldn't have gotten it at the casino. The restaurant was closed and a sign on the door read "Cook Wanted." The casino, a little the worse for wear but cleaned up and with spaces waiting for new or repaired machines and tables, had already drawn a couple dozen gamblers. My green silk attracted a lot of curious stares.

I was on my way to the cashier's cage when I spotted Bernard, the flabby change guy who'd passed me the note. Maybe he'd know a good lunch place.

"You working a double shift or something?" I asked. He opened his mouth and closed it again. Not a sound leaked out.

He looked over his shoulder, twitchy with nerves at being seen with me. He couldn't have looked more guilty. Made me want to twist the knife by thanking him again for delivering the message, but I couldn't chance anyone overhearing.

"Some of our people never came back. I have to fill in." Eyes shifting all over the place.

I wasn't enjoying the conversation any more than he was, and had decided by then that he was the kind of short-lived spy who was bound to blow his cover, so I got to the point. Food. Bernard didn't think for even a second before he directed me, loudly, to "the Blue Chip Diner, the second-best eats in town."

"Thanks, see you, then," I said, escaping.

Monte was waiting for me. His gray eyebrows shot up at the sight of me in my torch suit. He gave me a friendly smile, smoothed back his sparse hair, and, taking my arm in his thin hand, led me inside the cage.

He actually seemed to know what he was doing. He had me

posing this way, that way, glancing over my shoulder, smiling, smoldering, head shots, full body, to the waist. He took his time. My stomach was growling.

Finally he was finished.

"Okay, Rica! That's just great. We got a bunch of good ones. You want to look them over?"

"I trust you, Monte." It was always more important to make a friend than it was to guard my ego. He smiled happily and escorted me out of the cage.

After I'd trotted upstairs and changed into normal clothing—a pair of denim pants and a blue striped shirt—I passed the restaurant again and saw that the help-wanted sign was gone and the doors were open. But since the new cook was a question mark and I'd rather not see Waldo again so soon, anyway, I decided that I might as well take Bernard's enthusiastic recommendation.

Outside the front door, a barker was urging passersby to "come in for a Blackjack win!" I remembered seeing him at the back door after the raid. He was wearing the same gold jumpsuit with white braid. When I passed him, I saw that his eyes were foggy and blind. He looked to be in his fifties, so he'd have been a child when the Poison began. Some of the chem-bombs did this to people. His nameplate said he was called Owen.

The Blue Chip was a small diner with a counter, a dozen booths and tables, three of them occupied, and a round table in the front window. One server, who had varicose veins and a black comb stuck through her dyed flat-brown hair, worked the tables; a fiftyish man took care of the register and probably the counter trade when there was some. He looked an awful lot like the change guy at the casino. Pale, bald, wearing a frayed pink shirt.

When I saw my breakfast, I was sure he was related to Bernard the spy. No one but a relative could have recommended the food there. The eggs over medium were a mess of broken yolk and crisped white. The toast and home fries were as damp and white as the man at the register. I ate what I could with lots of ketchup and hot sauce, left a decent tip on the counter, and took my check to the register where he was standing reading a newspaper.

"Enjoy your food?" The man took my money and laboriously counted out the change.

"Yes. Very good." He did a double take. Maybe no one had ever answered the question that way before. "Nice place you've got here."

He grinned, nodding happily. "Well, thanks. Haven't seen you around before." He raised one thin eyebrow in what I supposed was flirtation. He must have thought he was on a roll. "I'm Xavier Polsky."

"Rica Marin. New in town. Working over at Blackjack."

His puffy eyelids dropped, covering his thoughts. Was he connected with the Colemans' enemies, too, like the change guy, or did he just know that his clone was a spy? "Oh, yeah? They do real well over there. Working as a dealer?"

"No. Waiter. And singer, as soon as they open the room. Bernard, one of the change people? He recommended you."

He nodded, still looking at the counter. "No kidding. Well that's nice. Bernard's my cousin." Aha! "Nice of him to send you here, and nice that you're a singer. Maybe you'll come over and do a number once in a while, huh?" He laughed and looked up at me, raising that eyebrow again. I laughed too, and left it at that.

"I wonder, can you direct me to the newspaper office?"

He raised an arm and pointed east. "Right down the street here about a block and a half."

"Thanks." I turned to leave.

"Real nice people, those Colemans." He was definitely protesting too much, or he was scared of them.

"Yes, they seem to be." Nice. I started walking toward the door.

He called after me: "Well, you take care, then." I sent him a backward wave on my way out. I was a couple of buildings down from the diner when I noticed a poster tacked to the wall, a political poster for a candidate for Sierra Council. This was the first advertising I'd seen for the elections, which the poster said were about a month away. I glanced at the photo of the candidate and then looked again. I couldn't be sure, the quality of the photo wasn't great, but he looked a lot like one of the mercs who had attacked Blackjack.

The *Sierra Star*'s office was close to the center of town, housed in a two-story wooden building that looked like it hadn't been painted since the Poison. The front window had a new wooden frame, but that hadn't been painted, either. The chubby young blond woman in the front office sat me down at a table and brought all eight back issues for the past couple of months. I could tell she wanted to know what I was looking for, but was too polite or too well-trained to ask outright.

"Was there a particular time frame you wanted to look at?"

"No. Just wanted to see what's been going on around here lately."

"Oh. Well. Here they all are." She dropped the papers on the table. "Happy reading."

"Thank you."

After a half hour of flipping pages, I didn't have much more than I'd come in with. The mayor, a man named Arthur Madera, had been found a month before by Frank Holstein, the sheriff I was not supposed to contact. Frank had been on early morning patrol. Driving past a town park near the mayor's home, he saw a body hanging by the ankles from a low branch of a Douglas fir. When he investigated, he discovered the dead man was the mayor himself, with an old-fashioned bullet through his brain. It didn't look like intruders had broken into the house and nothing seemed to have been stolen, but the locals weren't ruling anything out. So he was either kidnapped and dragged to the park or grabbed while he was strolling on his own the night before or very early in the morning. In a random or a deliberate act of thievery or maybe not. There were no suspects.

Holstein might have found the body, but he hadn't found much of anything else. The mayor had been shot with a very old gun. Antique. A .38 police special. I wondered where they'd have found a thing like that. And gotten it working. Anyway, they shot him dead with it and then they hanged him upside down from a tree.

Hanging upside down from a tree. Interesting. A radical hugger–style killing. The fad had mostly died out back in the Forties, but it still happened from time to time, though not necessarily at the hands of huggers and not often, any more, as punishment for poison. Copycats, pranksters, and people who liked doing things the old-fashioned way. Sometimes they tied their victims up there alive and left them dangling, screaming and crying for help. I'd cut down one or two, myself.

Was he a toxie, I wondered? Did he own a factory? No, the story said he was a retired grocer.

It also said the mayor'd had no known enemies, which in itself seemed odd. The man was a politician. He had some power or was connected to someone who did. He had to have enemies.

There was no vice mayor, no official who could or would step quickly into the dead man's shoes. Replacing him would wait for September's election, and no one had yet agreed to run, at least not up until the night before, when the last edition of the *Star* had come out.

Just shows, I thought, how unnecessary government really is.

"That's really something, about the mayor," I said to the blond woman.

She shrugged. "Yeah. Sad. He was a nice man."

"Doesn't seem like anyone wants the job."

"Would you?"

"But who's running the town?"

She thought about that for a minute. "Pretty much runs itself, I guess. I kind of thought the Colemans—over at Blackjack?—would put up someone from their family, but maybe not."

"Why'd you think that?" Should I mention I worked there?

She shrugged. "They have a lot of, I guess you'd say, influence."

"They seem like good people. I just started working for them."

"Oh, yeah?" An involuntary glance at my hair. Maybe I should do those stripes, after all. For credibility. "I don't really know them well, but a lot of people like them."

"What about that other big casino? Scorsi's Luck. Don't they have influence, too?"

She looked like the thought had never occurred to her. "Scorsi? Well, maybe they do. Sure, I guess so."

I could see why the Scorsis thought the Colemans were out to grab power. They already had more than the Scorsis, at least in the eyes of this woman.

I was about to leave when a small man with salt-and-pepper hair appeared in a doorway behind the counter.

"Hello," he said. "New in town?"

"Yes. Working at Blackjack."

He nodded, which made me think he'd been listening to my conversation with the clerk. "That's great. I own this paper, name's Iggy Santos."

I told him mine. He peered at me. "We just got a picture of

you. For an ad. Singing in the lounge, right?"

I smiled modestly.

"Great people. Been friends with Samm for years. Samm Bakar—two *m*'s, three *a*'s." He grinned an editor's grin. "Blackjack's our biggest advertiser. I'll try to come and catch your act." He turned and disappeared back inside what I presumed was his office. I wondered who Samm Bakar was.

Just forty-five minutes before my meeting with Newt Scorsi, I headed back to the casino.

Still not as big a crowd as the day before; the raid had hurt business. I wondered how long it would be before the customers got over it.

The house sys in my room was blinking. The message had come in half an hour before. "Come see me in my office right away," Judith Coleman's voice said. I might be late for my meeting with Newt.

Again, the door was slightly ajar. I knocked.

"Come in."

Judith was sitting behind her desk. Today she was wearing a purple dress that made her look like a Santa Rosa plum. A man with a star on his chest was leaning against the window wall. He watched me walk in.

"Good. You got my message." She waved toward a guest chair. "Sit down. Frank, this is Rica, she's a new employee."

"And you were here last night?"

"Yes, I was."

Judith said, "Rica, this is Sheriff Frank Holstein." I'd already figured that out. "He's talking to everyone."

He shook my hand and studied my face like he could see right into my brain. I thought it was an affectation. He didn't look that smart. Holstein was a stocky, medium-size man with muscular arms and a flat stomach. His too-long brown hair—it fluffed over his ears—was combed up in front in a pompadour wave. His jumpsuit fit so well it must have been tailored. He swaggered over to the second guest chair and clamped his stubby hands on its back.

"What do you do here, Rica?" I told him. "Where were you when the bandits showed up?" I told him that, too, trying to sound friendly and helpful. He asked me who was in the casino that I could remember, and what I remembered of the battle and of the bandits themselves. I kept my answers minimal, not offering anything, certainly not saying I thought they were mercs. I couldn't be expected to know a merc from a bandit.

He straightened up, nodding like I'd given him something to think about.

"Okay. Well, thanks a lot. Judith? I'll get back to you when we find something. We'll get 'em."

"Thank you, Frank. I know you will." I doubted that she knew any such thing. I made a note of the blank expression she wore when she expressed confidence in the sheriff: this is how Judith looks when she's lying.

I stood. "Is that all?"

Judith shook her head and pointed at the chair again. She still wanted to talk to me—about what?

When Holstein was out the door, Judith looked directly at me. Her eyes, intense as Jo's but lighter, hazel, were wide open, unhooded by their circle of fat or the slightly drooping lids of early middle age.

"Jo tells me you taught Waldo a lesson." No smile, no clue of expression.

"It was a reflex. Life on the road . . ."

"Not everyone has such strong reflexes. Congratulations." Still no clue.

"Thank you."

"Jo says you sing a hell of a torch song." An odd and sudden change of subject. Where was the woman going with all this? "A secret sorrow, perhaps?"

Nervy. People didn't ask strangers such personal questions. My shock must have shown because the corners of Judith's mouth quirked in a tiny smile. But she didn't apologize; she waited. The queen of Tahoe, I thought with a quick flash of anger. Maybe I didn't like her, after all.

"Everyone has secret sorrows." A vague, evasive answer; a challenge I tossed right back at her.

"No. Everyone does not. Not so they can express them anyway. That's a talent. Shows a certain depth of character. I apologize for seeming to pry." She didn't look apologetic. "But I like to get to know the people who work here."

"I can understand that." I could, too. Especially if she had things to hide.

"And everyone is not capable of throwing a two-hundred-pound man to the floor, even one as weak as Waldo. Are you a fighter, Rica?"

"No, I wouldn't call myself a fighter." I could feel sweat collecting in my armpits. This was quite an interrogation.

"It's a violent world. You travel in it. How do you survive?"

"I try to avoid trouble. And I try to live by my wits."

"I suppose that so far, then, that's worked for you. But you're obviously capable of taking care of yourself. Blackjack has violent enemies. You saw that for yourself. Does that worry you? You work for us now. At some point you may have to help defend us. What do you think of that?"

Watch out. Too fast. Way too fast. Just last night, Jo had blandly insisted that the raiders were nothing but bandits. Bandits were everyone's enemy and so they were no one's. Now Judith was saying something else entirely. Odd that she'd open up to a stranger that way. She sounded like she was recruiting. Did she think she'd already bought my loyalty? Was she so arrogant that she assumed all her employees were loyal from day one? Bernard sure as hell wasn't.

If I said yes, I wanted to fight, would I be swept right up into the Coleman inner circle? Would it be that easy?

"I'm not sure what you're asking me. Do you expect more raids? I would certainly help to defend myself—and Blackjack—if it comes to that."

"But you didn't fight last night. Against the bandits. Only against Waldo." An edge of humor that seemed mildly unfriendly. I'd been careful not to join the battle, not to show I could fight. Possibly that was the wrong choice. Possibly I'd been so busy staying undercover that I'd I lost a chance to be a Coleman soldier from day one. I wasn't sure which way to go with this. I had to stay cool. Couldn't let her rattle me. For all I knew, getting me rattled was her entire purpose: see what the new girl's made of. For all I knew, she pulled this shit on everyone who came in the door. She was, after all—I felt my eyes darting toward the snow globes—a very strange woman.

"I'm a singer, a performer. I travel. I see my share of violence. I learned to take care of myself. But I didn't know what was going on last night. It took me completely by surprise. I didn't really even know who was who. And I have to say that as happy as I am to be working for you, I've never fought for anything but self defense."

"That's a reasonable answer, Rica. I hope you'll come to think of defending Blackjack as self-defense, but that's up to you. And I am grateful for the help you gave. You can go now."

Good thing. I was exhausted. And late for my meeting. I stood. "I hope you don't think I lack loyalty."

"Not at all." She smiled what seemed like an uncomplicated smile. There was no way I believed it.

"Good. Thanks."

★ ★ ★ ★ ★

Judith had shaken me a little, but any employee challenged so obliquely would react cautiously, so my tension didn't give anything away.

A few more customers had wandered back in, a scattering at the tables, a dozen or so at the slots. Maybe some of them hadn't even heard about the invasion; maybe the ones who had heard about it had managed to convince themselves the place was safe now.

Waldo came out of the restaurant. He walked aimlessly through the casino, stopping at the roulette table, staring at the spinning wheel. Scratching his stomach, wandering to the bar. He took a stool and raised his hand at the bartender, who nodded and poured him a beer. How did the lovely Waldo fit into all this? I couldn't imagine that grabby asshole being loyal to anyone.

I pushed out through the back door, heading for my car. I tried to tuck Judith's interrogation into a dark corner of my mind where it could cook a bit, and worked at focusing on my meeting with Newt.

I didn't know what Newt was planning to tell me, but I knew what I wanted to ask him. Were the mercs his? If so, what was the purpose of the attack? Was there a connection with the mayor's murder? How many people at Blackjack were actually working for Scorsi? Who were they? Would they be any use to me if I needed them?

But once I got to the subject of self-preservation, my mind couldn't help but kick Judith out of that dark corner and set her right out there in full daylight again.

What kind of game was she playing with me?

CHAPTER 8
TRAITORS. THEY'LL SELL US ALL.

The meeting place was two miles outside town. I was supposed to look for a boulder carved with the initials K.S.+R.L. inside a heart.

The heart was lopsided. The carving was weathered and barely readable, left there by some teenager who was now either old or dead. Depressing. I hate reminders of mortality—anyone's.

Just behind that boulder was a shiny new silver floater tucked in a stand of fir. A narrow trail led into the trees.

I found Newt Scorsi in a clearing, waiting under a rocky outcrop. He was slumped on a log, gnawing at an enormous sandwich that seemed to be made of an entire sourdough loaf. He sat up straighter and mumbled something that might have been a greeting, might have been "You're late." Hard to tell through the mouthful of bread.

He was no more than five feet six, gut-heavy with spindly arms and legs, his dust-brown and black hair cropped to half-inch bristle on his big head, the head balanced on a scrawny neck. He squinted at me and frowned, trying, I thought, to look shrewd and tough, succeeding only in looking hostile. Maybe he was socially inept, or maybe he didn't trust mercs.

Gran once told me, "Never trust a suspicious man." What about a suspicious woman? I'd asked. "Women," she said, "have more reasons for it."

I nodded back to him, returning the frown, meeting him eye

to eye. Okay, Newt, I was saying with a look, you don't scare me. So back off. He shifted his gaze. That was almost too easy.

"Are you sure no Colemans followed you?" he asked the trees behind me. "Blow your cover in the first week or however long you've been there—how long have you been there?" He took another large bite of his sandwich, jumped to his big feet, and paced around the clearing. A string of pink meat dangled from his lip as he chewed.

"Two days now. Why are you so worried? If I blow my cover, I'm the one in trouble—you don't have any cover to blow."

He swallowed. "Don't want them getting away with it. Maybe you can catch them and we can stop them."

"Them—that would be the Colemans. But tell me, what's the particular 'it' you don't want them to get away with? Sounds like they're doing a whole lot of things."

He nodded, took another bite, chewed, swallowed, sat down again, tapping his foot. Finally looked me in the eye. "They're doing whatever they can do. What they want is Sierra, all of it. And Redwood, too. I know that much. I'm not sure what the plan is beyond that. More consolidation, more countries all stuck together into their own big country? They're greedy and power mad, you know. Or they could take Redwood and Sierra and wrap the whole thing up and sell it to Rockymountain."

And then do what with the money? Move down to California? Take over Middle by paying off all their corrupt chiefs? Or Olympia? It was pretty there, if you didn't mind rain. No matter how I looked at what he was saying, it wasn't making a lot of sense.

"Why would they sell? If they're power mad, why would they go to Rocky and give up their power?"

"I told you, they're greedy. Traitors. They'll sell us all."

I repeated my question. "But why would they take all that power and then sell it to Rocky?"

"Jeez-us—I don't know!" he yelled, hopping up and pacing again, waving his sandwich. Hyper. A restless elf. He wasn't talking to the trees any more. "That's for you to find out. What do you think I'm paying you for?"

"Okay, okay." No point in pushing him over the edge. I'd hate to be in range if that big head exploded. He harrumphed and calmed down.

"I'm not sure which they really want, money or land," he said. "And maybe they've already got a deal to split the power with Rocky. But all the things they're doing to make money, to get people into strategic places . . . political office . . ." He waved his hand vaguely. "You'll see. They want to own the town so they can destroy the other casinos. They're training fighters, too. Soldiers." And looking for more, I thought, remembering that chat with Judith. "Those things mean they're after power. Power and money. What do people do with power and money?" He scowled at me, but went on before I could try to answer. "I'll tell you what they don't do. They don't sit back, say 'that was fun, now I'm going to take a nap.' We hear what we hear." He snapped off another chunk of sandwich, bouncing his heel in the rubble at the base of the rock. Crunch, crunch, crunch.

"Hear from who?"

"We got people."

People? More than one?

"You going to keep secrets from me, Newt? I already know you've got Bernard over at Blackjack. Who else?"

He shook his head. "Can't tell you that. Security. Got to protect my people. I'm paying you. I'll tell you what you need to know."

I opened my mouth to tell him to go to hell, thought better of it, and took a breath. No point in arguing with him, no point in asking him why he didn't trust me. I'm a merc. Judging by the crew who'd raided Blackjack, his experience with mercs could not have been reassuring. So aside from his probably having a congenital trust deficit, to be fair, he had reason to be careful. And there was a much bigger issue here.

Consolidation. A big country. Big trouble all over the place. Rocky pushing for population on one side, the Colemans building an empire on the other. If any of this was true, it needed to stop. I liked things the way they were. Liked my life the way it was. Well, mostly. But it was also possible that Newt was just plain paranoid, or that he only wanted to hassle and persecute the Colemans. The chief had sounded pretty neutral in her messages. If the Colemans were going after political power, that was not a crime. It was possible, too, that they were guilty of no more than petty moneymaking schemes. If they were skimming reals at the tables, I should be able to figure that out pretty fast, collect my pay, and go home to visit Gran for a week or two. Sit under a redwood tree and watch the ferns grow.

"They're your business rivals, isn't that right?"

He sighed. He could see where I was going with that. I was showing him I wasn't ready to trust him, either. "Yeah. But that's not the point. I'm not just trying to hurt a competitor. They want more than Scorsi's Luck. How many times do I have to explain?" He glared at me. I glared back, thinking: as many times as I ask, you potbellied big-nosed big-mouth garden gnome. "This is a war. I'm only trying to save Sierra, and I think Chief Graybel understands that or she wouldn't be working with me."

Newt Scorsi, savior? No. I couldn't see it. But if his suspicions stopped a power grab that could lead to consolidation, joining, that would be a good thing. How far would Newt's self-interest take him? I thought about the raid, the mercs. The beginning of Scorsi's war? But he was right about the chief. She had to at least be wondering about the Colemans or she wouldn't have gotten involved.

"Did you send those mercs to Blackjack last night?"

He looked sly and smiled at his sandwich. "They did a pretty good job from what I hear."

"The casino's fine. Missing a few runaway workers, a few broken machines. The customers are already coming back. Is that your plan for stopping the Colemans? Invading the place over and over again until they give up and go away?"

He flushed. I needed to put a lid on my sarcasm if I meant to keep this job. But there was something about the man that made me want to slap him around verbally.

There was that glare again. "Who says I did it at all? Now what I'd like is for you to stop asking me so many questions and find out some of the answers."

"I need more answers from you first. And please don't lie to me. It's obvious you were behind that merc attack. What was the point of it?"

"You'll see."

I kept my voice even, reasonable, soft. "You want me to help you or not?"

His bit his lip, angry, then shrugged, resigned. "Okay. The point is, I've got nothing to lose by doing it. We can sit around waiting for them to get strong enough to take us, or we can try to flush them out now, make them show what they're really about under all that leading-citizen shit. Come at us, show their army, way before they're ready."

Army. He was saying they had an army. Not just a few defenders.

"They'll show their strength and everyone will see."

So that was his plan. Force them to act aggressively and look bad, before they were able to follow through. But complicated plans that depended on the actions of others could have complicated failures, especially if the opponent was smarter.

"What if they don't bite?"

He shrugged again. "Then I've done some damage. Maybe scared them back for a while."

"You're sure about this army?"

He glanced around as if the trees were Coleman spies. "I even heard that they got an airplane, that it arrived a few days ago. But nobody who'll fly it for them, not yet anyway."

I thought of that Gullwing I'd seen heading west over Rocky. "What kind of plane?"

"Don't know."

Could be nothing, then. But if they did have a plane . . . I tried to get my mind around that. What would they do with it? My imagination went a little spotty then. Images from Gran's stories, terrorists flying over cities and dropping plagues on the people below them. No. I couldn't imagine the Colemans doing something like that. Would they threaten it? People would give almost anything to keep that from happening.

"Who knows? They could even be trying to get some tanks." Now this was beginning to sound like a fever dream. Tanks? Gran had mentioned seeing one of those, used by a survival cell that had once roamed the Redwood countryside. I'd never heard anyone else even use the word.

"What if you push them to fight and they beat you?"

"They won't! They're not strong enough yet. I told you!" More snapping. A testy little garden gnome.

He sounded so sure of that. He had to have something going for his side. More than I'd seen so far. "Tell me about your army, then. You have the dozen mercs you sent to Blackjack. What else?"

"You worry about their army. Not mine."

I needed the money. I really did. I didn't want to turn around and go all the way to New Orleans. If I quit now the chief would never hire me again. And I was also beginning to want to know if the Colemans were, truly, trying to take over a bigger block of territory. Because if they were, they might be looking toward the coast, and that was home to me.

Newt was another issue. He'd talked about exposing them. Scaring them back. I couldn't believe that was all he wanted. Surely he'd had fantasies about destroying his competition. Didn't everyone? And winners have a tendency to push to the next border.

"Okay. I can see why you want to keep the Colemans from taking over. But when we succeed in stopping them, what then?"

His eyes shifted back to me, and away again. He was thinking hard but not answering.

"You have some kind of plan in mind for Sierra, don't you?"

He wiped his mouth with the back of his hand and took another bite. Chewed. Swallowed. "Well not exactly a plan. We just want to keep ourselves from being conquered, merged. Keep Tahoe safe. Keep Sierra safe. Keep things the way they're supposed to be. That's all I want."

Oh, yes, Newt Scorsi was an altruist through and through. And, as a great Twentieth Century poet said, I am Marie of Roumania.

If the Colemans were raising an army, and Newt was raising an army, what we had, right here in Sierra, was something they used to call an arms race. I couldn't see anything but trouble in Sierra's future. I was wishing more and more that Sierra wasn't so close to Redwood, to that house up the trail, to Gran, her dog, her cats, and to that hammock in the trees.

But what it came down to, in the here and now, was the job I had to do. That job said the Colemans were the big threat, the one I needed to focus on. Not the lying, whining man who sat on the rock before me. He had gone for the sandwich again.

"Could you stop eating long enough to finish this conversation?"

"I'm hungry. Didn't have breakfast. Can't you let a man eat, for god's sake?" But he put the last of it down beside him on the rock.

"An army takes a lot of money to raise and maintain. And where are they hiding it?" They'd have to march around somewhere. And then there was the supposed airplane. I hadn't seen any planes since I'd arrived in Tahoe. It wouldn't be easy to hide one.

"They move it around, is what I think. As for money, they're smuggling vax. They're skimming at the tables. They're selling phony medicine. They've got money, lots of it. Money that belongs to Sierra. Tax money. Vax money. Health certificate money. They're going to get people into the government. And if they have enough time and enough money they won't have to worry about showing their military; it'll be too big to hide and they'll already own everything anyway."

It was true the Colemans didn't seem to be hurting for cash or vax.

"Who's in charge of this army?"

"Samm. He's doing it."

"Who's Samm?" Iggy Santos, at the *Sierra Star*, had mentioned that name. Samm Bakar. Two *m*'s, three *a*'s.

"Big guy. Dealer. But he's really more. He's getting people to join and training troops in secret and when they're ready . . ." He shrugged.

"So he's big—what else does he look like?" I was remembering the tall man who had been so involved in the battle the night before.

"Dark hair. With yellow stripes. Looks part Chinese or Indian or something. He's not even a Coleman but he came here when he was a kid; Judith took him in. Women like him." Newt looked disgusted. That had to be the man I remembered. "Samm and Jo and Judith, they're going to take over everything."

"Won't the law have something to say about that? What about

the sheriff? Won't he stop them?" I thought I already knew the answer to that.

"Frank? He's in their underwear."

"Well, but the chief—"

He snorted. "She sent you. She should have sent the guard." His wandering gaze settled for a moment on my face again. Angry and resentful. Was he the best the Scorsis had to offer?

"We need proof." She had a hundred or so cops at her disposal, if the council okayed their use. But they couldn't just act on rumor, dash in, lasers drawn, and shoot up Blackjack the way Newt had tried to do.

"She should have sent the guard," he repeated like a stubborn child.

"She can't do that, not without a vote in the Sierra Council. Maybe they'll do it if it's necessary. If it's a matter of war. Or insurrection or whatever you think it is."

"Somebody better do something."

I wanted to grab his shoulders and shake him. "That's why I'm here. If you didn't think one merc could do this job, why didn't you take your complaints to the Tahoe cabinet? I know the mayor's dead but what about the rest of them?"

"Half of them left town when the mayor was killed and the rest are just sitting around getting drunk."

"Who killed the mayor, anyway?" I guessed what his answer would be to that question.

"Samm. Or maybe Jo." He was looking at the trees again. "Who else would?" Who else? Those mercs Newt had working for him would kill just for fun.

I'd had enough of him. "All right, Newt. I'll do what I can for you. I'll get back to work now."

"Good idea. Before you go, I want to give you this." He held out his hand. In his palm was something that looked like a gray plastic button, no more than a quarter inch in diameter. I was impressed. I'd seen one or two of those. They were expensive and hard to get. I didn't own one yet. It was a syslink, made in Redwood. They connected with the sys but were much smaller, tiny enough to hide on the body or clothing with minimal chance of discovery. The first one I'd seen had been snapped onto a shirt and looked like all the other buttons. This one had a tiny hook on the edge and Stick-O on the back.

"Bet you've never seen one of these before." He looked smug.

I nodded. "I have." He sighed, irritated. "Haven't used one, though." That made him feel better.

"It's connected to my sys. You carry it. It'll vibrate when I need to reach you. Squeeze the hook, stick it in your ear and you'll hear me. It only goes one way. You can't talk back." He snickered.

I took it and dropped it in my shirt pocket. It stuck to the bottom. I'd check it over later to see how securely it would attach to my clothing. The hard part was going to be to keep from losing it until then.

He picked up the last of the sandwich and stuck it in his mouth. I was about to turn away when I decided I needed to make a small effort, at least, to be Newt Scorsi's pal. "By the way, that's a nice floater you've got there. One of the best Redwood makes, I think—it's a Helio Three, isn't it?"

He almost smiled. "You like it? Purrs like a cat, glides like a discus. New-grade glassy-metal, stop a bullet. What you got?"

I told him. He laughed. "Tell you what, you do a good job for me and I'll give you a bonus. What color Helio would you like?"

"Black would be nice." I actually prefer bright colors, but they're too easy to spot and remember.

I wasn't sure I believed he'd give me one, but the promise made me more interested in chasing down Newt Scorsi's enemies. Or his wild geese.

CHAPTER 9
CLINGING TOGETHER ON A BLOODSTAINED BED

"Well, Rica, I guess you're in Tahoe by now. I'm lying in the hammock up on the back hill, just listening to the eucalyptus curl its bark and drop its leaves. The messy stretch under the oak is noisy with birds rummaging in the dry brush." She'd sent while I was meeting with Newt. Her voice sounded relaxed "Francisco is snoring under the garden table, his tail wagging from time to time about some good dream or other. Oakland and Berkeley are lying on the roof below me, chattering and purring at the birds, probably hoping they'll just drop right into their mouths.

"I did a reading this morning and I got the Death card. Now, you and I both know that probably doesn't mean death but something's about to come to an end and that scares me when you're off spying so for god's sake be careful. I've been meditating on the reading and your safety. Doesn't feel right. I wish you'd just come home for a while. There'll always be another job. Love, Gran."

She was on that "come home" rant again. Whenever I was away for too long, she'd use those ratty old taped-together cards to hint that something dire was about to happen. I wondered how many times that day she'd laid them out on the rusty iron garden table before she got the Death card. I wished she'd toss the tarot in the nearest ditch and tend to her own life. Get a boyfriend. I hated it when she worried. I didn't really want her to love me less, but I needed to feel she was okay, happy, when

I wasn't home.

I was a little relieved that she wasn't there to jump right back into the argument, and I tried to reassure her in my return message. "Gran, I can't come home. This is a good job, not dangerous, and we need the money. I'll be home soon enough, maybe in a couple weeks, at most a month or so, I promise." I hoped it wouldn't take that long.

I stayed online, sitting on the edge of the bed, to send a report to the chief: I'd been hired at Blackjack. The mercs had attacked and torn the place apart and it was clear Scorsi was behind that. He talked about being in a war, had insisted that the Colemans were trying to take over Sierra and Redwood, but he didn't have anything solid to give me. I told her what he'd said about Blackjack's army and hints about his own and that he was expecting, hoping for, a reprisal. Her voice came on just as I was thinking I was finished and could sign off.

"Any evidence of that Blackjack army he's talking about? Or his own?"

"Not yet. I'll track it down if there is one. From what I've seen so far, I wouldn't be surprised if they had some kind of home guard, if only to protect them from Scorsi's jealousy. But the people I saw fighting the mercs seemed mostly to be casino employees defending their turf. As for Newt, he must have more than those dozen mercs or he wouldn't be goading the Colemans."

"Does he have anything you could turn into proof about the Colemans breaking the law? He made accusations and demanded a merc, but . . ." She sighed loudly.

"He's not telling me everything he knows, but it's also possible he knows even less than he says he does. By the way, he's burned you didn't send the guard instead of just me."

A brief pause, then:

"I know Newt's not too appealing, but be careful. The Colemans are no angels. Jo's ambitious and Judith's smarter than most people."

Apparently she didn't think his complaint about the guard worth addressing. But why the pause. Had she considered it?

I mentioned something else I'd been wondering about. "There's no government here. Why doesn't Sierra come into Tahoe and take it over?"

"How would we do that? By force? By appointing a mayor? No one would like that. Besides, the problem's on the way to being fixed. The Colemans have promised to see to it that a new mayor is elected."

The Colemans? And that was all right with her? "But then they'll have their own mayor, won't they? And if they're really doing the things you think . . ."

"I don't know what they're doing. That's what you're there to find out. And for now, they're doing what we need them to do. We can't really interfere with local politics for no good reason."

Talk about wandering in circles. We don't trust the Colemans, we think Newt Scorsi may be right when he says they're trying to control the town or maybe the world, but we won't fill the current political vacuum because the Colemans are going to do it. Prove they have an army, prove they're up to no good, skimming and stealing and god knows what else, prove they killed the last mayor, and then maybe we'd dare to tell them to stay home and mind the casino.

I wanted to ask the chief what she was afraid of, but it went without saying. Power. Power that might, eventually, take her job away.

I told her I'd be in touch. She said thanks and we both went on with our business. I scrolled down my messages and learned the New Orleans assignment was still waiting for someone to take it. There were no more messages from Iowa. The chief there was probably dead or running for his life. A possible new job—a feeler from Desert about some "disruptive" godders they wanted me to check out. What did that mean? Godders could be anything from mild smiling windbags to intolerant toxies to mass murderers, as some of them had been during the Poison. There weren't a lot of the killer ones left, as far as I knew. Just enough to be trouble. I told the people in Desert I'd get in touch with them when I finished this job.

While I'd been reporting to the chief, Gran had come back from wherever she'd gone and sent more message. Not voice this time. Text. Because when she got very serious she preferred to nag with the written word. For some reason, she thought I'd read when I wouldn't listen. Or would pay more attention to what I read. Maybe she was right.

"We could get along with less money. Our needs are really very small. I worry about your lack of peacefulness. You can't be happy swimming in a pool of adrenaline. Find someone. Bring him or her back here and we'll make do. Nobody's getting sick any more. And if you get killed you can't bring home money anyway. So what if?"

She knew better. My mother—her daughter—and my father died when I was little because we couldn't afford the vax. She was just twenty-three and he was twenty-two. They got very sick, dengue, Gran told me later, a virulent strain some lab had developed so they could study it and fight it if terrorists developed it, too. Something crazy like that. Anyway, a bunch of thieves, looters, and lunatics decided to break into the lab and look for black market–bound plague vaccine somebody thought they had there. They didn't, but the thieves carried the dengue out with them and managed to spread it all over the North Bay. I was barely four years old, but I've never been able to lose the image of my parents, clinging together on a bloodstained bed, bleeding from their eyes, mouths, noses . . . even now, just letting it back into my mind for an instant, I saw them everywhere

I looked in this room at Blackjack, heard my own baby screams, felt Gran's hands pulling me away. I choked, my throat closing on a cry that brought me back to the here and now. I fell back against the pillows.

They were gone. Their kisses, their hugs, their voices, the home-smell of them.

No one could save them. There was no vax that Gran could buy and it was too late anyway. We were more than a decade into the Poison, then. Everyone dead or sick or dying. No medicine. We all four went to the hostel, where the doctors did what they could, but there was no help. Gran and I didn't get very sick, and we survived. She told me later that a couple of weeks after my parents died, and we had gone home, a mob set fire to the hostel thinking that would kill the disease. There were still sick and helpless patients there. Like lepers stashed away out of sight, feared, hated. Killed.

There was vax to be bought now. But it would only protect people who could afford to buy it.

I couldn't earn enough any other way, and Gran was seventy-five. Healthy, but it's not like she'd ever earned much. She'd trained as a lawyer while she raised my mother, starting her practice only a few years before the world changed. She'd been involved, for a while back in the late Thirties, in setting up a local council in Western Redwood. Worked for several years in the six-member faction-crippled excuse for government for almost no pay. Managed to buy a house—they ranged from cheap to free—that had never been abandoned and didn't need much rebuilding. Food and clothing took the rest of the money.

She always had a little power, a few enemies, a lot of friends.

One year, when I was just fifteen, a fellow council-member sent a dose of vax our way as a favor. That was the same year I earned us some food helping to scavenge materials from abandoned houses that had been burned, vandalized, or already partly cannibalized and were too far gone to even try to save. We found the remains of a family of three in one of them, butchered, probably by a gang of bandits who had rampaged through the year before.

Eventually, Gran got bounced for being part of the wrong faction, did this and that around the periphery. And as she'd gotten older she'd drifted into what she called the "woo-woo" culture of the Bay Area. Bits of Buddhism and astrology, palmistry, meditation, nature worship. But making a real living? Not her strength. I had to do it for both of us.

It was crazy to think we could just settle down in our woodsy little hollow and live happily and safely ever after. The only people who were safe were the ones who could buy the vax. I didn't plan on losing either one of us to some hideous plague. Maybe things were better because all the most vulnerable people had already gotten sick and died or were doing it now and maybe those who were left had mutated or started out immune or got that way, but no one had proved any of that to me.

There were a lot of times when I would have loved to give up the merc life, go home and maybe open a theater or a club. I got tired of the spying and the lying and the fighting and, occasionally, the killing. More than tired. But I didn't really have a choice, did I?

I sat up again and sent a quick reply.

"What if? What if the moon crashes into the bay or Mount Tam erupts? What if, hell, Gran. Let me do my job in peace, and I'll have peacefulness."

She must have been waiting for my answer this time because she was right back at me, and this time it was her voice coming through.

"Oh, the hell with it, Rica. I tried. Have fun. Do good and be bad. 'Bye for now."

" 'Bye, Gran."

He was dealing seven stud at the center table, his
yellow-striped black hair shining in the light of the chandelier
that hung over his head. This had to be the dealer, the adopted
Coleman, that Newt had been talking about. Samm. The big
man who had fought so well against the mercs. He wasn't
wearing a nametag. Was that because everyone knew him? I
still had a few minutes before my restaurant shift, so I leaned
against the rail that separated the poker tables from the slots
and watched.

He had four players. A fat man who looked like he was upset
about something, his face red and sweaty; a guy in a cheap
shiny suit who showed no emotion at all; a woman close to
Gran's age who was drinking beer as if she were thirsty; and a
woman with a long scar down her cheek, a glass of something
brown, no ice, at her elbow, who looked more relaxed than any
of them.

Samm noticed me. He nodded, smiling. I did the same.

"Want to join us?"

"Only have a few minutes. Maybe another time."

"You work here, don't you?" He was dealing seven stud as he
spoke.

"In the restaurant."

He dealt the first up card. An ace, a five, an eight, a jack. The
beer drinker had the ace. She tossed in some chips. The scar-
faced woman with the five folded, lifted her glass and swallowed, grimacing as the brown stuff went down her throat.
Whisky? Brandy? Something strong.

"Thought I saw you helping out last night."

I shrugged modestly.

"You're Rica Marin, the one who's going to sing in the

lounge. Pair of eights bets."

"Soon as it's open."

"I'm Samm Bakar. I'll come and see you. Pair of aces show-ing."

Flirtatious, gorgeous man. Those cheekbones were astonish-ing. The almond eyes a light brown or maybe hazel. So this was the general. He didn't speak again, concentrating on his job, but he glanced at me once or twice in a friendly way. So did the scarred woman.

Time to get to work. I was almost at the restaurant door when I heard my name being called. Turning, I saw Jo headed toward me.

"I saw you at Samm's table, but you took off so fast . . . I wanted to tell you. The lounge is opening Saturday night. I as-sume you'll be ready?

"Sure." As ready as I'd ever be.

"Good. Did you enjoy watching Samm deal?"

There was that quirky little smile again. Alpha bitch, sees all.

"I like poker. Maybe one of these nights I'll play a few hands."

"Aha. Checking out the action, then. Well, see you Saturday night."

She turned and walked away.

Showtime. It was really going to happen then. I hadn't been sure.

Waldo greeted me with a scowl.

"I've been told I have to change your shift because you're go-ing to be singing in the lounge. Not very convenient."

"I'm sorry." Like hell.

"You'll have to work a split shift until I get it figured out. Early dinner to eight-thirty, back again after the show."

"Okay." I wasn't going to show him that a split shift was "not very convenient."

"And with Drew injured I'm short a busser. Lizzie will help, but you'll have to bus your own tables until we find someone."

I nodded. A demotion of sorts. One step up, one step down. Waldo would never forgive me for tossing him.

CHAPTER 10
A FIXER WOULD MAKE A POPULAR CANDIDATE

Jo was first to arrive at the meeting that evening and took the corner of the flower-patterned couch nearest to Judith's desk. Deep red was not Jo's favorite color, and a childhood failure with a petunia bed she'd forgotten to water had left her feeling uneasy and somehow guilty at the sight of flowered fabric. But the couch was comfortable, not too soft, and provided a good power position, at Judith's right, for any discussion.

No one was there yet but Judith, sitting behind her desk scribbling on a notepad. She looked up and smiled, waving the pad.

"Making some notes for the treaty." She flipped the page over. "And some points we need to consider about that attack the other night."

Samm pushed the door open, followed by Drew and—Lizzie. What was she doing there? Samm and Drew took the chairs at either end of the long coffee table. The girl headed toward the couch where Jo sat.

"Lizzie?" She stopped, still standing, eyes focused on Jo's face, a frown creasing her brow. Jo hadn't meant to sound so surprised, it just slipped out. She was still young for a family business meeting. Wasn't she? Had Jo missed something? She caught Judith's eye. Judith gave the tiniest lift of the eyebrows, a barely visible "what could I do?" shrug.

"I told Mother it was time, Aunt Jo. I'm seventeen." She lifted her chin, eyes still meeting Jo's in a look that was half defiance, half plea. Lips tight, she added grimly: "And I think that killing a merc makes me a grownup." She shifted her gaze toward her mother, then sidelong again to Jo, and sat beside Jo on the couch.

Jo considered arguing that point. Killing might make you a lot of things but it didn't make you a grownup. Lizzie must have noticed the flicker of doubt on Jo's face because she glanced at Drew, sitting next to Samm, his solid stocky body young-looking next to Samm's long-muscled build, his bright blue eyes watching his sister. He looked tired, holding his bandaged arm close in the sling. He nodded.

"She's earned it, Aunt Jo."

Jo was surprised at his response. The two were competitive and he liked to make a point of being the older brother. But then, she'd killed the merc to save him. He probably thought he owed her.

What did Samm think? He was like an older brother to Lizzie, too. Was she the only one who felt uncomfortable with Lizzie's grab at adulthood? Apparently. He was just sitting there, a quizzical lift to his eyebrows, as if he was wondering what Jo's problem was.

Well, what was it? Protectiveness? The bite of awareness of her own age, the reminder that she was approaching forty, now that Lizzie was suddenly not a child? With the promise and threat of so much changing and about to change, she wanted her family to stay the same.

Lizzie brought her back from her wanderings with a light touch of fingers on her forearm. Jo looked up. Lizzie grinned. "Everybody knows I'm smarter than Drew." Drew snorted. Jo laughed. Just like Lizzie to use a joke to punctuate—and puncture—emotion.

Samm smiled but shifted restlessly. As always, he wanted to get on with it. He spoke quietly but abruptly. "I've got something for the agenda, Judith. I just heard about a border incident. One of my soldiers has a brother in the guard. He told him about it."

Wonderful, Jo thought. A soldier. Somebody's brother. As usual, her spies were ten paces behind everyone else.

Judith glanced down at her notes. "I've got the treaty. Intelligence. Military report. Response to aggression. Political candidates. I'd say a border incident comes under several of those headings. What did you hear?"

"Bunch of Rockies tried to come through. A dozen or so. The border guard didn't like the look of them, so he asked a lot of questions."

"The look of them?" Jo asked.

"They were loud, pushy, and they were wearing long coats. He made one of them take his off and he was dressed in some kind of uniform. Khaki."

"Rocky military?"

"Well, that's the thing. Military, probably, but one of them tried to talk the guard into going back with them and making babies, and another one was spouting some crap about the immorality of Sierra."

Judith stared at Jo, who blurted, "Military, breeders, and godders, all together?"

As long as Rocky was split into factions, their bluster was limited to infighting. She hoped this was just a fluke, a gang of rejects, and not a first sign of an alliance.

"I'll find someone I can send," she said. "I haven't heard anything about this from the people I have there now." Brave word, "people." Jo had two spies in Rocky. Looked like she'd have to be deploying more. Just when she needed to focus on Scorsi. "What finally happened between the guard and the Rockies?"

"Some of the Rockies had guns, and waved them around

threateningly, but the guard called for help and the Rockies turned around and headed east again. No way to know if they sneaked in some other way."

Everyone sat silent for a moment. Then Judith broke the spell by asking, "Anyone else got anything they want to report?" Jo knew that Judith wasn't downplaying the subject of Rocky. But their eastern neighbor had been posturing and puffing for a long time. A mixed mob of hoodlums in khaki didn't necessarily mean anything.

"I've got something," Drew said. "Waldo."

Judith's mouth twisted. "What about him?"

"He knows when we're having meetings. Every time we have one he's even lazier and meaner at work. He's always watching. The host station has a great view of these stairs. I'm sure he knows we're in here now. He always makes some remark to me. Like 'I'm a Coleman, too.' Or 'What's the big secret this time?' I don't know that it's such a good idea to leave him out of everything."

Jo knew Waldo also hated that Samm, who was not born a Coleman, was part of the inner circle while he was an outsider.

"Too bad," she said. "But that's not going to change. I don't trust him. I think he's capable of selling information to Scorsi."

Judith nodded. "Or stupidly blurting something we don't want blurted."

Jo added: "Or telling a secret to a woman to impress her."

"He'll just have to keep not liking it, Drew," Judith said. "Even if he had something to contribute to the discussion, it wouldn't be a good idea."

"But Mom, if he's burned all the time, doesn't that make him more likely to do something against us?"

Judith shrugged again. "Yes or no, either one." Jo smiled. Exactly. She remembered a time when they'd tried to make Waldo feel like a Coleman in more than name. But he'd said something to Frank about skimming tax money and they'd been forced to start paying the sheriff a percentage. They'd kept him in the dark since then, and the only way they held his supposed loyalty and kept his mouth shut was by letting him keep his well-paying, high-status job. He was an irritation they lived with, like a poison-oak rash that never went away.

Judith was careful to ease away from talk of Waldo in a way that didn't make Drew feel his words were being dismissed along with the topic. "Drew, you're absolutely right about him. He's crawling with resentment. This is something we've been deciding and re-deciding for years. But unless we want to kill him, there's not much we can do." Drew laughed nervously, as if he wasn't really sure she was making a joke. Lizzie studied her mother's face for a clue. Samm looked only mildly interested. He didn't have to deal directly with Waldo, and he avoided him. Jo had often thought killing him would be the best solution, but Judith said they couldn't kill their own cousin.

"But that does bring up another topic, Drew," Judith went on. "I wanted to ask you about someone else you work with. The new woman, Rica—what do you think of her?"

The boy—well, he really wasn't a boy anymore—blushed. Uh oh! Not that Jo couldn't understand it.

"I think she's great. Nice. And smart. And I loved that she tossed Waldo."

"Jo? What do you think?"

Jo hoped she wasn't blushing, too.

"I like her. But there's a lot there to wonder about. She's smart, and she goes deep. Why do you ask?"

"I don't know. I like the way she carries herself, I think she might be, well, helpful. But I don't know how and I don't trust it. I ran her through a verbal maze about Blackjack having enemies, and loyalty, all that kind of thing. She didn't bullshit me but she looked nervous and then she slid right through and out the door. We need good people, and she seems smarter than she needs to be to work at the jobs she works. She might want more. So Drew, when you go back to the restaurant, keep an eye on her."

He nodded eagerly. This was an assignment he obviously liked.

So Judith had hinted to Rica that Blackjack might have more to offer a smart woman than casino work. She did that kind of thing sometimes, hinted at hidden power and a hidden agenda with near-strangers. Jo knew that it was deliberate and never because of lack of caution. Judith believed that rumors were good; that they created confusion and speculation among their enemies. And for those who were not their enemies, rumors built mystique. Judith believed in mystique as a political weapon.

And she wasn't wrong. One thing Jo's people in Rocky had noticed—the Coleman name was known there. Through spying or gossip or both. If Rocky believed the Colemans were creating a buffer in Tahoe, the rich and well-defended gateway to Sierra, if they saw only the image and didn't bore too deeply, they'd be less likely to try to move in. But she didn't want Rocky slipping any other kinds of tentacles, political, military, or economic, into Sierra. Not before the Colemans had a chance to take over.

Consolidation was coming, one way or another. The countries would merge and grow large. She didn't like the way Rocky governed itself; xenophobic, overrun with godders and cops and stiff with laws, hostile, tight-assed. She sure as hell didn't want people like that governing Tahoe and Sierra.

What a trio we are, Jo thought. Judith and her mystique. Samm and his army and his drive to war. And Jo? Well, like Judith and Machiavelli, she believed it was essential to make yourself legendary. And like Samm and Machiavelli, she believed the foundation of power was both good laws and good arms, to inspire both love and fear. And there was so much more. The old expression: hearts and minds. Get to people where they lived, their homes, their health, their sense of powerlessness. Make them believe you could deliver them out of bondage, discontent, or dispersal. Bondage to the vax and those who could get it for them, discontent with weakness and fear and dispersal into nonfunctioning or malfunctioning little countries.

Samm was reporting. He was planning on running a training all day Saturday. Weapons practice, tactics, hand-to-hand. He said he now had a total of forty-eight fighters, up a few from the last time he'd reported. Hardly an army, but more than a police force. Of course, they had no idea how many of those soldiers would actually fight if it came to that, or how many of them would fight for the Colemans.

Samm's next words sounded like he'd been reading her mind. "Thing is, I can't give you a real count. Don't know how many of them are really ours, how many are in Scorsi's pay."

Judith laughed. They all knew that was not a problem. The army could be full of spies for all Jo cared. Scorsi would be so busy getting reports from renegade soldiers he might forget to concentrate on winning people over, on giving and getting economic and political favors.

Lizzie was biting her lip, scowling, puzzled by something. She burst out: "I don't understand why he would send those mercs against us if he knows we have an army. With fifty fighters we could level his stupid casino."

Jo answered. "Knowing Newt, he probably thought he'd scare us off. Show us he has an army too." Jo hated him. Back when they'd been teenagers, he'd tried to rape her. She'd hurt him badly. Broken his hand and his nose. He was the one person in the world she thought of as a personal enemy, besides the bandits who'd murdered her mother as her father lay dying of plague. Mother had been trying to defend the vax she'd just bought on the black market. Judith was a young woman at the time, Jo a child. Jo had run out the back of the house when she heard Judith screaming. When she'd crept back later she found her sister bleeding, ravaged, and her mother shot through the heart. Their father died two days later.

That was thirty years ago. Those bandits were probably dead by now. But Newt was still alive.

"Which brings us to the next item on our agenda. Samm, you had something to say about the merc invasion."

"I do, and Lizzie's already brought it up. If we're ever going to use our fighters I think we should do it now. Go back at him, tear Scorsi's Luck apart. Scare off his customers and give him some real damage to deal with. He sends a few mercs at us, we send four dozen soldiers—or however many are real—at him. Might be a way to find out who's loyal, come to think of it. Teach him a lesson. Back him off. I'd really like to show him what happens when he jumps us."

Uh oh, Jo thought. We'd better cool this off. Judith opened her mouth but before she or Jo had a chance to speak, Lizzie jumped in, her face glowing with excitement.

"I think that's a really tribal idea!"

"Yeah," Drew agreed, glancing ruefully at his injured arm. "Stop him dead right now, no more trouble from that bunch."

"No. We don't want to do that," Jo said, sitting forward, hands clasped. "Samm, you know we don't."

"Why not? This was an outright act of aggression." Samm tilted his chair back on its hind legs, crossing his arms, looking calm but stubborn.

"We don't want to do it because his little attack wasn't much more than a provocation. He wants us to fight back with everything we have so he can see what it is we do have. And he'll try very hard to make us look like bullies in the process. I wouldn't put it past him to shove women and children in with his mercs. Enough of those get hurt we'll lose a lot, politically."

It was an old and despicable ploy, and it always worked.

Judith nodded. "For now, I'll go with Jo on that. Let Newt look like a hoodlum while we keep on making friends. Pretend that we want peace, that we're above his crap. Because we have important things to do for Sierra." She slapped her notepad. "Which brings us to the treaty. We present him with a plan for peace. An alliance between the two families." Samm grinned. He thought the treaty idea was funny. He liked it.

Lizzie spoke up again. "I know you've talked about this, but I don't know why you want to do it now." She turned to Jo. "Do you want the Scorsis to think they scared us?"

Jo laughed. "No one else will think that. Fine if he does. We just rattle on about everyone benefiting financially if we work together."

"It's okay, Liz," Drew said. "This might be fun."

"Work together how?" Lizzie still looked doubtful.

"Well, that's the trick. We need to be so vague the agreement is meaningless, but convince him with one or two small concessions that we mean it. For instance, we say that we agree not to attack or damage each other's businesses. Then we say that in consideration of that, Blackjack agrees to return to negotiations about the Gold Bug." The Gold Bug was a very small casino down on Stateline, right next to Scorsi's Luck. The Colemans owned sixty percent of it and the rest was owned by Newt and a few other investors. Newt wanted it. He wanted to own more of his side of town. When Judith had refused to sell all of their percentage to him, he bought out the other small shareholders and then tried to negotiate enough of the rest so he would have the controlling interest. Judith had ignored his offers.

There wasn't much more to it than that. A few little bits and pieces of a few more shops. Judith read her notes, Jo added some thoughts, including a clause that said they would continue discussing several other deals Scorsi wanted. She knew they'd never get to them. The treaty was just a ploy, a move to keep Scorsi at bay a little longer and keep him out of their hair. It might or might not work.

In half an hour they had a draft. Lizzie, grinning with approval now, declared it "dark."

Jo asked, "How do we negotiate this thing, Judith?"

"I think we send it to them—hand-carry it—and wait for a reaction."

Drew brightened. "Let me be the messenger. They can send Ky and you can send me." Kyron Scorsi was Newt's nephew. About Drew's age. "We can meet somewhere and I'll hand it to him. Then if they want to answer, we can meet again. Neutral back-and-forth until the real negotiations start."

The first time Jo and Judith had mentioned a treaty, Drew had been interested. If it ever got to real negotiations, Jo knew he'd enjoy taking part. Maybe he'd be a diplomat someday, when they truly had use for such a person.

But this courier job? It could be dangerous and Drew was a one-armed man. "I like it. Except, Drew, you're injured. Kyron's a tough guy. He might decide to slap you around just for fun."

"I'll go with him, Jo," Lizzie said, scowling fiercely. Jo was beginning to worry that Lizzie's act of violence, horrified as she had seemed at the time, had given her a taste for it. She was eager to go after the Scorsis, one way or another. Like Samm. Did Jo now have two warriors to hold back?

"Could we?" Drew obviously was in love with his courier idea.

Jo decided not to argue, since Judith didn't seem to mind. It was agreed that Drew and Liz could carry the treaty.

Judith flipped to a new page in her notepad. "What's going on at the intelligence end of things, Jo?"

"Obviously, since we didn't see either the attack on Blackjack or the border raid coming, we could do better." They had a half-dozen people working at Scorsi's Luck. Unfortunately, they didn't seem to be doing a very good job; none of them had gotten close enough to the family to learn about the plan for the attack on Blackjack. She needed more people, or smarter people. Jo would try to come up with ideas, but wanted input from the others. They promised they would think about it.

"Finally, then," Judith said, "the mayor race. The election's in a month. We need to come up with a candidate—a willing one." They all laughed. Nobody wanted to end up hanging dead and upside down from a tree.

Samm stopped scowling about their incompetent spies and brightened. "I may have someone. One of my soldiers. Her name is Hannah Karlow. You may have seen her at the poker tables. Thin woman, long scar on her cheek." Well, thought Jo. She's a busy one. "She mentioned it to me last night at the table. Only half-joking, I think."

"I know her," Jo added. "I just talked to her a couple days ago myself. She's a fixer. I asked her to get the elevator running again. She actually promised to do it soon. Maybe she even will."

Samm nodded. "A fixer would make a popular candidate."

"I know she's one of your soldiers, but how well do you know her? Do you think we can trust her?" Was she really theirs and would she stay theirs? She didn't need to trust a fixer or even a soldier, but a mayor? That could matter.

"I don't know for sure. We can have her watched for a few days, see what we pick up."

That sounded good. "Okay," Jo said. "Let's do that." A few days might not tell them much, but if it didn't work out with Hannah one of them would have to go after the office. She wanted to avoid running herself, or trying to convince Judith or Samm to run. They all had too much to do right now and other campaigns to think about. There were a few employees they were sure they could run for other offices, but a fixer-soldier would carry a lot of charisma, and charisma was what won elections. Charisma and fear. And even though no one else was running yet, she was assuming someone would.

A flood of almost sexual pleasure washed through her. Intelligence was frustrating—especially when it didn't work or only worked sometimes. Like love. But the game of politics? Better than romance. More fun than poker. More interesting than twenty-one. She'd studied propaganda, negative versus positive campaigning, charisma and core issues, promises—a chicken in every pot—made and delivered or made and reneged on, the outsider as threat. Fear. Drew had once sat talking to her about the election of 2016, before the breakup. A man named Cooper, from Utah or Wyoming, she couldn't remember which, had run for president preaching hate under the guise of protective leadership, deliberately stirring up fear of terrorism or moral destruction by anyone who was the least bit unlike whoever Cooper was talking to at the time.

He'd won, and become president. He was assassinated less than a year later by a man who didn't seem to belong to any group at all. But Jo never forgot, after that history lesson from her nephew, that Cooper had won. And while she didn't think she'd ever try to turn one group of Sierrans against another, or Sierra against Redwood, she didn't have to look far to find someone Sierrans could worry about. She didn't mind raising an alarm about Rockymountain. Or, rather, having her candidates do it.

Jo pulled herself out of her cheerful thoughts of political gamesmanship and noticed Drew was looking pale. "If there's nothing else, I think Drew needs to rest."

"Good idea," Judith said. "Drew, when are you planning on going back to work?"

"Waldo wants me to go in tomorrow."

"That seems too soon."

"Maybe, Mom." He grinned. "But you do want me to keep an eye on Rica, after all."

Jo laughed. That was obviously going to be a hardship for him.

CHAPTER 11
WHO KNOWS WHAT KIND OF DIRT HE'S GOT INSIDE HIM?

Ky Scorsi was nowhere in sight. Just like that germ to be late. He and Lizzie were a few minutes early. It was always better to get there first, stake out your territory, get a fix on the field. Ky was stupid. Arrogant. This was exactly the kind of shit that was going to beat the Scorsis in the end.

Drew liked working with Liz. She didn't always agree with him, but once she got past her first questions and decided he was mostly right, she'd usually let him take the lead.

A quick survey of the beach, a quicker discussion, and they put themselves into play. Drew led his sister close to the water's edge, but not too close. They'd both learned in childhood never to turn their backs on a Scorsi, never to let a Scorsi back them into any kind of corner. They sat on a log, worn so smooth it must have floated in, that was far enough from the woods beyond the sand that no one could sneak up on them and far enough from the water to leave room for maneuver.

Position was one thing, attitude was another. Lizzie sat straddling the log, half-facing the woods, alert but pretending not to be. Drew stood beside her facing the lake, casually skimming rocks across its bright surface. Lizzie jabbed her elbow into his ribs and he turned to see Ky emerging from the woods, followed by two of his younger cousins.

It figured. Ky wouldn't have the guts to meet them alone.

He was grinning smugly, ambling toward them in that way he had: long, loose, gangly, all bones, and no brain. "Hey, Cole-

117

man! What happened to your arm?"

Billy Scorsi, who was Lizzie's age, snorted like a horse, and Newt Junior guffawed. Newt was only fifteen but he looked and acted a lot like his father. He had a big head, and it bobbed on his skinny neck when he laughed. Like a marionette, Drew thought. He was laughing and bobbing now. Billy had always been thick, but he seemed to be going to fat lately, and his frizzy orange hair needed cutting.

"I got bit by a mosquito, Ky. Guess we'll have to send some big fish to clean out the larvae."

Billy looked confused for a moment, wrinkling his freckled nose; then he seemed to figure out what Drew meant by fish and larvae and spat into the sand, scowling. He and Newt both looked at Ky, waiting for him to come up with an answer.

Drew kept a scornful look on his face, but he was worried. Three of them. Even with room to move, they could surround and herd him and Liz like dogs with deer. Back when they were nine or so, Ky and a couple of his friends had trapped Drew at the lake's edge one morning and backed him into deep cold water. He could swim, but all three of them had jumped him and held him under. He'd fought hard, managed to get his face into the air and screamed for help. Luckily, a group of tourists from Redwood had seen what was going on and three big men had pulled the boys off him and brought him back to shore, exhausted, nearly drowned, and humiliated enough to hate Ky forever.

Not the kind of trick anyone was going to play on him twice. He skirted the log and moved a few paces closer to the woods. The Colemans and the Scorsis were now equally placed along the beach and he was still near enough to his sister to work as a team.

Ky took a step closer to Drew. "Yeah, well . . . that's big talk, Coleman. But I hear your little sister had to save you from one of the big bad mosquitoes. Is that why you brought her along today?"

Lizzie moved closer to Drew.

Drew laughed. Ky had walked right into that one. "To save me from a mosquito?" Was that Billy growling? What a weird kid. "Looks like you brought the whole pond, tough guy."

Ky glared. The discussion was taxing his brain. Drew thought it was fun, but he could feel Lizzie, too, getting edgy beside him.

Okay, the mosquito metaphor was turning a little tiresome and he wasn't sure how far he could stretch it. Time to move on.

"Why don't we just get down to business?"

Ky agreed immediately, obviously relieved. "Yeah. Why don't we. My uncle says you want to give us some kind of piece of paper." Newt Junior nodded. Billy spat in the sand again.

Drew pulled the folded treaty proposal out of his shirt pocket and held it toward Ky. Ky waited. Drew didn't move. Ky glanced at Lizzie, smoothed his greasy dark hair and leered. Drew felt heat creeping over his neck and face—don't even think about my sister you running sore! Then Ky stepped forward just far enough to grab the two sheets of paper from Drew and backed a few paces toward the log, putting it behind him. His brow furrowed as he read, scratching his scalp. After what felt like five minutes of reading and scratching, he crumpled the sheets and jammed them into his hip pocket. If he'd had his way, Drew guessed, he'd have tossed the treaty at them. But he must have been under strict orders to bring it back.

He swaggered forward again, the two cousins moving with him.

"This is a pile of shit. Everything in there is a lie."

Lizzie spoke up, still calm. "We don't lie. Samm and Jo and our mother . . ."

"Samm?" Ky snickered, looking Lizzie up and down. Bastard. Drew wanted to kill him. "He was born in a hostel. Who knows what kind of dirt he's got inside him?"

Drew could feel Lizzie trembling at his side. She spoke again before he had a chance to. "He wasn't born there. He went there with his mother. She died. They let him out."

Billy growled again. "You mean he escaped."

"Yeah," Ky said, "escaped. Everybody knows that." He moved closer to Lizzie and the others followed, the three Scorsis a triangle with Ky at the point. "He's dirt. And Jo's a slut. And you're a whore. And you go back and tell your fat old mother—"

Drew's breath caught in his throat. He barely had time to take in the last insult before Lizzie's fist connected with Ky's nose. Blood poured down his lip and smeared his chin, dripping onto his denim shirt. He stumbled back, falling against the log, blood gushing from his nostrils, tears streaming from his eyes, and pulled a small handgun from his jacket, waving it wildly, blindly, in the general direction of the Colemans. Lizzie got ahead of Billy and Newt, who were aiming themselves at Drew, and kicked Billy in the groin. He fell to his knees screaming. Newt Junior pulled a buck knife from his pocket and started doing a cautious dance around Lizzie, that ugly head bobbing. Drew lunged past the howling Billy, pulled the pistol from Ky's distracted grip, and smashed him over the ear with it.

Good. That felt good. Drew could breathe again. Ky grunted and dropped to the ground, his mouth open. But Drew's roar, ripping from his throat like nothing he'd ever felt before, drowned out whatever other sound Ky might have made. Maybe Ky would stop breathing altogether. Had he? No time to worry about that. Newt came at him with the knife and Drew had to threaten to shoot him before he'd stop. Billy saw the gun in Drew's hand, stumbled to his feet, and ran for the woods, but Newt Junior, red-faced with rage, wasn't retreating. He was screaming obscenities and jabbing the knife at the air in front of him. Too stupid to run, Drew thought. But Drew wasn't.

Drew stuck the gun in his waistband, under his shirt. He grabbed Lizzie's arm, yelled, "Enough of this shit!" Lizzie didn't hold back, she let him yank her away, and the two of them got the hell out of there. They stopped running about halfway back to Blackjack and stopped, leaning against a redwood fence to catch their breath.

Drew had ignored his two-day-old arm injury during the quick struggle with Ky and he was still so flushed with adrenaline that the abused wound didn't hurt—yet. But he thought he'd felt something tear and there was a small spot of blood on his sling.

Lizzie was gasping for breath and laughing. "That was sooo dark! Drew, wasn't that the darkest?"

What the hell did she think was so funny? His arm was beginning to throb, then burn, and he wanted her to just shut the hell up.

"Liz! What kind of asshole trick was that? Why'd you start a fight?"

"Hey, Ky's the one who started it!" Lizzie was grinning. She was going to start laughing again, he knew it.

"But I think I killed him." Hitting Ky had felt good at the time, but now he was getting scared.

"No you didn't. I saw him move right before we ran."

That was a relief.

"Well, but really, all he did was say something stupid. And all we had to do was look injured and innocent and go away shaking our heads. But no, you have to punch the nickel-ante valley-boy and make him pull a gun." Lizzie had always been a bit impulsive, and Drew had covered for her more than once. But nothing like this. This was over the line.

"I didn't make him—"

"And then that asshole, Newt. And Billy! Did you hear that spotty freak growling? You don't want to mess with those guys, Liz. They don't get over it."

Lizzie shrugged. "I'm not afraid of them."

"You should be. And I'm not lying to Mom this time, either. You tell her what happened."

She glared at him. "Including the fact that you hit Ky so hard you thought he was dead?"

"He had a gun. I had to do something before he shot someone." That was true, but it sure wasn't all of it. He knew it and so did she.

She sighed. They were supposed to be trying to fool the Scorsis into thinking they were worried, or at least conciliatory. And breaking Ky's nose, maybe his head, and Billy's balls, was pretty far from conciliation. Not only that, Mother had ordered them to report fully and accurately on whatever happened and whatever was said. She'd know if they were hiding something. They'd have to tell her. All of it. She would push until she got the whole story, Drew knew, including the exact insult that had set Lizzie off. Not slut, not whore—fat old mother, that was what had done it.

Lizzie was biting her lip, not laughing any more. It was clear she was as reluctant to face their mother with this story as he was, now that the violent rush was over.

"Well, we don't have to say we hit them first, do we?"

Lizzie was living in a dreamworld. He shook his head. "Evasion won't work. You should know that by now."

"It's not evasion! We just don't have to tell her everything that happened exactly as it happened. We delivered the treaty, after all."

Always the same. Lizzie would do something risky and then she'd be afraid of Mother's disapproval. She'd start lying. Loyally, he'd keep silent. Then Mother would find the lie and they'd both be in trouble. More trouble than the truth would ever have brought them. And that had been for little things like staying out after curfew. This was bigger. He wanted her to trust him with missions. He was worried about Lizzie's unthinking violence, afraid she'd get herself into something she couldn't get out of, some place and time when no one was there to help. He was enraged that Ky had said what he'd said and acted the way he had with Lizzie, and that Lizzie had reacted as she had and that both of them had made him so crazy he wanted to kill Ky. What had happened to his self-control?

"I'm not going along this time, Lizzie. We screwed up and she has to know what happened. What really happened."

By the time they got home, he'd worked it out in his head. It was just a fight. Not a smart fight, not a strategic one, but understandable. He'd had a moment's rage. Everyone did. The guy was drooling at his sister and trying to kill her, all at once! And they'd done their job, after all. The treaty proposal was delivered and look! Blackjack was jammed with customers again. The merc attack had put only a two-day dent in the business. Lots of people tossing their coins and bills into the slots, braving the tables, losing their money, looking hypnotized and self-satisfied.

Drew played a slot once in a while, just for fun, but he didn't understand why people would throw away all their money this way, and some did. Sad for them, but Tahoe was what it was. One of a kind, too. Vegas, over in Rocky, burned down by godders long ago, and Reno shriveled to nothing but a bandit camp.

But Tahoe was still here. Still beautiful and open for business. He would do anything to protect it from people like Ky. Maybe someday again, if Mother and Jo and Samm had things the way they wanted, Tahoe would be like it was long ago. Elevators rising a dozen floors and more, carrying hundreds of people. The lots full of big cars. It made him feel better to think of the long range. Little mistakes like today, they'd just fade away.

He glanced at Lizzie. She was worried about what Mother would say, but he could tell she didn't really feel bad about what had happened.

They walked slowly, both of them reluctant to reach Mother's office. Through the bell clanging, the laughter, the intensity of customers focused entirely on the machines or the cards or the table in front of them, up the stairs to the mezzanine.

Drew knocked and they walked in. Jo was sitting on the couch drinking something from a cup. Probably some of Mother's imported tea. Mother, holding a glass of beer, sat behind her ten-foot desk, squeezed into her oversized chair, big and round and powerful in a purple dress.

"Look at them, Jo. Bad news, I'd guess. You didn't lose the treaty, did you?"

"No," Lizzie said. "We delivered it." Drew waited for her to go on. She didn't. It had to be obvious to his mother and Aunt Jo that something uncomfortable hung between them. They stood there, in front of Mother's desk. They didn't sit and she didn't invite them to.

Jo laughed, deep and soft, brushing a speck of lint off the front of her blue brocade vest, crossing one strong velvet-knickered leg over the other. "You delivered it, that's good. Whatever else happened probably won't matter in the end, kids. But we need to know."

Lizzie glanced at Drew. He glared at her. She glared back, but capitulated. "It was my fault, I guess. Go ahead, Drew, tell them. You probably remember it better than I do." He probably did. After all, he'd only been crazy for a minute or two.

He reached under his shirt, pulled the gun out of his waistband, and laid it on his mother's desk. Her eyes widened. Jo jumped to her feet, strode the three steps to the desk, picked the gun up, and turned it over in her hands.

"Nice," she said. "Fairly new. Where'd you find the weapon?" She took it back to the couch and sat again, looking at it.

Her appreciation for his trophy made telling the story a little easier. Leaving out exactly what Ky had said, he told them there was an insult that started the fight, and explained how they'd defended themselves against the Scorsis' weapons. He didn't leave out the part about smashing Ky's head, even though he really wanted to.

Mother was scowling. "And what exactly was the insult that started this off?"

"He called us names." Drew hoped she'd leave it at that, but of course he knew she wouldn't.

"Names? What names?" She would push to the very end. He couldn't bring himself to say it.

Lizzie spoke up, finally. "He said you were old and fat, that Jo is a slut and I'm a whore and that Samm is hostel dirt."

Mother's mouth twitched, the way it did when she stopped a smile. She shook her big head, the gray curls bobbing, the amethyst earrings dancing and flashing, and shot a glare at Liz.

"Well, damn, Lizzie, I am old and fat." She hesitated. "Maybe not so old. And the rest is just words. There's no place for a fast temper when you're delivering a peace proposal." She let the irony of the situation shine from her eyes, but Drew noticed his mother was studying Lizzie's face, maybe thinking what he'd been thinking about her new quickness to violence.

"I know. I'm sorry. But I thought Ky was going to do something besides just act stupid and I could see him bashing Drew on the arm or, I don't know . . . something."

"But there wasn't any bashing until you bashed, isn't that what you're saying?" Mother didn't look angry any more. She didn't look amused, either. Just thoughtful.

Lizzie nodded, looking at her feet. "That's right. I bashed first."

Jo was studying Drew's arm. He followed her gaze. The blood on his sling was obvious, a quarter-real-sized spot of deep red on the white cloth.

"Looks like you popped a stitch, Drew. Better show it to the doc."

Drew nodded, relieved that she was so calm about it.

Mother was still glaring at Lizzie. "I'm glad you can take care of yourself, Liz. But next time think before you swing." She ran a thick finger over the smooth surface of a snow globe and her face relaxed.

"Now tell me this. In the heat of battle, you didn't let slip any information, did you? Didn't give them any reason to think that maybe we weren't serious about the treaty?"

"No, Mother!" Lizzie looked indignant.

"Well, fine then. And Ky took the treaty with him?"

"He stuck it in his pocket," Drew said.

"Good. I'll message Newt and make sure he got it."

"And next time . . ." Jo began. Mother held up her big hand. Drew wondered what she thought Jo was planning to say. Next time take prisoners? He suppressed a smile.

"Next time, children," she said, "just deliver the damned message. You're not emissaries, you know. You're not negotiating the damned treaties. You're not fighting any wars for my honor or anyone else's. You're just—"

"Couriers," Lizzie said.

Which, Drew thought, was a very good segue to something he'd been wanting to talk to her about. Maybe this wasn't the best time to bring it up, standing there in semidisgrace. But she'd brought it up, in a way. He was nineteen. And he was old enough to do more than carry pieces of paper.

"Mom, can we talk about some more—" His eyes slid toward

his sister and away again. She'd be jealous. She might ruin everything by making some demands herself. "Adult assignments for me? I know Samm would have me in—"

"I know. You want to train with Samm's army. Starting tomorrow." He knew she didn't really want him to, not yet.

"Yes. Starting tomorrow."

She sighed, glanced at Jo, who shrugged, leaving it to her. "Okay, Drew. Now go get your dinner."

"But not me?" Lizzie interjected. "Can I go tomorrow, too?"

Crap, Drew thought. She's just a kid. She's got no business even asking. What if Mother changed her mind about him?

"No, Lizzie. We'll talk about it, but it's too soon."

Drew shot a look at his sister. She was scowling at him, her lips tight. He knew one of these days he'd be the target of a tirade—I'm a better fighter, I've proved myself, if you're in the army I should be, too—but for now, she was silent.

Drew and Lizzie left their mother's office. He headed for the restaurant to do his half shift, and Lizzie—well, he never knew where she was going unless she was going with him.

CHAPTER 12
YOU'RE A FIXER?
I'M IMPRESSED.

No question about it, I didn't like Newt Scorsi. But I'd certainly worked for people I didn't like before. Chiefs were often corrupt or stupid. Private citizens who hired mercenaries or instigated the hiring were not always the most upstanding. But then, neither was I.

There were his decidedly unattractive personal qualities—I hoped I'd never have to watch him eat again—but my skin-scratchy dislike went beyond that. The more I thought about it the more sure I was that he was so devious as to be dangerous.

Although only the change guy Bernard had exposed himself to me as a Scorsi spy, or at least someone who did odd jobs for Scorsi, Newt had said that he had "people" in the Coleman camp. Either he was bragging and turning one man into many, or he was hiding people from me. I doubted it was, as he'd said, to protect them. Just as likely it was so that someone I didn't suspect could kill me if he decided I had to go. In any case I had this ugly picture of a dozen amateur mercenaries floating around Blackjack crashing into each other, none of them knowing the other was a spy, none of them trusted or trusting, making my job tougher than it should have been.

Even if Scorsi was not a fool he was the type who sometimes thought "smart" involved elaborate, unnecessary, and convoluted schemes and secrets.

Did Bernard know if there were others? Did he know who they were? Did any of them know?

I wondered if I shouldn't spend some time shadowing Newt and finding out what he was really up to, but the prospect was not nearly as appealing as getting to know Samm better and I would certainly have to do that to get some idea of what this supposed army was all about. If it even existed.

A couple of hours before my shift was due to start I headed for the casino. Sure enough, Samm was working the center table, second of three. I stationed myself behind the railing, not playing, just watching, pretending I was getting some pointers on the great game of poker. Not that I couldn't use pointers. I lean more toward the slots than the tables. I get enough conflict in my work. Enough bluffing, too.

I'd first noticed Samm's height and physical power during the merc raid. Watching him now, I could see that even his dealing had a casual strength about it. Nothing sloppy or indecisive in his movements. The man in charge of the military. The general. That was what Newt Scorsi had called him. A pretentious title, considering the probable size of the well-hidden and possibly mythical army. Then again, for all I knew, half the people in Tahoe were secret Coleman foot soldiers. And the other half? What were they? Neutral? Scorsi fans? Unaware of any rivalry at all?

Samm smiled and nodded to me. "Sit down, Rica. Plenty of room tonight."

"I don't want to play, just watch."

"Sit down anyway." He patted the empty chair beside him. His smile was sweet, his dark eyes warm. If I hadn't seen him fighting off mercs I'd have wondered if he was a soldier at all.

A scrawny black-haired man with a day's growth of dirty-looking beard that didn't hide the smallpox pits, wearing a too-big rusty black jacket, watched me take the seat between him and Samm.

He grinned. Dirty teeth. "Yeah. Sit down and be my luck."

The slightly-less-used-up greasy blond specimen sitting next to him on the other side laughed. "Forget it, Willy. She's house luck. She works here." He leered at me. "Noticed you in the restaurant the other night, miss. And now I see your picture's up outside the lounge. Pretty. Word is you sing real good. Is that true?"

I hadn't realized the poster was up. I'd have to take a look. And word? Already? Jo wasn't wasting any time in pumping up business.

"Thanks. I guess it's true. But I'll leave that up to the audience to decide, once I actually give a performance."

Samm was dealing seven stud. An orange-haired woman of about thirty-five was showing a pair of aces, the potbellied man next to her three on a straight. He raised her bet by twenty dollars. Willy and his friend folded.

"Wonder if I could learn to do that," I said, watching Samm's strong, graceful brown hands dole out the last up cards. I wasn't really interested in being a dealer, but I was looking to spend time with the general, and I also wanted to get a feel for when he was around and when he might be out doing things I needed to track. From what I'd been able to observe, Samm worked the tables between five and midnight, same as my hours, which gave him a lot of free daylight to do other things. And if Newt wasn't entirely full of shit, what he had to be doing some of the time was meeting with his troops, training and recruiting, or supervising the training and recruiting.

"You want to learn to deal?" I nodded. He smiled at me again. "I don't see why not. Doesn't take a genius." He laughed. "Not that I don't think you're a genius. You know the game?"

"I've played a few times."

"Win?" He grinned. He had the most beautiful cheekbones. And his eyes weren't really all that dark. Hazel. Deep hazel.

"Mostly lost. And the times I've watched the tables here I've noticed some pretty sharp players." Dirty-face and Blondie preened. The potbellied man looked alarmed. The woman just looked bored. "I guess you've been doing this a long time, Samm?"

"A few years."

"Always for the Colemans?"

"Yep. Always." Dirty-face had bet too much for Potbelly. He folded.

"They're good people to work for," I said.

That earned me a smile and a nod. Dirty-face picked up a nice pot.

"Sure are. Glad you like it here." He was dealing again. "You know, I'd like to hear you sing. I'll bet I could get someone to take over for me a while one evening."

I said it would be lovely if he came to the opening the next night.

He nodded. "Maybe a glass of something together afterward?" Potbelly snorted.

"Good idea."

But it was still his days I wanted to know about. I stood up, as if I were leaving, then pretended to have a second thought. "Maybe you could give me some lessons in dealing sometime soon. What day would work for you?"

"Not tomorrow. I won't be here. How about I let you know?"

Perfect. Now all I had to do was find out what would be keeping him so busy. Only one way to do that: follow him.

I'd heard the Colemans had apartments on the second floor. I hadn't seen anyone but other employees and hotel guests on the third floor and Samm was more like family, so I was guessing his place was on the second floor, where I really had no business being. But I could station myself down in the casino, in a spot where I could watch the doors, early enough in the morning to catch him leaving.

When I'd climbed the stairs to the third floor and pushed open the door into the hallway, I noticed that the elevator doors were open and someone was fiddling with the wiring. A tall skinny woman. The scar-faced woman I'd seen playing poker the day before.

She looked over at me and smiled. The smile deepened the long mark on her left cheek, a white gash that ran from sharp cheekbone to craggy jaw. She wore her hair chin-length and un-striped; it hung lank around her starved face. Her eyes were sharp and dark and radiated ambivalence. Friendly. Angry. Warm. Cold.

"Are they fixing the elevator?" I asked, rather stupidly.

"I am."

"Oh, sorry. You're a fixer? I'm impressed."

She shrugged, but she looked pleased. "What's your name?" she asked.

"Rica."

"Hello, Rica. I'm Hannah. There's a sign outside the lounge that says Rica Marin will be singing there tomorrow night. There's a photo, too. Looks like you. I guess it must be?"

"Yep. That's me."

She flashed an even bigger smile. "Now I'm impressed."

Injuries like the one that had left the scar on Hannah's face were common. There were a lot of scarred people around. The borders could get nasty from time to time, some bandits were meaner than others, ordinary people were driven past the edge of violence when vax or food were involved. But Hannah's scar was not a disfigurement, somehow. She wore it well. Like a pirate or one of those Twentieth Century Nazis with their saber scars. It added mystery and interest to a face that was stark and worn-looking, eroded like sandstone.

"Should I come and hear you sing, Rica?" She said it as if she wanted me to invite her, so I did. I didn't know why I should get to know this woman but she seemed to want to get to know me. Maybe she was more than a fixer. It occurred to me for a second that she might be a spy for Scorsi, making a connection. But I thought she looked too much like a spy to actually be one.

When I got to the restaurant, Timmy told me that Drew was going to work as a server each evening while I performed and Lizzie was taking over some of the bussing part time. Lizzie was already there, cleaning off table two.

"What about days off?" I asked. We all seemed to be working seven days a week. Even Drew, with his wounded arm, was already putting in time again.

I'd prodded Waldo about the schedule the day before. I hadn't gotten an answer. He'd muttered, "Days off . . ." Then he mumbled something about figuring that out.

"Well, sweetie, Waldo has promised to write out a schedule. Everyone, days, nights, whatever, doing no more than six shifts a week. God knows when he'll actually do it. Of course if he were more willing to work, we'd have enough people to cover the serving and bussing twenty-four hours and get days off too."

I was wondering why the Colemans were leaving so much management up to Waldo. They seemed to be thoughtful and generous employers. Waldo was a tox-bag. It didn't match. Now that there were two young Colemans working there, and presumably talking about their jobs to the higher-ups in the family, would things change?

The night before I'd noticed the whole herd of Colemans and Coleman adjuncts—Jo, Samm, Drew and Lizzie—walking past the door of the restaurant. I faked a trip to the restroom to see where they were going. They all went up to Judith's office and closed the door. And I'd also noticed that Waldo had watched them and hadn't looked happy about it. Whatever they were talking about, he wasn't in on it. So even if he was untouchable he wasn't part of the inner circle.

Why was this man no one liked running the restaurant in the first place? Maybe Waldo had something on Judith or some other Coleman.

So. He was pissed off and jealous, nasty and lazy. An outsider who had something on the Colemans. Sounded to me like a man who could be bought. If I got desperate enough, I could always give that a try. I'd have to be end-of-the-road desperate, though. Traitors who can be bought tend to sell their wares to everyone.

Chapter 13
Ragtag Bunch of Shitheads

Five o'clock Saturday morning, dressed in drab and gnawing on a stale hard roll I'd saved from the restaurant the night before, I peered out my open door, scanning the hallway. No one was there. I quick-stepped to the stairs.

I knew it was going to be hard to be invisible down in the casino. I couldn't fade into a crowd if there was no crowd. Some employees would be wandering around but at this hour even the most obsessive gamblers were more likely to be eating breakfast or sleeping than hitting the slots. It couldn't be helped. I had no idea when Samm would be leaving.

How early did Samm's army rise? Didn't all armies crawl out of bed before dawn? Was I going to be early enough?

Sure enough, the casino was nearly empty. I didn't know if anyone was noticing me, because I was very busy avoiding the eye contact that would make me memorable. With any luck, the few customers and early-shift workers would either not notice, not care enough to remember, or assume that insomnia had driven me downstairs. I'd thought to get a roll of nickels after my restaurant shift the night before, so not even the change people would be forced to notice my presence at this weird hour.

I stationed myself as unobtrusively as I could, at the last of a line of nickel poker slots, a vantage point from where I could see both the front and back doors, and waited to see what happened.

At least there was no sign of Jo or Drew or Lizzie or Judith anywhere around, although I hadn't seriously expected Judith to be up and moving.

Huddled at my machine, pretending to be invisible, hoping I wouldn't win a noisy jackpot, I began to play, slowly, trying to lose. Jacks or better, draw. This was all going to be a terrible waste of energy if Samm had an all-day date with a nubile shopkeeper.

A pair of tens. I dumped one and got a pair of queens. Wonderful. I didn't want to win, so I was sure to get great hands.

I drew to an inside straight and lost a nickel to the house.

Whoa! Three kings. I dumped all three of them and got a handful of garbage. That was more like it.

A pair of twos, a king, a jack, and a four. What should I do? Keep the king and jack or keep the twos? I kept one of the twos and the four, and drew a three and a five—and an eight.

Four hearts. Tossed them all.

I went on this way for nearly an hour before, finally, Samm came striding through the casino. I slid around the side of my slot, putting the row between me and him. He didn't even look around, just aimed for the back door.

This part wasn't going to be easy, either. Insomnia was one thing, following him was something else. I'd have to be slick and casual. The second he was outside, I sidled to a bank of slots next to the door and scanned the parking lot. The angle wasn't good; I didn't see him. I walked aimlessly, idly, yawning, past the doorway, and spotted him, over on the right, unlocking a yellow floater. Pretty. But my dark green Electra was better: less noticeable.

I was parked in the next row over; I'd either have to walk past him to get to my car or wait until he was on his way out of the lot. I was afraid of losing him but waiting was the only way.

I couldn't risk his seeing me. Some scenario that was: Oh, look, there's Rica, at dawn, getting into her car. And damned if she isn't following me. He'd be catching me in his rearview all the way to the meeting or whatever it was. And maybe using me for target practice once we got there.

I edged up to the side of the door and watched as he started his floater and eased it out of the row, heading toward the north exit. When he turned right onto the street, I shoved the casino door open and dashed to my car, hit the lock and the starter and careened to the street.

He was already two blocks down, three cars ahead, but in the sparse early morning traffic the bright yellow floater wasn't hard to follow even at that distance.

At the end of the old strip, traffic thinned even more. Only one vehicle between us now. And half a mile into the outskirts, I lost the cover of that last car, dropped back, feinted a turn, and circled around to follow again. If he turned off while I was doing that, I'd lose him entirely.

That almost happened. I barely caught sight of him turning left onto a northbound road.

The low sun was burning off the morning mist. His floater practically glowed in the light. Once again, with no other cars for cover, I had to take a chance on losing him. I stopped at the corner, counted to ten, and went looking for him again.

There he was. Dead ahead. Another straight two miles on rutted and pockmarked asphalt and then right onto a curving dirt road. This was both good and bad. Even though the floater never touched the surface its blowers raised dust, which was good. I could follow the dust. But the bad part: my tires raised dust, too. I had to stay even farther back, hiding behind the curves. And he had the advantage of a smooth ride on a rough road while I navigated a long, slow, dusty, bumpy three miles into deep woods wilderness. I consoled myself that at least it wasn't winter. I probably would have run nose-first into a ten-foot drift by now.

I coasted around a curve and saw him much too close ahead, pulling off into a tall stand of pines at the edge of deeper woods. He stopped. I jammed into reverse, backed up a few dozen yards, and found cover beneath an enormous fir nesting in a snarl of ripe blackberry. I reached into the dashbox for face-camo, smearing green and brown all over my forehead, cheeks, and chin. Stepping out of the car, I got myself caught up in the thorns. Nothing nastier than blackberry. I swear the stuff has a hostile mind. Dressed for the morning chill, I managed to mostly avoid getting punctured, but one thorn caught me on the back of my hand and another barely missed my left eye, ripping a hot scratch along my cheekbone. I choked back a curse. Berries spotted my dust-brown jacket. Squinting, ducking my head to protect my face, trying to work fast despite all the precautions, I covered the car with vines and branches and a dirty camo tarp I kept stowed in the back.

Hopscotching along, tree to tree, I got within a dozen yards of his parking spot and shot a quick look through the brush toward his car. He, too, had pulled out a tarp, tossing it over the top of his floater. He finished tying it down securely and marched off into the woods. Just like in the casino, he didn't look around, he just aimed where he was going. He must have felt safer than he was. I admired his confidence and enjoyed my superiority all at once.

I sneaked closer. It wasn't until I was right up on his car that I could see that others were also parked there, hidden under the trees, some draped with tarps, some buried in branches and vines. Several cars, mostly not floaters—the general had more money than his troops—a truck or maybe two. The woods were thick and I couldn't tell how far in on either side cars might be hidden. There was even an eight-seater bus, covered with tarps and branches, but still pretty hard to miss once you were under the trees.

I'd never have known this spot existed at all if I hadn't been following someone who was going there on purpose. There were no houses anywhere near, not for miles. Barely a road. A few old ruts with summer-brown weeds stretched across them like rags. I was betting these were the only cars that had come down this way for years.

Reminding myself that Samm might not be the last to arrive, that others might come behind me, I surveyed the path ahead, tension knotting my shoulders and stiffening my neck. I forced my shoulders down, rolled my head from side to side, and crept after him. Staying under cover, stepping quiet on the needles and trying to avoid the crackling dead branches, watching my back, my sides, and the brambles and brush ahead, I followed a rough trail that was no more than a line of dirt where the needles had been kicked away. Again, good and bad. If I followed the trail, I risked coming up on someone or having someone come up behind me. On the other hand, the trail was quieter and faster than stumbling through the underbrush. So I stuck with it until, a hundred or so paces in, I heard voices dead ahead, maybe twenty yards. Too close. The stale roll refluxed into my throat. I veered to the right, off into the brush, and began picking my way carefully and slowly toward them.

The trees and brush were thinning ahead. I couldn't see any movement yet, but the hum of a laser pistol sent a cold draft through to my bones. Nothing near me looked zapped but even so I dropped, crouching, then crawling to the edge of the wood, squinting out into a large clearing.

Samm was there with at least four dozen people. Five of the women held laser pistols, burning holes in a painted cloth target strung between two trees at the other side of the open space a good fifty yards away. Some of the others were watching. One blond young woman with a strong swimmer's build, early twenties I guessed—she looked familiar, did she work in the casino bar? No, she was a dealer. I'd seen her talking to that big bald guy the night of the raid. What was her name?—stepped up and aimed a sleek little gun, squeezed the trigger and burned through the bull's-eye, a little puff of smoke announcing the hit.

"Great shot, Emmy!" the next woman yelled, clapping her on the shoulder and taking her place. Emmy stepped back, smiling.

Samm was talking to a small group of men and women who held a variety of weapons, everything from laser guns to old pistols to swords to bows to staffs. Or maybe they were spears. Yes. Some staffs and some spears. Among them, cheerfully twirling an old pistol around her right index finger, was Hannah Karlow, the fixer.

Suddenly, loud voices and laughter erupted behind me on the trail, and the snapping and cracking and shuffling of someone crashing through the woods without stealth. I'd been so fascinated by the scene in the clearing that I'd closed the eyes on the back of my head. Stupid!

I slipped behind a tree and watched them arrive. The latecomers were Zack, the poker dealer; Monte, the head cashier; and Drew. Zack and Drew were both carrying canvas bags; Zack's looked heavy. Monte was carrying nothing but he was still having trouble keeping up, huffing and puffing. He wasn't young, in his late fifties, at least, with gray hair, and he looked like he needed to eat more. I didn't know how much time he'd spent struggling along in this army, but maybe a little more time would make him fit. Then again, it might kill him.

They passed me and broke into the clearing. Zack handed his bag to Samm. "Here you go, Sammy-boy." Was that how he talked to his "general?" Samm dropped it to the ground. It clanked. Drew kept his slung over his good shoulder, hanging on and smiling like holding that bag was making him happy.

Watching Drew at the restaurant, working with him, I'd gotten the impression of strength, the personal awkwardness of a normal nineteen-year-old mixing oddly with a watchful, quiet, almost studious depth. I liked him. He was sweet.

Samm smiled at the boy. "Drew. Welcome."

"Thanks. Lizzie's really burned that she couldn't come."

The two older men laughed and Zack said something about "growing up." Drew stuck out his chest and swaggered a bit, finally laying the sack he'd been holding at Samm's feet. Was this the first time Drew had been allowed to come to this adult place? He was acting very proud of being there, and Samm's welcome sounded significant.

Samm dropped Drew's bag on the ground alongside the other one. It didn't clank. He knelt next to the noisy one, loosened the ties, reached in, and pulled out a pistol that looked dull, even rusty, like it had been buried for thirty years. He and Zack talked a bit, too softly for me to hear, while Drew listened. They dumped the rest of the sack's contents on the ground. A couple dozen guns of various ages and styles, from what I could see.

Several of the troops came over to look. Hannah was one of the first, still twirling her pistol. Monte picked up a revolver, opened it, looked at it carefully, shook his head. Samm punched him on the shoulder, playful but, I thought, irritated by the small sign of doubt. The cashier shrugged, shoved all the guns back into their sack and dragged it to the side of the clearing, where he sat against a tree and began examining the weapons one by one. The bag that Drew had brought still lay on the ground, unopened.

The women with the lasers surrendered them to five other people. A knot of soldiers paired off for hand-to-hand, proceeding to huff and puff and crash into "the enemy," circle, and throw each other to the ground. Several men pulled out knives and swords, blunted with wooden sheaths, and ran at each

other, thrusting and parrying, while Drew and a couple of men
and women with large staffs tried to knock each other out. It all
looked painful and a little silly but they seemed to be having a
good time despite the bruises. At one point, Drew must have
thought he'd taken enough hits, because he went to try the laser
pistols. He wasn't as good as Emmy the dealer, but he got a
bull's-eye after three tries.

Samm talked with various of his soldiers, sat and scribbled
some notes with Zack and Drew and Monte, all the time with
one eye on the battles. Evaluating the troops every second.
Once I'd convinced myself that I was well-enough hidden, I
kept myself amused by placing bets on combatants. I bet that
Hannah would flatten the young, muscular man she was hand-
to-hand fighting with—he looked too cocky—and she did.

As soon as he yelled "enough!" she jumped up, breathing
hard, grinning, and looked around the field of battle.

Something caught her eye and she ran to a stack of weapons
leaning against a tree, pulling two wood-sheathed swords from
the tangle. Then she swung back around, carrying them across
the field.

"Samm!" she yelled. "Want to have a go?"

He turned from his notes, looking startled by the invitation,
but he got over his surprise quickly enough, laughed, and shook
his head.

"You can't beat me, Hannah."

"We won't know until I do it, will we?" She was laughing,
too.

He shrugged, grabbed one of the big swords out of her hands,
and in the next breath, brought it down across her shoulder.
She grunted. Red-faced, she jumped back and swung in a
horizontal arc, catching him at the side of the waist, hard. He
doubled over but recovered almost instantly, avoiding a
downward chop and thrusting his weapon into her belly. She

yelled, clutching her gut, but the cry of pain shifted mid-note into a roar. She straightened, looking taller than she had before, and went at him, thrusting, swinging, lunging. He fell back for a moment, feinted, feinted again, moving like a beautiful big dancer, graceful and powerful all at once, leaping and spinning. I could almost hear music. A big, crashing, Slavic dance. Western Asia. Eastern Europe. Whichever. Hannah gripped her sword with both hands, yelling like the spotty hordes were at her back, missed a final thrust—and Samm caught her at the side of the head, spinning her around, whacking her broadside across the back. She stumbled, dropped her sword, shook her head to clear it.

"Enough, Hannah?"

She stared at her weapon, lying on the ground.

"It seems that way, Samm." She laughed, but the sound was jagged, forced. When she looked back up at him I couldn't catch her expression from where I watched. But her voice was tight. "This time, anyway."

"Good fight," he said.

"Good fight," she answered.

He went back to his notes and she walked off toward the target practice, stiff-legged. She would have some physical pain that night, but I got the feeling her ego was hurting more.

The disorganized-looking play went on for perhaps another hour, or maybe it just seemed that way to me, lying in the dusty needles. I was beginning to think it was time for me to leave, that nothing new was happening, that I'd memorized enough faces, heard enough chat, when Samm shouted, once, twice, until everyone had heard and stopped what they were doing. They all ran to the middle of the clearing and lined up in neat ranks. The general alone stood separate, pacing back and forth in front of his troops.

"You're still a ragtag bunch of shitheads, but you're getting better. You're nowhere near ready to be an army, but you will, repeat will, be one by the end of the year. Are you working to recruit more fighters?"

They all screamed "Yes!"

"We need more of everything. Weapons, soldiers, dedication, training. Don't ever forget that. The more ready . . . fewer casualties . . . ultimate victory . . ." I'd stopped listening. A pep talk. I let his words sink to a drone in my head, focused on his neatly lined up troops, young and youngish and not-so-young at all, men and women, eager, fired up, ready to fight and die? Or ready to fight so they wouldn't die, just like I was? I tuned in to Samm again. Samm standing in front of them like something out of a heroic myth. He had the look and, as I'd seen during his battle with Hannah, he fought like a hero.

He was talking, now, in a slightly lower tone, which made it hard to hear. "Zack has set up the war-games plan for today . . . two opposing armies . . . all day . . . however long . . . the objective is the usual . . . trees . . ." He waved an arm toward some firs on a hillock to the east, where I could just make out what looked like a rough shed. The enemy castle?

Suddenly he called out: "Drew!" The boy came running, sack in hand. Samm spoke to him, quietly. Then he called out to Hannah and Zack. They came forward. Drew reached into the sack and began to pull out scarves, red ones and blue ones. Hannah took all the red ones, Zack the blue.

"Count off!" Samm yelled. The troops began to shout numbers and fall into two separate groups. Hannah and Zack distributed the "uniforms," which the soldiers tied around their necks.

A game of Capture the Shed. No need to stay for that. I had the information I'd come for. It was true. Blackjack, or at least Samm, was raising and training an army.

Now I needed to find out what they planned to do with it,

and when. Then I could tie up the package, hand it to Chief Graybel, and collect my pay.

I was just about to turn away and slink off down the path again when Hannah Karlow's eyes caught mine, dead on.

CHAPTER 14
YOU HAVE TO TRY
THE PORK BUNS

How had she spotted me, smeared with camo and tucked behind the leaves? There couldn't have been anything but my eyes showing. How had she managed to do that? Was she an eagle in disguise? A cat? Maybe she had caught a movement.

I held my breath, pulse racing, watching her, crawling slowly and carefully away from the edge of the clearing, expecting every second to hear her yell "Spy!" and see her point right at me. But she didn't.

She hasn't seen me, I decided. She was just staring into space and hadn't seen me at all. That had to be it.

She didn't call out, didn't point, didn't start to move my way. She just stood there, staring into my eyes, a smile brushing her thin-lipped mouth.

Hadn't seen me? Bullshit. She was looking right at me and doing nothing. She was no ordinary Blackjack soldier, not even an ordinary scar-faced gambling fixer. The problem: I knew what she wasn't, but I didn't know what she was.

I turned, rose into a crouch, and slithered away as fast and as silently as I could. When I'd gotten some distance between myself and the clearing full of Coleman army, I ran like crazy for my car, sweating in the dark and chilly woods, my ears tuned and damned near swiveling to catch any sound of pursuit.

Nothing.

Plowing back through the attacking berry patch, I yanked the tarp off my car, tossed it inside, slid into my seat, jabbed the starter, and pulled the disk sharply to the left, skittering out onto the road.

Still nothing. No shouts, no pursuing soldiers.

Gripping the disk hard to keep my shaking hands under control, I kept hearing the same words over and over again in my head: why did Hannah let me get away? Was she telling Samm right now that I'd been spying on the maneuvers? Was she keeping the information to herself for some reason I had yet to discover? I had to choose between three courses of action. Behave as if Hannah had not seen me, since Hannah seemed to be pretending that she hadn't; go to her with a good lie that justified my hiding outside the clearing; or give up on the job and go away. Or, if she told Samm she'd seen me, and he demanded to know what was going on, I could use the same lie on him I was planning to use on her. As soon as I figured out what the lie was.

Seemed like the best choice at this point was to be entirely innocent until challenged. After all, what could they do, kill me?

Outside the casino I noticed a flyer tacked up on the parking lot fence, advertising a medicine show. The flyer said "The Truth About Antibiotics! What the vaxmakers don't want you to know!" I couldn't guess what kind of "antibiotic" these people had, but the odds were that it had no more effect on the poison plagues than the old stuff had. "We got what you need! Cures everything from cancer to Ebola to dengue to warts and menstrual cramps. Only Costs Five to Stay Alive! Come hear the music, come see the magic, come and meet the survivors. You have our guarantee!"

All printed above a picture of a medicine bottle. The label read, "Omnicillin5." Underneath the bottle, today's date, the time, two p.m., and the place: right down the street near the

Blue Chip diner where I'd had the nasty breakfast that second day.

A dozen of the cheaply made black and white sheets were pasted the length of the fence. I'd have to check out the show, if I didn't have to fight my way out of town before then.

Owen, the blind barker, was on duty at the front door. I greeted him by name and told him mine, saying, "I work here." He nodded and smiled. Blind people hear a lot; I wondered if he ever heard anything that might be useful to me.

When I walked in, no one seemed to be watching for me. The change guy, Bernard, ignored me when I walked past him, but I didn't think that meant anything. He might have been a spy, or an errand boy, but he was a timid one, and he had seemed terrified of being associated with me in any way since the day I'd arrived.

"There you are!" the voice behind me crowed.

I know what it means to feel like your heart has stopped because I've had that sensation a few times before. But just like those other times, it really hadn't. I was alive enough to spin around, mouth dry, ready to fight.

I landed face to face with a smiling Timmy, Fredo right beside him. My stomach dropped back where it belonged, my heart speeding but functional. "We left you a message," Timmy added, "but maybe you didn't get it?"

My throat was tight. I managed to say, "Message?"

"Yes, on the house sys. And you obviously didn't get it, but it's okay because you're right on time. We're going out to lunch for Fredo's birthday. We'd love to have you come—do you like Chinese?"

I studied their faces until Fredo squirmed. "Is something wrong, Rica?" he asked. He focused on my cheek. "Oh, my, that's an angry scratch."

"No. Nothing's wrong." I touched my face. I needed to cover

that scratch with makeup.

This couldn't be a trap. It was too sideways. If the Colemans wanted to kill me, I reasoned, they wouldn't send Timmy and Fredo to do it, not with some elaborate chow fun scheme. They'd send someone up to my room at three a.m. and carry my body out in a money sack.

"I'd love to go to lunch with you. Just let me make a quick stop first. Give me ten minutes." They nodded and plunked themselves down on a couple of slot machine stools.

I wanted to let the chief know about the war games. I wasn't sure, yet, whether I should also tell her I had been spotted creeping around in the woods. I was reluctant to look clumsy this early in the game and I didn't know what game Hannah was playing, anyway.

I was hungry, I realized. Starving even. Sometimes I get that way when I've been scared half to death, after the nausea passes. I liked and trusted Timmy, and I had no reason to think that Fredo was anything but what he appeared to be. Lunch away would give me an excuse to put some time and space between myself and the casino, and see if I could find out more about Blackjack, about the Colemans, and possibly about Hannah Karlow. Anything I could learn about her would be helpful at this point.

I dashed to my room and closed the door. The chief answered immediately. I told her I'd followed Samm and watched their army on maneuvers.

"How many people?" the chief wanted to know

"Around fifty." I wanted to get back downstairs before Timmy and Fredo started wondering where I was. But the chief was more eager to get offline than I was.

"Good work. I have to go now. Keep at it." She was gone.

Keep at it? She hadn't bothered to ask where they held the war games or how good they looked or who was doing what.

She must have been heading toward some kind of emergency. Even if I'd been sure I wanted to tell her Hannah had seen me, I'd have had no chance to do it. And I still had to let Newt know there was, indeed, an army of sorts, just as he'd heard.

He wasn't answering so I left a message. I gave him what I'd given the chief, and a very general, nearly useless, description of the location. The chief's behavior had made me nervous and I wasn't sure I wanted Newt to have more than she did. My gut was telling me to hold back until I knew more. About everybody.

I didn't bother to check the house sys for the message from Tim—I was sure it would be there. I found my stage makeup and dabbed some on the scratch. Not bad. The entire side trip had taken twelve minutes and when I got back down to the casino, Tim and Fredo were still sitting on their stools, chatting happily, not the least put out by the wait.

The three of us walked out the front door and east along the old strip. I hadn't gone far in this direction before; I always seemed to be heading toward or over the old California line. Hadn't had much time for idle exploration.

King Yen was a few blocks from Blackjack, a nicely decorated place with flamboyant Chinese masks on the walls, gilded mirrors, a dozen black-iron-legged tables and chairs, and white cloth tablecloths and napkins.

It was just past noon, and about two-thirds of the tables were occupied. When we walked in a tall server swept past us carrying a tray of something that smelled wonderful. I caught a glimpse of rice and vegetables. Another Asian man, this one standing no higher than my shoulder, even shorter than Tim, approached with big red menus, smiling, and led us to a table in the back. He handed us the menus and left us alone.

"This is nice," I said, still wondering if Hannah Karlow would leap out from under a table and shoot me.

Fredo nodded. "You absolutely have to try the egg rolls. And the pork buns! You can't miss those."

Timmy smiled fondly, shaking his head. "Fredo eats meat all the time. It's so out of character for an animal-lover. He always feels bad about it."

I studied the menu. I could understand Fredo's problem. All my adult life I'd felt guilty for eating meat, even fish, but I couldn't seem to do without it. I guess I just didn't feel guilty enough. Or there was something about spending so much time running for my life that seemed to call for a carnivorous attitude.

We chose pork buns, happy family—fish and meat—vegetable egg rolls, and a tofu-vegetable dish. All of which suited me just fine.

"And a bottle of wine to celebrate Fredo's sixty-fifth!" Timmy insisted.

"Oh, sweetie, I'll nod off."

"Then you'll take a nap this afternoon. This is no time to worry about little things."

Fredo capitulated and we settled on a Napa chardonnay. Red's my preference, but the birthday boy had the choice. I thought I might have to take a nap myself to get through my debut in the lounge that night. I'd been up since before dawn on four hours sleep. Not to mention the stress of the eye-fight with Hannah. And now, wine. But I didn't want to spoil the celebration by begging off.

And still no Hannah or Zack or Samm leaping out of the kitchen, lasers blazing.

The minute we laid our menus down the server dashed over to take our order. He brought the wine immediately. Fredo tasted, nodded, and we filled our glasses.

"To my darling Fredo!" Timmy was so happy.

We all took a sip. Icy cold and not at all bad for white wine. I'd have heartburn later.

"How long have you two been together?"

"Twenty-seven years this May," Fredo said, his eyes glistening. Was I jealous? A little. Possibly.

Timmy was practically bouncing in his seat. What was going on with him? He seemed awfully excited for just a birthday lunch.

He burst out: "I just can't hold it any longer. I have the most wonderful surprise, something Fredo has always wanted."

Fredo's eyes grew wide. "Really?"

"I did it, Fredo. I bought us a house. And I can't wait to show it to you! You're going to just love it."

He had a right to be proud. On a server's pay, it would have been tough to save even the small amount of money it took to buy a house. When someone had one that was semilivable and wanted to sell, he wanted cash, payment in full. I'd heard that people used to put up a small percentage—if they could even afford to do that—and then borrow the rest, paying a house off for years and years. I couldn't imagine it. Houses as rare and expensive as diamonds. A crazy thought.

"Oh, Tim. We get three rooms free at Blackjack; isn't this awfully extravagant? Shouldn't we save the money for our retirement? It must have cost so much." But despite his protests, he was flushed, clearly thrilled.

"Not so much. And now you can have all the pets you want and Roberta and Harvey will have a yard."

"Roberta and Harvey?" They had children?

"Our cats," Fredo explained. "We had a dog, too, Oscar. But he got old and died. Just last year." Fredo's eyes looked damp, and he sighed. I reached over and squeezed his shoulder.

It had never occurred to me that people would have pets in their rooms at the casino. But this was a good opening to get onto the subject I wanted to explore.

"The Colemans don't mind if you have pets there?"

"Of course not," Fredo said. "Feel free to have a furry friend. They prefer that you keep it to one, because after all most of the employees have just one or two rooms. But they wouldn't dream of denying people the joy of pets. Judith had a dog until just a couple years ago. A litter mate of Oscar's."

"That's very sweet of them." It really was. Or smart.

Both Fredo and Timmy nodded vigorously.

"But we've always wanted a little cottage of our own, haven't we, Tim?"

"And Fredo has always wanted a houseful of strays. He's one of those people they just seem to find." He smiled affectionately at his partner. They were so cute, so sweet, I couldn't help but wonder again if this was some kind of trap. But I knew it wasn't. They were real. It was my life that wasn't real.

My sys vibrated and I excused myself to go to the toilet. They must have thought I had a very weak bladder.

The toilet was a one-seater, and empty. The call was from Newt.

"That location you gave me. I can't figure out where it is."

My gut was still urging me to play it close. "Sorry, I'll try to get a better fix on it. For now though, I got the impression they move the war games around, keep the location changing."

"Yeah? How'd you get that impression?" This wasn't making him trust me any more than he already did.

"Samm said something about letting them know where it would be next time." The lie sounded pretty good, even to me. For all I knew they did move it around and Samm had said exactly that, after I left.

He grunted. "About fifty soldiers, you say?" He sounded unhappy about it, which probably meant he hadn't thought there were so many.

"Yes."

"Okay. Keep me informed."

153

I flushed the toilet and went back to the table.

Our food had arrived. I picked up an egg roll and dipped it into the hot mustard. Thoughtfully, I said, "It constantly amazes me, how well the Colemans take care of their people. I know Waldo's related to them, but he's so . . . different."

Timmy snorted. "Different is a nice word for that bastard."

"And he seems so useless. Why do you think they keep him on?"

Timmy looked uncomfortable. "My guess is he knows things."

"Things?" Was my innocence overdone? I wasn't enjoying playing games with him.

"The Colemans are very powerful people." He'd lowered his voice. I could barely hear him. He leaned in closer. "And they could do a lot of good for Sierra. But you know, sometimes doing good means doing things that some people might not think are, well, good."

"Like what?"

He exhaled, loudly. "I don't really know. I'm just guessing that maybe sometimes . . . well I just don't know. You know what I mean. Politics." He nodded, definitively, conclusively, grabbing the spoon that rested in the tofu dish and helping himself to some. Fredo took a big bite out of a fragrant pork bun, rolling his eyes in ecstasy.

I pressed a little deeper. "But why would they trust him to keep secrets?" Did any of those secrets have to do with the mayor's murder? Could "doing good" include killing someone who the Colemans thought was bad for the town? "Sometimes secrets can be sold."

Tim studied me over a chopstick-load of tofu. "And he'd be the first one they'd suspect. Smarter for him to take what he gets from his family." That made some sense, and with Timmy looking at me harder than I wanted him to, it didn't seem like

154

the right moment to push. But I might not get a better one; I had to ask.

"I know the mayor was murdered. Was he bad for the town, do you think?"

Tim looked at me, surprised. "He was okay. Didn't do much. What are you asking me, Rica?"

I took a deep breath. "I heard someone saying that he thought the Colemans killed the mayor."

Tim giggled. He was more comfortable with the topic of murder than he was with the topic of politics. He poked at a piece of broccoli stem with his chopsticks. "Can't imagine why they'd do that. Far as I could tell, he never did anything without checking with them first."

I dropped my voice to a whisper. "What if he did something the Colemans didn't like?" I was frosting my naïveté with awe.

"I don't think so," Tim said. "At least not that I know. I thought he was pretty tight with Judith." He shrugged. "Seemed that way anyhow." He stuffed half a red-sauce-dipped egg roll into his mouth. "I remember she was the one who talked him into running."

"And unless I'm mistaken," Fredo said, "he was one of the casino's best customers. I don't actually know that he owed them anything, but I do know he ran a tab."

So he was either in debt to the Colemans or they were in debt to him.

I'd find no easy solution to the mayor's demise today. It was still possible the Colemans had done the man in, or, for all I knew, Scorsi himself did it. But the way things were in the world, his death might have been completely random. Almost anyone could have killed him for any reason. Some crazy hugger might have seen him trimming a hedge and decided he was a toxie. Some paranoid godder could have decided he was the devil. A fever-spot plaguey might have wandered out of the woods and hallucinated that the man was carrying vax.

I'd been wondering how to shift the topic to my worry of the moment, Hannah Karlow. Now Fredo had given me a strong segue.

"Speaking of good customers," I began, "I've noticed a number of interesting-looking regulars hanging around."

Timmy rolled his eyes. "Oh, yes, indeed."

I lowered my voice again. "One in particular. Says she's going to come and see my show. Her name's Hannah." Fredo scrunched up his eyes, trying to place her and failing. Timmy was chasing a hunk of carrot around his plate. "She's got a long scar on her cheek. Thin woman—"

"Oh, her!" Timmy cried, glancing archly at Fredo and back again at me. "So she's a fan of yours?"

I laughed, trying to sound modest. "Possibly."

"You're not . . . interested in her, are you?"

Not the way he meant. "Not really. But is there some reason I shouldn't be?"

"Well, I don't know her well enough to give you that kind of advice, sweetie, but she gives me the creepy-crawls. Something sly about that one."

Timmy was a wise man. But they barely knew her. No information to be had there. I ate some Happy Family and shifted to the medicine show, something that might also involve the Colemans, at least according to Newt Scorsi's accusations.

"I saw some flyers for a medicine show this afternoon. What's that about?"

Fredo was chewing. Tim was sipping delicately at the somewhat sour wine. He scowled, swallowed and answered. "It's a scam. They're crooks selling useless trash to scared people."

"Won't the sheriff chase them away, then? And why does the casino let them put flyers up on the fence?"

Timmy smiled grimly. "I think our friend the sheriff can barely remember that he should be finding out who killed the mayor. As if he's capable of doing that. As for the fence . . ." He shrugged.

"What about the fence?"

"Maybe Waldo put them up. The Colemans might not approve of what Waldo does, but they always seem to let him do it. And Judith, well, she's just glad the medicine shows don't pretend they're selling vax." Fredo nodded, looking grim. Timmy sighed. "That's how Judith's husband died. His original vax was phony garbage. Didn't matter how many boosters he got after that. The kids were little at the time. Terrible."

We sat there silent for a moment. For some reason, it hadn't occurred to me the Colemans might have seen hard times. Then Fredo broke in. "Anyway, I doubt Waldo put up the flyers himself. He's too lazy."

Timmy laughed. "You're right. Let's not talk about Waldo any more. It's curdling my tofu."

Okay, no more Waldo. The chief had told me she thought the sheriff belonged to the Colemans. I could check that out. I ate a prawn, sipped some wine

"You said 'our friend the sheriff'—is he a friend of the Colemans, too? Like the mayor was?"

Tim shot me a curious squint. Fredo spoke up. "The sheriff doesn't do anything that would hurt the Colemans." Tim was still giving me that squint. Time to back off.

"Well, Tahoe is a fascinating place, with lots to gossip about." I held up my glass. "But I'm more interested in Fredo's birthday. Here's to you, Fredo, Tim's love, my friend. And many happy returns!"

CHAPTER 15
A JUGGLER, AN ACROBAT, A MAN WITH A FIDDLE

I parted with Tim and Fredo after lunch, hugs all around, telling them I'd see them at work later. Meanwhile, my adrenaline was still pumping and the food had given me a boost. Despite the lack of sleep, I wasn't ready for a nap and most of all, I was not at all eager to go back to the casino. So I followed the flyers toward the Blue Chip diner and the corner where the medicine show was being held. I'd be right on time.

I'd been to a few of these extravaganzas in my life. Once, when I was a child in Redwood, up on top of Mount Tamalpais in the old stone amphitheater. They'd had a juggler, an acrobat, a man with a fiddle, and another man who talked fast and sold a lot of bottles of something, I couldn't remember the name, before the sheriff showed up and hauled the lot of them away. Once in Ontario, near the Toronto ruins. Another time, in Middle, in the Ozarks. In California, down near Los Angeles. In Rocky, on the smelly shore of the Salt Lake amid the ruins of a salt-processing plant. In Desert, right in the center of the inhabited cluster of Tucson.

Generally the locals shut them down pretty fast—the one in California was stopped in the middle of a knife-throwing act—but those last two times the show people had gotten away ahead of the law.

These con artists could be found pretty much everywhere on the continent, traveling by bus, truck, car caravan—the one in Middle was set up around a horse-drawn wagon. For all I knew, since I'd never been off North America, they were stealing money from suckers all over the world. I'd heard it was so. They all sold the cure for whatever ailed you, and they sold it cheap.

Usually, the base was feel-good alcohol, sugar, and flavoring. Sometimes they added herbs if they could scrounge some. Despite the low prices, there was lots of money to be made if you mixed up enough of the stuff and kept your costs low. People who couldn't buy vax and never so much as saw a doctor would try anything. Even though there didn't seem to be as many dying these days, and even though I knew the hostels were fewer and emptier, the memories were long and people were still afraid. I certainly was.

Running medicine shows was one of the crimes Chief Graybel had said the Colemans were accused of. But I just couldn't see them being involved in a cheap scam. Judith Coleman was tough and smart, but a heartless con woman? I didn't think so. And she probably had some very bad feelings about fake medicine. Jo? Well, she seemed driven and sharply focused. Possibly ruthless. But the shows were trashy, and she was anything but that. Samm? He was pretty much an unknown at this point. It just didn't feel right. Again, it seemed tacky. He had a big ego and I suspected he would think this kind of thing was unworthy of the general.

Skimming. Now that made sense. Not hard to do. Big money. And if they were taking a cut off the top before taxes, they didn't need to sell homemade liqueur for five reals a bottle.

It was possible that if I wormed my way into a dealing job, I could catch a glimpse of how they were doing it. It was also possible that the money was being misappropriated so skillfully I'd have to work as a cashier and a bookkeeper too, to prove anything at all. Why not? Tail generals, catch a murderer, deal with Newt, sing in the lounge, and handle four full-time shifts. All in a day's work.

I'd already caught them training an army, but the chief hadn't seemed interested in hearing the details of what I'd seen. Maybe they needed to march down Stateline shooting people before she could do anything. Maybe she wanted me to catch Jo drawing up a master plan to take over the world.

I was a few minutes early, but a scattering of people were already standing around, some of them excited, loud and happy, others with a "show me" smirk. Some of them were probably wondering if the sheriff would show up before they got a chance to buy or, even worse, before they got to see the show, but from what Timmy had said about the sheriff, I didn't think that was likely.

When the Omnicillin bus pulled up in front of the Blue Chip, it skidded in the gutter dust, stirring a cloud that made everyone cough. Maybe the medicine would help that. Clear the throat and soothe the nerves, if nothing else.

I glanced in the diner's window. Xavier was wiping down the counter, ignoring the fuss outside. He probably got a cut for not calling the cops.

The bus, including the windows, was painted in bright blue and yellow stripes—stripes for Tahoe? What would they use in Nebraska, funnel cloud shapes? Snowflakes for Northland? Icicles for Ontario? Jugs of moonshine for Middle?

The driver, a baggy-eyed dissipated-looking man who could have been forty-five or sixty-five, was crowned with a smudgy black top hat. A real antique. And when he trotted down the stairs carrying a folding table, I could see he was also wearing a seedy, faded black tuxedo that must have been older than he was. One assistant, a large fortyish woman wearing a long flowered cotton dress, helped him set up the table. Another, a young man of about thirty, almost clown-like with bright yellow hair and baggy pants that dragged on the ground—big floppy shoes and face paint would have finished the job—began bringing out signs and boxes of bottles. By now the crowd had grown. There must have been twenty people standing there, and more were coming.

When the younger man had finished setting up his displays, he went back into the bus and emerged carrying an ancient, stained accordion.

They seemed to be getting all their possessions from some Twentieth Century landfill. In Los Angeles.

He began to play a John Phillip Sousa march, of all things. I can barely tell them apart but I thought it was "Stars and Stripes Forever." And the fortyish woman, who had put on a straw hat, began to do an odd kind of dance-march to the music, tipping the hat in a salute every time she turned. When the song ended, she tossed her hat high into the air and caught it. The young clown-man cheered. A few spectators clapped.

The man in the top hat had set up an easel with a badly drawn poster that featured lopsided bottles of their wares in various colors. He took over once the hesitant applause stopped.

"We've got it right here, folks!" he yelled. "This is the real thing! The real medicine the government's hiding from you so their dealers can sell the vax—the vax you can't afford to buy! Selective breeding, that's what it is—steal from the poor and sell to the rich! Are you going to stand for that?" A few people mumbled "no." One woman laughed. It was the standard spiel, although his explanation of selective breeding was a little more muddled than most.

Omnicillin, he said, pointing at each of the bottles on the poster, came in six flavors—lime, lemon, cherry, blackberry, apple, and anise. These were all delicacies that any enterprising Redwooder could grow in his yard or pick along the road, but he didn't mention that. The cherry and apple were the same color.

At five reals a bottle, he said, you couldn't go wrong. He

began to rave about the curative properties of each flavor, sliding the first poster behind a second one that listed those properties in capital letters with lots of exclamation marks.

Lime and lemon cured colds, flu, and dengue. Cherry dealt with all kinds of immunodeficiencies, including AIDS and red-rash, and was also used in the treatment of measles, smallpox, and chicken pox. Blackberry was a specific for Ebola and black plague. Apple eradicated viral cancers and neutralized pesticide poisoning. Anise cured all new and as-yet-unnamed viruses as well as several other cancers, particularly melanoma.

All for five reals.

A fat man in a red suit—Santa Claus?—jumped down from the bus and began strumming a banjo. Sounded like bluegrass, but it was too fast. While he played, the man in the tux recited weirdly rhymed poetry—"melanoma, take-it-homa" was my favorite—about his medicine and about the conspiracy to keep vax prices high, and in the middle of all that, two young women, also wearing long flowered dresses, suddenly appeared in the bus doorway, leapt down the stairs, joined the large woman, and they all started doing a speedy can-can, back and forth in front of the audience, while the banjo and the accordion competed with each other trying to keep up with the dancers. It looked to me like they'd all had way too much Omnicillin. The guy in the tux had stopped reciting poetry to do business. The crowd had by now grown to perhaps three dozen people, and they were falling all over themselves to buy the stuff.

The young man had to put aside his accordion to climb back into the bus and carry down more bottles of Omnicillin. Santa Claus helped him.

We were half an hour into the noisy show; I was more and more sure that the sheriff was ignoring the scam, and, getting tired of the hysteria, I stepped off to the side, into the shade of an acacia tree. That was when I heard the man in the tux say,

"Hey, there, Waldo." Sure enough, there he was. My boss. Or one of my bosses, anyway. He didn't see me, which was just fine, and I slipped farther behind the tree.

Waldo grabbed the handrail and pulled his game leg up the bus steps, disappearing inside. The man in the tux turned over the sales to his assistants, and followed Waldo.

I stepped out from behind the tree and strolled casually around the bus, looking for an open window on the street side where the performers couldn't see me. One was cracked an inch or two. I crouched under it.

"Looks like you're going to sell quite a few dozen more before this ends." Waldo's voice. He didn't sound close to the window, but he wasn't bothering to whisper.

"Well, I suppose that's possible." A grunt. "Here. This should do it."

"I don't think so. You got a good crowd. You're gonna sell out."

Another grunt.

Waldo's voice again. "Yeah. More like it."

I heard the shuffle of feet heading toward the front of the bus and the exit door. Waldo hopped back down the stairs, shoving a fat wad of money into his pocket, grinning. He limped off through the crowd, slowly, swaggering a little, and considerably richer than he'd been before.

So Waldo had performed some service, and the cut was big enough to make the showman grumpy. Could be anything from letting them put up flyers to selling them food, but Timmy had said the Colemans pretty much let Waldo do as he pleased, so my best guess was that he was selling his influence: pay me and no one will bother you. Some of that wad might even be for the sheriff.

All medicine peddlers acted cheery and devil-may-care, just like this bunch. It was showmanship. But in most cases, you could tell by the nervous sweat, by the way their eyes scanned the street and the crowd, and by the way they stuck close to their wheels and rushed through the sales, that they were ready to toss their wares back into the wagon and take off fast at the first sign of cops.

Not these guys. No sweat, no nerves, no flickering eyes. They acted like they had plenty of time and nothing to worry about.

The flowered women were now doing less-than-graceful somersaults and splits, which was neither easy nor attractive in those long skirts, and the accordion and banjo were playing a medley of what sounded like Twentieth Century war songs. I recognized "Over There" and "Off We Go, into the Wild Blue Yonder" or whatever the title of that air force theme was.

Much as I was enjoying the show, I decided to follow Waldo.

He hadn't gone far. I nearly bumped into his back when he yanked open the door of the Blue Chip Diner. I peered in the window to see if he handed the proprietor a wad of reals, but I was so obvious standing there it made just as much sense to go in for a cup of tea and look dumb.

He sat at the counter, pulled out the wad of money, peeled off a twenty, and slapped it down.

"Gimme a coffee, Xavier." He slid the twenty across the counter.

Coffee. Wow. Big deal for a little dive. I didn't see any signs that said they had it. Probably only for the very special customers. Coffee wasn't just expensive, it was hard to get. Experiments with growing it in Sierra, Rocky, and Redwood hadn't produced anything very good, and the ships that brought it from South America and Hawaii were as likely to fall victim to pirates as make it through. Blackjack had a small supply of it, carefully sealed against the drying air; very few customers were willing to pay the price.

Xavier looked impressed, Waldo smug. For half a second, I

had wondered why he didn't just have a cup at his own restaurant, but their expressions told it all. Waldo was showing off. Xavier gave me a greasy smile, said he'd take my order in a minute, and went into the kitchen where presumably the precious stuff was kept. Waldo didn't even turn around to see who'd come in behind him.

I hadn't seen Waldo slipping Xavier an extra few reals tucked under the twenty, so if Xavier got a cut from the medicine show, it wasn't through Waldo. He probably collected from the guy in the top hat, too.

I sat down two stools from Waldo.

Finally, he noticed me. The smugness slid off his face, replaced by an irritated sneer.

"What are you doing here, Rica?"

"Just stopping in for a sandwich."

Why had I said that? Now I'd have to actually eat something there. I'd had lunch a little over an hour before and even if I'd been hungry I doubted I could choke down one of Xavier's creations.

When Xavier came back out with a cup and saucer, setting it almost reverently before Waldo, I asked him for a chicken sandwich.

I took one tiny bite. The bread was stale, the chicken boiled to dust, but I didn't have to eat it after all. Waldo drank his coffee quickly, without saying another word to me, and limped back out the door.

I waited a solid minute, letting him get a good head start, pretended I'd just remembered a very important engagement—"Oh, darn, got to go mumble mumble"—and said goodbye.

At Blackjack, Waldo went straight to the restaurant. He passed both the bar, where Jo was talking to the bartender, and the stairs to the mezzanine, where he might have found Judith. The money seemed to be all his.

The dealers at the two open poker tables were people I'd seen around the casino—a woman I'd noticed dealing blackjack once or twice, and a man named Quinn who worked in the cashier's cage. War-games fill-ins for Samm and Zack. It was not quite three o'clock and the army wasn't back yet.

I had two hours until my first shift at the restaurant. Just enough time for a mail check, a shower, and a nap. I was just about convinced by then that Hannah had told no one about seeing me at the war games.

I headed right for the hallway and the stairs to my room. I was passing the roulette wheel when I noticed Jo walking toward me. The doubt returned. Did she know? Had Hannah told her she'd caught me spying? Was Jo coming after me? Why would she do it alone? I held my breath.

She smiled, nodded, and passed right by, heading up toward Judith's office.

Hannah's work on the elevator had been interrupted that day for more important things. I wondered how long it would be before she had the time to finish it. Resigned to using the stairs for the rest of my stay, I showed them my contempt by taking them two at a time. At a quick glance, my room didn't look tossed or even touched. My sys was where I'd left it, rolled up in the pants. I couldn't see any signs that anyone had been there.

Shower first. I'd done a lot of sweating that day. As the water ran down my back, I thought about Hannah Karlow. She was an urgent problem. I had no idea where she stood on anything, or what it meant that, so far, she'd let me get away with spying on the training session, but I couldn't rely on her keeping the secret no matter what her reason was. I could say I wanted to join and was watching to see what it was like. Pretty weak, though. I couldn't imagine the Colemans falling for that one. And I couldn't imagine them being foolish enough to let a spy live.

I considered gunning Electra down the road to Redwood and home, but only briefly—a merc who runs away from danger loses the pay for that job and runs the risk of losing that client forever, possibly even losing the reputation that brings in future work and keeps her in vax.

So I would take a chance and stay, keep the Hannah problem to myself and give her no excuses, and let the chief message me if she wanted the rest of what I'd seen that day—what kinds of weapons, who was involved, where they held the maneuvers.

I dabbed disinfectant on the blackberry scratch, wrapped a robe around myself, pulled out my sys, and punched up my mail.

Nothing much new. Some Middle chief I'd never heard of who had some kind of problem with godders; his message was pretty vague and he sounded angry, arrogant, and in a big hurry. I didn't answer him. Gran had sent me a meditation that consisted mostly of repetitious statements about how happy I was. She must have been right because I caught myself smiling as I read it.

Thinking about my happiness, I went to bed. I had an hour and a half to sleep.

I got nearly all the way through the first part of my shift at the restaurant with no one coming to haul me away and toss me in a casino dungeon. Waldo was his usual surly self, Lizzie was friendly in a self-absorbed adolescent way, and Jo came in for a quick dinner and didn't shoot me. On the contrary, she gave me a very sweet smile, asked me to sit with her for a moment, and told me the piano player would meet me half an hour before showtime so we could run through the music. Since she hadn't mentioned an accompanist before and I had been so preoccupied I hadn't thought to ask, I'd been ready to bring in some instrumental capsules. This was better, if he was any good.

She also said she'd heard from a lot of customers that they'd be there for the show.

"Word's getting around, Rica. You're bringing us business even before your show opens. We may want to do two shows a night soon." Timmy—she was sitting at one of his tables—overheard that last line when he brought her a glass of red wine and a menu. He beamed like I was his daughter. Fredo came in and started doing setups at my tables. He was going to be filling in for me during my performance.

A little while after Jo had left the restaurant, Drew showed up. His clothes were dusty, his face pale; he looked tired and was holding his injured arm stiffly. While Timmy was bringing him his dinner, Samm walked in and dropped into a chair next to Drew. And ten minutes behind Samm, Hannah, who sat alone across the room, at one of my tables.

The warriors were back from the front, hungry, dirty, and exhausted. Samm looked broody, Drew happy and a little sick. Hannah gave me a sly smile, and asked for a half bottle of Sonoma merlot. I studied her eyes, looking for a clue. She smirked and examined the plain white tablecloth as if she were reading it.

When I came back with the wine, she glanced toward Samm and Drew and spoke softly to me, still smiling.

"Rica, you need to be more careful." Sly and conspiratorial. I handed her the menu; she passed it back to me without looking. "I'll have the chicken."

CHAPTER 16
THE PARKING LOT WILL BE PRIVATE ENOUGH

Drew was worn out. His arm hurt; he was hungry and sick to his stomach all at once. He'd tried to take it easy, not push too hard, do more observing than fighting, but during the last attack on the outpost he'd forgotten he was wounded, thrown himself on a Red soldier, and fallen right on his bad arm. It hadn't stopped throbbing ever since. Blue had won and Zack had complimented him on that last run for the shed, but maybe Mother was right and it was too soon to be out there abusing his messed-up body.

Lizzie came to his table with a basket of bread.

"You look like shit, Drew."

"Thanks."

"You're an asshole. You should have waited. I told you not to go today!" she slammed the bread down and marched away.

She was just jealous. It was really chewing at her that everyone said she was too young to be a soldier. And she was getting more snappish every day.

She'd always been edgy, prone to trouble, but it seemed like killing the merc had cut something loose in her. Something that went deeper. She was fierce. Wild. Had she always been that way, underneath? She'd been upset enough when she'd killed the man, but then she seemed to settle in and accept it. She could be dealing with guilt by making it normal to be violent. Or it could be pride. She felt she had something to live up to. If everyone thought she was a killer, she had to be one. He knew that sometimes people took their own reputations too seriously.

He wished he could make her understand that she'd killed because she had to, and leave it at that, but she absolutely refused to talk about it.

Rica was still working, not time for her show yet. He'd sat down at the first table he came to, sick, unthinking, and instantly regretted it. He'd sat at one of Timmy's stations. That blew his chance to have a casual word or two with Rica. Oh, well. He didn't feel too dashing anyway. Not up to impressing her. Still, he couldn't help but wonder what she'd think if she'd been able to see him training that day. He'd run fast, knocked down several opponents with a staff, shot a pistol with some accuracy. All with one arm. All with pain weighing him down. But when he'd landed on the bad arm tears had poured down his face, and he was glad she hadn't seen that.

He sighed. Who was he kidding? She probably thought he was way too young for her, if she thought of him at all. She smiled over at him just a moment before Samm came stumping in and threw himself down next to Drew. What a beautiful smile.

"Good work today, Drew. How's the arm?"

"Okay," he lied. Drew noticed Samm had glanced toward Rica and felt an instant of triumph. She'd smiled at Drew; she hadn't even noticed Samm. Then Hannah came in and sat down at one of Rica's tables. They talked for a minute, Rica looking stiff and angry. He wondered what that was about.

I stared at Hannah, willing her to say more. She didn't. And I couldn't drag her out of the restaurant and demand she tell me what was going on, what kind of game she was playing. I'd have to talk to her later, somewhere private.

"You want chicken. Sure. Fine. I want to talk to you."

"I'm flattered."

More games.

"Meet me at my car in the parking lot after my second shift. About one o'clock." I described the Electra and where it was parked.

She gave me another coy smile. "Your car? What about your room?"

I shot her my best glare. What did the bitch have in mind, sexual extortion? "The parking lot will be private enough."

Jo sat in her office doodling on a notepad. She had a lot to think about. Samm had promised to talk to Hannah Karlow today, during training, about running for mayor.

So far there weren't any other candidates, but it was only a matter of time before Newt ran someone. She had little doubt that he was responsible for Madera's strange and spectacular murder, and he wouldn't do that just to hand the office over to someone else he didn't like. Up until now, though, there'd been no pressing reason for him to act. He was coasting, in that lazy way of his. No friend of the Colemans was in charge, so no one had to be. But once he saw that Hannah was running and Blackjack was backing her, he'd start looking for a candidate of his own.

She couldn't think who that would be. Neither of his brothers was up to campaigning, let alone doing the job. He'd probably run himself. The thought made her laugh out loud. He wasn't pretty and he wasn't likeable and the people who bothered to vote would probably not vote for him. Hannah wasn't pretty either, but she was a fixer. That carried a lot of weight. The mayor race was looking good.

She had a few other offices to think about, too, including seats on the Sierra Council. Fortunately she still owned the sheriff, for whatever that was worth. He was harder to kill than Madera, with his guns and his deputy, and so far no one had tried. Even Scorsi didn't see him as much of a threat. As far as

Jo was concerned, his willingness to belong to the Colemans was his only good quality, but for now that would have to be enough. One of these days she'd find someone who could actually do the job.

Too many places she wanted to put people, too few who were loyal and smart and capable.

Which brought Rica to mind. Beautiful, smart Rica. She wanted her to stay at Blackjack for any number of reasons. Earlier that day, when she'd passed her walking through the casino, Jo had thought there'd been a break in her stride, a hesitation. She looked tense, watchful. Jo had smiled and nodded at her and Rica seemed to relax. Probably just nervous about her opening night. She should have stopped, talked to her, reassured her, but she'd been thinking about Hannah.

She'd have to do it later. She'd try to make a point of it.

What she needed now, though, was a session with Judith. From what Samm had said about Hannah's temperament and attitude, she had no reason to believe the woman wouldn't accept the invitation to run for the mayor's office, and the backing it took to run, and they had a campaign to plan and money to allocate. They also had to set up a meeting and get to know Hannah better.

A good soldier, a good fixer, that was all fine, but Jo wanted to know more about why she might want to be mayor of Tahoe, and what kind of future she saw for the town.

CHAPTER 17
WORLD ON A STRING,
ASS IN A SLING

The long midnight blue sequined dress was not one I wore often. I preferred to perform in light, floating blouse and pants, usually. But I thought my debut at Blackjack, and the debut of its lounge, called for something slinkier. I was doing mid-Twentieth Century standards, including World War Two. It wouldn't hurt to look like a chanteuse from a noir film.

Of course, those chanteuses were always in big trouble and sometimes got murdered.

Gran had started her movie collection when she was a teenager and the noirs were already creaky with age by then; she'd pushed me to watch some of them when she thought I was old enough. Art, she said, the art of black and white cinema.

At first I'd hated them. They were, as the name implied, dark. I was a sad little kid to start with and I didn't understand why Gran, whom I loved absolutely and who I knew absolutely loved me, would want me to be even more depressed. The clothing in the movies was strange and formal, with the men in those baggy suits and the women wearing spiky-heeled shoes and tight skirts that must have made it hard to walk. The language was archaic, so I didn't always understand what the characters were saying. But gradually, the eerie combination of low-key passion, bitterness, and danger took hold of my imagination, and the crowds of people on the streets, the miles of huge buildings, none of them in ruins, the easy and casual movement through a world that was treacherous and primitive and civilized

173

at the same time, worked on my imagination and helped me to understand Gran's sense of loss. I fell in love with the sleaze and the music and the stars. Lupino. Stanwyck. MacMurray. Ladd. Bang-bang you're dead.

I turned to the mirror in my tiny dressing room. The midnight blue looked good. I practiced looking noir, world-weary, Twentieth Century, until I thought I had it right, and made my way backstage.

Curiosity and novelty had, as Jo promised, brought a pretty decent crowd to the lounge for its opening night. Peering out from behind the curtain, I counted twenty-nine customers in a room that could hold forty. If they liked the show they'd come back and bring their friends.

I noticed Drew in the doorway. He slid into a chair at the back, disappearing into the shadows holding his wounded arm close to his side. Hannah Karlow was there, too. You'd have thought that after a hard day on the battlefield they'd have both been ready for bed by now. I could barely see Drew, but Hannah's worn-out face didn't look any different than usual. She'd agreed readily to the meeting later and now she'd come early enough to get a table up front. Once again, she was by herself, drinking a glass of red wine. I was surprised by a stab of pity. I'd disliked her almost at first sight and I guessed a lot of other people felt that way, too. That made her even more alone than I was.

The piano player, Andy, was the big bald man I'd seen talking to Emmy, the pretty young dealer, the night of the raid. As I'd discovered that day, she was also a soldier who was a good hand with a pistol. Andy was a bartender. I hadn't seen him at the clearing. More the indoor type, I guessed.

He was wearing a jumpsuit that was all wrong for this night's show, I'd asked him if he had anything period to wear next time, one of those suits or a tuxedo or something, and he'd looked at me like I'd asked him to drink from a dead-pond. I shrugged and smiled to show that it didn't really matter, and he relaxed.

He told me Jo had only talked to him about the show late that afternoon, but he was good enough so the half hour she'd given us to get used to each other was almost enough. We'd run through some songs together. To my relief he was a good musician, knew several of the songs, and picked up the others quickly from the sheet music and by ear, so I was happy enough to go with the yellow jump that made him look like a big round piece of bald lemon candy.

Because this was opening night, Jo had said she'd do the introductions. And there she was, suddenly, striding toward the stage, lace collar and cuffs, purple knickers. She got the crowd's attention by walking in; she didn't have to quiet them when she jumped up onto the stage wearing a wider, friendlier smile than I'd seen before. Jo liked an audience.

The intro was short and sweet, just like Jo herself.

"Ladies and gentlemen, I want to welcome you on behalf of the Coleman family to the new Blackjack lounge." Hannah Karlow applauded, and the others joined in. Jo held up her hands.

"You're going to love what we have for you. Andy Woolly, at the piano—a lot of you know him from the bar." Laughter and enthusiastic applause all around. "And a really exciting talent, first time in Tahoe—Rica Marin!" She waved me onto the stage and hopped down. The crowd, again led by Hannah, applauded, but only politely this time. After all, they might not like me. They didn't know yet. Jo had stopped at the door and was standing there watching, her arms folded across her pretty ruffled chest, making me feel nervous.

Once I got into the first song or two, I settled down. I glided through "I'll Be Seeing You," slow and soft, and they loved it.

All romance and tragedy for the next hour. Andy and I had only a couple of rough spots, a near miracle considering how little rehearsal we'd had.

Sometime during "I'll Walk Alone," I realized Jo had taken a table off to the side.

The waiter, a new guy hired for the lounge, finally spotted Drew in his dark corner and bounced over to him.

"Beer," Drew said, dropping his voice into a rougher register. "Coleman Ale. The draft." He was old enough, and Mom let him drink beer, but for some stupid reason he wanted this waiter to think he was older. Why would he care what he thought? The waiter winked at him and went off to get the beer. What was that about? Did the guy wink at every young man who came in? Did he think Drew was interested in him? Did he know who Drew was? Did he think maybe the boss's kid was too young to be drinking? Was the wink meant to tell Drew he was letting it slide? Or did he smell the nervous sweat oozing out of his pores? Could he tell that Drew was barely able to sit quiet in his chair waiting for Rica to come out and sing?

He'd tried to sneak away when Lizzy wasn't looking, but of course she'd noticed, so he had to lie to her. He told her he was going to lie down for a while. He probably should have, but as Samm so often said, time for rest when I'm dead. He just wanted to watch Rica from a dark corner and hear her and build up some dreams for later. Funny thing. He usually liked dark-haired girls. Dark-haired women. Well, this was the first actual woman. Shit. This was really stupid. If Lizzie ever guessed he was in love with Rica she'd torture him or even worse, try to help.

It wasn't that he thought she'd tell anyone. He had too much on her for that. But she'd be jabbing and poking and driving him sideways and he didn't want even one person knowing, let alone Lizzie.

It must be almost time for the show. He made an effort to relax his neck and shoulders, trying not to feel his exhaustion, trying to find a comfortable way to hold his injured arm.

Rica was a mystery. He had this feeling, you know, this feeling that something secret was going on inside. But she made him feel good. She was tall enough for a woman but still shorter than he was. That was more important than age, wasn't it? Her auburn hair fell in her blue eyes sometimes, eyes full of smiles and secrets. How could they hold all that?

He wanted to sit in the dark and watch her and pretend . . . things.

The waiter brought Drew's glass of beer and zigzagged his way back to the bar. The place was crowded. Nearly full. Must have been thirty-five people there. He glanced around, trying to look sophisticated, like he did this all the time. That was when he noticed Samm, sitting right up front. Had Samm seen him come in? He didn't think so.

This made it hard. Drew was torn. He could sit with Samm. Or he could sit back here and watch Rica, alone. He'd never done anything like this with Samm, gone to a show or a bar or anything men did. He could do it. Just get up, stroll over there all tough and slow, drop into a chair. Sit with the starriest and darkest man in Tahoe. That would be so tribal.

But if he sat with Samm, he'd have to be really careful to hide his feelings about Rica. He wasn't sure he could do that yet. He hadn't practiced enough. Shit.

So he just sat there. Then he resigned himself to just sitting there. Then, a couple of minutes after he'd succeeded in soothing his frustration by reminding himself that this was what he'd intended to do all along, Jo walked into the spotlight at center stage and introduced Rica, who was wearing a dress covered with blue shiny stuff that hid everything and hid nothing at all.

She smiled. His throat tightened. He coughed. The crowd applauded.

"Tonight I'm going to take you all the way back, more than a hundred years, to World War Two and the middle of the Twentieth Century. A long time ago, when millions of people heard these songs, and sang them, and thought about the ones they loved."

Drew loved her even more. He was fascinated by that war and that century. What an amazing time. So crowded, so itchy for bigger and better tech. World on a string, ass in a sling, his mother said sometimes. And romantic and violent and kind of spotty and they really thought they had everything tied down, really thought the USA was forever. He wondered: how could all those people have gone through the wars they went through, with countries swallowing countries and spitting them out again, and think that anything in their over-organized, chaotic, inefficient, and smug too-big world would last? But it must have been really exciting.

Rica started singing. He hadn't caught the name of the song, maybe she never said it, but it started with the lines, "Kiss me once, kiss me twice, kiss me once again, it's been a long, long, time . . ."

He took a deep breath. The way she sang "kiss" sounded like a kiss. He felt warm. No, hot.

He leaned back, trying to find room for himself in his clothes. Someone brushed past his chair, startling him.

Jo. She hadn't seemed to notice him, just walked right by, her eyes on the stage. She glanced toward Samm, he thought, and turned, deliberately going the other way, choosing a table way over on the right side. What was that about? Had they had an argument? Not that he knew about. He focused on Rica again until her song ended. The audience clapped and cheered, warming up. She smiled, waited for the appreciation to die down, and said, "This one's called 'I'll Be Seeing You.' "

He'd heard the song somewhere, once before. Sad. Did she have tears in her eyes? They looked glittery, soft. He thought he would melt into his chair or explode, he didn't know which. He closed his eyes for a moment, then opened them and let them drift over to Jo, and then to Samm.

Both completely engrossed, very still. The three of them made a triangle, Samm at the front, Jo at the side, Drew at the back. Each of them alone, and, it seemed, deliberately alone.

A triangle? Were they all there for the same reason? No. Couldn't be. Samm maybe. Samm was a soldier, a real man, not some drooling virgin godder. Why would he not want Rica? But Jo? Of course not. Jo hadn't had anyone in a long time. Didn't seem to want to. Too much in her head. He couldn't see her with Rica. No, there was no way Jo would be interested in Rica or Rica in Jo. Samm, maybe. Probably.

Was that better or worse? He didn't know. The beer tasted bitter. His stomach hurt. How could he compete with Samm? Or Jo? Unless Rica liked young guys. Some older women did, he knew that. There had been that tourist from Rocky, that one time. But just the one time, because the day after, she went home again.

He was disappointed when the show ended. And burned when he saw Samm stand up and pull out a chair at his table for Rica, even though he hadn't planned on doing that himself. He glanced at Jo. She was watching, just like he was. He shoved his chair back, nearly tipping it over, and left the lounge.

Rica looked good and sounded good, and she knew how to deliver a song. It took an actor to do that so well.

Which worried Jo. Rica could be concealing anything. What that anything might be, Jo couldn't even begin to guess and she was probably wasting mental fuel thinking about it. She was just here to check out the performance. Beyond that, she needed all the focus she could muster and she didn't want distraction. Needed to set up a real government. Needed to get the Scorsis off her back. She wanted to fight Scorsis. Especially Newt. She hadn't had the pleasure of injuring him for many years, and she'd always regretted not hurting him more than she had.

Rica was an impulse she needed to control. She didn't have time to be sitting here watching this beautiful woman sing, and having paranoid fantasies about that woman. Or any kind of fantasies, for that matter.

And Samm! What was he doing here? He was supposed to be dealing poker. Sitting up in front, too. And Drew, for god's sake. She'd pretended she hadn't seen him, huddled back there in the dark, where she'd been thinking of sitting. Let him think no one noticed he was there, let him have the last of his adolescence without adult interference. He'd be an adult soon enough.

What kind of adult? She didn't see him as a soldier, even if he thought he wanted to do that now. He was so much like his mother. A thinker. A governor. Jo was beginning to see Lizzie as a more likely successor to Samm, if they ever needed one, than Drew would be. If she could calm down a little.

Her eyes wandered around the room, catching the excitement of the audience, and focused again on Rica, singing about sadness and love up there on the stage. The hell with sadness. The hell with love. Love hadn't worked for her and sadness was just plain useless.

She had more important things to do. Sometimes she wished that it were all over now. That they had already taken control of Tahoe, and used that base to go for all of Sierra and Redwood.

But they'd barely begun. They could run into some heavy opposition if they weren't careful. She didn't want to alarm the Sierra Council and end up having to take on the guard. The elections next month were key. If she could get a couple more of her own elected to the council, and turn the chief, as she thought she could, the people she had inside now thought Sierra would fall to Coleman power easily enough. All of it could be done peacefully. If she had to shed some Scorsi blood to get to the peaceful part, well, that was a shame.

Then came Redwood. She would show them that they needed protection from Rocky, and that Sierra was their buffer. It shouldn't be hard to do; no one liked Rocky, with its lurking spies and self-righteous tourists. She was convinced that the country to the east would be a danger some day soon. And the offer of cheap vax would buy a lot of support among Redwooders who didn't believe in the Rocky threat.

She and Judith would organize everything, end the chaos. Build a big, strong country. No more messy little bits and pieces. No more vax black market, no more poison or provincial ignorance. Like it used to be, only smarter.

People were the hard part. Samm was an icon, but like so many icons, he was vain and impatient. Judith was careful, more careful, sometimes, than Jo thought was necessary. Drew? Soon. Lizzie? Eventually. Who else? Her eyes followed her thoughts back to Rica. Too clever to be working as a server, even as a server-entertainer. The brain and spirit she saw there were wildly attractive, but she didn't trust it.

And that was why she had one of her spies checking up on her.

Jo smiled to herself again. If nothing else, it always paid to know whatever you could about a woman you thought you might want. Sometimes she wondered which she enjoyed more: chasing political power or pursuing a lover. It was a great game either way.

Rica had finished her war medley and was singing "Somewhere over the Rainbow." Why can't you fly over the rainbow, pretty Rica? Maybe you can. Amazing. She made even that ancient warhorse sound like a torch song. Who was this woman torching for, anyway? Truly, if this was all an act, she was capable of any kind of deception.

And Jo had no time for this!

At the end of the set, Rica took her bows and accepted Samm's invitation to join him at his table. Jo glanced back, toward the table where Drew sat. He was watching Rica with Samm, she thought, but it was too dark in that corner to see his face. She guessed it was not wearing an expression of benign interest, of admiration for the handsome couple. Or maybe that was just her own mood. No, it was his, too. He lurched to his feet, nearly breaking the chair. Leaving.

Jo wasn't about to do that.

The applause got less and less polite through the show and more and more enthusiastic. I even saw tears glittering in the eyes of an old woman sitting up front. The crowd was clapping wildly; I heard a sharp whistle or two. Hannah stood, still applauding, and like a wave rising, the rest of the room followed suit. Jo was smiling broadly, nodding at me. This was great—I was a hit!

Someone yelled encore and I obliged. I sang two more songs before they'd let me quit.

When the crowd began to wander back out to the casino, Hannah stood. Tall. Maybe six feet. The wiry body, the long white scar, the ready way she held herself. She looked like a hard-driven merc to me. She caught my eye and grinned. I glared back at her and she just kept grinning. The moment of pity I'd felt earlier was irretrievable, and I thought it was probably a good thing.

Was she or was she not going to out me with the Colemans? She hadn't so far, unless they were playing some unfathomable game with me. I intended to find out later that night in the parking lot.

Right now, though, there was Samm. I was about to have a chance to talk to him over a drink. If Hannah had so much as hinted to him that I needed to be watched, I should be able to see the suspicion in his behavior. And if that was not an issue, he might trust me enough to tell me something useful about the Colemans. How should I approach our conversation? The open-ended personal question, after the introductory chat? Of course I'd done this kind of thing a thousand times before, looking for information. Women sometimes saw through my fiery, fascinating-and-yet-attentive-redhead act; men usually wanted to believe it. But this man seemed sharper than most, more watchful. I joined him at his table.

"Great performance, Rica."

"Thanks, Samm." I took the chair he offered. We both sat. "I was so happy to see a good crowd here. Hope I don't chase them away." I laughed. Modest, humorous yet begging for re-assurance, compassion. People tend to trust and like those they can reassure, those who ask for support. I learned that a long time ago, the honest way, by needing and asking.

His strong face relaxed, the lines around his mouth softening. "The place was full, Rica. Not an empty table that I could see. You pulled in a crowd, and they love you. The room might end up being too small."

I gave him a warm smile. It wasn't hard to do.

Samm didn't look suspicious, not at all. I asked him a few inconsequential questions: how long have you known the Colemans, how many nights a week do you work the poker table, how long have you been doing it, that kind of thing. I was just about to segue into some deeper chat about the casino, the Colemans, find a way to mention Hannah, when we were interrupted by a soft dark voice saying hello.

Jo. Damn. But didn't she look good. Samm didn't invite her to sit but I realized that if I didn't she'd think I was after Samm. Or worse, wanted to talk to him alone. I couldn't let her believe either of those things.

"Sit down, Jo. Join us. I can't stay long anyway." It was true. I needed to get back to the restaurant for my second shift. She pulled up a chair. Okay, maybe I could learn something by playing them off against each other. Make it look like a double flirtation, no problem there, and get to know more about each of them in the process. Maybe even set up a tiny rivalry that could open someone up. Put someone off guard. I wondered if Jo was ever off guard. Probably not.

Then I had a truly uncomfortable thought: were these two doing this deliberately? Working together to find out more about me? Oh, hell, that was just stupid. They had no reason to do that. Too elaborate. All they had to do was say, "Why were you spying on the war games?"

I preferred to assume that all this interest in me was based on lust, even if the assumption was dangerous.

We talked about music and Tahoe and the casino business and even my supposed desire to learn to be a dealer. I never did find a way to bring Hannah into the conversation.

Five minutes after my second restaurant shift, I opened my car door and slid inside, leaving the passenger side locked. Hannah came out the back door and moved toward my car. I watched her. She walked like she knew she was being watched, glancing casually at a car here, a bus there, up at the moon. Too tall, too thin, too self-conscious. Gangly, that was the word. Like a teenage boy whose legs had grown too fast. But people built that way could be strong and wiry and have a long reach in a fight.

I cracked my window. She started to walk around the car to

the passenger side. I didn't want her in the car.

"Just come over here and talk to me," I told her, getting out again and standing so she wouldn't tower over me quite so much. She shrugged and grinned and came back around.

"Anyone ever tell you that you sound a little like June Christie—they used to call her 'the misty Miss Christie.' Way back."

Way way back. "Actually, I have been told that once or twice." By people who really knew their jazz standards. But I wasn't about to compliment Hannah, and I kept the upper hand by implying that her observation was not original and I was not impressed by it.

"What's going on, Hannah?" Was there any way I could be wrong about her seeing me hiding in the trees? I didn't think so, but just in case, I played it close. "We both know you saw me." I was careful not to say where.

"No harm in you being there. You work for the Colemans, right? Just curious, probably. Why didn't you come on in and join us?" She was laughing at me. I don't usually mind that; this time I did.

"Stop playing games, Hannah."

She smirked, reached over, and chucked me under the chin. I wanted to stomp her instep, but I slapped her hand away instead. She had the nerve to laugh.

"Why didn't you tell Samm I was there?"

She studied my face for a moment. "Flying blind, aren't you? Well, that's Newt. Tight with information. Fact is, we do both work for the same people, Rica. I mean the ones we really work for."

Well, that explained it. And I was relieved. At least I wouldn't be dealing with blackmail. Or maybe I would anyway. What kind of merc was she? There was the kind who did the job she was hired to do and never betrayed anyone connected to her employer. And there was the kind who would play anyone off against anyone else, make the people she was spying on believe that she was really loyal to them. Or to get something she wanted from a fellow spy.

All I could do was ask. She'd lie, but her face might betray her.

"And what are you going to do about it, Hannah? Let me do my job or turn me in to get points with the Colemans?"

"If I was going to do that, wouldn't I have done it already?"

"That's not an answer."

"Well, Miss Torchy, that's the only answer you're going to get." There was that smirk again. Miss Torchy indeed. Bitch. "Want to go get a late supper somewhere? Somewhere besides Blackjack?"

I closed my car window and locked the door. "I don't think so, Hannah." I walked back toward Blackjack. I felt like I had driving across Iowa. Not enough eyes in the back of my head.

CHAPTER 18
DOUBLE CHRISTIAN ALL
OVER THE LANDSCAPE

Before I dropped onto my mattress that night I shoved the bed against the doorway. Even though I guessed that anyone who wanted to come after me would have done it by now, I thought I'd sleep better if I wasn't worried about assassins picking my lock. I sent two messages, one to Newt Scorsi and one to Chief Graybel. The one to Newt: Thanks for the offer to perform at your casino. I'd like to hear more. Wednesday morning at ten a.m.

I wanted to talk to him about Hannah, among other things. I didn't include a meeting place. If he couldn't figure out I meant the same clearing we'd used the first time he'd have to message me.

As for the chief, I had decided I couldn't trust Hannah, even if we did work for the same man, and, reluctant as I was to do it, I had to send a warning that I might need help. I wrote:

Stand by. Double Christian all over the landscape. May need your prayers.

Double-crosses, may need to be extricated. No action yet.

It was only good form. The last thing she wanted was for me to be captured and questioned. She served the council. She liked to keep her covert operations disconnected from what she thought of as her power base, her job, because spying could fail as often as not and too many failures, made public, could put her out of work.

She wouldn't trust any merc to keep her mouth shut if things

187

got bad, and for good reason. I never knew a merc who was willing to die under torture rather than expose an employer. Only a terrorist or a martyr would do a crazy thing like that. The trick was not to be captured at all, and, of course, not to die.

Damned tox-bag Newt and his skinny razor blade of a double agent.

I was tired, but still quivering from the double dose of adrenaline—the show and the tense meeting with Hannah Karlow. If I thought about either of those things I'd never get to sleep, and I really needed some rest after this long and raggedy day, so I put them out of my mind. Instead, I found myself lying in bed thinking about Samm and Jo.

It was a real shame I'd had no time alone with either one of them. If my songs had made that woman in the audience cry, maybe they'd also softened up Samm or Jo. Soften up, open up. No such luck. The conversation was light and friendly; they were charming and attentive and interested in my life. I gave them a good story, based narrowly on truth, embellished with fantasy jobs like the one on the Riverboat Queen, and then I had to go back to work.

Samm's image drifted away on a cloud of twitchy weariness and Jo remained, hovering in my mind.

Jo didn't seem to be anything like Sylvia. Sylvia was an artist. Jo was a—what? Politician? Sylvia was blond, with hair like white sand, and she was soft and sweet and smelled like spicy nasturtium. Jo was dark, demanding, with hard and angry edges, even if she spoke softly, moved softly. And she smelled like cut grass. The sweetness and fear that coexisted so touchingly in Sylvia were both missing. Well, that might not be fair. Jo had been tender and loving with Drew when he was wounded. Just because she hadn't shown her soft side to me . . .

Sylvia needed love and needed to feel safe in love. Jo? She

needed admiration. She needed followers and comrades and flawless performance and probably sex. But a warm kiss? A loving touch? Safety? No, that didn't seem to have much currency in Jo's life. I saw no sign of anyone who gave her those things.

It was possible that I was drawn to her because she was different. Or because really, under the swagger and in her soul, she wasn't different from Sylvia at all.

The attraction was powerful. The dangerous glint in her eye. The dry hint of humor that I guessed could spin wilder and wilder webs of laughter and excitement. Maybe it was because she was bad enough, and dangerous enough, and challenge enough, to take my mind off Sylvia entirely for a while.

I needed to stay away from her. She could drag me in over my head.

I was investigating her family. I could practically taste her ruthlessness and I wanted to kiss her ear, nuzzle her neck. I wanted her to put her hands on my shoulders and pull me close and kiss me and lead me off to her bed. Well! That was clear enough. But why? Because Sylvia wouldn't, and probably never would again. Because she couldn't forgive and couldn't trust me. And because she'd made a life without me and was determined to be as faithful to that life as I had not been to her.

I didn't know what I would do if Jo came closer. If we became lovers and I was faced with the choice of turning her over to the chief or letting her get away with whatever crimes she was committing. It would be easier to let myself follow my safer inclination toward the exotic and beautiful Samm, who seemed less complex and less threatening, except that it might not be any easier to turn him in. So all in all, the course of action seemed to be prescribed. Stay away from both of them, make friends with Samm—I didn't think I could with Jo, the heat was too intense—and do my job.

And consider the possibility of traveling to Sylvia's house

when this was all over and shooting her husband. No, of course not that. Going to her house and what? Begging her to follow me around the countryside like a nomad. She'd love that. Sylvia and her little house tucked in the woods. Sylvia and her safe little house and the lover she controlled and dominated with her love. Well, she could stay with Gran while I worked.

But she had no reason to want me back. It had been a long time and a dozen lives and what I could offer she didn't want.

A dozen lives.

A dozen years anyway. We'd been young then. She was a dancer. Both of us scraping for a low-level living, afraid all the time of the dying around us. I met someone. A man, a little older, sweet, funny, kind, who said I could make enough money for vax for me and Gran and Sylvia if I went to work as a merc. We liked each other. He would teach me, get me started, he said. I told Sylvia I could make enough for all of us, to protect all of us, but I would have to travel. She said no, it was dangerous, I couldn't go without her and she wouldn't come along. I said I was going to do it, that I believed I had to. She said if I went it would be for good. It was a terrible and catastrophic night, there in the last bedroom we ever shared. The only fight we ever had. She packed some clothes and walked out.

Maybe she knew that I was being seduced in more ways than one, but I didn't know it yet. Not until I ran grief-torn to my mentor and he comforted me.

I went off to be a merc, with the man who became my lover for a time. And while I was learning useful things, and terrible things, Sylvia found safety and married it.

Oh, Sylvia. If you can love that idiot you're living with why can't you love this idiot who blew our love all to hell?

Come on, Sylvia, be a sport. I swear I've learned my lesson.

All of my lessons, whatever they are.

I'm a liar. I don't have any idea what I have or have not

learned. And as hard as I keep trying to reach her, she pretends she's not there.

Jo wasn't so sure about Hannah Karlow. She trusted Samm's judgment about many things, but not about women. And not about politics. She and Judith had scheduled a morning meeting with Hannah to see where she stood and where her ambitions and loyalties, if any, truly lay.

The fixer was early, standing outside Judith's locked office when Jo arrived. They nodded to each other, stood silent, and waited. Karlow didn't seem uncomfortable with the silence; that was good and bad. Jo hated people who couldn't tolerate silence, had to chatter mindlessly, and Hannah seemed to understand that without Judith present, nothing of substance would be discussed. On the other hand, it might mean she didn't think Jo had power, and that was bad.

Right on time, at exactly nine o'clock, Judith hove into view, Drew beside her.

"Good morning," Judith said, opening the door to her office and ushering them inside. Judith sat behind her big desk, Jo at her right hand. Hannah took the remaining chair, across the expanse of the desk, farther away and in the line of fire of two sets of deliberately intense eyes. "You've met my son, Drew?" Karlow nodded and smiled. Drew nodded back and sat on the couch. He was an observer, there to learn, not an active partici-pant.

Judith got right to it.

"Samm says you might be interested in running for mayor."

Hannah smiled, deepening her scar. Not obsequious, Jo noticed, but relaxed, cool. She would have preferred obsequi-ous.

"Might be. Depends on what kind of support I'd have."

Ah, Jo thought. The what's-in-it-for-me factor.

Judith shot back: "Why do you want to be mayor? And what kind of support are you talking about?"

A blink, a second's hesitation. "The town can't go on forever without one. I like the idea of doing it better than it's been done before." Both Jo and Judith waited for more. "What I mean is, government interests me. I think with the right support I could do some good things here."

Jo fixed her with a deliberately bland look. She still hadn't defined "support." "Like what?"

Hannah sent a bland look right back at her. "I think we could figure that out together."

Jo fiddled with a snow globe, the one that was a model of Blackjack. "You know what happened to the last mayor. Were you here then?" Hannah nodded. "He was a friend of ours. You're a friend of ours. He was murdered. Why aren't you afraid you'll be murdered, too?" Jo watched Hannah's face carefully. No change of expression.

She had a fast, smug answer. "If I were afraid of being killed I wouldn't have joined Samm's army. Some things go beyond that kind of fear."

Lots of things, Jo thought. Loyalty. Ambition. Greed. She wouldn't bet on loyalty, not unless Karlow was in love with Samm. And she doubted that very much.

She opened her mouth, ready with a question, but Judith beat her to it: "Like what? What goes beyond fear?"

"Vision."

"Whose vision?"

"I think I agree with yours."

"Really?" Jo prodded. "And what do you think our vision is?"

Karlow was silent for a moment. Jo was sure she was only pretending to think. She thought this woman had come to the meeting with a full script ready in her mind.

"I like the way you run things, the way you treat your people.

And I like that you're raising an army. That means you want to spread your influence."

"Armies are for conquest," Judith shot back. "Not influence. Speak plainly. Stop sounding like a diplomat. Do you or do you not want power?"

Karlow grinned. "Yes, I do."

"Why?"

"Because I think I would handle it well and I would like it."

Jo nodded. Good. She wanted power. They could give it to her, or make her think they had. It didn't matter, at this point anyway, whether they could trust her or not. She would do, as a candidate. They'd put her in office and keep her convinced they were building her road to power. She would serve them as long as she thought it was in her interest. If she veered off their road, they could deal with her. And if someone else assassinated her, it would be no great loss. Satisfying. A good morning's work.

She glanced at Judith, who returned the look and nodded.

"My sister and I need to discuss it, Hannah," Judith said. "Stick around. Come back in an hour."

The gaunt woman stood, dismissed. She looked pleased with herself "One hour," she said.

Jo watched her go out the door. When it shut behind her, she said, "Do you trust her?"

"Hell no. But she's not as smart as she thinks she is. We're throwing her a title and a few perks and she thinks we're giving her control." She grinned. "Samm told me she wants to learn to fly the plane. Asked for lessons the minute she saw it. He's letting the merc who delivered it teach her." Jo didn't much like the idea of Hannah Karlow flying a Gullwing over their heads. "If she's grateful enough, she'll be useful. What do you think, Drew?"

"I don't like her." He looked worried.

Jo laughed. "I think that's smart." Drew was a good judge of people. "Did you notice—she didn't even ask why we wanted her to be our candidate."

Judith smiled and shook her head. "Oh, she's probably afraid that if she asks too many questions we'll decide we don't need a mayor at all."

Jo laughed again, reached over and patted Judith's shoulder. "Well, that's done. Do you want me back here in an hour?"

"No, I'll give her the good news."

"Then I'll go roust Samm, tell him we've decided." Samm had begged off this meeting. He already knew what he thought about Hannah Karlow. He thought she was tough and he thought she could be bought.

"Good." Judith looked from Jo to Drew. "See me back here at noon, then. Both of you. And tell Samm, and Lizzie, too, if she's interested. We need to start putting together our mayoral campaign."

Lizzie had gone off that morning hiking with friends, but had made Drew promise to tell her all about the Karlow interview. She was interested, just not enough to give up a good hike.

He needed to get out for a while, too. He stuck a book in his pocket, a biography of Golda Meir, and headed for the lake.

This Hannah Karlow . . . good soldier, strange woman. He wondered if there was any way the wrong mayor could mess things up. But then, what was a wrong mayor?

Lately, he'd been thinking a lot about his family's plans. Sometimes he had doubts about his mother's drive for power, his aunt's drive to consolidate little countries into bigger ones. He wasn't sure it was a good idea to start out on that road, even if he trusted them to do the right thing.

Big countries made irresistible targets for big terrorists. Big markets made big toxies. These were problems they had no firsthand experience with, and history showed what such problems could do.

Oh, they had straggler causies and crazies wandering the roads but even the godders who had started so much of the Poison couldn't scrape together the followers or the targets to take a bite out of what was left, and just as often were targets themselves. Just yell "terrorist" and they were dead or heading for the border.

Someone had tried to blow up a glassy-metal molding factory in California a few years ago. They made parts for cars and buses and the few planes that were put together at a Redwood plant when the parts made it that far north without being stolen. But the people who lived nearby, who kept a watch on the factory, ready to protest the slightest hint of toxic sloppiness, eyes sharp for terror, too, took the would-be bomber into a field and shot at him until he blew himself up, blasting a crater in a patch of onions. No one ever found out what point he was trying to make.

Drew sat on a bench off to the side, the picnic tables at his back, the wide blue lake to his left, remembering the last time he'd been there. The stupid fight with the Scorsi boys. He opened his book, read a paragraph, set it down beside him.

His mother and Jo, and Samm, too, were so sure that consolidation was right, and the time was now. But Drew didn't trust political ideas to take real people into account. He'd always thought that political systems tended to rely on people being either stupider and meaner than they were, or smarter and better than they were.

He would stand with family, and he would see. He would watch as things changed, if they did, and make up his own mind. For now, he recognized that he didn't know. He thought it was a complex question that he hadn't quite figured out the answer to yet

What he did know, right now, was that he didn't like Hannah

Karlow. He opened his book again.

Newt was late to our meeting, but at least this time he wasn't dragging a giant sandwich along with him. He swaggered into the clearing looking impatient, an important man called for a small purpose.

"This wasn't convenient, Rica. What exactly is it you want to talk to me about? I have business to take care of." His big head rolled back on his skinny neck and he eyed me from under his puffy lids.

"Yeah. So do I. I told you I needed to know who else you've got at Blackjack besides Bernard. It would have been especially helpful to know about Hannah Karlow."

"Why? You've got your own job to do. She has hers." So she'd told me the truth, about that, anyway. He sat down on the rock beside me and broke a pebble from its surface.

"What about Waldo?"

He looked at me as if I'd suddenly started spinning a plate of chicken on my head. "What about him?"

"Does he give you information?"

Newt laughed. A rusty sound. "He doesn't have any. That's a really stupid question. Waldo is nothing. Haven't you figured that out yet? Is that what you got me out here for?"

"I have to know who's safe and who isn't. I have to know what else is going on. You sent me to spy on the army. I didn't know Hannah was doing the same thing." Silly sack of drool.

He snickered. "She's really got Samm in her pocket. He's going to let her learn to fly their airplane." He glanced up at me, sidelong. "She found out they really do have one."

Why did Samm trust that bitch? Was it true? I needed to find out if there really was a plane. "Where do they keep it? The plane?"

He looked exasperated, unsure. "At the airport."

"Where's that?"

He picked up a stick and drew a map in the dirt. I studied it for a minute, asked a couple of questions, and felt I could probably find the field. He said it was ten minutes south of Stateline, south of the lake.

"Okay." I tried to sound reasonable, calm. "If you've got the army covered, I can focus on something else."

"You need to focus on everything." He was scraping at the boulder with the pebble. Scrape, scrape, scrape . . . "You're the only one the chief sent. I wanted someone here who was official. That's you. I've got people who are loyal to me here and there but . . ." He shrugged. "Well, they're just there because they're there." He screwed up his forehead, having a hard time explaining his lack of organization to me. Scrape . . . scrape.

I slapped the pebble out of his hand. It shot across the clearing. He stared at me, his blubbery lips hanging open.

"You can't . . . !"

"I did. Now I want a list of everyone you've got at Blackjack and what their jobs are."

He squinted at me. "Not a chance! Why should I trust you?"

"Because you're paying me. And I'm a merc."

"Not good enough. I've got a lot of plans, a lot of things going on. And I'm the only one who knows about all of them." He stood up. "And that's the way it's going to stay. You know about Bernard, so you can use him if you need to. And now you know about Hannah. Make the Colemans love you. Become a Coleman. That's your job." He swaggered back out of the clearing again and I sat there stewing.

So my job was being lovable.

I drove back to the casino and pulled into the parking lot in time for lunch. The restaurant was about half-full. Tim was working the shift with Drew and one of the regular day people.

"Hi, Rica! You look annoyed. Everything okay?"

My irritation with Newt must be showing. I shifted gears and gave him a peck on the cheek. "Everything's fine. Just thinking about tonight's show."

I sat at a table near the restaurant door. Just as I was ordering a club sandwich and an orange juice—expensive but worth it—I noticed Jo and Samm walk by together. Drew noticed them, too, glanced at the clock, and told Timmy he had to take a break for a while. He took off his apron, stashed it behind the host station, earning a glare from Waldo, and ran off after them. They walked up the stairs to Judith's office.

Another big Coleman meeting. Again, without Waldo. I wondered what this one was about.

"Drew was in a hurry," I said casually to Tim, when he brought my small glass of juice.

"Meeting. Family meeting. Big doings today I hear."

"Oh? What kind of big doings?"

Timmy arched an eyebrow. "Seems that one of our regulars is going to run for mayor of Tahoe, and the Coleman family, well, let me just say it's their candidate of choice. And they're going to start working on a campaign. That's what Drew told me, anyway."

"The candidate—anyone I know?" He hadn't said "employee." He'd said "regular," meaning a customer.

"Yes indeed. You were asking us about her just yesterday."

Juice went down the wrong way. I coughed. It burned its way up through my nose. "Not Hannah Karlow?"

"Why not?"

Was it possible? That Blackjack was running a Scorsi spy as their candidate for mayor?

Newt must have known about this when I'd seen him earlier, but as usual, he was letting me find out for myself.

Maybe I was underestimating him. Or overestimating the

Colemans. It was reassuring that smart as the Colemans were, they weren't mind readers and they could be fooled by a good spy.

CHAPTER 19
IT'S NOT LIKE SHE'S OUR CANDIDATE OR ANYTHING

This was news I could give the chief. Hannah Karlow, supposedly working for Newt Scorsi, was the Colemans' candidate for mayor in a one-candidate race.

On my way to the stairs, I noticed Samm wasn't working but Drew was hanging around Zack's poker table, sitting back from the action on a slot machine stool. I moved up beside him. The game was moving fast; Zack was working hard.

"Learning to deal?" I hadn't intended to startle Drew, but he jumped when I spoke and stared at me for a moment before answering.

"Yeah. Mom wants me to learn all the jobs."

"There's a lot to learn." Was it my imagination, or had he shifted slightly away from me, just an inch or two? And was that a blush on his downy young cheek?

I stood there with him, silent. Worrying about his discomfort. What, if anything, did it have to do with me?

"So you're going to stay with casino work?"

He looked surprised that I would even ask such a thing. "Yeah. Of course."

"No interest in anything outside the casino?"

"Like what?"

"Well, I hear someone's running for mayor here in town. Any interest in anything like that? When you get a little older?"

"Politics?" His gaze was more direct now, as if he were trying to see inside my head. Why? Because he thought I was seeing inside his? "Don't know. Maybe."

"You're smart enough."

His blush spread and in that instant I knew he had a crush on me. Now that was a dilemma. I liked the kid. A crush might make it easier to get information from him. I'd feel like a rat, but feeling like a rat was part of my job, sometimes, and I'd have to live with it, wouldn't I? I could hang onto that crush just enough, and damp it down just enough to use it without tearing his young heart out. Couldn't I? Probably not.

"What do you think of the new candidate, this Hannah Karlow woman? Have you heard she's running?"

"Yeah, I knew that. How'd you find out so fast?"

I grinned, innocent. "News gets around."

He laughed. "Timmy."

I shrugged. "So what do you think of her?"

"She's pretty well known around town. Any fixer would be, but she's a good one. She can get a broken slot up and running faster than, well, fast. Came in real handy after that raid the other day. And the elevator's running now." She must have finished the job while I was out.

The hand ended, one of the players raked in a good-sized pot, and Zack started dealing again.

Drew watched the table, but kept praising Hannah. "She fixes everything from toilets to cars from what I've heard. She does work for all the casinos."

Yes, I thought wryly. She certainly does. Nothing like a fixer to get inside everyone's works. Not mine, though.

Despite Drew's positive words, his body language—a doubtful tilt of the head, a tension in the shoulders—told me he wasn't sure about Hannah.

"Do you think she'll get elected?"

He shrugged. "She's known. And I haven't heard anyone else is running." Drew turned back to watch the poker play again.

Less comfortable talking about politics than about fixing.

I watched with him for a few minutes, not wanting to push the conversation too hard. Then I got back to it.

"Is that usually the way it is, just one candidate?"

"If someone else wants to run, he can, but . . ." He hesitated. I waited for the rest of his sentence. It didn't come.

"I heard that your family is supporting Karlow. They've got a lot of influence here in town, don't they?"

"Sure."

"And I hear the Scorsis are your competitors. Why wouldn't they support a candidate, too? Another one?"

He took a deep breath and, keeping his eyes on the poker table, rolled out what sounded like a party line. "Well, it's not like she's our candidate or anything. She's running and we're supporting her. If someone else wants to run, and Newt Scorsi wants to support that other person, that's up to him, isn't it?"

"Of course." I tossed it off like I didn't much care. But there was no mistaking the kid's slightly embarrassed look. He knew better, knew she was their candidate, and he wasn't happy that he had to lie to me. I didn't much like making him unhappy.

"I like Hannah," I said. He nodded, noncommittal. "I'm thinking of working on her campaign. Guess I'll talk to her about it." I turned and moved away. "See you later, Drew."

"Yeah. Later."

So Drew wasn't crazy about Hannah. Was he the only one in his family who could see through her or did they all feel the same way? Hannah could be stepping into a killer-ants' nest. They were running her but watching her. If they caught her at anything dicey she might want to toss me onto the hill as a diversion.

I took the finally-moving elevator up to the third floor and retrieved my sys from the pants where I kept it hidden. Holding it in my palm, I stared at it for a moment. Maybe I shouldn't be keeping it in my room. Or my car. Maybe I needed to find a tree somewhere in the woods and stash it inside.

The way this assignment was going, some damned squirrel would find it and bury it.

For the umpteenth time, I was wishing I knew how sophisticated Blackjack's techspy system was, or if the casino even had one, and how thoroughly they watched their employees. The path the chief and I used was routed through ringers and baffles, but I couldn't be absolutely sure that a sniffer hadn't been planted. I'd run the squeeze a couple of times and hadn't found anything. That was all I could do, along with using a lot of code.

The chief didn't answer so I left her a message. What I told her was this: "Thinking of getting involved in politics here. A friend named Hannah Karlow is going to be running for mayor, with the support of my boss. She's a keeper."

"Keeper" was our code word for double agent. To rhyme with sleeper.

I lay back on my bed and let things run through my mind again, hoping the fog would start to clear. Had Newt Scorsi killed Madera so he could run a candidate of his own undercover as a Coleman candidate? Was he that smart? I thought, and a scratchy thought it was, that maybe, under his secretive, slimy exterior, he could, indeed, have a real plan going.

The whole thing was giving me a headache.

The Colemans were making a mistake, that was clear. Judith should be running for mayor. Jo. But then, a candidate could be defeated, tossed out of office, neutralized politically, or even killed. It was safer and stronger to be the power behind the candidate. To fill the public offices, including the appointed town cabinet, with your own people and run things from behind the scenes. That way, you weren't the one who got killed, or exposed as a fraud or a crook. That way, your power could go on, and on, and on.

Or Jo planned to go for something wider-ranging than mayor of Tahoe. That wasn't the only job on the ballot. Some of the council seats would be opening up. I didn't know a lot about Sierra politics; I certainly didn't know how many council members she already controlled and what it would take to own the majority.

I left another message for the chief: How many knights do the queens own? That was as vague as I could get without dumbfounding her. We didn't have a code word for the council; I hadn't thought we'd need one. But I knew they met at a round table. And "the queens" was a term I thought she wouldn't have much trouble with.

Okay. That was done. I dropped my sys in my pocket and went back out to the elevator. I had plenty of time to look for the airport, sniff around, and get back in time for my shift.

The airport wasn't that easy to find.

After driving south of Stateline for ten minutes, I still saw nothing but a screen of trees and brush beside the road. If there was a field in there somewhere, I couldn't tell. The signs that must have pointed the way years ago were all gone now, scavenged or lying somewhere in the underbrush, rusting away. There weren't enough planes flying for anyone to bother maintaining or replacing them. The few people who did fly would know where the airport was, and no one else would care.

Then I got my first hint: a fence. New-looking, eight feet tall, solid wood, visible behind the trees. I drove another five minutes. The fence ended and there was nothing but trees again.

Somewhere, there had to be an opening. I pulled up alongside the road, nosing into the brush as far as I could, and began walking back along the fence.

There it was. An iron latch with a lock hanging open from it.

Sloppy, but I could have climbed over if I'd needed to. And a barely car-sized opening in the brush and trees. I yanked the latch and the gate swung open. Tarmac. A couple of hangars. The place looked deserted, but I decided not to make a stir by bringing Electra through, just in case someone was around.

The airport had one runway, a road parallel to that, and connecting roads I thought were called "taxiways" where the planes moved from still to slow to position to fast enough to move to the runway and finally take off. Or something like that. Gran had shown me a small abandoned fallen-down airport once, up in Sonoma County, and explained some of it.

Several buildings stood at the back of the field. "Stood" was a relative term. One small building looked like it had been an office of some kind, a long time ago. The windows were boarded up, a quarter of the roof rotted and fallen away. Two hangars that seemed to have most of their parts loomed over big piles of what must once have been other hangars.

There was no cover of any kind between me and the hangars, so I ran across the runway, listening tensely for a shout, and skidded to a stop in front of the nearest one. The front was missing. It was empty. Moving to the next one, close by, I saw that it was complete and completely closed up. A new-looking patch was screwed to one wall. I walked around the side and found a small, human-sized door. A big, new-looking padlock hung from a shiny hasp, but there was a window. Boarded up from the outside, and not very well. It hadn't occurred to me to bring a crowbar, but those piles of collapsed hangars might offer something I could use. No one seemed to be around. I had time to do some breaking and entering.

I went to the closest pile and began shifting pieces.

Ouch. Okay, I'd be leaving some of my blood behind. I hadn't thought to bring work gloves, either.

After several minutes of hard labor, nicks, scratches, and

strains, I unearthed concrete rubble and—luck at last! A loose piece of rebar sticking out of the chunks. I grabbed hold of it, wiggled it, pulled, and it came free. A three-foot rod.

One of the boards on the hangar window had a knot in it. I jabbed at it until the knot fell out, leaving a small hole. Couldn't see anything through it, but it gave me a place to stick the rebar. The board came away, and it was easy to get leverage on the others. I could see why the knothole hadn't let me get a look inside; the window was opaque with dirt. No other way. I covered my face with my shirt and swung the rebar, shattering the glass.

It was in there, all right. Cutest little Gullwing II. Pristine. Just like the one that had so frustrated the Rocky border guard. Probably, I thought, the very same one.

I propped the boards back across the window again and managed to stick a couple of nails back in their original holes. Anyone who went inside would see the broken glass, but at least no one could tell at a casual glance, from the outside, that someone had come by to have a look.

On the way back, I checked my sys; no answer from the chief. Then it buzzed. Not the chief, though. Gran.

"Rica! I'm so glad I caught you."

"Hi, Gran. Something wrong?"

"Not here. But what's going on there?"

Uh oh. Reading the cards again.

"Nothing much. Just working on the case. Listen, Gran, I've only got a few minutes. I'm on my way back to the restaurant."

"What restaurant?"

She didn't usually ask a lot of questions about my cases until I was safely finished with them. I realized I'd told her almost nothing about Blackjack and what was going on in Tahoe. I gave her a quick rundown and said it was all a lot of fun.

So I exaggerated.

I also said there was some question that this casino clan might be skimming a little tax money. That was all, just some possible theft. Nothing dangerous. I didn't mention any dead mayors or gorgeous soldiers or wildly attractive would-be dictators.

"I did a reading—"

"Gran! More Death cards?"

"Never mind, Miss Skeptical. No, not the Death card this time. There's a queen of pentacles and an Empress and the outcome is the Tower of Destruction. Sounds like two very dangerous women to me, or at least one. There's also swords all over the place. A knight—that means a soldier, but with the Tower involved it could mean war, or at least a powerful conflict. And then you've got the page of swords. And the ten. Spies. Trouble."

That was scary. Sometimes Gran and her cards came too close to truth.

"Gran, I am a spy. And there are other spies here. And yes, there's a soldier. More than one. But there won't be any Tower of Destruction. What's that mean, anyway? Isn't it sometimes good, like the Death card?"

She'd read the cards for me hundreds of times but I always managed to forget what they mean.

"Yes. I suppose it can be. It can also mean a terrible catastrophe."

"Can't it also mean a powerful change that leads to enlightenment?" Gotcha.

"It can. But . . ."

What was this dramatic pause for?

"But you've also got the Devil. In the environment."

As a matter of fact, my environment seemed to be strewn with devils, but I wasn't going to tell her that.

"Look, love, that's what I do. Joust with devils. Don't worry."

"I am going to worry. I think I'll have a consultation with Macris."

Macris, John Macris, was an astrologer she'd known since before the Poison. He insisted on being known only by his last name. He was a silly man, but handsome, with long gray hair. Gran adored him.

"You go ahead and do that; just don't tell me what he has to say."

"You are a stubborn woman, Rica. Always good to have fair warning."

When I got to my room I saw that the casino sys was blinking. I had a message from Hannah Karlow.

"Tell the housekeeper your toilet is broken."

CHAPTER 20
YOUR PISS IS DRIBBLING
DOWN YOUR LEG, MACHA

She'd sent the message while I was snooping around the airport. Good. We had a lot to talk about. I told housekeeping that the toilet needed fixing right away. In an hour and a half I'd be in the restaurant serving early dinners to daytime gamblers.

Twenty minutes later, she knocked on the door.

"What's this about, Hannah?"

She held up her hand, pulled out a sniffer, and stalked slowly around the room.

"There's nothing here," I told her. "I checked the first night."

"Run a squeeze lately?" She smirked at me. I hadn't since I'd gotten back that day, but I was damned if I'd admit that to her. I gave her a neutral disgusted look.

"Okay," she said finally, walking back in from the bathroom "All clear." No new bugs, no nothing.

She helped herself to my bed, fluffing up the pillows, propping them against the headboard, stretching out her long skinny legs.

I took the one comfortable chair in the room and glared at her.

"You're too good at singing to wait tables."

"Is that what you want to talk about?"

"You've already got a lot of fans, me included."

"I'm flattered." I wished she'd get to the point.

"Maybe if you talked to Newt, he'd put you on as an

entertainer in his bar and you wouldn't have to waste your time doing the menial crap."

"Not wasting my time would be nice," I growled pointedly. "But I'd rather work here for now." I had no idea what she was after. She could have been trying to replace me as the spy in the Coleman camp, or giving me an opening to work for the Colemans as a spy at Scorsi's. "What exactly are you getting at?"

"Nothing. Just talking. What do you think of Jo Coleman?"

I continued to glare at her. "You're staging a fake toilet-fix so we can sit here and gossip? Pardon me, so you can lie down and gossip?"

She laughed. "Just answer the question."

"Why the hell should I? I've got questions for you."

"Trade?"

"Me first."

She looked me up and down. If she was trying to be provocative it wasn't working. I was just plain provoked. "Okay."

"You're a fixer and a mayoral candidate and a spy for Newt, but why are you working for him? Is it for the good pay or is it loyalty?" I wasn't sure which would make her more dangerous.

She shook her head. "Funny. A merc asking a merc about loyalty. Of course I'm loyal. He's paying me. And he's not the one trying to conquer the world. I'm not in favor of people conquering the world." She grinned so I'd know she was bullshitting. I thought she'd love to own the world, herself.

"Are you really learning to fly the Colemans' Gullwing?"

She shook her head. "That's two questions, Rica. Now it's your turn to answer one of mine—what do you think of Jo?"

"I'll answer it when you tell me why you're asking."

Fast as a snake, but without a rattle of warning, she was on me. Off the bed and flat up against me, her strong, long-fingered hand wrapped around my throat, shoving me and my chair to the wall. I brought my arm up, hard, ripping her fingers away from me, and kicked her left knee, which buckled for only a second. She fell back a pace, though, as I sprang to my feet, her eyes glittering, tongue-tip showing between her lips. Snake. Did she lie in the sun to warm her blood? My neck hurt—she'd yanked it when I'd knocked her away—and I could only hope her knee hurt as badly.

We stood facing each other. I could feel that my lip was curled in a snarl, but she was smiling.

"What the fuck was that about, bitch?" I wanted to kick her again, smash her face. I held my hands ready and aimed arrows at her eyes.

"Just checking your reflexes."

"You're crazy. Tell me, do the Colemans know you're crazy?"

"I don't know if they care. Do you?"

I didn't bother to answer. "Maybe you need to get out of here."

"No, let's finish talking. You wanted to know why I was asking you about Jo." She walked back to the bed, careful not to limp, but I could see the stiffness. Good. "I think you know these people better than I do. I can't read Judith at all. I don't think her boy likes me. Samm seems to trust me. But Jo—are you lovers? Are you planning to become lovers?"

"We're not and I have no plans."

"What about Samm?"

"No. Not him, either."

"Well, maybe you can help me scope Jo out. Is it your experience with her that she conceals a lot or is she just what she appears to be? Smart but not careful? Ambitious but a little soft?"

"I have no idea." And if I did, I wouldn't tell you, nutbucket.

"I think you should seduce her. I think you'd have better luck at it than I would and it would look more innocent."

"You telling me what to do? Last time I looked, I wasn't working for you, Hannah."

"Maybe you should be."

I walked to the door and opened it. She didn't move. "It was just a suggestion," she said, "the thing about Jo. But you should keep in mind that it would gain me a lot of trust with the Colemans if I told them you were a spy."

"You think you can force me to make love to Jo? Look, Hannah. I'm holding the door for you."

"I just want you to know that I'll use my leverage unless you do what I say." There was that corpse-like grin again.

"I have as much leverage over you as you have over me. Now you do what I say and get the hell out of my room."

I was very tired of this pissing contest. First the physical attack, now this. Maybe these tactics had worked for her in the past; they weren't going to work now. She hadn't won the fight, and she needed to know I'd out her in a flash if she tried to out me. As far as I was concerned, we had a stalemate.

She stood, but she didn't walk toward the door.

"I told you to get out. Now run along and run for mayor. I'll let you do that as long as you behave."

"So I guess you think we've got a tie, here, huh?"

"I guess so."

"I'm good at tie-breakers."

"Your piss is dribbling down your leg, macha."

She laughed and walked, carefully, out the door.

I was on my way to the restaurant, passing the front doors. I had just noticed Jo strolling toward me when a crash, an animal scream, and the agonized yipping of a dog turned me in my path and hurled me out the door, past Owen the blind barker.

The animal was large and black, a mass of curly hair. It was lying in the street, in front of a white floater with a red smear on the hood, crying and trying to stand, but it couldn't put weight on its right shoulder, where the fur was matted with blood. It struggled partway up, leaning on its left front paw, and then fell again, crying. A man stood beside the car, cursing.

"Look at my car! Look what he did to my car! Goddamn dog!"

I knelt beside the dog. "There's nothing wrong with your car a washing won't take care of." Even a deer couldn't dent the glassy this floater was made of; a sixty-pound dog sure hadn't.

"Who owns the damned thing, anyway? I hurt my head on the disk and my car will need washing. Someone needs to pay."

No one anywhere nearby admitted to owning the dog. His eyes were wild, flashing white from the mat of black hair, and he was lying there whimpering. I approached the driver.

"The dog is not mine but I'll find the owner. Have you called anyone? A veterinarian?"

"Fuck you, lady!" He was young, maybe twenty-five, and he stank of alcohol. Arrogant prick was probably a tourist from Rocky. I wanted to hit him but there were more important things to do. I turned back to the dog. Jo was beside him now, putting her jacket over the quivering black body. She reached to stroke his head and he snapped at her in pain and fear, but his teeth didn't connect. She touched the top of his head; he laid it down on the street, closed his eyes and groaned. One of the Blackjack cashiers came out to see what was going on, ducked back inside, and came out again with a tall man I knew was a cocktail server. They both stationed themselves in the street, directing traffic around the idiot's car, Jo, and the trembling black dog.

"Rica," Jo said, "get the doctor. Just punch 'doc' on any casino sys. He'll come himself or find the vet."

"I want to talk to the owner! My head hurts." I could see the tiniest reddish mark on his forehead. Like a pimple. Maybe it was a pimple. "And I want to be paid for my car."

"I'll find the owner for you," I lied. "Just stick around." I thought he was probably stupid enough to do that. I leaned down toward Jo, muttering, "I'll call the sheriff, too." She nodded, not looking up from the dog, crooning to him softly.

The doctor said he'd leave a call for the vet and also come himself, just in case the vet was tending an animal and didn't check in for a while. A deputy answered at the sheriff's office.

"This is Rica Marin over at Blackjack. There's a drunk driver stopped in the middle of the street outside our front door. Right near the dog he hit. He's screaming and yelling. I think he's violent. He may be crazy. If the dog has an owner he might want to press charges. If not, I will. At any rate, he should be taken off the road before he kills someone."

The deputy, who sounded smarter than Frank himself, said she'd be right there.

When I passed Owen on my way out again, I noticed that his face looked pinched, anxious. I stopped to tell him what was going on.

He nodded. "I gathered most of that. You're a nice woman, Rica. I was afraid he was going to start hurting people next. Anything I can do?" I told him things were under control and the deputy would arrive soon. He looked relieved.

The drunk driver was sitting on his hood, on the side without blood, glaring at Jo.

"How's the dog?" I asked her

"Alive. In shock, but maybe okay. Shoulder looks broken, but I can't really tell."

"Doc's on the way. So's the sheriff."

Jo smiled at me, and it was a sweet sight indeed. "Good."

"I'm due at the restaurant now."

"Stick around for a few minutes. It's okay. You've earned the right to see this finished."

The deputy got there first. Marty Kaiser, her nametag said.

She ordered the ranting driver to pull his car to the curb. When he'd done that, she told him to shut up, get out, and walk the center line. He wobbled along the line cursing the dog. She told him to shut up again and when he wouldn't stop yelling, cuffed him, told us she'd have the car hauled away, and took him off to jail, still carrying on, indignant now that the dog, the real criminal, wasn't being arrested. Or was it the owner he was complaining about? I liked this deputy's style. If Jo wanted to replace Frank, she'd be the one.

Doc and the vet arrived at about the same time, and between them, strapped the shoulder down and got the yowling, snapping dog onto a stretcher, out of the street, and into the casino. Jo invited them to lay the dog out on the carpet, blood and all. The vet was a young man, about thirty, with broad shoulders and a wide, cheerful face. He got a better look at the dog than I had and announced she was a young female.

"Never saw this little girl around here before. If she's got a human he never brought her to me. Quite a specimen, though."

"Of what?" I asked.

"Looks like a standard poodle, maybe a mix. Scrawny. Dehydrated. Paws are a mess. She's been wandering for a while." He'd given the dog a shot of some kind and she had calmed, then drifted into sleep. He took the temporary wrap off the shoulder, set it, and put a cast on it, binding her forequarters in a way I was sure she'd object to when she woke. It was right about then that Drew and Lizzie showed up. I told them what had happened. Lizzie turned red with anger when she heard about the driver; Drew scowled.

Other than the broken shoulder, the vet said, the dog seemed to be okay. But she'd need care. Who would be responsible?

"We will," Jo said, not hesitating for a second. "Lizzie's especially good with animals. Shouldn't be hard to find a home for a dog who might be a full breed. And she's pretty and seems smart and gentle. How about giving her a haircut while she's under? She smells bad and we won't be bathing her any time soon except maybe with a sponge."

So Jo was both compassionate and practical. What a combination.

The vet laughed. "I'm no groomer, but the closest one I know of is in Oakland. Guess I can do a little something to make this young lady more adoptable."

He'd already shaved the shoulder and foreleg to put on the cast. He asked for some scissors. Lizzie ran to her mother's office and brought some back. Using those, and his own clippers, he gave the snoring dog a simple short haircut. Two of the cleaners showed up just as he was finishing, one with a broom, a big waste can, and a dustpan, the other with a vacuum and a bottle of liquid cleaner.

The pooch was skinny, her hip bones protruding, and she had a few sores where the long fuzzy fur had matted. But she was handsomely built. The vet looked at her teeth and said she was about two years old.

"She'll sleep for a couple of hours. See to it that she drinks plenty of water and give her little bits of food, several small meals a day, until she gets built up a bit."

Jo turned to Lizzie. "Hear that, Liz?"

"Heard it, Jo." Lizzie was grinning. She looked eager to start.

These damned Colemans. Hard not to like them.

Jo turned and met my eyes. "Good job, Rica. I guess you can go to the restaurant now. If Waldo has any complaints about your lateness, send him to me."

I was hoping he'd complain. He glared, but he didn't say anything.

CHAPTER 21
HE'S AFTER HER UNDERSIDE

Drew was lying in his room reading an old history book he'd scavenged from a trash box up at Zephyr Cove. It was published in 2015. Not very good, badly written, and barely edited, if at all, but it was published right on the edge of the time when the world began to collapse, right after the Euros started trying to expel all their Muslims. Like a new Inquisition. The authors of the book, a pair of professors from Montana, clearly believed the expulsion was necessary, and therefore a good idea. Drew, with the benefit of hindsight, knew that it hadn't worked.

Things got much worse. Trying to curb the sporadic terrorism only brought more insane violence in reaction. More bombings and killings and poisonings, and then the dissolutions started. France. Spain. Germany and Britain. The Scandinavians and Slavs didn't try to expel anyone, but the violence and death crossed their borders. The United States fell, less than a year after the assassination of the last president. All by 2023. It took another couple of years for the rest of the world to run to chaos. China had been the last holdout.

"Drew!" Banging on the door. Lizzie. Home from school. What did she want, anyway? A man could hardly take the time to think any more. He swung his legs to the floor, still carrying the book, and went to open the door.

"What?" He didn't invite her in.

She looked antsy, hopping from one leg to the other like a

little kid. "I want to talk to you about something I heard at school."

Oh good. High school gossip. "What?" he said again, still patient but showing his disinterest by glancing down at his book.

"Don't just stand there saying 'what,' slug-boy. Let me in. It's about Billy Scorsi."

He sighed. Jesus. That spotty nutbucket? What was he up to now? Drew really didn't care.

"Oh, please—you want to talk about Billy?" But she was flushed and scowling. He opened the door wider and his sister came in and threw herself on the bed. Drew slipped a bookmark, the jack of diamonds, into his book and set it on the desk, dropping into a chair and folding his arms across his chest like an impatient parent.

"Okay. What?" He sighed when she laughed at his third "what," then grinned back. He knew he was acting like a Newt.

"I heard from Nancy Tricot that he was bragging to her about how he was going to 'get' Hannah Karlow. He's after Nancy's underside, you know." That was more than Drew wanted to know. Billy was sick-fish ugly as well as crazy and Nancy was kind of cute, for a seventeen-year-old.

"Go on, please, but leave off the sex part." She smirked. She was such a kid. Two years could make a big difference.

"He was talking about how she was our candidate for mayor and he was going to do everybody a big favor and get rid of her. That was the way he put it, she said. 'Get rid' of her. And here's the other interesting part. Even though she insisted Billy didn't exactly in so many words say so, she got the feeling he was hinting he might have had something to do with Mayor Madera's killing."

"He's just bragging. I can't imagine Newt Scorsi would send a scroop like Billy to kill Madera."

She thought about that for a moment. "You're right. But maybe he didn't send him, Drew."

That struck him. Was it possible? He didn't think Billy could have gone off on his own and done something that big, but he could see Ky or Newt Junior or both of them deciding it would be fun to kill someone and using the family as an excuse. And he could absolutely see Billy hanging the body from a tree.

He nodded. He was glad he'd listened to Lizzie. This could be nothing, a rash-ass trying to make an impression. Or it could be important. "I think we should talk to Mom. And Jo. Tell them what you heard."

Jo looked around the room. Samm was there, this time. He was worried, she could tell, his brow furrowed, his eyes downcast. Judith, too, was taking what Lizzie had heard very seriously. She made the kid repeat every word Nancy had said to her and asked everyone, in turn, what they thought of the gossip.

Drew said he thought it could all be true, true that Billy was going to try to kill Hannah, and true that the boys had killed Madera. But, he said, it was hard to know what might be true with Billy, since he was a braggart as well as beyond strange. Lizzie nodded energetically when he said that.

Jo hadn't been aware that those Scorsi kids were so over the line, but Drew and Liz would know. Yet another generation to worry about.

Samm's response was simple: "We need to find out." He was aiming that at Jo, she knew. And her corps of barely awake spies.

Judith, too, was looking at her, waiting. Time for her to say something.

"I think we at least consider it as a possibility. We need to tell Hannah to watch her backside. I'll put someone to watching the boys, Billy in particular." She had only one operative working at Scorsi's Luck who she thought might be sharp enough to do this job. A dealer. He hated Newt, but he was old and arthritic. If he agreed to do harder and more dangerous work, he'd probably want more money, and she didn't know how long he'd hold up, following kids around.

Samm responded with a nod. "I think she can take care of herself, better than poor old Madera could. You want me to tell her, or will you?"

"I will."

"All right, then," Judith said, glancing at the papers on her desk. But Jo had something she wanted to talk about before they all went back to the day's work.

She'd heard just that afternoon, out on the floor, that a number of godders had been spotted crossing the border into Sierra.

"If they were ordinary Rockies," she said, "I'd guess they were just running away from home." Samm laughed. "But they don't seem to be. Word is that some of them are talking about coming to 'bring the light' to Sierra. Looks like just another idiot crusade, but it's possible that Rocky's sending them in as spies."

Samm laughed. "Godders don't spy. They rant . . ." Then he understood where she was going, and sat forward, looking more interested.

"And corrupt elections with threats, or throw bombs," Jo said. "Godders sent by Rocky. We need to do anything we can to show what a threat Rocky is." Samm nodded.

"What exactly did you have in mind?" Judith asked.

"This might be the time to push for an anti-godder law, talk about it in our campaigns and really go for it when we have a more solid hold, after the election. A law that gets rid of them and keeps them out, or at least creates a lot of noise about getting rid of them. Enough noise to make the Rocky threat clear to Redwood, and to the voters." Enough to get things stirred up, anyway.

Drew was staring at her.

"What is it, Drew?"

"That might not be a good idea. Think about what happened back in the Teens. I was just today reading—"

"What happened in the Teens? What's it got to do with now, anyway?" Samm was puzzled and impatient. He often was with Drew's references to what Samm thought of as ancient history. Lizzie rolled her eyes. But Jo and, when it suited her, Judith, believed in that old cliché: those who don't know history are doomed to repeat it.

"The crazies got crazier. And stronger. And things got a lot worse."

"Well, we won't let that happen," Samm said.

Jo smiled reassuringly at Drew but it didn't seem to help. Maybe she needed to rethink that idea about an anti-godder law.

I had noticed—I always made a point to—that the Colemans were having yet another family meeting that afternoon. Everybody looked painfully serious. Even Samm looked upset. When I got to the restaurant for my first shift, I saw Drew and Lizzie huddled with Timmy.

Timmy would have made a wonderful spy, if he'd had the temperament and the duplicity for it. He knew how to keep his finger on the pulse of things without being threatening. I didn't know if he ever learned anything important, anything the Colemans were trying to keep quiet, but sometimes simple gossip held more information than people knew it held. Tim would feel free to pass it on to me if I didn't act too eager. I'd have to have a little chat with him sometime that night. When all this was over, I hoped he'd forgive me for using him this way. I thought that depended on how things worked out.

It was a couple hours before business quieted down enough to casually approach him.

He poured me a cup of tea and we sat for a five-minute break while Drew and Lizzie covered the room. Waldo was sitting in the kitchen eating. Or sleeping. I wasn't interested enough to go back there and find out.

"So," I said, stretching and rolling my shoulders. "What's new?"

He was dying to tell me.

"Well, I heard just tonight that the Scorsis are going to try to kill Hannah Karlow!"

My mind raced in a fast circle, taking little nips at the information. What? What was he talking about? "Really? Because she's running for mayor?" I pasted a bored look on my face. "Or because she's ugly?"

Timmy clucked at me for the nasty remark. "Because she's the Coleman's mayor." This was strange. The Scorsis knew better. Unless they knew something I didn't—that Hannah was turning. Certainly possible, if she thought there was an advantage to it. A sudden image flashed across my mind: Hannah running down the street with the Scorsis chasing her and me running the opposite way with the Colemans on my tail.

I nodded, trying to look wise. "That makes me wonder, Tim. Do you think they killed the old mayor, too?"

"Probably. He favored the Colemans."

"Favored them how?"

"Oh, you know. All kinds of little ways."

"Like what?"

"Well . . ." he laughed. "He made one of the streets outside Newt's casino one way. Inconvenient for customers, cut his traffic down. Another time—now I don't know for sure he was behind this—there was some problem with Newt's liquor license."

Wow. Enough of those "little" things and Newt would be apoplectic. I could just see him having the man killed and then trying to blame it on the Colemans.

"Where'd you hear about this? About Hannah?"

"Lizzie and Drew. One of the Scorsi boys was bragging at school, to some girl, that he was going to get rid of Karlow."

"A boy bragging to a girl? That's news." I laughed.

Tim laughed, too. "I know what you mean, Rica, but the kids think it could be real."

Drew seemed like a careful young man who wouldn't believe something just because it was exciting or showed an enemy in a bad light.

If there really was such an assassination in the works, I knew what I had to do. Much as I would have preferred to let someone else shoot her off my back, that would not be the best move if I wanted to keep the Colemans from getting more powerful. With Hannah as their candidate, even their mayor, they were crippled. If she were killed, they might find a real one.

So far, she hadn't outed me to the Colemans, possibly because she enjoyed holding the threat over my head. If I got to her, warned her, saved her nasty life, she might decide to be my pal. She might even tell me the truth about who she was working for, and stop messing with me.

CHAPTER 22
A GENTLE TUG, SO SUBTLE
I HESITATED

Jo found Hannah in the casino's storage room tearing down a battered poker slot, one of the casualties of the raid. She was so engrossed she didn't hear Jo come in and jumped when she spoke her name.

"Whoa! What's up?" Hannah gave her only a quick, smiling glance and focused again on the slot's innards. "This is the last of them, if you're wondering."

"Good—but that's not why I'm here. The kids heard a rumor that may or may not mean anything. Lizzie heard it. At school."

Hannah laid down the Phillips head screw driver and turned to give Jo her full attention. "What kind of rumor?" She wasn't smiling any more. She looked tense around the jaw.

"That the Scorsis are going to try to kill you. I don't know if they mean to do it before you're elected or after, don't even know if it's true. I just thought you should be warned."

Her eyebrows lifted and her eyes shifted away, off to the side, thoughtful. "Any particular Scorsi? Or do they plan to send a platoon of mercs after me?" She didn't look worried. That was reassuring. She thought she could handle it.

"What Liz heard was that Billy was going to do it. Newt's nephew. He's around Lizzie's age."

Hannah grinned. "All by himself?"

Jo shrugged. Maybe Hannah was a little too cocky.

"I'll keep my eyes open, Jo."

"Do you want someone keeping an eye on you? We could

give you a bodyguard."

"No!" Sharp, definitive. Almost angry. Jo wondered about that. Too much pride? "Not necessary. Don't want people thinking the candidate is scared. Send someone with me when I make speeches, maybe, but that's all." Hannah thought for a moment. Jo stayed silent, wondering what was coming out of that thin-lipped mouth next. "In fact, maybe I should mention it in my speeches. Not name names or anything, but say I heard someone wanted to kill me, joke about it, show everyone they can't scare me off, can't stop me. People love that kind of shit."

Sounded like a good plan. Except . . . "Why not name names?"

Her eyes shifted away again. "Well, it's better that way. If I say this kid is making threats, so what, right? But if I don't say, people will assume it's the Scorsis. Right? All of them, trying to kill me?"

Jo thought Hannah's thinking was a bit tortured, but okay, why not? She wasn't so sure about letting her wander around alone and vulnerable, but it was what she wanted; she seemed to have a plan for using the problem as propaganda, and she could be replaced if she had to be.

"That sounds good. But don't act cocky, okay? Just brave."

Hannah shot Jo a sharp look; a corner of her mouth quirked. "You think I'm cocky, Jo?"

"I don't care whether you're cocky or not. Just don't act that way. People don't like it, and we're trying to get you elected." She turned to go.

"Okay, Jo," Hannah said. "You're the boss." Jo wished she hadn't turned away so fast. She couldn't tell much from the flat tone, but she would have loved to see her expression when she said that. She was guessing that Hannah didn't like the idea of anyone being her boss.

On her way back into the heart of the casino, Jo saw Rica,

heading toward the restaurant for her first shift. If she kept pulling in crowds at the lounge, they'd have to find another server
for the restaurant. Rica deserved at least to work there less than
full time.

She moved gracefully. She was taller than Jo, bigger through
the hips, womanly. She looked strong, and that red hair. Sea-
green eyes. But the mouth, that was the best. Full. Soft. Jo
sighed. Damn it. Even Machiavelli must have spent some time
chasing love.

Jo had been heading toward the bar to check on some overdue
and probably missing beer orders. It was too bad they had to
come all the way from San Francisco. Even with no-name
trucks, beer was a favorite target of bandits. But that could
wait. She changed direction, heading toward Judith's office.
They needed to send out word that Blackjack needed help in
the restaurant. She'd like to give Rica some good news that
night. She really would.

Hannah hadn't shown up at the restaurant for dinner, but I
wasn't worried about finding her to warn her. She was in my
line of vision too much of the time as it was.

And there she was again, in the lounge, sitting near the stage,
close enough to leer at me. Jo came in a few minutes later and
took a table off to the side, just as she had the night before. She
looked good, as always. Dressed in a less businesslike outfit
than her usual knickers and vest, wearing a simple white shirt
over long gray-blue flowing pants. Silk? Mine were black velvet.
Drew slipped in right before the spotlight hit me, sitting at the
back again. Samm wasn't there. I guessed it was because Zack
was nursing a sprained finger and couldn't relieve him at the
table. At least that was the late news from Timmy.

The place was full again, impressive for a Monday night.

I'd decided for this third performance to lean a little less heavily on the tragic love and a little more on the seductive. Less of the "Autumn Leaves" genre and more of the "Besame Mucho." Sung slowly and with a jazz edge. Not ready to work myself out of mid-Twentieth yet. After the first few nights, something from the very early Twenty-First would be good. Norah Jones. Dido. Confusion and obsession. I thought that would work for me really well right about now.

At one point during one of my steamier numbers, I flicked a look toward Jo and she smiled back at me. That smile went right through me. It was all I could do not to squirm. What was it, anyway? Her power? Her look? Her confidence? All of that, but mostly she was just plain sexy. Even when she wasn't talking to me, that soft voice ran through my mind.

After my second encore, when the audience finally began to leave, I caught Hannah's eye and stepped down off the stage. This was my chance to warn her about the danger she might be in. I stopped when I realized that Jo was walking toward me.

"Another astonishing performance, Rica." There was that smile again.

"Thank you, Jo."

"Take a walk with me."

Hannah knew I wanted to talk to her. She'd have to keep. If I was late getting back to the restaurant, I didn't care. We strolled out into the casino together.

"Let's get some real air."

I nodded. For just a second I wondered again if my cover was blown, but somehow it didn't feel like she was taking me to an ambush.

We went out the back door into the parking lot, all the way to the edge where a stand of fir bordered a small park. Alone. Outside, in the dark night.

I thought of asking if something was wrong but decided silence was the best choice. Especially since my throat was feeling constricted. The combination of attraction and tension was winding me tight as a godder. It was all I could do to keep my walk relaxed and smooth.

She stopped beside the trunk of a large fir, and leaned her back against it.

"I think we're asking you to do too much, Rica. A split shift at the restaurant and singing in the lounge, too."

She was speaking very softly. I moved closer. To hear her better.

"A dinner shift and a show. That's enough. In fact, we might want to expand the show or do a second one every night. In which case, I don't see how you could work in the restaurant at all."

If I were really a waitress-singer, I'd be worried about losing the tip money. I took a deep breath, catching a scent of something from her skin—lilac?

"I need what I make in the restaurant. Would you—"

"Don't worry about that. We're making money with the lounge, because of you. We'll pay you more."

"This is wonderful, Jo." Two shows a night, and no Waldo.

"It might take us a while to find a replacement, but I wanted you to know we're working on it."

And then she reached out and took my hand. A gentle tug, so subtle I hesitated before I responded and moved even closer, only inches away. Another bit of pressure on my hand and I was kissing her, pressing against her, pushing her against the bark of the tree. She stroked my back. My hair. My hands slid down to her hips. Too fast. I stopped, pulled back. Too much. I could barely breathe. I wasn't ready to lose control. She was watching me, only the slightest hint of a smile in her eyes.

"Guess it's time to get you back to the restaurant. For now."

Like an idiot I turned too fast, and stumbled. She touched my arm, then took her hand away.

I don't really remember walking back to the casino. Just inside the door, she took my hand again and squeezed it.

"I'll let you know how the hunt for a replacement goes."

"Good. Yes."

Our hands separated and she walked away. Too easily, I thought with a stab of hurt that I instantly hated myself for. But I couldn't resist watching her for a moment before heading back toward the lounge, my tiny dressing room, and my restaurant clothes. I'd gone only a few steps when I noticed Drew standing at the lounge door, watching me. His face was flushed, his lips tight. He swung away and disappeared inside the restaurant.

Unless he'd followed us, he would only have seen the two of us going out into the parking lot to talk. But when I showed up for my shift he was too polite. I suspected he'd seen more. Wonderful. Injured feelings and now guilt. I really needed to pull myself together.

It wasn't until Hannah entered the restaurant that I realized I'd forgotten about her. She sat at one of my tables.

"Coffee, and a piece of the cheesecake, please, Rica." I scribbled down the order. Before I had a chance to tell her about the assassination rumor, she said, "What's going on between you and Jo?" Had the sexual tension been that obvious?

"Nothing."

"Didn't look like nothing." She grinned, deepening the scar.

No reason not to give her a partial story. "She wants to do two shows a night, cut back my hours in the restaurant."

Hannah squinted at me, studying my face, obviously trying to see if anything else was there. But I'm an actor, and I played the role. She shrugged. Time to change the subject and tell her what she needed to hear, before my façade and my lie slipped.

"There's a rumor that the Scorsis are going to kill you, Hannah."

She didn't even look surprised. She shook her head. "They're just planting stories. Gives me points with the Colemans. Trust." Of course, that was probably it. Newt was giving his spy credibility. Probably.

"You're sure that's what it's about?"

She shrugged again. "What else? That's certainly my best guess. Are you worried about me?" That nasty smirk again.

"Guess? You mean Newt is spreading rumors about killing you and he hasn't told you what he's doing?"

She laughed, her face relaxing in real amusement. "Thanks for caring, Rica. Maybe I should ask him. But you know damned well Newt never tells anybody anything."

That was certainly true. But something didn't smell right. First a mayor and now a mayoral candidate. Sounded like a pattern to me.

CHAPTER 23
THEY SWAGGERED AND SNORTED FOR ABOUT A MILE

The next day, I called Newt.

"What do you want, Rica?"

"I need to meet with you."

"Too busy. Just do your work."

"It's about your assassination plot against Hannah."

Silence for a moment. Then, "I'll get back to you." And he was gone.

He might get back to me, he might not. I'd go right to the source: Billy, whoever he was. I wasn't sure what I'd do when I found him, but I was always good at playing by ear.

I didn't feel comfortable paying a visit to Scorsi's Luck; if someone from Blackjack saw me there they might get nervous. But I couldn't think of any other way to find a Scorsi I didn't know. I cornered the sleazy change guy, Bernard, behind the quarter-real slots.

"I need to talk to Billy Scorsi, Bernard. Where can I find him?"

Bernard slid closer to the wall, his eyes shooting in all directions. "School, unless he's cutting."

"Where's the school?" He gave me directions and started sidling away again. "What time does it let out?"

"Two o'clock."

"What's he look like?"

"Orange hair. Big freckles." Bernard was whispering now. I

could barely hear him above the casino noise. "He's kind of fat."

"Who would he be hanging out with?"

"How would I know that?" I waited. He twitched. This man brought out the sadist in me. "Well, I've seen him around with his cousins a lot. Ky. Newt Junior."

"Describe them."

"Ky's taller. Darker hair. Older. Newt Junior looks like his dad. I've got work to do. Let me go." His voice rose on the last word.

I had enough to move ahead with. It was one-thirty. I headed for the school. From what I'd heard there were only a dozen or so kids roughly Lizzie's age. An orange-haired, freckle-covered Scorsi shouldn't be that hard to pick out.

I felt like a pervert, skulking around and waiting for children to come out the doors. I was hoping no responsible adult would notice me, trying to stay out of sight around the corner of the building, leaning against the chipped, tan-painted siding.

Ten seconds after the bell finally rang, the noisy kids erupted in clumps through the doors like bad milk. Or tapioca, depending on your perspective, I supposed. The school was kindergarten through twelfth grade, so there were a good four-five dozen kids all together. I saw an ugly little Newt clone dash out the door in a rush of hyperalertness. Big head. Bug eyes. Skinny little legs. Brown hair. He hung around, tossing a soccer ball against the side of the building, tapping his foot. Pacing. If he'd had a potbelly and a sandwich in his hand the picture would have been complete.

Was the clone waiting for someone? And where was Billy Scorsi? Detention? I wouldn't be surprised.

A little while later, an older boy, dark hair, not bad looking but sullen, strolled up from a side street carrying a pack and grabbed the ball, tossing it back at Junior, who grunted when it hit him in the gut and tossed it back. They went on that way for a time, using the ball as a weapon against each other, until a chubby kid with flaming hair and big blobby freckles clomped out the door. Billy. Bernard was pretty good at describing people.

I'd had a vague thought about striking up a conversation with him, but it looked like now was not the time. He was too well insulated by relatives.

The big kid tossed the ball at Billy's head; he ducked and it shot past his ear. Little Newt—what a disgusting thought that was—guffawed and grabbed the ball and they all began to walk away from the school.

I waited until they'd gone a block and started following them. If I couldn't talk to Billy I could at least see where he was going, get some idea of what he was like. They were doing a lot of laughing, a lot of loud swearing; nothing other boys at that wretched stage of development didn't do. Where did they get these odd ideas of manhood? Their fathers? Their mothers? Each other, passed from child to child like a bad cold?

I thought they might go to their home casino; maybe they worked there. After all, the Coleman kids worked.

Instead, they walked past it. I was trying to be unobtrusive, but like most teenagers, they were aware of very little outside themselves, so I really didn't need to worry.

Then I realized that someone else was following them. He'd slipped in between me and the boys from a side street. He, too, was trying to be unobtrusive, ducking in and out of doorways like a villain in a bad play. He was an older man, small, with gray hair. Someone else was keeping an eye on the Scorsi boys. Had to be Jo. Thinking about her brought a twinge that I decided not to name or even examine.

They swaggered and snorted for about a mile until they came

to a park with a stand of pines, a line of firs along the back, and a few oaks.

The big kid, he must have been Ky, opened his pack and pulled out a coil of heavy rope. They all snorted and swaggered some more. Junior blew his nose on the ground. Ky pointed to a brushy area near the oak and Junior crawled into it, clawing at the dirt for a while. I was some distance away so it was hard to see what he was doing, but after Junior had finished scrabbling around in there, Ky handed him the coil of rope. He stashed it in the brush.

As I watched from nearly a block way, I was recalling a photo from the local newspaper that had showed the oak tree Madera had been strung up in. Now, California live oaks of a certain size and age all pretty much look the same, but this one was the right size and seemed to have similar branches at the same height from the ground.

The boys began walking back toward me, toward their casino. I turned and tucked myself into a food store entry and watched them as they went by, the elderly spy right behind them. The boys looked pleased with themselves. So did the spy.

It looked to me like the Scorsi spawn were arranging the setting for a murder.

I had to talk to Hannah again. Even if she seemed to trust Newt, for some reason, the scene I'd just witnessed might poke a small hole in her arrogance.

It didn't matter whether Newt was involved or not, although I thought he must be. It was just as possible these young gangsters had no idea Hannah worked for Newt. That they thought she really was the Colemans' candidate, and were planning to kill her to win status. And they were either copying someone else's killing style or repeating their own.

Hannah was in the storage room working on a slot machine.

Its innards were all over the work table.

She gave me an up and down look. I was beginning to think she flirted to be annoying. "What a nice surprise. Looking for me?"

I shoved some slot parts to the side and hoisted myself up. "We need to talk." Too late, I realized that was the kind of thing lovers said. There was that smirk again. "About the fact that your life is in danger."

She shook her head. "I thought you already told me that."

"But you didn't believe me."

"Kid bullshit. Billy Scorsi is a moron."

"He may be a moron but I just saw him with two of his cousins messing around an oak tree that looked a lot like the one Madera was found hanging from. And they were stashing a rope in the bushes."

Her raggedy brown eyebrows lifted. She went to the door and looked out. Reassured that no one was lurking, she came back to the table. "Three of them, huh? Guess I better talk to Newt, after all."

Good. Then I wouldn't have to. She actually looked worried for the first time, dropping the cad-with-the-ladies act. I disliked her a little less.

"How did you manage to see the boys doing those things?"

"Accident." I hopped down from the table.

She laughed. The cad had returned. "Are you watching my back, Rica?"

I turned and gave her the nastiest sneer I could come up with. "Not a chance."

I slept late the next morning. Neither Jo nor Samm had showed up at the lounge the night before. Neither did Hannah. She must have been busy straightening things out with Newt and the boys. Drew slipped in briefly once. Maybe I was losing my charm. The only one I truly regretted was Jo. I wanted another encounter with her, and I wanted this one to end less abruptly.

The house sys showed no message from Jo saying they'd hired a replacement to work under Waldo. Maybe Timmy had some news. Patience might be a virtue but I'm convinced it's an unhealthy one, like chastity.

My own sys held an interesting message from Newt:

"Stop everything. Meet at noon."

Everything?

After a quick breakfast at the casino I headed out to our little trysting spot. No more than ten minutes late.

This time we met near our cars; I never had a chance to get all the way to the clearing before he stopped me.

"You're late."

"Just got the message."

"This won't take long." His eyes shifted away. "I want you to stop looking into the mayor's murder."

Aha. "Why is that?"

"You don't need to know."

"So it wasn't the Colemans who did it?"

He took a deep breath. "Just stay away from it. Concentrate on their army and their skimming. And any inside information from the family. I hear you've gotten close to Jo." Hannah must have told him that.

"I wouldn't say 'close', but I'm watching her." I sure was. "About the army, hardly seems like you need me there, since you've got Hannah on the inside."

"I know that!" he snapped.

"Unless you don't trust her?"

"I do. Much as I trust anyone. Always good to have two pairs of eyes." He got into his floater. "Just stay away from the mayor thing."

"Happy to."

It seemed pretty obvious what was going on. Hannah had talked to him, told him what the boys were doing at the oak tree. I doubted she gave me the credit: she probably said she saw them there. Newt went to them. Told them Hannah was a Scorsi loyal, leave her alone. And found out or at least now suspected that his little gang of hereditary felons had killed the mayor. I hated giving up on the idea that Newt was behind both plots, but there it was.

So Hannah was safe, which meant that I still needed to deal with her. Oh well. One more act to this side show. I had to send a message to the chief and pass on the names of the mayor's killers. Whether she did anything with it or not was up to her. Jailing juvenile Scorsis was not in my contract.

Lizzie needed help with her history class. Drew was sitting with her on a park bench back of the parking lot, looking at her book and her notes. The topic was the Industrial Revolution.

"It's so irrelevant to the way things are now!" she complained.

"No, it's not. Nothing is. You need to understand how it happened the first time. So you can understand why things happened the way they did and how they're going to happen next time."

She sighed. Drew read through her sketchy notes and skimmed the chapter she was working on. Lizzie sighed even louder, and spoke suddenly:

"Something funny is going on with Billy."

He didn't raise his eyes from the book. "Like what?"

"Well, you know how he was saying he was going to off Hannah?" Drew nodded. "Well, he isn't saying that any more. Not only is he not bragging about doing it, he's denying he ever said it and going around looking all secretive and wise. What an asshole!"

"What do you think it's about?"

"I don't know."

Neither did he. If the Scorsis had been planning to kill her it made a certain amount of sense, since she was the Colemans' candidate. If they'd changed their minds, what did that mean?

"I think I want to find out," Lizzie said.

Drew studied his sister's face. She was getting that flushed, excited look again. "How you going to do that?"

"I'll beat it out of him. He's made of dog shit."

He knew he'd never talk her out of going after Billy. She'd been muttering about those Scorsi boys since their fight over the treaty. And she wasn't wrong. There might be something they needed to know hidden under Billy's craziness. But she was looking for trouble and he didn't want her finding it alone.

"I'll go with you. Is there some way you can isolate him? Lure him off where I could meet you. A couple of threats . . . he's not real brave. Probably won't even have to hit him." He hoped they wouldn't. He didn't want violence if a peaceful way could be found.

"Lure him?" Lizzie laughed. "That sounds slimy. But probably easy enough. I'll catch him outside of school tomorrow and snare him in my evil web. Heh heh heh." She wiggled her eyebrows evilly.

He scowled at her. "We'll make a plan. I'll be there to cover you."

"Okay, Drew. Just don't tell Mom—or anyone else, okay?"

He didn't think he would.

Driving back from the meeting with Newt, I noticed an unusual sight at the intersection of Stateline and Highway 50: right there at the corner, four new-looking floaters, including an open truck, had pulled up in a line at the curb. A dozen people, six men, six women, all young and all dressed in khaki, were milling around the cars. A party of rich tourists from California? Unlikely. People from Los Angeles didn't tend to wear khaki, and were even less likely to all wear the same color. The outfits looked almost, but not quite, like uniforms: neatly creased pants and soft-looking shirts, open at the neck. Shiny black shoes.

I pulled over, on the other side of the street, to watch.

Three of the men were hauling lengths of something out of the back of the truck. Lumber. Pieces of a framework. They laid them down on the sidewalk and began fitting them together. Two women and another man unloaded plyboard of some sort and brought it to the men snapping the framework together. A few bangs with a hammer and the platform, a small stage, one step up, was finished. They stuck a folding table in one corner of it. Like a medicine show, but the outfits were all wrong.

They didn't keep me waiting long for an answer. Next to the table, they added a large sandwich-board sign that read:

"Money! Land! Homes! We'll pay you! Come to Rocky and raise a family! Sign Up now!"

Rocky had sent this strange little army to Tahoe to buy Sierrans. I'd never seen anything like this before and it scared me to see it now.

Two men and one woman jumped up on the platform. They had bundles of papers under their arms, which they set on the table. By now, a few curious people were crowding around. One of the men began to shout at the spectators.

"Tired of never having enough money? Tired of having to earn your way with hard work in a country where there's never enough work to find?

"Have you heard of the richer place on the other side of these mountains, ladies and gentlemen?"

By now the little soldiers from Rocky had put up more sandwich boards with the word "Money!" printed on them. The crowd was growing. A dozen. Two dozen.

"Rockymountain is a rich country, but it's more than rich, it's a true land of opportunity. Rockymountain wants you. It wants you badly enough to pay you to come, to pay your way, to give you land and homes and nest eggs. Security! Financial stability! Plenty of work, plenty of money to go around. Why waste your lives here?

"Rocky is looking for people to settle and raise children and build families and towns. We have the money to pay you to have children, pay for their education, their food, their family homes." Worse and worse.

"We have the money, the land, the will, the drive, and the government to take care of you for the rest of your lives!" Nobody had that much money. I wondered what the new citizens would have to do to pay the government back.

The crowd had grown. A couple of dozen people were listening intently and more were drifting up to the table, some of them looking hypnotized, their mouths dropping open whenever he shouted "money!"

A street show where the actors were both selling and buying. Selling an idea. Buying people for the great land of Rocky. It looked like a few Sierrans were seriously considering selling themselves.

But that wasn't the worst of it.

Several more of the khaki-clads jumped up onto the stage—how many would it hold? One of them was carrying something white. He wrapped it around his shoulders. A robe of sorts. Uh-oh. He aimed a fierce eye at first one and then another member of the audience, roaring in a thunderous baritone that "Rocky is where God lives! Come to the light!" I felt a shiver up my spine. Soldiers, breeders, and godders—together? Not good. I was surprised that the weight of their self-righteousness alone didn't collapse the stage.

A sheriff's car pulled up alongside the floaters. Frank. He got out of his car and sauntered around it to the platform. The robed godder, his white holiness floating around his military khaki, jumped down to meet him, smiling. Frank wasn't smiling. They talked for a moment; Frank went back to his car, sat with his legs sticking out the open door, and pulled out a sys. He called someone. Nodding, shaking his head, looking confused, doubtful. Nodding again, shrugging. What was that about? Who had he called? Then he sat for a moment, watching the recruiters, before he called someone else. During all this, the Rockies were cheerfully waving contracts around and chatting up the citizens, several of whom were signing on. Most of the others, though, had stepped back again, eyeing Frank, waiting to see what happened.

A few minutes later, Frank's deputy, Marty, showed up with a closed truck. They both drew their guns. Frank approached the recruiters and barked some orders. They didn't move. Their odds were good at a dozen to two. I was on the edge of helping, my door half-open. I'd rather liked the deputy's style when she'd arrested the drunk driver. And these people made my flesh crawl. They needed to be stopped.

Then one of the khakis pulled a laser pistol from inside his shirt. He didn't have a chance to use it. The deputy shot him first. After that—maybe none of the others had weapons—they lined up and let the two cops pat them down. No, no more weapons. Frank and his helper began herding the Rockies into the back of the truck. I closed my door.

Jo was thinking about the spy report she'd gotten the night before. The Scorsi brats had gone to the tree where the mayor had been hung, done a lot of laughing, and messed with a piece of rope, which they stuck under a nearby bush. Was the threat to Hannah just a game or were the boys rehearsing and preparing for her murder? She sent a message, telling Hannah what her man had seen.

She'd just stuck her sys in her pocket when it began to vibrate. "Jo, this is Frank."

"Yes, Frank?" As if she wouldn't recognize that voice, oily and gravelly all at the same time. Like wet rocks.

He told her a team of Rockies was running a recruitment on Stateline. "For people who'll go there and have babies or some damned thing. They're paying them to go. Khakis, but they've got godders with them. Thought I'd check with you, let you know I'm about to roust them."

Jo wondered if this was the mixed group that had caused the ruckus at the border a few days ago. Supposedly, that bunch had been turned back, but they could have found another way in. And there was also the gang of godders someone had seen more recently. These recruiters could be any or all of those. Too damned many Rockies. But she didn't want them hustled out of town so quickly.

She thought for no more than a few seconds. "No. Arrest them. Call your deputy and take them in."

"Huh? What charge?"

"I don't know. Slavery. Baby-buying. Terrorism. And after you lock them up, tell Iggy Santos that you've arrested a band of Rocky spies and recruiters and you're questioning them. Tell him you'll have more information for the paper by his Friday deadline."

"What questions should I ask them?"

"I don't care. What's their favorite color. Hold them for a couple of days, I'll write out what you should tell Santos then."

This was perfect. Rockies crossing the border into Sierra, coming right into their town, offering a dubious deal. They were here to buy people! And godders in the group. This was a first, all the way around. She laughed. Judith was going to love it.

She pulled out her sys and began to compose what the sheriff would tell the newspaper.

"The spies from Rockymountain admitted they were here to recruit or kidnap citizens of Sierra and to gather information for a future military invasion that would include terrorist acts by godders . . ." Maybe not strictly true, but true enough at its core. Godders with military connections would kill people.

The problem was, what should they do with them? She couldn't just kill them outright. Even Samm might balk at slaughter and it wouldn't look good if someone found out. She couldn't keep them jailed or execute them as spies without a trial. She knew things like that happened in other countries, but not in Sierra. And a trial without proof would blunt the drama, cast doubt, and drag on until after the election.

She added another line. "They were deported on Friday, escorted to the border, and told to take a message back to Rocky: Sierra is strong, alert, and ready to defend itself."

Her sys vibrated again. It was Frank.

"One of them, a khaki godder, he pulled a gun and we killed him!"

Even better. "Tell Santos a godder terrorist was killed trying to shoot you."

CHAPTER 24
THE NERVE OF
THOSE PEOPLE

Drew was getting antsy. School had been out for twenty minutes. He was waiting in the copse behind the Winner's Tavern, just like they'd decided. Neutral territory, pretty much on Billy's way home but far enough from both Scorsi's Luck and the school. The place could always be relied on for loud music, and its patrons tended to be both noisy and oblivious. He was standing behind a fir tree. His nerves were going right to his bladder, but he was sure the minute he opened his pants they'd show up. He did it anyway. They didn't show up.

Where was she? Maybe Billy was smarter than they thought and had figured out Lizzie couldn't possibly want anything from him he'd want to give her no matter how she acted. The whole idea was nauseating anyway. His sister, wiggling and jiggling for Billy. He felt his face flush, then, and like a nasty little burr, a thought of Rica and Jo stabbed at him. He'd felt like a real asshole for doing it, but he'd followed them, seen them kissing. He hadn't watched the whole thing, just the start. He both did and did not want to see more and he was afraid if he stood there longer, they'd spot him. He had dashed back into the casino, his stomach burning, his groin alive, his mind spinning in anger and misery. The memory today brought back both the pain in his gut and the arousal. He bit his lip, willing it all away, out of his mind and his body.

Then he heard voices, one of them Lizzie's.

"Ky? I don't think so, Billy. It's pretty obvious you're the real leader. You knew when to end that fight the other day." Was Billy really dumb enough to swallow this crap? Just a couple of days ago, she'd kicked him in the balls. Now she was drooling all over him. But yeah, Billy was dumb enough, and horny enough, to believe anything she said.

"Well, Ky's mumble mumble mumble . . ."

She giggled. He couldn't believe he was hearing his sister giggle. "Come on, I think it's kind of exciting that our folks wouldn't like . . . Like Romeo and Juliet or something . . ."

Billy snorted. Just as he strutted past the fir tree, Drew slung his arm around the boy's neck and pulled him backward behind the tree, deeper into the copse. Yelling as loud as he could with Drew's forearm choking him, fighting with both hands and both feet, Billy was spitting and growling like a feral orange tomcat. Drew didn't let go. The heavy beat of the music from inside the tavern bounced off the trees. Drew swore he could see the leaves shaking.

Lizzie punched Billy in his puffy stomach. He grunted and tears shot from his eyes. He sagged, but Drew held tight, knowing Billy could start up again any time.

Lizzie waved her fist under Billy's nose and spoke just loudly enough to be heard over the yells and shrieks and drumbeats coming from the tavern. "Okay, what's the story, scroop? A couple days ago you were going to get Hannah Karlow. Now you're not. What's going on? You better talk. Now."

"We'll make you guys pay for this. Lizzie, you're gonna be really sorry. You're gonna put out for all of us when—" He strained forward.

Blam! Her fist hit his nose and blood gushed. He screamed and sagged again.

"Easy, Liz." Drew didn't want them to use up all their best stuff, certainly didn't want the disgusting little shit to pass out. "Just tell us, Billy. What changed your mind?"

"Nothing changed anything." He was mumbling, barely opening his mouth. It must have hurt to move any part of his face. "I was just kidding around, before. About the killing."

Lizzie hit him in the ear. His head snapped to the side. "You're lying."

He glared at her, coughed, and whimpered, "You'll never hear it from me."

"Hear what!" Lizzie roared, raising her fist again.

"Not talking." He clamped his lips shut. Drew was surprised. He never would have thought the freckled freak could hold out this well. How much more did he have in him?

She punched him in the stomach again, hard, and his lunch spilled out of his mouth. Tears streamed down his cheeks, mixing with the blood and snot from his nose. Sickening. Drew didn't like any of this. He was glad his fist wasn't smashing into that ugly mess. Lizzie didn't seem to mind.

"No one will ever know who told us," Drew said.

Billy spat on the ground and mumbled, "Fuck you." Lizzie's fist hit him squarely in the teeth.

"Damn! Ouch!" she yelled, shaking her hand. The knuckles were bleeding. "I don't want to keep hurting you, Billy. I don't want to do anything worse than what I've done so far. But I swear I'll cut off your balls if you don't tell us." Drew was shocked. His little sister. Not so little any more. Was she actually carrying a knife? He hoped not. No. He didn't believe her.

But Billy did. Finally, he gave it up, crying. Terrified. A seventeen-year-old kid, not a brave soldier. Drew had to wonder how long he himself would have lasted under Lizzie's torture.

"You think you know so much? You don't know nothin'. We were going to kill her because we thought she works for you guys and we don't want no fuckin' Blackjack Coleman mayor. But Newt heard about it and stopped us. She really works for us. When we found that out, it made everything different."

As bad as this was, Drew couldn't squelch that "I told you so" feeling. He couldn't wait to tell his mother he'd been right. He didn't like Hannah. And she was a spy. In their army, in their family. Lizzie's face was red with rage.

He released Billy's neck and Billy ran.

Lizzie swung around, snarling, "What'd you do that for, Drew!"

"Because he told us."

"But now he's going to warn Hannah."

"I doubt it. To do that, he'd have to admit that he caved. He won't want to."

Lizzie was sucking on a tooth-gashed knuckle. She spat and nodded. "You're smart, Drew. Smart as Mom."

That made him feel good. He wasn't completely happy that they'd made a mess out of Billy, but the results were worth it. And he did feel smart. At the same time, he wasn't sure Billy really would be afraid to confess he'd outed Hannah. He thought—hoped—he wouldn't have the guts, but he'd only pretended to be sure of it to make Lizzie feel better about letting him go.

What else could they have done, anyway? What was Lizzie planning on doing to keep him from talking? He didn't want to know.

"Thanks. We'd better get home and let everyone know."

Jo and Judith had been sitting in Judith's office for the past hour discussing the Rocky issue and considering their political options.

Frank had already told Iggy Santos that the spies were in jail and being questioned, but of course, everyone knew that. And everyone would be waiting to hear what the Rockies had to say. The paper would come out on Saturday afternoon, the day after Frank escorted them to the border. Judith had agreed that they needed to avoid a trial. They could not kill them in town and it would be almost as obvious to arrange an "accident" en route. The double dose of propaganda the incident was creating was well worth any minor threat this particular bunch of causies might pose. To Rocky: take your recruiters back and shove them. To the citizens of Sierra: Rocky's out to get us.

The candidate issue was not quite as complicated but harder to resolve.

Jo was putting together a list of contests and candidates and once again was all too aware that she needed more people who were both trustworthy and free of other essential duties. There was that old saw: need something done, ask a busy person. But there were limits to the practicality of that.

"Up for election, mayor and cabinet, some seats on the Sierra Council."

Judith nodded, staring into the depths of a snow globe, tapping it and watching the white stuff lift and fall on the petals of the single red rose. Jo found that snow globe disorienting. She always expected to see the rose freeze and shrivel.

She continued. "We've got Hannah Karlow. That takes care of the mayor. I've talked to Zack about the cabinet. He's smart and loyal. I'd really like to send him to the council but Samm says he needs him as a lieutenant. He doesn't want to lose him even the one or two days a week the council meets in Hangtown. Monte—he'd be solid on the council." Judith nodded again, jotting a note, probably something about who could help out or even be promoted to Monte's head cashier job. "And have you thought any more about Drew?"

There were three open seats on the seven-seat council. The cabinet would pretty much belong to whoever was elected mayor, as always.

They'd discussed Drew as a possibility for the cabinet or the council, but they hadn't said anything to him yet. He had a full schedule already and she wasn't sure what part of it could be sacrificed. He was working in the restaurant and was about to learn bartending and poker and blackjack dealing. Samm said he was a good soldier, but Jo saw him as something more. He had a quiet about him, a depth. He thought about government and history and he had his doubts about Jo and Judith's vision of the future. Jo liked his questioning. When he came to agree with her, and she was convinced that he would, he'd be a very strong leader. The only drawback was his extreme youth; he'd be easier to appoint to the cabinet than he would be to elect to the council.

"I have. Let's talk to him. About the cabinet."

"That's what I was thinking. But we still need to run someone for those council seats." Of the four members who were not up for reelection, one was clearly in Newt's camp, two solidly in Jo's, one stubbornly pretending there were no sides. If she could elect two more she would control the council with four reliable votes out of seven, no matter who won the third vacant seat. She had to do it, because if Newt managed to take two new seats, the count would be three, three, and one. Deadlock with a seventh who could go any way at all on any given issue.

"I think it may be time," Judith said, "for us to consider moving actively, openly, into the hierarchy. I think I should run."

Jo choked back her first shocked reaction, taking a moment to think. Judith would make a terrific candidate, with her obvious leadership and presence. And no one had, so far, tried to kill any council members. But there was no guarantee the job would stay safe, especially if the Colemans had a majority. Jo would rather take a chance on her own life than Judith's. The thought of losing Judith made her feel weak and sick. She wasn't sure she could keep going. And what about Drew and Lizzie?

Judith was watching her. She laughed. "Nobody's going to kill me, Jo."

"What makes you so sure? Maybe it would be better if I ran. If we can't find anyone else," she added quickly. "It wouldn't keep me away from Tahoe that much. And it's not even a two-hour ride if you need me."

Judith tapped that damned rose snow globe again. She sighed. "I'd prefer to keep us both out of it, but I don't think that's possible. I'm the logical choice for now. I just don't see you as a legislator. You do better behind the scenes, planning and plotting."

That was true. If Jo was going to run for anything it would be mayor. She knew she'd find the slow negotiating and wheedling and blather of the council irritating. She wanted a job where she would just tell people what to do and they'd do it.

Jo shook her head. "Maybe we do need to be more public. But I don't like it being you up there as a target."

"That's sweet, Jo." Jo gave her a look that a few decades before would have been incomplete without a protruding tongue. "But who else would you suggest? Samm doesn't have the temperament for politics."

"Oh, my god, no!" They both laughed this time. "As a tribal chief, maybe . . ."

"So we've got Monte to run for council, and me. We need one more to cover all three seats. Let's sleep on it for a night. Someone will come to mind." They couldn't sleep on it any longer than that; they wanted to hold some kind of rally to coincide with the spy revelation, so they could get people revved up over that and connect the threat with the ability of the Coleman candidates to deal with the threat.

"Okay. That leaves the cabinet." The current five-member group included two friends and two employees. Madera had also appointed a token Scorsi cousin. She could go or stay; she was ineffectual and rarely showed up for meetings. Even if she expressed interest in a vote she would be unlikely to carry the rest of them with her. She was the perfect opposition member. Jo wanted to keep Doc on the cabinet, but it would be good to replace at least a couple of the other lame ducks so the town government could look revitalized. "I've been thinking about Timmy."

Judith looked up from her globe, brightening. "That's a wonderful idea! He has maturity, stability, charm. Everyone knows him. I love it."

Jo sat back, pleased. Drew and Timmy on the cabinet. Perfect. "I'll ask him. When will you file?"

"Today. Actually, I'm looking forward to it. Trips to Hang-town, building alliances, playing the grande dame. I'm glad you talked me into it."

They were still laughing about that when Drew and Lizzie came through the door, sweating and flushed. Lizzie's hands were a mess.

"Is that blood on your shirt, Liz?" Jo was sure it was. What was the girl doing now? And Drew—his collar was ripped nearly off.

"Yes. And wait until you hear—"

"Sit down." Judith looked stern. "And tell me whose blood it is."

"Billy Scorsi's. But you'll be glad when you hear what we found out." The kids threw themselves onto the couch, side by side, Drew watching his sister. "Hannah Karlow is a spy for Newt Scorsi."

Jo felt bile rise in her throat. Oh shit. Samm had been off the mark on that one. Why hadn't she seen it? Against her own uneasiness, she'd convinced herself the fixer would do.

Okay, who are we going to run for mayor now? Maybe, she thought wryly, I can convince one of the Rocky recruiters to take the job. On pain of death.

Lizzie told the entire story of how they'd broken Billy. Judith didn't look pleased, but she wasn't angry, either. They had done what had to be done, on their own initiative. Jo didn't want to discourage that any more than her sister did. Because, after all, they'd succeeded.

She pulled her sys out of her vest pocket and punched in Samm's numbers. He had to know about Hannah right away. And they had to decide what to do with her. Kill her? Offer her more money than Newt was paying?

They had to find her first. Jo hadn't seen her around the casino, she realized, since the night before.

There was only one word for Tim and Fredo's cottage: cute.

We'd gone to lunch again at our Chinese place and then I'd driven them to the house so I could see it.

The chief topic of conversation was, of course, the arrest of the Rocky spies. I told them I'd seen the whole thing, including the shooting. Timmy was just full of stories about what was going on at the jail. The spies, he said, were being interrogated. And the word was that they were confessing to some pretty terrible things. He'd heard that one of them had said they were doing reconnaissance for an invasion Rocky was planning. I was seriously wishing I could be in on those interrogations. I had no reason to disbelieve what Timmy had heard, but I had to wonder, just a little, when he said the information had come from Drew by way of Jo.

"Imagine!" he said. "The nerve of those people. Just let them try it!"

The house was on the northern edge of town. Small, two little bedrooms, a twelve-by-fifteen living room with a nice stone fireplace. Old. Built before the regs that demanded pellet-burning stoves.

Oh, yeah, that had really helped a lot. It wasn't wood smoke that ended the world.

The yard was big and backed up to woods. Pines flanked the front walk. A picket fence, for god's sake.

The house had needed paint, inside and out, but the inside had been finished the day before. I caught a whiff when we clomped in.

"Tomorrow he's going to start painting the outside!" Fred was clearly ecstatic. Tim had found the money to actually hire a neighbor, a handyman named Daniel, to paint the place for them.

I wandered through the rooms. Nice sim-wood floors. Not old enough or new enough for the real thing. At least it didn't have that ridiculous carpet you found in a lot of the relics, stained and smelly, holding decades of bad memories and pet piss. In the too-bright yellow kitchen, the faucet leaked, and the sink was stained with rust. I suggested that Hannah could probably take care of that for them. Timmy thought that was funny.

"Maybe. Some time next year when she runs out of bigger jobs. We'll have to let Daniel give it a try."

I couldn't decide whether I was jealous of their domesticity or glad to be free of it. I suppose, if I were as happy with someone as they were with each other, I would want to nest. Both Sylvia and Jo passed through my mind. What an idiot I could be.

I was fiddling with the fireplace damper in the living room when the button-sized sys-link Newt had insisted I carry "in case of emergency" vibrated. This was the first time he'd used it. Could be important. I strolled aimlessly around the corner, back into the kitchen, flicked it on, and stuck it in my ear.

"This is all your fault, Rica! Hannah's gone. Gone! I told the boys not to kill her, she's ours, but now she says she doesn't trust them not to blabber. She says everyone is watching everyone else, following everyone else. That Jo had someone following the boys. Last straw, she says. She isn't hanging around waiting for the Colemans to find out and kill her." He took in a ragged breath. Since this device was listen-only, I couldn't respond. "So! Now! You're going to have to make up for this by working twice as hard, taking her place. I want you to join their army right away. And another thing. Hannah said they never had those war games anywhere but the one place, they don't move them around. You lied to me." Oops. I waited for more. He seemed to be gone.

I flicked the "heard-you" button with my fingernail and stuck the thing back in my pocket.

Was I supposed to run for mayor, too?

I couldn't wait to get back to Blackjack and see if the Colemans knew she was gone. It amused me to think that she might have literally flown the coop in the Gullwing. But I didn't really care how she left, I was just delighted that she was gone.

Samm had commandeered Drew and a dozen of his other soldiers, left Zack running the poker tables, and searched for Hannah through the afternoon. Jo, waiting in her own office for word, was not surprised when he reported that she was nowhere they'd looked. Not in the storage room fixing slots, not in the bar, not at the poker table, not in her motel room, and nowhere on the strip. They'd prowled through Scorsi's Luck, earning glares and gasps of surprise, even opened Newt Scorsi's office door, slamming it back against the wall, to find him deep in conversation with his brother, Larry, Billy's father. They got out fast when he called for help. No time for a fight. They had a fugitive to catch.

They'd even gone out to the airfield; the plane was still there.

Somehow, Hannah must have known that they'd found her out. Or guessed. She was smart. Maybe she'd heard that the kids beat up Billy. Or saw him afterward. Maybe she even saw them coming back to Blackjack after the fight. Lizzie's bleeding knuckles, the spatter, Drew's torn shirt. It wouldn't take many pieces of the puzzle. A word, a look, and any cautious merc would get out while she could.

In any case, she was gone. Now who the hell was Jo going to run for mayor?

What about Waldo? She wouldn't care much if someone offed him and she thought he was, underneath it all, loyal to the family in his way. He'd probably do as he was told, unless the instructions involved women.

But no, she just couldn't bring herself to do it. Watching him swagger around town would be more than she could bear.

Timmy? She'd never forgive herself if he got hurt. He was so trusting, not to mention small, old, and effectively one-armed. Oh, hell. She needed some air, needed to clear her head. She locked the office door behind her and trotted down the stairs.

She was striding through the casino, intent on the exit, when Zack waved her over to his table.

"What's on, Zack?"

"Got a problem now, huh, Jo? No mayor?"

"It's a problem, Zack."

"I'd as soon do that as sit around with the cabinet, yakking about nothing. A mayor gets to do things, give executive orders, right?" He grinned at her, his ice-blue eyes sharp and humorous.

"You volunteering?" Not a bad idea. And this was a man who could take care of himself pretty well. How would Samm feel about it?

Zack was smart enough to know she'd be wondering that.

"Why not? I can still stay close to the army, be where Samm needs me. Maybe I can talk Samm into taking a cabinet job."

Jo burst out laughing. "You do that and I'll give you a raise."

Samm wouldn't go for it, she knew. But with Drew, Tim, Doc, and Andy, they had four already.

She still needed a third candidate for the council.

Samm had mentioned that young blackjack dealer, Emmy. Early twenties, only, but very smart. He said she was interested in politics and admired the Colemans. She'd been there for six months now, done several jobs and worked her way up to the table. He said she was a rock and that the gamblers, men and women, loved her. Jo hesitated. Samm had recommended Hannah, too. But she had a better feeling about Emmy. She'd consider her, talk to her, see what was what. Monte, the grayhair; Judith, imposing matriarch; and the strong, good-looking, charismatic youngster. Not a bad slate.

And then there was Rica. What could she talk her into? The thought made her smile, and led to other ideas that she pushed to a far corner of her mind, if only for the time being.

Chapter 25
Huddled over a Scarred Table

When I got to the restaurant later that afternoon Timmy dashed up to me, a big grin smeared across his sweet pink face.

"Have you heard about Hannah?"

"You mean her disappearing?" Was that what was making him so happy? I knew he didn't like her much, but this seemed extreme.

"Oh, you know about it then." He looked slightly disappointed. "But there's more!" He was beaming again. "Drew says Zack has volunteered to be the mayoral candidate. And Judith and Jo want me to be on the Tahoe cabinet! Isn't that exciting?"

"Very." This was all moving pretty fast. Timmy in politics. The cabinet would be keeping few secrets.

"And Drew is going for the cabinet, too, and he says Judith is probably running for council."

"Not Samm? Not Jo?"

"Well, not Jo, anyway. Drew thinks Zack might want Samm with him on the cabinet, though."

Samm was big and pretty and a popular man. He would inspire confidence in the voters, help Zack win the election. But Warrior Samm on the cabinet? He was bigger than life in so many ways, it was hard to picture him sitting in meetings.

As for Jo, someone had to run the casino, especially if Judith won a seat on the council. But I didn't think that was the only reason she was sticking around the home shop.

Judith was the queen and Jo seemed more like the power behind the throne. She wouldn't run for office unless she had to; she'd rather plan and coordinate everyone else's plotting and warring than fight for votes or policy right out in public. Yes, indeed, it could take a lot of time and energy to draw up a master plan for world conquest. The thought made me laugh: Jo, huddled over a scarred table with only a candle to light a dark room, poring over a map of the western half of the continent, her sensual mouth sneering, connecting all the people and all the pieces, laughing evilly. Kind of sexy, actually. Right there at that table with her pretty hands in everything at once. Timmy was looking at me oddly. I stopped laughing. I needed to stop picturing her body parts.

A party of three sat at one of Tim's tables. "Well, more gossip later . . ." He dashed across the room.

Drew on the cabinet. So young. I wondered if he really wanted the job. He was smart and thoughtful, but maybe they were pushing him to do something he didn't want to do. Maybe his moodiness wasn't about me at all. I didn't want it to be about me, so I liked my newly conceived alternative. He and Lizzie were, after all, heirs to the casino. They were going to teach him more than dealing and serving and managing. They were grooming him for power. Pushing him. I could stop taking his unhappy look personally.

I scanned the restaurant for him. He was bussing one of my tables, Lizzie cleaning up another one nearby. Drew was down to just a couple of hours a night in the restaurant now, working the rest of the time at the tables and the bar.

And Lizzie? The girl was only seventeen. What did they have in mind for her?

What did Drew and Lizzie have in mind for themselves?

When Samm came in for a quick meal I was reminded that

Newt expected me to join Samm's army now that Hannah was gone. Crap. How was I supposed to conceal my merc-level skills with weapons and hand-to-hand if I was playing soldier for the Colemans? Even more important, how was I supposed to admit I even knew there was an army?

I handed him a menu and he smiled up at me. Dazzling. You just didn't see perfect teeth like that every day. His family might have died in a hostel, but their genes didn't seem to be at fault. He took the menu and grabbed my hand, kissing it. I must have looked stupidly startled because he laughed.

"Sorry, Rica. But it was irresistible." Like his charm. I smiled back at him. What a mixture this man was. Strength and beauty. Brains and spirit. I wondered about his love life. He was alone so much. He flirted with me, but he never followed through. It had occurred to me early on that he might be in love with Jo, but I was beginning to think he simply wasn't interested in romance. What about sex? I'd noticed him with a woman or two, walking, sitting next to him when he was dealing. But no one consistently. I guessed he just took it as he found it.

He glanced at the menu. "What's good today?"

Jo was sitting at her desk stewing about her candidates list. She'd left a message for Emmy but hadn't gotten an answer back yet. She liked the roster she had, but she'd have a problem if someone backed out. If she did need to run herself, she'd prefer the cabinet. She wouldn't have to campaign, just take the job when Zack won. And it wouldn't be much work.

More and more she was wondering about Rica as a candidate. But she hadn't been around very long and Jo still didn't know if she could trust her. The spies she'd asked to check on her hadn't reported back yet.

And what about the other side? What were the Scorsis doing? She had messages out to her sagging network at Scorsi's Luck, telling them to find out what they could right damned now. Surely Newt had plans for more than just the one council candidate he'd put up posters for. With Hannah gone, he wouldn't let the Colemans walk off with the mayor's office. He'd run someone. He'd be lining up people for the cabinet, and trying to find someone to send to Hangtown.

This was more than an election, it was a war. How safe would her candidates be? Would she have to kill off some of his? She'd rather defeat them with bribes and miscounts and stolen ballots and double and triple and dead-guy voting. She wasn't above any of that, certainly, if it looked like one of her own might lose. And she thought that she could get money to the right people when it came to counting the votes, if she had to.

Her head hurt. She rubbed her temples. Closed her eyes.

She wasn't getting enough intelligence, didn't feel they were building enough strength. She had a small army training and a few people working at Scorsi's Luck as spies, and it wasn't enough. She should have known, long ago, that it was the Scorsi boys who killed Madera. She should have known that Hannah was a spy.

How could she light a fire under her people? Her thoughts flickered toward Rica again. Judith had been right to prod her early on, see if she had interest in real work. But she hadn't gotten any kind of answer. She might be a good candidate. But she might also be useful as a spy. Scorsi had a small stage in his bar that was used from time to time by unfunny comedians and untalented musicians. Maybe Rica could interest him in having a singer on her nights off.

Fantasy. She hardly knew the woman. It took real talent to be a good spy. Good enough to do the job and stay alive. Newt was a fool but not an idiot. He'd be suspicious of anyone coming to him from Blackjack. Her sys buzzed.

Amazing. It was one of her people at Scorsi's.

"I found something out."

Good for you. "What is it?"

"Well, it won't be a secret much longer, but I thought you'd want to know as soon as possible."

Oh for god's sake. "Yes. Tell me what it is."

"Newt's going to run for mayor. And his brother Larry?" Billy's arrogant, overdressed father. "He's going to run for the council." Two council candidates, then. Larry and the merc.

"Anything else?"

"No."

"Good work." She clicked off. She couldn't help thinking it: killing Newt's candidates was looking more attractive. The world would not miss either Larry or the merc. She wasn't sure whether she should laugh or cry. She needed to be stronger. She needed a vacation or at least a nap.

There was a knock on the door. For just a second, she considered telling whoever it was to go away.

"Come in."

The door swung open and the big black poodle hopped in on three legs, grinning a dog grin. Followed by Liz, who wore a proud mama smile.

"Look how great she's doing, Jo!"

Jo reached down to pat the dog's head, gently. "Very good, Liz. Just don't let her overdo it, okay?"

"Okay. What are you doing?"

"Wondering why only one of our spies at Blackjack came up with the information that Newt's going to run for mayor and his brother Larry's running for council." Lizzie raised her eyebrows but didn't interrupt. "Wondering—what do you think of Rica Marin, Lizzie? Do you think she can be trusted?"

Lizzie sat down on the easy chair next to the desk. The dog lowered herself to the floor with a grunt and a little squeaking cry of pain.

"I never thought about it, I guess. How could we find out?"

"I don't know, exactly." Did she really want both kids watching Rica's every move, tripping over her in the lounge? Probably not a good idea. She should try to keep Lizzie out of that for now.

"Drew's watching her, right?" Lizzie asked.

Jo hadn't gotten any feedback from Drew.

"Yes. And I've got someone trying to check on her. Never mind, I'm just thinking."

"Okay." Liz got up again. "Well, I've got some homework. Come on, Soldier."

The dog struggled to get back on her feet. Lizzie placed an arm under her hindquarters and helped her.

So she'd named the dog Soldier. Lizzie seemed to be staking out her own territory in the family. Another year and she'd be wanting to fight alongside Samm.

Jo's netsys buzzed again. She punched on and saw that she had a message from one of the people she had working from the Delta west into Redwood. About time she'd heard from one of them.

Rica, it turned out, had never worked on the Riverboat Queen. She had in fact, according to a border guard the spy knew, come to Blackjack traveling from the East. That was all he had so far, but he thought there'd be more.

Jo couldn't wait to hear the rest, depressing as it might be.

"Hurry that information up, if you can."

"I'll try."

Meanwhile, she'd have to step back a few paces in her pursuit of Rica as a candidate and as something more, as well.

That night, Jo did show up at the lounge and took a table near the front. She watched me very carefully, but something felt off. The heat was gone. I felt like I was being observed, more evaluated than enjoyed. What had happened? Had I somehow made a fool of myself in her eyes out on the parking lot that night?

When the set was over, she gave me a quick smile and took off. I was disappointed, and I was worried.

But after all, I told myself, trying to stiffen my upper lip, Jo had a lot to do, with the casino, the elections, world domination. She couldn't spend all her time pinned against fir trees.

Chapter 26
I Sure Would Like to Be
Cannon Fodder

Jo was finally letting herself go to bed, climbing under the covers, but her sys buzzed at her from its place on the nightstand.

Emmy.

"Hi, Jo! I'm so flattered that you want me to run for the Sierra Council. Do you think I could actually win?"

Nice kid. Too humble.

"We'd support you. I think you could win. How about it?" She knew she should be chattier, but it was late and she just wanted an answer so she could get on with it.

"Well, okay, if you think—yes. I'd be honored."

"Good. I'll talk to you more about it tomorrow."

"Oh! Did I wake you?"

"No. But let's talk tomorrow when we're fresh."

Emmy agreed and once again Jo settled herself in for sleep. Good. Another candidate for the slate. She needed to rest. Then, tomorrow, she could start planning speeches and advertising.

But her mind wouldn't let her relax enough to sleep.

Jo had caught Rica's puzzled look as she was leaving the lounge. Well, good. Let her wonder, let her get nervous. She'd lied. Why she had lied remained to be seen. Maybe she didn't have any decent references and a friend had faked one so she could get a job.

But she could be a spy. Newt was apparently better than she'd thought he was at placing spies in Blackjack. She knew he

264

wanted to find something he could take to the law, stop them from doing what they were doing with their army, their political forays. She'd heard the rumors: the Scorsis had accused them of skimming from the tables, holding back tax money that belonged to Tahoe and Sierra. They'd accused them of a lot of other things, too, but that was the one that worried her. It was true.

No one but Jo, Judith, and Monte knew how much they took and exactly how it was done. A little record-fiddling. A steady ten percent of the cash slipped into a separate safe once every day at the same hour, five a.m., when Monte was alone in the cage and business was slowest. The dealers never had to dirty their hands and she never had to worry about people new to the tables. They skimmed enough to build an army and pay spies, to convince loyal people to take office, and bribe a few others into being loyal for a while anyway. Enough to put up campaign posters and set up rallies.

In the short run, she didn't like skimming because it took tax money from things that needed doing. The hostels were still always looking for money. Sometimes the streets needed repair so the locals, and tourists not rich enough for floaters, could drive their old heaps around. And the sidewalks. You didn't want customers falling on their butts. Money the Colemans took wasn't available for those things.

But in the long run, the temporary diversion of funds would bring tremendous returns. Once they were truly in charge, everything would get done.

When everyone could get vax, when the competition for small territories was over, when even the poorest could build decent lives and populations could grow again, and when she and Judith could run the day-to-day business of the town and the country and eventually a bigger country, people would be better off. She'd see to it. Meanwhile, she invested in that future and looked the other way, while the sheriff looked the other way when small crimes were committed. The sheriff took bribes from drivers who'd had too little sleep and too much alcohol. The medicine shows entertained people and gave them hope. Waldo took medicine show profits. The amounts were small and it kept him happy, and out of worse kinds of trouble that might affect the family's plans.

Things just had to work better. When they didn't, people died.

She would never forget the famine of '48. She was a teenager and Judith barely thirty. The local crops had failed and a lot of people had starved because bandits ruled the roads and stole whatever Sierra tried to import.

Just a few years ago, no new cars were available from Redwood because the factory had trouble getting parts from the glassy-metal molder in California. The people who lost their jobs had started a riot that only ended when some of them were killed. Even now, half the products made in Redwood didn't make it over the mountain roads. Always the bandits waiting to intercept and the petty officials taking their cuts and the little rivalries using up the resources and ingenuity.

A country didn't have to be as big as the old United States, but a merging of Redwood and Sierra would be a good start. Then they could not only defend their territory against the posturing Rocky, they could fight for it and own it. Sierra, Redwood, Rocky, then add California. They could do anything with a country that size. Build anything.

Life and death. Vax and food. And Rocky. That's what her candidates would run on. Sierra couldn't afford to lose people to their recruiters and couldn't afford to see Rocky get stronger and bigger. Life and death. Vax, food, self-defense. Wonderful timing. She hoped they'd send in some more of their khaki-godder scouts. Scare people. Make them angry. With any luck,

Newt would be slow to get on the anti-Rocky bandwagon. And even if he caught on fast enough to use it, she didn't think she'd have trouble convincing the citizens that the Colemans were more capable of defending the country. If she had no other choice, if she wanted to pump up Rocky's threat and Coleman strength, she'd march Samm's army down the street with a brass band and recruit from the spectators.

Of course, Samm had wanted to do that a while ago. Show his army, turn recruiting into a circus. Draw Newt out of the woodwork. Have a war for control right inside Sierra and get it over with. But even a little war would do a lot of damage. Fields would be burned. Small industries trying to start up would be buried, their resources stolen. War didn't leave much behind. Jo wanted everything still there when she took it over, and she wanted to be responsible for as few deaths as possible.

Once, a long time ago, those crazy Twentieth Century people had designed something called a smart bomb that left the buildings and transport and just killed all the people. Smart? Hardly. Aside from being despicable, anyone left would be really, really angry. Hatred would bring you down eventually, just like fear would.

Her solution was politics. Worming people into the fabric of power.

It was all falling into place in her mind, the recruiters from Rocky supplying the last bit.

As she drifted into a half dream, Rica showed up like a memory. Where did she fit? Was she just an opportunist with a fake reference? Was she a cop sent there to find out if Jo and Judith were skimming money? Was she a spy sent by Newt Scorsi?

Best to operate as if she were a danger. And for the time being, not let her know directly that she was under suspicion. Rica had made friends with Tim and Fredo. She would ask Tim to do a little spying on the possible spy. She hoped she'd hear something more from her man out west, and soon.

I'd never gotten a return message from the chief about the boys undoubtedly being the mayor's killers. I thought she'd missed it somehow, so I sent it again.

Her response came in the time it took me to brush my teeth and get undressed.

"That leaves the army and skimming. Keep me informed." Click off. I'd never known her to be this abrupt. She didn't seem to want to talk to me. What secret was she holding? Oh, the hell with it, that was just plain paranoid. She was busy, or tired, or lost her lover, or caught a cold.

Ah, yes. The army. I was under Newt's orders to join up. It was true that peeking at them from behind trees wouldn't give me the whole picture. I would ask Samm to let me in. All I had to do was figure out a way to explain how I knew it existed. Neither Timmy nor Drew had ever mentioned it to me. If I could twist one of them into doing that, it would help.

The sys buzzed again. Gran. I didn't want to get into it with her right then so I let the sound run. In case it was something important, I'd listen to it the minute she went away. The message ended in less than a minute. I retrieved it.

"Rica, dear, I hope you're being careful. I consulted with Macris—"

Yes. That was what I was afraid of.

"—and he said the transits are very difficult for you."

No shit.

"He said there is danger to you and also to someone close to you. Violence is coming. Betrayal. Now I know you don't believe it. I don't know why you don't. You've gotten true warnings before."

A few. A few ambiguous ones, anyway.

"So be very careful. And get back to me as soon as you can."

I would. Much later that night when I knew she'd be asleep and I could just leave a message. I adored her; I wanted to talk to her. But not right now. Not when things were looking so, well—difficult. I could fake cheer and confidence for a quick send, but not in a real conversation.

Before I went to sleep, I sent a message to Sylvia: "What's new in your life?" She wouldn't answer, not live, not ever, and not in text either, but still, what if she did? I knew she wouldn't say "leave me alone." She had never been that direct. Which I thought, when my obsession was at its strongest, had to mean she was ambivalent. Of course when my brain was working I understood that it didn't have to mean that at all.

I'd promised to get up that morning and help Timmy and Fredo move. Nothing heavy; they'd hired some underemployed local muscle for that and everything but the two of them and their cats was already at the house. I was going to help them unpack and organize.

The first thing Timmy said to me when he and Fredo, juggling a carrier with the yowling cats inside, climbed into my car, was: "Did you hear about Newt?" Had he run away, too? No such luck, I was sure.

"Newt Scorsi?" I didn't want to seem too familiar with who he was.

"Yes of course. What other Newt have you heard of?"

I just shook my head.

"Well, he's going to run for mayor!"

I was stunned. I couldn't imagine how that ugly, nasty gnome could hope to win. Kill Zack? Steal votes?

"Well," I said, as calmly as I could manage, "that ought to make it an interesting contest."

When we got to the house, the handyman Daniel was already there, standing on a ladder shoved into some tarp-covered shrubs and slapping a coat of white on the stucco. Fredo unlocked the door; we walked into a daunting mess. The living room was filled with boxes and furniture placed haphazardly but, I realized after a quick look, all of it had been dropped in the appropriate rooms.

"Drew said he'd come," Timmy said, "but he ended up having to do something else today. Lizzie promised to help after school. Such nice children."

My ears perked up at the "something else."

We worked for a couple hours, shared the lunch Fredo had packed with the painter, a man with a shy smile, red ears, and a day's beard, laughed and listened to music, watched Roberta and Harvey tiptoeing around the rooms looking spooked and going all puffy at the slightest noise, pawed through boxes and hung clothing and put musty old books and capsules and doodads on shelves.

Lizzie showed up around three. She'd left Soldier at home because, she said, she didn't think she should walk so far yet. She jumped right in, unpacking bathroom boxes and filling the drawers and medicine cabinet with more skin creams and shampoos and unguents than I'd ever seen in one house before. They could have opened a notions market right there.

From time to time during the day, Newt as mayor of Tahoe oozed into my mind, a disturbing image.

Toward the end of the afternoon, I found myself staring at the inside of a kitchen cabinet, wondering what I was supposed to be doing. A box of dishes sat near my feet, but there was something else . . .

Oh, right. Timmy wanted shelf paper down first. I rummaged in the box with the garbage bags and wrapping paper. There it was. Sky blue with little white flowers.

Fredo struggled into the kitchen carrying a large rattling box of pots and pans.

"Fredo, have you seen the scissors?"

He dropped the box in the middle of the tiled floor, sighing. "Let me think. Oh. Yes. They'll be in here." He pushed a box labeled "mess drawer" out from under the table with his foot, squatted, and pulled it open. He lifted out can openers, corkscrews, whetstones, chopsticks, graters, nut picks, and laid them on the brown tile counter, finally uncovering a yellow-handled scissors. "Here you are, sweetie."

"It was nice of Drew to offer to help," I said. "What was it he had to do today?" Very casual. I couldn't care less.

Fredo waved a hand vaguely. "Oh, you know . . ."

I smiled and cocked my head, waiting.

"Come to think of it, I don't know. Maybe he went with the sheriff's escort party. They took the Rockies to the border this morning." That was interesting. "But maybe he didn't." He pivoted toward the doorway and yelled, "Timmy! What was Drew doing today that was so important?"

Timmy appeared in the doorway. His eyes flickered toward me and back to Fredo. "Who knows? He's nineteen. Probably has to do with a girl." A quick smile, and he cocked his head at me. "Rica? Take a walk with me, honey."

A walk? Why would we take a walk now? I waved the scissors. "I was just going to start—"

"Plenty of time for that. Come on."

I followed him out through the living room onto the small front deck. We sat on the steps.

He took my hand. "I wanted to thank you again for helping today." He hesitated, then gave me a quick hug and a peck on the cheek. I gripped his pointed little chin and returned the kiss. The affection was real between us, we both felt it, but why did he look so sad?

"You're a good friend, Rica." He looked away. He seemed to be gathering strength to say something that would go along with that sad face, and I didn't want to hear it.

He turned back to me, still avoiding my eyes. "You want to know what Drew is doing today. Why?"

My mind flashed to Hannah. She had told Timmy. No, they weren't friends. She had told someone who had told him. I stopped myself again. No. Timmy was worried about Drew's crush on me and wanted to talk about it. I had to say something. This was going to be hard. I did my best to look innocent, puzzled, but my heart wasn't in it.

"Just chit-chat, Tim. I know how much Drew likes you. I was a little surprised that he did something else today." Then, with no idea of where this conversation was going, I turned it back on him. "What's so serious about all this? Is there something I should know that nobody's saying? Some secret I stepped on a corner of?"

Timmy wasn't as good at the game as I was. He flushed and looked away. Did I see tears in his eyes?

"No secret." He picked a spray of pine needles off the step and began to play with it, twisting it around his index finger. "But there's a lot going on around here, with all the elections and things. And those mercs who invaded the casino. And the dead mayor. And who's running for what and who wants who to do what."

"Yes. But it feels like there are things going on that no one's talking about." I hunkered down, leaning closer to him, and put my hand on his knee. Clumsily, self-consciously. "People disappearing all day and no one saying why. Hannah taking off suddenly that way." I forced myself to grin and shrug. "I'm as curious as the next person, Tim. I'd rather be in on the secrets than on the outside. Anyone would."

He nodded, but I didn't think he was buying it. I was in trouble. I might as well have been trying to lie to Gran. But I kept going. I had groundwork to lay. I had no options.

"Listen, Tim, when I first came here, Judith talked to me about defending Blackjack. It was all pretty vague. I just thought she was talking about protecting the place from more raids. But then I overheard something in the restaurant the other night. Well, actually, it was a while ago. And I've wondered about it ever since." I hesitated, as if I were reluctant to let him in on the secret.

"Overheard?" He cast a quick sideways glance. "From who?"

"I don't know who they were and I don't remember much about them. A couple of men. They weren't at one of my tables. And I didn't hear much. Just what one of them said to the other one. Something about how many guns the army had."

Timmy nodded again, looked straight at me, and said, "You don't remember who they were or what they looked like?"

"No." This, I knew, was possible but barely believable. In a population of a couple thousand, including tourists, you tended to remember faces and you were pretty sure to see them again.

"And they were talking about an army?"

"Yes. And they mentioned Samm's name."

Timmy sighed and leaned away from me. My hand slipped off his knee. "Where are you going with all this, Rica?"

"Do the Colemans have an army?" He didn't answer. Desperately, quickly: "Because I like it here, and I think Judith and Jo would keep me around longer if I got more, well, you know, involved."

"You want to join an army?" He didn't say "the" army. He was being careful not to admit there was one.

"I'd like to see what it's about." I nodded enthusiastically and pumped up the energy in my voice.

"If you think Samm has something to do with it, why don't you talk to him? Or Drew?" There was that hint of dampness in his eyes again.

"I didn't want to be too pushy, since I can see this is not

something everyone knows about." Limp. Amateurish. Tim shook his head.

"Rica, I love you to pieces. I want us to be friends. And so I'm not going to talk to you about this anymore." He stood up. "It's almost time to go to work, now. Let's just do that."

During the five-minute drive back to Blackjack with Tim, I chatted about Waldo, sneered about Hannah, but Tim was quiet. When we got to the casino, he trudged toward the restaurant and I went to my room to change.

I didn't know what to believe and Timmy's sadness hung over my thoughts, brushing at them like a black velvet curtain. The idea that I had somehow lost Timmy's trust sent me into a fit of irrational misery. Irrational because I deserved to lose it. His life and Fredo's, their loyalty, were bound up in Blackjack. Was I really as disgusted with being a spy as I felt today?

I couldn't think about that for very long, so I began hunting for less depressing explanations for his behavior. Maybe someone had told him to talk about the army with no one, and he felt bad that he couldn't answer my questions. I laughed out loud. That was just pathetic. I knew there was more to it than that. Jo seemed colder, Tim was unhappy about something, and all the hairs on my spy pelt were standing on end.

Still, I either had to keep trying or quit the job. I'd have to find my information somewhere else. I needed an informant I didn't feel rotten about using. Someone stronger than Tim. Someone who didn't remind me of Gran. If my cover was not yet entirely blown I'd made a mistake by sneaking around talking to an employee. It was better to bluff, to go right to the top like an honest woman.

I would talk to Samm, that night, when the soldiers returned from what I assumed was another day of war games.

Let's see . . . Hey, Samm, I heard you're raising an illegal army and gee, I sure would like to be cannon fodder for dear old Blackjack . . .

I wondered how far I could stretch the role, how convincing I could be about my passion to be part of the group. Could I derail whatever suspicions there were about me or was it past that?

There was no doubt I'd been rushing things. This was no ordinary job spying on ordinary people. It would have been safer to hang around for several months getting deep inside the family. But Newt wouldn't wait—and keep paying—for that, not with elections coming up in just a few weeks, and the chief seemed to be losing interest. Unless I decided to give up making merc wages for half a year, I didn't have that kind of time. And I was already too deep inside the family for my own comfort.

I was buttoning my white shirt when my sys buzzed. Gran. The real one.

"Hi, dear, just saying hello. Everything okay?"

"Everything's fine, Gran. How are things at home?"

"I drank too much Sonoma red with Petra last night."

Petra was another one of her old political friends.

"Wish I'd been with you. Sounds like fun."

"It was. She told me the funniest story about something that happened over in Berkeley yesterday."

Lots of funny things happened there. A long tradition, Gran said.

"What happened?"

"Well, it was only partly funny. A bunch of foreigners were run out of town for trying to buy people. Can you imagine?"

Uh oh. I felt a chill. "Foreigners?"

"From Rocky, that's what Petra said. Wearing strange uniforms! And she said some of them talked like godders. That's the part that isn't funny. First they tried to get the mayor and a couple of her cabinet members to make a deal with them.

Something about putting a lot of volunteers from Rocky on the police force or the sheriff's department. Something like that." Gran tended to let details slip away from her. "The mayor told them three cops were enough and they kept pushing. They kept saying, 'but we'll work for free.' Until the mayor told them to go swimming in a dead-pond. Then, you'll never guess what they did."

"You said they tried to buy people." I was due in the restaurant in five minutes, but I wanted to hear every word of this.

"Yes! They went right out on the road and tried to buy a woman and her two children. Offered her money to move to Rocky! She hit one of them with her walking stick, they had the nerve to complain to the cops, and the cops told them to go home to their own obnoxious country. I guess they did."

Scratchy assholes. I told her we'd had our own bunch of Rocky drones in jail in Tahoe for the past couple of days, and that the sheriff had taken them to the eastern border that morning.

"Not the same ones, then. Curious. Well, I have to go feed the fur-folk."

"And I have to feed some humans. Talk to you soon, Gran."

There were way too many Rockies wandering around the western countries.

CHAPTER 27
DIDN'T MERCS EVER RETIRE?

"Jo, I just can't do this!" Timmy was actually wringing his hands. She'd never seen anyone do that before. It was remarkably irritating.

"Did you even try?"

"Yes, of course. She was at my house, helping us move in for god's sake. And she asked why Drew wasn't there."

"I assume you didn't tell her he was training with the army."

"Jo!"

She knew she sounded sarcastic; he didn't deserve that. She was feeling frustrated about Rica. She still hadn't heard anything more from her western spy. Now she was not only feeling ambivalent about Rica, she was feeling guilty about treating Timmy this way. Jo didn't like messy feelings. Yes or no, love or hate, win or lose. That was how she liked things to be. And damned if they ever were.

She softened her tone. "Well, what did you say, and what did she say and how did it feel to you?"

His eyes flickered downward. She knew she shouldn't trust whatever he said next. "Like a friend asking a friend . . . about a friend." He looked back up into her eyes again, begging. "I can't spy on her. I like her. Do you really think she's a spy?"

Jo shrugged. "Could be." Oh, the hell with it. "Yes, I think she might be. And I think you think she might be, too, or you wouldn't be so damned hysterical about it." The poor little man looked miserable.

"Well, who do you think she's spying for?"

Was it possible she was working for Rocky? No. She just couldn't see it. Still, if Rica was a merc she'd work for anyone. No. Rica wouldn't work for Rocky. Yes, no, maybe.

"Newt." That seemed the most likely.

He looked truly shocked. "No. Rica could never work for that creature."

"I hope not."

"You're not going to hurt her or anything, are you?"

"Timmy, how evil do you think I am?" She was evil enough. If she were sure that Rica was a threat to the Coleman plans, she'd have to get rid of her somehow. But it wouldn't be easy. And she suspected, as well, that Rica wouldn't just disappear the way Hannah had. Hannah looked tougher, but Rica had something better inside her.

"I don't think you're evil. Not at all. You know that. But you are determined." He hesitated. "I would do anything for you, Jo. But I never said I would be any good at this kind of thing. Any more than I'd be a good soldier."

He was just too decent. She wondered, now, whether it would be a good idea, after all, to put him on the cabinet. Could a man that decent be an effective politician? As long as it was the cabinet, and not the council, probably. A support position for the mayor, rather than an elective office with power of its own.

Yes. He'd be fine on the cabinet.

"Okay, Tim. Don't worry about it any more. Go on to work." He dashed off, happy to be out of the corner she'd put him in.

She needed to put the Rica question aside for a while to deal with the day's election business. Monte had drawn up some rough posters for Zack's candidacy, as well as his own, Emmy's, and Judith's. She needed to take a look at them and make any changes she thought they needed. They were stacked on the easel in the corner. She stood and walked over to them. Judith's was simple, strong. "Judith Coleman. A leader who will stand for Tahoe in Hangtown. Vax for all!" The posters were new but they were out of date already. They needed to lean on the protection angle, but Monte didn't know yet that the Rockies had "confessed" to being point men for an invasion. That news would come out the next day, Saturday. After "Hangtown," she added the words "and keep Sierra safe from her enemies."

She carried the roughs to her desk to work on them.

Zack's poster for the mayor's race focused on the town's economic health. That was an important part of the job and she didn't want the people to think he'd forgotten it, but she added: "Tahoe, the first line of defense for Sierra." Not strictly true geographically, but true in terms of strength. And then, she wrote, Zack was "A strong man to draw that line in the snow."

Smiling to herself, she read her handiwork again. Not bad. The snow wouldn't start falling for a couple of months, but the image was good anyway.

Iggy Santos had promised her the front page of Saturday's *Sierra Star* would be dedicated to the confession of the captured Rockies, with sidebars on how people felt about that danger, including quotes from Judith and Samm. As concerned citizens. Sometime in the next few days she'd renew Blackjack's order for a month of full-page ads. They had a good arrangement.

Once the paper was out, the candidates would have something to roar about besides vax. Then, on Sunday, the posters would go up.

She called the Lucky Buck motel, letting them know she'd be renting their courtyard for some town meetings and rallies, starting Monday. By Monday, the town would be nicely revved up. She clipped a note to Judith's poster, telling Monte to add flyers announcing Monday's rally and hang them right above the posters.

As she was stacking them back on the easel, her sys buzzed.

It was the spy she'd had checking on Rica.

"Jo, I talked to a guy who knows a guy who says Rica Marin is a merc. He was involved in a job she did in Redwood a couple years ago. She was using a different name that time, but the description is exact and he says he knew her as Rica, too. I think you can safely bet you've got a merc there. The woman he met lived in Redwood, north of San Francisco."

So that was that. "Thanks, Theo. Anything more?"

"No, 'fraid that's it."

She'd have to make sure she kept Theo happy. He did good work.

They signed off. Brainlessly, she caught herself hoping that Rica was in Tahoe because she was taking some time off or even quitting the merc business. Didn't mercs ever retire? Surely they must. Rica was probably in her late thirties, like Jo. Maybe she wanted to leave spying to younger women.

She laughed at herself, out loud. Sure. Strong, healthy, smart people like Rica always quit jobs that paid big money so they could work in a casino for a tenth of the pay. Happened every day.

Now Jo needed to find out for sure who Rica was working for: Newt, the chief, or Rocky. Again, though, she refused to believe it was Rocky. Especially if Rica was from Redwood. Newt on his own was a strong possibility even if Timmy found it hard to believe. Mercs didn't always know the people they hired out to before they started. As for the chief, she generally tried to do her job, and she wanted to keep it. But if she was involved, Jo thought she was probably being pushed by Newt and wouldn't have come after Blackjack on her own. She had bets to hedge so close to the elections.

First of all, the chief would be more worried about the council coming in than about the current council, which had only a month left in office. Not really enough time to remove her even if they thought she was ignoring blatant lawbreaking. They'd have to act fast, the neutrals would have to go along, and the whole lame duck bunch, with the exception of Newt's pet councilmember, would need to be more motivated than they probably were to spend their last few weeks making enemies.

Jo was sure the Colemans would win the elections. If Graybel thought so too, she'd be careful about offending them.

But then, she didn't know what Graybel was thinking. She also didn't know whether she'd want to keep the woman in her job once she and Judith controlled the council. She was competent, but she needed to be strong and loyal, too. And compliant. Frank with brains.

Rica was giving Jo a way to get some answers about the chief, so she might as well just bull right into it. She reached her immediately

"Good evening, Helen. This is Jo Coleman."

"Jo! Nice to hear from you." Jo knew that was halfway true, anyway. "What can I do for you?"

"I've just found out that there's a strong possibility that someone who's working in the casino is really a merc. Her name is Rica Marin. Would you know anything about that?"

She grinned at the full five seconds of silence that followed. Now she was sure the chief was involved in the spying, which made it even more unlikely that Rica'd been sent by Rocky. That, at least, was a relief.

"What makes you think she's there as a merc?"

"It's probable."

"Hmm." The chief was buying time. "Who do you think she's working for?"

What Jo wanted to say at that point was "I think she's working for you." But she controlled herself.

What she did say was, "I don't know. Just thought I'd check with you and see if you'd heard anything about her or what she's doing here. I have no idea why she'd be working in our casino."

"No. This is the first time I've heard the name. I haven't heard a thing about her." Of course she had, if only because Rica was the star of Blackjack's lounge. That was a stupid lie. Jo waited, silent, to see if she could make the chief even more uncomfortable.

"Got another incoming. Let me know what you find out, Jo." And she was gone.

If the chief was one of Rica's employers, as her tense silences and quick escape indicated she was, she now had fair warning that her spy had been outed.

She could tell Rica, pull her off the job, and send her home. That would protect Rica but it would also expose Graybel's role in sending a spy against the Colemans. One conversation between Jo and the chief and Rica was gone. Obvious.

On the other hand, if she was herself feeling busted and was willing to sacrifice her merc to save herself, she might not tell her at all. That would put Rica in danger and protect the chief. It would show that the chief was afraid of the Colemans, that she believed that Jo and Judith were not far from wielding the kind of power that could either give a job to, or take it away from, a regional chief.

What she did depended on how politic she was at heart and how duplicitous she was willing to be.

Should be interesting to watch. Would Rica stay, or would she leave?

And if she stayed, what was she going to do about her?

I had to come up with a good reason I could give Samm for wanting to join his army. If he asked how I'd found out that there was one, I'd mumble vaguely, say, as I'd said to Timmy, that I'd overheard something, and look like I didn't want to betray a confidence.

But my motive for joining had to sound viable. I didn't know whether the army job paid anything, but if it did, that would certainly give any server-singer a motive to play soldier. Better to sound practical than to babble about loyalty I'd had no time to feel.

He showed up at his poker table later that evening; he was there dealing when I finished my show.

"Hey, Samm." He looked up, those dark, sloping, Asian eyes a little tired but still shooting plenty of flash. The full lips smiled at me. I couldn't see any suspicion in his look. "Can I talk to you for a minute?"

He nodded, waving a dealer over from an empty blackjack table. I fell into step beside him; we walked toward the covering noise of the slots.

"What can I do for you, Rica?" The words were a sexual challenge. Tempting. Even more tempting because there was always that hint of laughing at himself. I liked the man. I wondered what he'd do if I responded to his dare.

"I've heard you have a military corps of some kind. Police? Mercs? I'm not sure. I'd like to find out more about it. See if it's something I might want to do." I shrugged self-deprecatingly. "Or if it's something I could do."

He gazed at a clanging slot. Not a blush, not a shift in the cast of his mouth or eyes. Nothing. He acted like he wasn't surprised I'd heard about it. Maybe it was less of a secret than I thought.

"Why would you want to?"

"For the money. I heard it paid."

"It does. But not a lot."

"For the excitement, too. I love singing, but sometimes I want to get out and do something more physical. More adventurous. I'd like to learn more about combat or protection or whatever it is you do." I tossed him a subtle smile. "It's a dangerous world."

"That it is. How'd you find out we had some troops?"

I shrugged again. "I would have been more surprised if you didn't. Especially after that merc attack. If that kind of thing happens often, you couldn't just sit still for it. You and the Colemans have a lot to protect." That sounded pretty good.

He studied my face. The scrutiny was almost intimidating. He knew I hadn't answered his question, and he was trying to make up his mind whether to challenge the omission or not. He decided not to.

"Tomorrow. I'll meet you at the back door at seven a.m. and take you to where we're training. You won't get much sleep tonight, after working until one." A quick flash of smile. I smiled back.

I nodded. "I'll meet you."

So I had to be taken to the site. Could be standard procedure with new members, trying to conceal the location from someone he didn't trust yet.

He turned back toward his table. "Sorry I missed your show tonight. Don't be late in the morning."

"I won't."

Up in my room, later, I left a message about the army for Newt, and called the chief. She answered.

"Something going on, Rica?" She sounded tense or irritated.

"I wanted you to know I'm about to join the Coleman army."

"You are?" A moment's silence. "That's good, Rica." Why did she keep saying my name that way? She sounded like she was rehearsing some kind of speech that was all bad news.

"Is there something wrong?" I asked. Again, she hesitated. The sys was flashing. Another message was coming through. It was Newt. He could wait.

"No, of course not. But I don't have to tell you—be careful. You're heading into dangerous territory now."

I'd been in dangerous territory all along. What was so different about now? "Do you know something I don't know?"

"No!" She almost barked. "Sorry, I have to go."

Should I be getting as twitchy as she sounded? I'd always trusted Helen Graybel and she'd never failed to pay, never lied to me that I knew of. But there had been a lot of strange little pieces of one-on-one that day. Jo's near-avoidance. Timmy's coolness and probing. Samm's apparently easy acceptance that I knew there was an army. Now this. None of it had to mean anything, no single piece was a strong indicator of trouble. But all together, at the very least, it hinted something was off. Maybe it had nothing to do with me. Maybe each of these people was having some kind of problem. The more I tried to think that was the case the more I called myself a liar.

So whatever each of them was doing, whatever each was thinking about me, I needed to look so innocent that mere suspicion would drift away. And hope there was nothing more to it than that. The chief's behavior worried me the most.

But it was the message from Newt that really stunned me.

"When Hannah comes back, you be ready to help her or I'm not paying you. And oh yes," he cackled, "you may have to talk her out of killing you, first. She doesn't like that you took her job."

When Hannah comes back? Killing me? I was in no mood to deal with his craziness. I called the chief again. She wasn't answering. I left a few words. "Possible you may be covering the whole tab now."

CHAPTER 28
OURS. THEIRS. MINE.

The chief called a couple of hours after I'd gone to bed.

"What did you mean by your message? About the tab?"

"Newt seems to be blaming me for Hannah leaving. Says she's going to kill me. I'm thinking he doesn't want to pay me."

"Didn't you say he told you to join the Coleman army? Did he recant on that?"

"No."

"I talked to him last night. He's still in. Just very, very burned. Panicky. He was relying on Hannah." She hesitated. Cleared her throat. "I think you should consider dropping this whole thing. Take the money you've made. Get out while you can. I would have no problem with that."

"Because of Hannah? Not a chance." I could handle that woman. My pride wouldn't let me run from her. Awfully nice of the chief, though. Too nice.

Again, there was that silence. "What are you not telling me, Graybel?"

"Just watch your backside."

"Even when you're behind me?"

"Yes." And she was gone.

Okay, a tox-bomb didn't have to fall on me. My best guess: the Colemans had found out something, she knew it, and she was afraid to cross them.

Yes. I was sure. That was the only conclusion I could come to, with the puzzle pieces glued. Glued by her obvious and sudden step-back. Come to think of it she had just given me another important bit of information. She'd told me not to trust her, which meant I never should, or would, again. My only consolation—it was three a.m. She wasn't sleeping too well.

So the people I was spying on knew more about me than was safe. One of my bosses wouldn't mind if I was murdered, and the other one was hiding dangerous information.

Usually, money bought at least a piece of my loyalty. Not this time. Loyalty is paid in loyalty. Money with treachery behind it earns nothing. Newt aside, I didn't believe any longer that the chief really wanted to know what Jo and Judith were up to.

I still had the attractive option of hopping into Electra and scooting away from this mess. But I felt nowhere near finished. Those Rockies wheeling around my turf had me scared to death, even more scared than I was of what the chief wasn't telling me. Redwood needed to stay the way it was. Independent from the Colemans, and from Rocky, too. I didn't think there was much I could do about Rocky with the Colemans standing in the middle doing god knew what, so I had to deal with them first.

If I did manage to get real evidence against them before I ran out of time, what would I do with what I learned? Take it to the Sierra Council? They could already be in the Coleman pocket, like the chief. Take it to Redwood? Redwood didn't have an army and none of the chiefs there had ever sent me to spy on another country. I'd need a lot of proof that there was a threat from Sierra before they'd even agree to be suspicious.

And I wasn't feeling too great about my skills as a merc. I'd turned in a miserable performance that day. Maybe the worst ever. But it was the only way I knew to stay alive.

And I wondered how alive I'd stay running around Tahoe with a target on my back.

Drew was dressing for the day's training. He was also stewing about Jo and Rica. He didn't hate either one of them. He was just upset. He'd been busy dealing with Lizzie and Billy and the Hannah issue, but the sight of Jo and Rica together had come back to haunt him at night, all week long.

Of course. It was going to be either Samm or Jo, if not both of them. Why had he ever thought she could be interested in him? He was just a kid to her. He'd been stupid, getting all messy. He knew what his mother would say—hell, he knew what Jo would say. "Find a nice girl your own age."

Shit. There were maybe five or six dozen girls anywhere close to his age living in and around Tahoe, and most of them were dumb. Or taken. Or not his type. He'd dated some of them and at best he'd been bored. Maybe what he needed to do was go someplace bigger. Just get the hell out of Tahoe. Sacramento was too small. San Francisco. Somewhere in the whole Bay Area there must be someone who would make him feel the way Rica did. He wasn't so sure he wanted to hang around anyway. Not sure his mother and Jo were right about things.

But if they succeeded, they'd own the Bay Area, too, along with the rest of Redwood. Not like he could get away from his family by heading west. His head was beginning to hurt.

East, then? No, certainly not to Rocky. North to Olympia? Seattle had a thousand people. That might work.

Oh, who was he kidding. Who'd watch out for Lizzie? He had a duty to his mother, too. And to Samm. And, he guessed, Jo. She kept telling him he was a born leader, a man who would govern, like his mother.

Maybe Rica would get tired of Jo, or Jo would get all tangled up in her head and forget about Rica. He hadn't seen them together since that night. Maybe in a couple of years, Rica would see him as a man. He sighed. A couple of years.

Running away like a dumb little kid . . . it still sounded appealing, he had to admit. But it wouldn't solve anything.

I was there, at the back door, at seven that morning. Samm showed up a couple of minutes later. He was wearing the clothing I'd seen him in when I'd spied on the training. Heavy denim pants, khaki work shirt, boots. Nothing like his casino-dandy clothes. I noticed that there were dark roots at the base of his blond stripes, and wondered what he'd look like if his hair grew out. I had for some reason always seen him as a blond man with olive skin, even though I knew it wasn't the case.

He looked me over. I was wearing tough, protective clothing, too. He nodded his approval. Did he think I'd come in a sequined dress? He put his arm around my shoulder and gave me a quick hug. Would he have done that if I were under suspicion? Maybe he was a better actor than I was.

Zack walked up, carrying a sack that clanked. Guns, probably. "We ready?"

"Drew's coming with us." And as he said it, Drew, his arm still wrapped in bandages but swinging freely, strode toward us. He was looking very serious. Older, somehow. He nodded.

"Good morning, Rica."

"Good morning, Drew." Wow. He was getting more formal with me all the time. I caught myself hoping it wouldn't be too long before we could be comfortable with each other again, and realized that might never happen. Now I also had to worry whether his stiffness came from his crush on me or from knowing that I was a spy.

Drew, Zack, and I went out the door after Samm, following him to his floater. Zack and Samm seemed cheerful, eager. Drew sat silently beside me, looking out the window.

"How's your arm, Drew?"

"Good." He seemed to gather himself up, make his shoulders

broader. "I was surprised when Samm said you'd be going with us today."

"Well, those Rockies . . . we're awfully close to their border here."

Zack looked back at us from his seat beside Samm. "At least that bunch that came to town is out of here, now."

I'd heard that from Fredo the day before. "Good thing," I said.

He nodded. "Frank told them if they talked, he'd take them to the border instead of kill them. So they talked."

"What'd they say?"

"All I heard is that they admitted they were spies and that Rocky was planning an invasion. And that it'll all be in the paper today." He grinned. "Iggy even interviewed Samm about it. Prominent citizen Samm Bakar . . ."

My stomach sank. Was this true? An invasion? Oh shit. Why did Zack look so cheerful about it?

"I don't understand why he'd let them go then," I said.

Drew shrugged. "We try not to kill people here." That was re-assuring. Was it true? And what did "try" mean? "Besides," Zack added, "trials cost money and take time and we never execute anyone without a trial."

Abruptly, then, Drew changed the subject.

"Isn't it going to be tough on you, Rica, doing this? You work so late every night."

"Waldo says he'll take me off the second shift in a couple of days. As soon as they can schedule the replacement. Then I'll be doing two shows and finishing earlier." Not much earlier. Probably by midnight.

Waldo had told me he'd found a server himself this time. Said it with a sneer. Guess he decided he didn't want to work with another one of Judith's choices, like me.

"Good. That's good." He turned to look out the window again.

"So, Jo. What are we going to do about our singing spy?" The sisters were having breakfast together in Judith's office. They'd talked only briefly the night before.

"Good question."

Judith shook her head, her striped curls bobbing. "The chief should tell her what you said."

Jo knew what Judith meant. They'd always thought Graybel was a good cop. If Rica was hers and Scorsi's, and she was sure she was, the decent thing for the chief to do was let Rica know the Colemans knew she was a spy. "If she tells her, she tells her. If Rica disappears, well, that's that." She didn't want her to leave.

"I'm not sure I'm thinking clearly enough about all this, Judith. I have to admit, I like Rica."

"I do, too, but I suspect you mean a different kind of 'like' than I do." Judith smiled. "Here's some clearer thinking, then: she's a merc. That means she's not ideologically opposed to what we're doing, she's just in it for the reals. Which means she can, possibly, be turned. A better solution than shooting her, given your feelings." Not so much a smile as a smirking challenge, Jo thought. The irritating big sister who peeked out from behind all those years from time to time.

"The hell with my feelings. She'd be an asset."

"You don't have to convince me."

"Samm says she came to him about joining the army. He took her with them today. I told him, spy or not, we don't have much hope of keeping the army a secret after Hannah, anyway. So I said let's give her a little field test as a soldier. Just don't give her a gun."

Judith laughed. "It might be best, for now, not to mention

any of this to the kids. They're brighter than the Scorsi brats, but they're still kids. Lizzie's been pretty emotional lately."

Lizzie, yes, but Drew? "I can't help but think Drew should know, Judith. He's taking on a lot of adult jobs these days. He seems to be friends with Rica, too."

"Well . . . I'll think about it." Judith tapped her index finger nail on the Blackjack snow globe. The white stuff swirled. "She's smart, Jo. Even if the chief says nothing, I think she's going to figure it out."

The ride in Samm's floater was a lot smoother than the one I'd taken in my own car to this same spot a week ago. Samm pulled into the trees. We all climbed out and he tarped the floater. I could see other cars tucked into the foliage here and there, some across the road. I caught myself before I started marching down the path. I wasn't supposed to know where I was going. Samm led the way, Zack after him, then Drew, then me, at the rear. Fitting behavior for a newcomer, bringing up the rear.

The few dozen people I'd seen in this clearing the last time were all there already—except for Hannah, of course, and a couple of dealers who showed up right behind us. Samm walked around, talking to people, slapping a few backs. Monte, looking pale and depressed, as usual, pawed through the bag of guns, as he had the first time, nodded something that looked like approval, and handed them back to Zack, who passed them out. He didn't give me one. Either guns had to be earned or word had been passed down that I couldn't be trusted with firepower. Then it occurred to me that this would be a really good way to get rid of a spy: an "accident" on the mock battlefield. I pushed that thought away. What was I going to do, spend the whole day hiding behind a tree?

Drew stood chatting with the two dealers. One of them, the

blond-and-red-striped young woman with swimmer's shoulders and an athletic stance—Emmy, that was her name—was looking at him, I thought, with something more than camaraderie. I was thinking about joining them when I noticed he seemed to be flirting back, and decided not to cramp his style. Although I thought she was a little old for him. She must have been twenty-five.

Zack was folding the now-empty weapons bag. I was about to approach him, see if I could get him into a chat, when Samm sauntered to the middle of the clearing and held up his hands.

"Let's start with a little easy hand-to-hand. Half an hour. Pick an opponent. After that, we'll do some shooting. Then we'll split into teams for the war games. I've got a detailed plan here for orange team. Black team will have to deal with that, find a way to outmaneuver them. So"—he grinned—"black will be competing against orange this time. And me. The scarves are in the hut. We'll pass them out after target practice."

He was just starting to say something about the hand-to-hand when the woods behind him erupted into screams, howls, yells, ululations—and a mob broke through into the clearing, men and women waving guns, knives, and clubs, and knocking down everyone in their path. At first I thought it might be a surprise part of Samm's game plan.

But it definitely was not. Near the front of this mob, or army, or whatever it was, Hannah Karlow ran, waving a gun in her left hand and a sword in her right, heading straight for Samm. Newt had said she was planning to kill me, but Samm seemed to be first on her list.

I ran toward Samm as he turned to face her, but veered off and looked for someone else to help when I saw that Zack was already at his side.

The blond dealer was standing wide-eyed near the hut, her focus shifting all over the place, a sword dangling from her limp hand. She looked confused, as I'd been for a moment, and she was acting like she thought this was, truly, a war game and nobody had given her the rules. An ugly muscle-bound hairball of a man was galloping right at her, in his hand a club studded with spikes.

Drew was running toward her, but he was farther away than I was.

"Emmy!" He was yelling. "Emmy! This is real! Run!" I heard gunshots, laser hisses, and one shot burned close by my right ear. Weaponless, I grabbed a spear I spotted leaning against a tree and aimed myself at the attacking toxie. I'd never held a spear in my hand before and I knew I couldn't throw one hard enough or accurately enough to kill him even at close range. So I ran between him and Emmy, hoping he'd be slower with that club than I was with the spear, and shoved it through his chest, blood gushing, drenching my right arm and shoulder.

The club came down when he did, the spikes tearing at the flesh of my left forearm. Too much blood. Way too much blood. But it was my left arm, so I could still fight.

I turned and saw one of our other dealers splayed in the choking dust. He was holding a laser pistol in what I could only assume, from the bullet hole in his forehead, was a dead hand. Now, there was a weapon I could use. I knelt, pried his fingers away, and swung around in a crouch. Where was that bitch Hannah? There, taking aim at someone—Zack? Drew? No—she was arcing the gun toward me! I squeezed my pistol's button just as someone crashed into me from behind. My aim was knocked to the side and I barely winged her right hand. Good enough to stop her for a minute anyway. She dropped to her knees, trying to grab her laser with her left. How good was she? Could she shoot with either hand?

I glanced behind me. Nothing to deal with there. The blow to my back had come from a grappling pair and Blackjack's guy, a cashier I recognized, name of Quinn, definitely had the upper hand, as well as a knife to the throat of a thick blond woman who looked like she'd spent her life swallowing too much alcohol and seeing too much ugliness.

I'd lost track of Samm—there he was. Crouched behind a shrub shooting at Hannah, who had recovered, scrambled to her feet, and was now firing back, left-handed, from behind a tree at the head of the trail from the road. A dozen dead lay sprawled on the ground, some ours, some theirs, and Hannah's remaining army was in retreat, falling back under a roaring charge and heavy fire from our troops, led by Zack, Drew, and Samm, and, now, Emmy, who had finally recognized that this was no game. Probably when she noticed the dead guys. I revised my estimate of her age downward. More like twenty-one.

I ran to join them, firing at everything human and semi-human that moved ahead of us. We were still taking fire ourselves. Samm, at my right, fell into the crackling brush at the edge of the trees with a wound to the leg. I heard a grunt and a cry somewhere near me on the left, but was too busy to look. We tore through the woods in pursuit and broke out onto the road. The enemy was already stirring up the brown dust with their escape cars.

Goddamn Hannah got away.

It took a while to find everyone in the woods and in the clearing who needed help or could be helped. We'd lost five soldiers, including poor Monte and the cashier whose pistol I'd taken. Hannah's troops had carried off all of theirs who were wounded, nothing left of them but the dead. No one to take prisoner. Emmy was laser-burned in the side, but would be okay. Samm's leg wound looked pretty bad. I saw a pool of vomit near his head. Zack tied a tourniquet around his thigh and Drew got through to the doctor on a small sys he was carrying—almost as small as mine. Doc was on his way to us now, he said. Drew had blood on the side of his head but didn't seem to notice. Several others were limping or bleeding or both. I was in the process of binding Emmy's wound when she looked at my arm and did a double take.

"Rica, your arm looks worse than my side." Bullshit, I thought, you were shot. I was just—

I glanced down at my arm and, like Emmy, looked again.

I wasn't thrilled with the sight. The forearm was swollen with bruises, deeply punctured, and the ugly merc had also managed in his death drop to inflict two four-inch gashes. And now that I was looking at them, the wounds were starting to hurt really badly.

For some reason the reality of those marks of battle focused me enough to make me realize where my mind had been through the fight.

Our troops. We lost five . . . The Enemy.

Unless Hannah was taking over, she was Newt's. These soldiers were his.

But even though he was supposedly still paying me, I clearly no longer thought of myself as his. I'd fought with Blackjack's army. I'd killed for them. I had blood all over me. Ours. Theirs. Mine.

CHAPTER 29
I GUESS YOU COULD CALL
IT BONDAGE

After he'd taken care of our most immediate medical needs, like bandages, pressure dressings, and painkillers, Doc followed us all back to the casino to finish the job. Samm couldn't drive his floater; his leg was bad, burned through at the calf by a laser. He was sweating with pain. Zack took the two of us back, along with Emmy, who offered to come along to help.

My arm throbbed. Doc had packed it tight and said he'd do the stitches in a cleaner environment. He ordered both Samm and me to go immediately to our rooms, Samm accompanied by Zack, Emmy taking care of me until he got to us.

I walked into Blackjack, woozy but upright; Emmy and Zack carried Samm. Doc came in right behind. I tried to avoid the eyes of the casino customers, not wanting to attract any questions because I didn't feel like giving answers. But the gasps and whispers followed us and I caught a few horrified stares and noticed several tourists heading for the doors. How many of these people had been around when the mercs invaded the place the week before? This could be one scare too many for them. Certainly the locals would be passing stories around within the hour.

Emmy was very nice to me, pushing the elevator button, asking me if it "hurt really bad." Yes, I said. It did. I was tempted to tough it out, bullshit a little, but I suddenly realized I didn't have the energy. I hadn't lost a lot of blood but my legs felt weak and I was considering the need to curl up on the floor.

In my room, she helped me take my half-shredded shirt off the rest of the way and wrapped a robe around my shoulders.

"Lie down. Right now."

I laughed. "Yes, ma'am."

She smiled back, barely. "Sorry. It makes me nervous and a little sick to see people get hurt."

"Won't that make it hard to be a soldier?" The second I asked that, I was sorry. After all, my problem with blood didn't exactly make it easy to be a merc. Yet I managed.

"No." She shook her head, hard, as if she were trying to convince herself. "It will not."

A protective wave swept over me. She was just a kid. Trying to do the right thing, or her version of it. Once again, it was clear the Colemans commanded a great deal of loyalty from some of their people. I'd been trying, and had so far failed, to find a reason why they shouldn't.

"Good for you. I'm sure you'll do fine." I realized then how patronizing that sounded but she just nodded and I let it go. I didn't think I could do better at the moment.

She brought me water and sat down in the chair beside the bed, silent, waiting with me. A few minutes later, there was a knock on the door. She went to open it and Jo strode in, nodding to Emmy and not stopping until she was standing right beside me, looking down, her eyes strafing my body in a disturbingly asexual inspection. Well, screw you, too, gorgeous.

"I heard you were wounded." She gazed at my bandaged arm. There was no need to answer; it certainly wasn't a question. "Is it bad?"

"No."

"Tell me the truth." Was she worried I wouldn't be able to work? Hoping I'd be incapacitated? "What exactly is wrong with it?"

"A few punctures and a couple of gashes."

She nodded. "What'd they hit you with?"

I described the club. There was no softness, no compassion in her face. She either made a habit of concealing emotion under difficult circumstances or she'd gotten over me really fast.

"How is Samm?" I asked.

"He's fine," she said, watching my reaction. Maybe she didn't want to admit the general was in trouble.

"No, he's not," I snapped. "I was there, remember? I came back here in the car with him. It's your turn to tell me the truth."

She studied my face for a moment, trying, I thought, to decide how to react to what—my insubordination?

A softening, then. She'd decided. "Not so good. It's a bad wound. Doc is working on him now. He'll be okay, but . . ." She shrugged. All the time she spoke, she watched me. Searching for some clue to my attitude. It wasn't hard for me to look upset about Samm, and that seemed to satisfy her.

Another knock on the door. I hoped it was Doc. I was ready to get past the stitching and whatever other misery he had in store for me. Again, Emmy went to open it. This time, Lizzie came rushing in, followed by the big limping black dog. Her cast was filthy. Lizzie's name was scrawled on the side of it in black paint or ink. The dog wagged a couple of times and dropped in a furry heap on the floor.

"Hey, Rica. I heard you got hurt, too. You okay?"

"Sure."

That satisfied her. She had other priorities. "Jo, Drew told me you were in here with Rica. I want to talk to you right now."

Jo's eyes slid to me, then back to Lizzie. There had been no trust in that look. "About what?"

"I'm seventeen. I'll be eighteen in a few months—"

"Eight months, Liz."

"So what?" Nyah nyah. She was still a kid, for sure. "This is happening right now and you know I'm strong enough and smart enough and all I need is the training, and . . ." Her tirade slowed, fizzled. "Please, Aunt Jo. I want to help. I want to fight. Emmy's doing it." She tossed a challenging look toward the young soldier.

"Emmy's twenty—what, Em?"

"Two." Emmy responded.

"She's twenty-two. Five years older than you."

"You can't make me sit around like some little kid. I just won't do it, Jo! You can't make me do it."

Jo sighed. She seemed trapped by the girl's adamancy. "Tell you what, honey. If your mother says you can start training—I didn't say fighting, just training—I'll go along with it. If Samm says it's okay."

The girl fell into the chair Emmy had vacated. The dog hauled herself to her feet, limped over, and dropped with a sigh beside Lizzie.

"She won't agree if you don't. You can't just bounce me back and forth that way." Wow. These Colemans learned stubborn and righteous at a young age. But even though Jo was taking Lizzie's demands seriously, she wasn't giving in.

"Talk to her, then come to me. And Samm."

"Can't talk to Samm. Doc wants him to sleep."

Jo gave Lizzie a warning look: stop arguing. The kid got up and left the room, trailed by the dog. I could understand their not wanting Lizzie to get involved in the army, but if things really began to explode, there wouldn't be a way to keep her out of it short of sending her away. Everyone would be in it one way or another. Just like I had been back at the clearing. And now there was the added threat of Rocky's invasion plans. I had to find out more about that.

Jo took the chair that first Emmy and then Liz had sat in.

"Emmy, could you go see how Samm is doing?" It was a fairly obvious ploy to get her out of the room, leaving us alone. I was feeling helpless. My arm weighed a hundred pounds and burned like laser-fire. My legs were weak. I couldn't even imagine standing up, let alone defending myself.

After Emmy had gone out, closing the door behind her, Jo contemplated her thumbs for a moment. When she raised her eyes to me again I thought I saw some sweetness in them, but I didn't know what to believe, what to feel, and her eyes iced over again almost immediately.

"When was the last time you talked to Chief Graybel, Rica?"

Oh, plague-shit. Did she really know I was working for the chief or was this a trick to get me to admit I was? I fast-played my conversation with Graybel the night before. Jo knew something. But I didn't know how much and it just wasn't in me to give up so fast.

"Chief Graybel?" Duh.

Jo smiled and shook her head. "Try again, Rica. When was the last time you talked to Newt Scorsi?"

Still not ready to quit. You show me yours, first, Jo-baby. "What's going on, Jo. What are you saying?"

"I know your reference from the Riverboat Queen was phony. I know you're a merc."

"I've done a lot of things for a living, Jo."

A flash of anger. "That may be, but at the least you're a liar, aren't you? Tell me who hired you. And tell me why you're here. Tell me all of it and do it right damned now. I don't have the time or the inclination to be patient with liars or traitors or game players."

I had to give her something. "Okay, I am a merc. I've known the chief for years. She just wanted me to spend some time here, see if there was any truth to the accusation that you or someone in your family killed Mayor Madera."

This time, her sigh was loud, an exasperated explosion of air. "The chief doesn't give a toxie's ass about Mayor Madera."

"And other things. The medicine shows. She wanted me to see who was behind them."

"What else?"

My arm was on fire and my head was pounding. My stomach was in knots. But adrenaline was making my legs feel stronger. The right one twitched. I considered jumping up, knocking her down with my good arm, running out the door, and getting the hell out of Tahoe. I tensed, and at that moment, someone knocked and Doc came strolling in. He stopped abruptly, seeing and feeling the tension.

"Can you give me a few more minutes, Doc?" Jo said.

He pursed his lips. Amazing to see someone hesitate even briefly over a request from Jo. He looked at my bandaged arm. Blood was showing through the white gauze. He nodded slowly but he didn't leave. Jo showed no impatience. She respected this man.

"How's the bleeding, Rica?"

I considered telling him I'd bleed to death if he didn't tend to my arm right that minute, but I thought Jo might order him to leave anyway. And there was no way to know how far his independence went. Might as well see it through with Jo.

"I'll be okay for a bit."

"Okay. I'll be back in five-ten minutes." He wasn't comfortable leaving, but he did it anyway.

After the door had closed behind him Jo started right in again.

"What else, Rica?"

And again I tensed, ready to take off. She noticed.

"Rica, forget it. I've got people out in the hall and you're not in perfect shape. Just settle down."

I did. A little. How many people? I could still . . .

"Here's how I see it happening, Rica. The chief wouldn't have hired you on her own." The chief had never, as far as I knew, been reluctant to use mercs to investigate problems. Which probably meant Jo thought she'd be reluctant to investigate problems that had to do with the Colemans. "And I don't believe Newt would have, either. So I think he demanded the chief check things out. Pushed her into it. He's got his own spies, but they're not worth much. Except for Hannah. She was pretty good. You, Rica, you're better."

"Thanks." Except that I'd gotten caught. That brought up deep questions about my skill. Still, not much point in hanging onto self-doubt. And there really wasn't much point, either, in making any more denials. If I had to crash past her and her guards at the door, I could do it somehow, even with one arm, I thought. And it wasn't like I was betraying people who hadn't betrayed me. So I started talking.

"Yes. Newt wants to find out what you're doing. And the chief contacted me. And I haven't told either one of them very much."

She sneered. Good. It was not attractive. I needed that.

"Oh, and why not?"

"Because I don't know very much yet." That was hard to admit, but might sound as true as it was. The rest just poured from me. I was tired and I wanted my arm sewed up and it didn't matter. She already had most of it figured out. "And because Newt is a—he's never trusted me, and he's an idiot. I don't like him, don't want to help him. The whole time I was fighting in that clearing today I kept thinking of his soldiers as 'the enemy.' And the chief? Is she the one who betrayed me?"

"No."

"But she knew you were at least suspicious, didn't she?"

"Yes."

"And she didn't tell me. Oh, she hinted around, suggested I

might want to leave town. But she didn't tell me." Odd how good it felt to be telling someone the truth. Even Jo. Or particularly Jo. I was a disgrace to my trade.

"You came here to spy on us, Rica. Why shouldn't I just kill you now?" She didn't sound as hard as she was trying to sound.

"Because I fought for you today. Because I'd rather be working for you." What I didn't add was that I wanted to know exactly what the Colemans had in mind for our corner of the world, for Gran and all her crazy friends. "Because I've been working for an asshole and a political weasel. I could leave, go home, let them flail around in their own mud, let you finish Newt off. Or I could pretend to still be working for Newt while I'm really working for you." More or less. Jo was smart. She would know I had my own reasons for supposedly turning. Would she care?

She laughed, loudly this time, truly amused. I hoped. "You just told me he doesn't trust you."

"But he still ordered me to join your army."

"He did?" I nodded. "Have you had a chance to report to him about it yet?"

"Look at me! Do you really think I've had a chance to do anything except get hurt?"

She crossed her legs and gazed out the window. Very casual. So in charge. So confident. "And the chief? What about her deal with Newt? What's she going to think when I let you hang around, and what's she going to tell him?"

"She wouldn't tell me I was in danger. I assume that's because she doesn't want to get on your bad side. Why would she tell Newt what was going on? Why would she do anything at all?"

"I think you're right about that. We're pretty sure the chief isn't going to tell him." She laughed. "And why should I trust you?"

You shouldn't. "Because I'm a merc without an employer. The chief betrayed me and I don't want to work for Newt. And because . . ." I thought about it. Because what? "I'm not sure why you're doing the things you're doing, I don't even know what it is you're doing, but I know you're decent to your people. You treat them well. That tells me something." It felt good to be able to string together a few truths.

"What is it you think we might be doing?"

"I don't know. Building power, I suppose."

"It's more than that, Rica. There's danger in the world, and it's growing here. Rocky sent spies; they want to invade and take over. Everything's changing, or on the verge of it. I just heard that there's a movement over in China toward reintegration, and rumors about Australia. If it's happening in other places, we can't fall behind. That's dangerous. And we can't let Rocky do it for us."

"China? That's a long way away." As far away as Stockholm. They'd been gobbling borders for a decade and we'd felt no ripples on this side of the world. Not yet, anyway.

"But a sign of change. And there are changes in Oceania, too." But signs don't mean reality. These were straw men. Excuses?

She'd said, "we can't fall behind here." So the Colemans really were trying to create a larger country. A much larger country. Because others were doing it. A country that could implode in bloody death . . . I realized I'd stopped breathing. I took a breath. She noticed, her eyes narrowing. I tried to calm myself. Chaos, balkanization. Those were good for me. Order was not. I could never make enough money as somebody's beat cop or acting or singing. I liked things the way they were.

"How are you planning to defend against the changes in other places?" This was not just a matter of defense. It was a matter of the Colemans grabbing Sierra and Redwood first.

She stood up. "I'm not ready to tell you that. I'm going to talk you over with Judith, with Samm. Meanwhile, consider yourself under house arrest." The look she gave me at that instant sent a rush of heat to my groin. "I guess you could call it bondage." A slow smile. I could feel the heat crawling up my chest, into my neck and face like one of Gran's hot flashes, way back when.

When she opened the door, Doc came in. they nodded to each other.

I had a lot to think about while he sewed me up.

CHAPTER 30
DEAD WATER LACED WITH INDUSTRIAL ACID

On her way out, Jo said something to someone outside the door, and Emmy came back in, a worry line between her brows, her blue eyes puzzled.

"Jo told me to search you for weapons, Rica, so . . ." Doc stepped away from the bed, only a slight lift of the eyebrows betraying his surprise. She frisked me and found the state-of-the-art laser in my boot. That left one in my car, one in the closet. Her mouth opened as if she wanted to say something, but she didn't. The doc didn't react at all; his eyebrows were back where they belonged. Like he was a million miles away. Maybe this was the way he handled being in the pay of the Colemans: removing himself from the scene emotionally in case something bad happened. He could also be hiding sympathy for me, and there might be some way I could use that.

As Emmy backed off, he returned to the bedside, shook two pills out of a little vial and told me to swallow them.

"For the pain."

Not a chance. The pain wasn't that bad and I didn't want to be doped. "No, thanks. I'll be okay—"

Emmy cut me off. "Jo said to be sure you take your pain pills."

"You heard her," Doc said. "Don't make me force-feed them to you." He smiled like he was kidding, but I didn't think he was. So much for any help from him.

I was hoping I'd convinced Jo I was on her side now, but I

wouldn't have blamed her if she thought I was nine-tenths medicine show. If she wanted me drugged I was more determined than ever to stay alert. Doc watched while I slipped the pills between my lips. I tucked them into my cheek. I'd spit them out when everyone went away.

Except that they started to dissolve almost immediately. They tasted like dead water laced with industrial acid. This job was cursed.

Now Emmy was moving about, opening drawers, patting the clothing inside. She found the only other weapon I'd hidden in my room, another laser. They'd probably want to search my car, too. Or try to. They'd have to break into it, first. I'd had it fitted with a super-lock, keyed to my handprint, that would give them some trouble. I could only hope they wouldn't wreck the car in the process. And if they did get in, they'd be disappointed. All they'd find would be a few more weapons, including my last laser, a few wallets with various amounts of cash, some dried food. A capsule player.

My sys was still hidden in those pants in my closet. It was no longer a secret that I had access to very nice tech, but I didn't want to lose the sys and, with it, any chance I had to call for help. She went to the closet, ran her hands along the clothing hanging there. Including the pants where I'd hidden the sys. She didn't find it, shut the closet door, looked under the bed, scowled, said "Excuse me," and went out again.

When the doctor finally left, many stitches later, I was alone in the room. I could hear my guards chatting with each other, shuffling around. Sitting, standing, shoving a chair back against the wall. All I heard were mumbles; I'd have to get up and listen at the door if I wanted to distinguish more than a word or two.

I felt pretty good. The pills had dulled the pain. I was stitched and bandaged and on the edge of starting to heal. The punctures hurt the worst. Especially the one near my elbow. Still, the joint was intact. I'd been lucky. I swung my legs over the edge of the bed. Oops. Dizzy.

I stood and tottered to the door, the sleeve the doc had slashed to the shoulder flapping around my arm. Steadying myself with a hand on the wall, I pressed my ear against the wood.

Emmy's voice. "Mumble how long we have to mumble."

A man I couldn't identify. One of the cashiers, maybe, I didn't remember his name. Oh yeah. Quinn. I'd seen him in the clearing during the battle. He answered, "Till someone else mumble mumble." Somebody sat down hard on a chair, scraping the leg against the floor.

"Why is she mumble?"

"Spy. That's what Zack says."

A surprised "Oh!" from Emmy.

"I don't get it," Quinn said. "She fought mumble."

"What else would a spy do?" Her words were loud and clear this time. She sounded angry. Hey, Emmy! Let's not forget that I saved your life!

I pulled the door open, not a thought in my head about what I'd do out there. I wanted to be gone, one way or another. Jo had drugged me and Emmy sounded like she might shoot me on sight. I'd fight my way past them. I'd make my stand in Redwood. I'd—what was I doing? They both jumped, he out of his chair, tipping it to the floor. Yes, it was Quinn, all right. Pale blond, almost white hair, streaked with bright pink. Fuzzy white eyebrows. About forty years old. He was scrambling to get upright again. I realized that he'd gotten blurry and that I was staring at him for no reason. I yanked my stuporous eyes away from him and toward Emmy, who was pulling a pistol out of the waistband of her pants.

She looked really burned, glaring at me, her lips tight. "Rica, you just go back in your room and go to bed. Doctor's orders." She pointed the gun at my midsection.

"Emmy . . ."

"You heard me, Rica. I don't want to hurt you." That was nice. I didn't want to hurt her, either, unless I had to, in which case . . .

Only not right now. A sudden wave of dizziness. Nausea. My head felt thick and full of lumpy pea soup, like the stuff I'd eaten at that motel in Nebraska, and my legs wobbled even when I was standing still.

"I'm supposed to be training my replacement in the restaurant." That was pathetic. They didn't say, oh, well, in that case, go ahead downstairs, Rica. Instead, silent, they watched me like I was melting on the floor. Another thought. "What time is it? I have to do a show tonight." I knew I wasn't making any sense but my mouth kept talking anyway. Hoping something would change, reality would shift and they'd let me stagger away.

They both looked at me like my mind was gone.

"It's just past noon," Quinn said. "I don't know if you'll be performing tonight," he added, reasonably, gently. Talking to a lunatic.

The pills that had dissolved in my mouth had left it feeling slick and nasty. It suddenly occurred to me that I'd left the room without my sys. How could I go anywhere without that?

No weapons, no brain, and body unstable. But I couldn't stay here, totally helpless. Everything in me, or what was left of me, rebelled at that helplessness. I staggered back into my room and closed the door, and went right for my sys.

The chief had betrayed me, but there wasn't anyone else I could call for help. I made it, slowly, to the closet, dug my sys out of the pants, and, closing myself in, putting two doors between me and my guards, called the chief. No answer.

"Get me the hell out of here, Graybel. I don't care how, as long as I'm alive. Wounded in battle with Scorsi forces today, drugged, weaponless. Confined to my room. Come and get me."

Even as I spoke the words, I doubted there was any point in saying them. She was afraid to cross the Colemans directly, maybe always had been. I suspected that she was listening to my message and deciding, right now, that it wouldn't be smart to help me. As for Newt, even if he still thought I was working for him he wouldn't do anything, either, no point in asking. I was no good to him if I left, and now I was a failure who needed help. I wouldn't find any there.

I dropped my sys into my pants pocket and forced my mind to focus on getting away. The window seemed to be out of the question. There was nothing like a fire escape and I'd never been able to get it open more than eight inches. I tried it again, though, heaving at it, stumbled over my own feet and fell to the floor. I could break it. Would the guards hear that? Did I have enough sheets and blankets and towels to make a three-story rope? And if I did, could I shimmy down the stupid thing with one good arm? After all, I was drugged past pain. The question then became, could I shimmy down the stupid thing without falling on my befuddled head? I figured my odds were fifty-fifty. That Jo would or would not decide to kill me, and that I would or would not fall on my head. Even if I got as far as my car, I'd have to avoid crashing into the nearest tree.

I didn't get a chance to try any of it. The door opened again and the Coleman sisters walked in, shutting it firmly behind them. I'd already been searched, so after a second's panic, I relaxed. They wouldn't do it again so they wouldn't find the sys in my pocket. Unless of course it buzzed. The panic came back. I really wasn't thinking clearly.

"How are you feeling, Rica?" Judith asked. She was carrying

a newspaper.

"Fine." I was still sitting on the floor near the window.

She laughed. "You look like hell."

"Thanks." What was this, some kind of softening-up torture?

"Here"—she reached down, took my good arm, and helped me to the bed, laying the paper beside me—"something to entertain you. You can read all about how the Rockies are planning to invade."

I glanced at the big black headline: Rocky Planning Conquest of Sierra and Redwood!

"Jo and I have been discussing your future." And whether I had one, I thought. "What were you getting paid for this invasion of our privacy?" What a quaint way to put it. I told her, adding a few hundred reals for good measure. She glanced at Jo and sat down in the bedside chair.

"Sounds a little high, Rica," Jo said, one eyebrow raised. Don't try to be sexy right now, Jo, I was thinking. It won't work. I shrugged, and felt it in my arm. I managed not to groan.

Jo was watching me. I didn't say anything. Judith didn't say anything. Finally, Jo spoke again. "We'll pay you that much and promise not to kill you for spying on us. All you have to do is work for us. Against Newt. Against Rocky. And you'll have to prove yourself, prove we can trust you. After all, you could take this offer to Newt and get even more from him."

"I doubt that," I said. "But you need to tell me: what are you after that I can help you get?" The bed was soft. The adrenaline my body had mustered to take me to the hallway, the closet, and the window had seeped away. I tried to raise my right foot. Nothing more than a twitch.

She laughed. "I'm not ready to lay out a master plan for you, Rica. You'll do whatever bits and pieces we need done. By the time you've proven yourself, and we trust you, you'll have figured out whatever you have to know." Judith nodded her approval of Jo's obfuscation.

"Prove myself how?"

"First of all, the easy part: who does Newt have inside Blackjack? You must know. Tell us. Second, tell us where his army trains. Or rather"—she tossed a sneer toward Judith—"his little band of grubby mercenaries. If you don't know, find out. We need to know their strengths and weaknesses and when they can be attacked, quietly, on their own ground, just like Hannah did to us. Beyond those two things, we're still working out how to use your services. We'll be watching everything you do and we'll see what you're not doing. So you can be sure that we'll figure it out soon enough if you're poisonous."

Damn Newt and his secrecy. I didn't have a lot to give them, even if I were sure I wanted to. I hesitated for only a second. I didn't want to be responsible for anyone's death, not even Bernard's, but I had to give Jo someone, and he was the only one I was sure about. Maybe she wouldn't kill him.

"The only one I know is Bernard, the change guy. Pale? Scared-looking?" Jo looked grim. "Newt used him as a messenger once, when I first arrived. I don't think he's much of a danger."

"Bernard, huh?" She shook her head. "I don't think he's dangerous either. Not any more. He quit right after Hannah left." Wonderful. The one name I had was useless. "That's it? You don't know about anyone else?" She didn't look like she believed me.

"Newt wouldn't tell me anything. Either he never trusts anyone or he doesn't trust me. I've told you that before." I was trying for strong, but wondered if I sounded whiny. "And I haven't seen any signs from anyone else." My head was pounding and my vision fogging again. I was falling miles lying down, spinning in my own head like a drunk.

"We need more. You need more. To protect yourself as well as the rest of us. You're absolutely sure you don't know anyone besides Bernard?"

"Absolutely sure." This was like one of those old psychological tests where they asked you the same question more than once to try to trip you up. "I only know two names. There was Hannah, and there was Bernard. I asked Newt and he wouldn't tell me, but I know there have to be others."

"Of course there are. And if that's all you can give us . . ." Jo squinted doubtfully at me.

"I'm sure you can find the rest of them if you really try to, Rica," Judith said. Her voice sounded ominous and gentle all at once.

Get the rest of the names and find out everything there was to know about Newt's army while I was pretending to be Newt's spy and getting inside the Coleman army and working at their casino. I could do that.

Apparently I'd said some of that out loud, because Judith responded, smiling that irritating wise smile.

"You'll be very busy, Rica, but you'll also be collecting two stacks of reals." She stood. "For now, I think you need a nap. We'll talk again later. Or Jo will talk with you."

"Nap? How do I know you won't kill me in my sleep?" I clamped my mouth shut; stomach acid was threatening to erupt. Lovely pills, Doc. Thanks.

Jo answered that. "Three reasons. At this point, you don't know anything the Scorsis don't already know about us. Or the chief. All you can do is run. You'll either do that or you won't. And we've decided that you could be an asset. You haven't exactly gone undetected here—sloppy on the backstory, Rica— but you're smart and Samm says you're a helluva fighter, saved some of our troops, did some damage."

"That's two reasons."

Jo rolled her eyes. "Drugged to the hair follicles and you're still pushing."

Judith smiled. "The third reason you'll know that we won't kill you, Rica, is this: the guards are gone. You're free to do whatever you want to do. Run back to Newt. Or run back to Redwood." I hated that image, me running, scampering like a scared bug. "Or you can stay here and recuperate and start work in a day or two spying on Newt. For us. Your choice." And spying on the Colemans from within, for myself.

I tried to get up, and managed to roll over. Again, Judith took my arm.

"The door," I said. She pulled me up. I nearly toppled. Jo put an arm around my waist and between them they got me there. I opened it and looked out. No one was there. The guards were gone.

They helped me back to bed. I fell on it with relief. "You should know," I said, "that both my guards know why they were guarding me. I heard Quinn tell Emmy I was a spy, that Zack told him."

Jo nodded. "We'll cover it. We'll take care of it. No one here is going to talk, or act like we don't trust you, like you're not one of us."

That was reassuring. Under this arrangement, I might not have the Colemans actively using me for target practice, but I could easily have Hannah and Newt trying to kill me.

The guards weren't out there. I could leave. But I couldn't keep my eyes open, couldn't even sit upright without help.

"Let me sleep on it." I think I said that, anyway.

I sank into the pillows. The two women turned and walked toward the door. I never saw them close it.

When I woke and looked at the clock, three hours had passed. The chief hadn't gotten back to me. I tried her again. No answer. I left another message. This one said, "No longer working for you. No longer want your help getting away." And then, for insurance: "Say nothing to Newt or the Colemans won't like you." I could feel my lip curl as I spoke.

The newspaper was lying beside me. I lifted it, glanced through the story about the Rockies. The headline pretty much told it. The main story was about a confession from two of the "recruiters" that the spying was a prelude to war and conquest of all the land to the Coast. My land. There was nothing about when that war would start. The scariest part of it: they bragged about a coalition of khakis, godders, and breeders.

Swinging my legs over the edge of the bed, I tested my stability. Hardly dizzy at all. I stood. Not bad. I sent a message to Gran.

"The Rockies who came here were arrested and confessed to being spies, in advance of war. They say Rocky is uniting their factions and planning an invasion, here and in Redwood. Talk to everyone you know who still has any power. Macris. Petra. Let them know they need to get their butts in gear, get people organized, make some plans, prepare to defend. I'll send more as I find it out."

I crossed the room to the door and opened it. There was a guard out there again, one of the change people. They'd lied to me.

"Hi," she said brightly, tossing her brown and black hair. "I see you're awake."

"Very clever," I grumped. "Why are you here?"

She laughed. "I was supposed to hang around and see if you needed anything. Judith wants you in her office as soon as you can walk okay. You going to need help getting there?"

"Absolutely not." Would she insist? Was she a guard in puppy disguise?

"Okay. You take care, then." She trotted off down the hall. I stared after her. For a flash, I thought again of leaving. This was my chance to run. I could go back to Redwood and help organize—oh, hell. No. I really couldn't. Rocky might be a danger, but so were the Colemans. Did I want Redwood overrun by Rockies or Sierrans? Was it going to come down to a choice?

I was beginning to think the Colemans really meant it. They wanted me working for them. And I wanted to work for the Colemans for more than one reason. I loved the torch-singing gig, I had to admit. Jo and Samm and Judith—three kinds of attraction. Not only that, but if it was true that someone had to keep my world safe from Jo, I was the only one in a position to do it. To paraphrase that Victorian admonition to women: I closed my eyes and thought of Redwood.

I'd made my decision, I just needed to accept it.

Picking my way carefully down the hall to the elevator, good hand brushing the wall, I wondered what Judith had in mind. Pushing the down-button I was glad, now, that Hannah had been so good at her fixer job.

The sling was yanking at my neck. I'd have to get that thing off as soon as possible.

CHAPTER 31
AMELIA WAS NOT A TOTAL IDIOT

Judith looked up at me and smiled. It seemed sincere. But of course she couldn't trust me yet, any more than I trusted her.

"Feeling better?"

"Yes, thanks." I sat in the guest chair, even though she hadn't invited me to. She didn't blink. She may have been powerful, but she was secure enough about it that she didn't demand obeisance.

The drugs had worn off; the arm had a long way to go. Sitting felt a lot better than standing. I still hadn't changed my shirt and wasn't looking forward to trying.

"Think you're up to running through a quick training with your restaurant replacement?" I wondered why Waldo couldn't take care of that, under the circumstances, but maybe it was because he wasn't so good with people. Once again I'd either spoken aloud or Judith had read my thoughts. She answered my question. "Waldo hired her and I want to be sure she's up to the job."

"Sure." My arm hurt. Badly. That hole below my elbow felt like the bubbling chem-pit I'd seen once in Middle. Doc had left me a packet of what he'd said were milder painkillers, but I'd stuck them in a drawer.

"Of course we won't expect you to go back to the restaurant until the arm is healed. Maybe you won't have to go back there at all, if things work out. Two shows a night and the work you do for us."

Sounded like heaven. I just nodded; I know I must have looked pleased, because I was. I'd still be very cautious about believing everything I heard, but it really did look like they were giving me a fair try.

"Speaking of that work I'm supposed to do for you, I don't see how I can do it without a weapon. You've taken mine." No need to mention the ones in my car.

She laughed. "Did you think we wouldn't check your car, Rica? Quite an arsenal you had in there. We took the guns, left the cash and other things. Here. You can have this one back." She reached into a desk drawer and pulled out the laser pistol Emmy had taken from me earlier.

"You're appropriating the others?"

"For now."

I wasn't happy about it and wasn't so sure I'd ever get them back. From what I'd seen, the Colemans could use all the good weapons they could find or steal.

"What about my car? Did you wreck it?"

Judith looked shocked. "Of course not! And we've already had the lock repaired." She changed the subject. "Do you think you could do an hour tonight in the lounge?"

"Yes. I think I could." I wanted to. Didn't want to lose my fan base. I thought I could sit and sing, with a minimum of arm movement. I had a shirt with big flowing sleeves. I'd get myself dressed somehow.

"Wonderful. Head on down to the restaurant now." She tapped a button on her desk sys. "Waldo, she's on her way."

She looked at me expectantly. I stood. I must have winced. Her gaze sharpened. "You sure you can do the show?"

"I'll get plenty of rest before then." I left her office and picked my way down the stairs from the mezzanine. Going up those stairs had hurt, going down made my head fuzzy. Still some drugs dancing in my brain. I never did understand how anyone could like that feeling.

Timmy came running to meet me in the restaurant. "Oh, Rica, my dear girl. I'm so sorry! How is your poor arm? I'm so sorry!" He was, indeed, very sorry. Timmy still cared about me, even though he probably knew by now that I was a Scorsi spy, exposed and turned. Drew and Lizzie talked to him freely, and I suspected everyone else did, too. He had to be one of the people Jo trusted to keep quiet about the whole thing now. He leaned closer and whispered, "And I'm glad that you're . . . um, you know. Now." I wasn't sure what he meant but he seemed to know he didn't have to be suspicious of me any more, for whatever reason.

"Thanks, Tim. I'm supposed to see Waldo?"

He scowled. "Oh yes, your replacement. They're in the kitchen. Be careful about going in there. No telling what awful sight you'll see." Now did that mean what I thought it did?

I knocked on the swinging kitchen door, heard a grunt and a grudging "Okay, come on in." I did that and there was Waldo, sitting on a worktable beside, very close beside, the woman from the medicine show. Not one of the two young ones, but the large fortyish one who'd done the can-can with the other two. She wasn't wearing the flowered dress and big floppy straw hat now, though. She was wearing the restaurant black and white, and no hat. Waldo spoke to me but his eyes stayed on her.

"Rica, this is Amelia. She's going to take your place serving." Amazing. But then, who wouldn't give up a life on the road for the divine Waldo?

Amelia giggled and blushed and cuddled close against Waldo's side. His nostrils flared. "Pleased to meet you, Rica," she said.

I silently thanked Timmy for warning me about walking right into the kitchen. It was bad enough seeing Waldo sitting there with a woman. I couldn't imagine what else they'd been doing. Well, I could, but I didn't want to.

Despite her very strange taste in men, Amelia was not a total idiot. I shadowed her, dropping into a chair now and then when standing was more than my arm or fuzzy brain could bear, for about half an hour, and she did just fine as a server. She was reasonably fast, only messed up one order, and flirted with everyone enough to get good tips.

"You're doing great, Amelia," I told her. "Just keep doing what you're doing." After Waldo finished seating a party of three, I went to him with the same news.

"Of course she's doing fine," he barked at me. "And no pesky split shifts to deal with, either. I don't need you any more, Rica."

Waldo was telling me to get lost. His face blurred as my mind focused on this perfect reality. They really were cutting me loose from the restaurant. I never had to work for Waldo again. A rush of warm pleasure, almost sexual, swept over me. I moved in close, nose to nose. He blanched and backed away, his ugly butt bumping into the host station. I stepped forward, following him, only inches away again. "Then everybody's happy, aren't we, Waldo?"

Drew didn't get it. He'd been told to keep an eye on Rica and he had. Then he'd seen Jo keeping more than an eye on her. Then he'd noticed that Jo was acting cold to her, even more suspicious, it looked like to him. And now, just as suddenly, his mother and his aunt were talking about her like she was their pal again. He'd even heard Jo mention, in passing, maybe, but it seemed significant, that she might make a good candidate. What was going on and why the hell didn't he know about it?

He decided to find Jo and make her tell him what was going on.

She wasn't in her office, and Mother's office was empty. He went back down the stairs again, heading for the cashier's cage. She might be there.

On the way, he was surprised to see that Emmy was setting up her blackjack table. She flashed him a smile.

"Didn't think you'd be working today, Emmy. How's your side?" He knew she'd been grazed, at least, and that Rica had probably saved her from something much worse.

"Hardly hurts. I'm just filling in for a couple of hours." She laughed. "Then I think I'll go to bed." What a pretty laugh she had. He'd never noticed that before. He smiled back at her. Nice. Really nice.

"Well, guess I'll see you around." That was just stupid, but she smiled and nodded. "Oh, you haven't seen Jo, have you?" She shook her head. A couple of players drifted up to the table. "Okay, well—" He started to turn away.

"See you around, Drew." Was she making fun of him? No. She wasn't. Her look was friendly and . . . warm, even.

Quinn was working the cashier's cage. He told Drew that Jo had cut him loose from Samm's hallway post for a couple hours; she was sitting at his bedside last time he'd seen her.

He heard them laughing from outside the door.

Samm was pale. A full plate of food sat untouched on his nightstand.

"Hey, Drew! Did you come to wipe the sick guy's brow?"

Drew ignored the snappish sound of Samm's words. "How you doing, Samm?"

"I'll do better when I can get out of this bed."

Jo sighed. "You did. You hopped across the room an hour ago, you damned fool."

Samm glared at her.

"He's a rotten patient," Jo said. Samm shrugged.

Drew turned to her. "Can I talk to you?"

"Sure."

"You don't have to get up and leave, Samm," he said with a little grin. "You can hear it."

"Thanks. Friend." A grudging half smile.

He jumped right in. No sense hesitating. "You're keeping something from me. About Rica. I want to know what it is."

Her eyes dropped to her lap. She fiddled with her thumbs. "Jo—"

"Okay. We're trying to keep this as small as possible, cut the leak factor. But you're right. You should know. You can't say anything to anyone, not even Lizzie."

He nodded, impatient. Not even to Lizzie. That was hard, but she was still a kid, after all. And a hothead. She might lose her temper, open her mouth.

Jo started slowly, talking about how she'd seen that Rica was smart, and knew how to fight, and so she wondered about her. Remember how she'd asked him to keep an eye on her? She set some people on her trail, looking into the story Rica'd told on her résumé, and discovered she wasn't who she said she was.

Drew listened, shocked but not speaking, not interrupting even for a question. For two days, Jo and his mother had known Rica was probably a merc and possibly a Scorsi spy, and had never told him. He had to bite back the anger, listening, wanting to hear it all.

They didn't completely trust Rica, couldn't now, not for a long time, but they wanted her to work for them and they were going to try it.

"She's a good fighter. That skirmish this morning proves it. And we can use smart, strong, charismatic people," Jo finished.

Yeah, Rica was all of those things. And more. To him, to Jo, to Samm.

He turned back to Samm. "You knew this?" Samm nodded. "And you took a chance on letting her into the army?"

"A calculated chance, Drew. Worth the gamble." Samm looked embarrassed, though. Jo had convinced him. Jo had forced him to keep the secret.

He stayed silent, letting the first angry words slide back down his throat, thinking, weighing. He let his eyes rest first on Samm's face, then on Jo's. He didn't hide the hurt and anger; he wanted them to see it and know he was dealing with it as an adult. Jo seemed embarrassed, too. Good. She should be. Treating him like a child.

Finally he spoke, softly. "I wish you'd seen fit to trust me with this information. Both of you. All three of you." He wanted them to know they'd lost his trust, and to worry that they'd lost it for good. "You should have told me." Good, that sounded strong, not whiny.

"Drew—" Jo began.

"I know your reasons. I've heard them. I know Scorsi can't find out she's turned. If she really has. I know all that. And I can understand your not wanting Liz to know. She's pretty fast-burning these days. But you're the one who's always saying I'm a born leader. That I'll have a big responsibility in the future of this family. I can fight for Blackjack and for the Colemans and take a seat on the Tahoe cabinet and contribute ideas in meetings and get involved in planning and actions and help you run candidates for office. I can do all those things."

"Yes, you—" Jo began.

He held up his hand. He'd never before in his life stopped Jo from speaking. It felt good. "But the truth is I can't. Not if I can't trust you. Not if I'm getting some of the information some of the time." It hurt so much to say that. It was all he could do to keep from crying. And he could tell by the look that passed between Samm and Jo that it hurt them, too. He was only sorry his mother wasn't there to share the pain.

★ ★ ★ ★ ★

Jo felt sick. The boy—no, he wasn't a boy any more. Drew was right. His eyes, locked on hers again, were bright with stifled tears. But she let hers come. They ran down her cheeks, dripped off her chin. She heard Samm groan. She didn't turn away from Drew, but held the look between them.

They had been wrong, she and Judith. So caught up in the intrigue they'd lost Drew's trust. So caught up in how smart they were they'd hurt and insulted one of the strongest members of their clan. Stupid. But they were all new to this, weren't they? Juggling so much . . . Excuses. Stupid. Useless. He should have been one of the first to know.

It hadn't even occurred to her, or to Judith, apparently, that this could hurt Drew, damage his trust so badly. Why hadn't they thought of that? She was so busy worrying about everything else. Monte's death on the field was the latest blow. She had to find someone else to run for the council in his place. The moment she thought of that, she chided herself. The last thing Drew needed to see right then was her loss of focus on him.

"We made a mistake, Drew. We were trying to be careful, make sure everything worked out. It was hard to figure out how to deal with it and I can see that we did the wrong thing." She knew what had to be done now. "You'll be all right for a while, Samm, won't you? I'll send Quinn or Andy back up in case you need anything." Samm shook his head. He knew perfectly well that Jo had scheduled what he called "twenty-four-hour nursemaid service." At least he wasn't objecting to it.

"Sure. I'll be fine."

She touched Drew's shoulder, gingerly. "Come on, Drew. Let's go see your mother and set this right. I can promise you right now I will trust you and confide in you completely, from this point on. Please forgive me."

He sighed. He didn't speak. She let him sit there, thinking

about it. His hesitation was real; Drew didn't play games like that.

Her tears had stopped, but they nearly started again when he said softly, "Okay. Let's go see her."

I asked Amelia to get me a sandwich and carried it to the elevator, knowing I'd better lie down for a while again until my show. On impulse, though, I stopped at Samm's room. I wanted to see how he was doing.

Andy, my accompanist, was sitting in the chair outside Samm's room, reading the latest issue of the *Sierra Star*.

"Guard duty?" I said. What for? Was Samm that hard to keep in his room?

Andy laughed. "Nurse duty. Jo wants to be sure that Samm has no excuse to get up. And don't worry, Quinn'll take over for me later. I hear we're doing a show." He glanced at my sling.

"Show must go on," I said. He groaned.

I knocked, and Samm's voice, strong enough, told me to come in. He looked surprised to see me—or was he afraid I'd come there to finish the job on him? I didn't know how much, or how little, to expect from any of them.

"Rica! How's your arm?"

"Okay. Your leg?"

"Better." I sat on the bedside chair. "You fought well, Rica. Saved some lives. Thank you."

"You're welcome." What else could I say? This felt awkward. "But that's my job now."

He laughed. "Just don't quit your night job."

I laughed with him. "I don't know how to take that."

"In all the best possible ways." He reached toward his nightstand for a glass of water that was sitting there. I got to it first and handed it to him, then raised my hand and brushed a yellow lock of hair out of his eyes.

He gave me a pale version of the flirtatious Samm smile. "Thanks, gorgeous. That Hannah, she's something to behold, isn't she?"

"Gorgeous yourself. It looked like she was going right for you from the start. Even if Newt does think she hates me."

"If that's what Newt thinks, watch your back. She's good at her work, too."

"I will. Anything I can get you before I go? Want a bite of my sandwich?"

He laughed again. "Nothing, thanks. Be careful, Rica, and get some rest." I stood, leaned over the bed, and kissed his damp forehead. Then I kissed his lips.

"You, too, Samm."

"I should get wounded more often." There was a hint of that old leer again. I was glad to see it.

As I made my way slowly back toward the elevator I was thinking it would be nice to be able to believe in these people, nice to think that their cause was my cause. And I couldn't.

I didn't care about saving Newt Scorsi's scrawny ass or doing a job for a traitorous chief, but there was no doubt that the Colemans were dangerous, and I suspected that the more I found out about them the more disturbing the knowledge would be.

No sense worrying about that yet. As Gran always said, "Sufficient unto the day is the evil thereof." I had no idea what or who she was quoting but I tried to keep those words in mind as much as I could.

Right now, on this day, it was all I could do to pretend I had moved completely to the Colemans' side of whatever war it was they were fighting. And sing in the lounge. And get healthy again.

Judith handled it well, of course. Once she got over looking startled that the problem had even arisen, she was honestly contrite and completely open, even if she kept her words short and to the point as always.

"I don't know how to explain it, Drew, other than to say we lost track of who was a grownup around here. This is new. You just grew up."

"You noticed," Drew muttered, teen-like.

"We've gotten into certain habits. I talk to Jo and Samm about everything. We talk to each other. While you and Liz were kids, well, you were kids. But you're not any more and our habits need to change. They will. Now, they have. Okay?"

He nodded. "Okay."

"So stick around for a minute, I'm going to lean on Jo. Maybe you can help me."

Uh oh. What now? Jo didn't feel like being leaned on. She had enough problems to solve.

Judith swung her chair around to face Jo directly. "We have to get this election campaign crap going."

Well, that was irritating. "I haven't been thinking about much of anything else, Judith."

"But now we've lost Monte and I don't think you've come up with the most obvious solution to that loss. If you had, I'd have heard about it." Drew was watching his mother, alert, sitting forward in his chair. Jo knew, suddenly, what was coming.

"Me."

Judith nodded. "You."

"I thought we'd agreed that I could do more in other ways."

"That's changed. We need a candidate for council to replace Monte." She looked down at her desk and sighed. When she looked up again her eyes were damp. She'd always liked Monte. They were old and good friends. "I need you to join me there."

Jo felt as if they were constantly reinventing government. Judith was president, she was secretary of state. Judith was the queen, Jo the prime minister. How was she supposed to be secretary of state and senator too? Their models would have to be older, it seemed. This new world, with so few people, demanded something else. Chieftain and village elders? In Tahoe, maybe. But what about all of Sierra? And ultimately, Sierra-Redwood, and . . .

Get the right laws passed, as council members, and they could set it up any way they wanted to.

"Jo?" Judith broke her train of thought. She looked up. Judith and Drew were watching her, Drew with a little smile.

"Oh, all right. Maybe Drew can help me write my speeches."

Judith laughed. "Zack's already conscripted him. Drew needs to focus on the mayor race and his own cabinet job. I thought you and I would work on our council race speeches together. How's the plan for the rally going?" Judith was actually enjoying this, Jo realized. She liked the idea of running for office. Maybe her enthusiasm would be contagious.

CHAPTER 32
THE PAINFUL HUG OF A HUGE MERC

"Newt, am I still working for you or not?"

He hesitated. "Yes."

I'd started to drift off, but when Newt's ugly face popped into my mind, it came with the thought that I needed to get some action going in his direction before I could rest. For a moment I wondered if I should use the room sys for everything now to keep the Colemans in the dark about the one I'd been hiding from them. I decided they'd probably guessed I had my own equipment and didn't much care that Emmy's search hadn't turned it up.

"Are you aware," I snarled at Scorsi, "of what happened at the Coleman war games today?"

"Yes."

"Are you aware that I was wounded?"

"No. How bad are your wounds?" I couldn't hear anything in his voice, not worry, not concern, not even pleasure.

"I'll be okay. I'm recuperating. Thanks for asking."

"Don't be snotty with me. It couldn't be helped. I heard you got in the way."

So he did know I was hurt. "Excuse me? I got in the way?" How much indignation could I pack into my voice? "I was doing what I was supposed to be doing, working for you, spying on the Coleman army. How can I do that and not get in the way? How about letting your people know they're not supposed to kill me?"

"They don't all know you're a spy. Do you want everyone knowing you're a spy?"

"Well, the thing is, I'm definitely operating at a disadvantage. You owe me more information. I want to know who else is working for you here so I can go to them for help if I need to. Or at least let them know we're on the same side. Because it certainly looks like I need to defend myself against your people as well as the Colemans."

He was silent. Thinking about it.

"How do I know I can trust you with their names?"

"Give them mine."

"Why should I do any of this?"

"Because Hannah's gone and I'm your best spy." I didn't even know if that was true, but it was all I had. He was silent again. Then:

"Okay. There are only two people working at Blackjack now. Bernard disappeared. I heard he got scared when the Colemans found out about Hannah. There's Yulie, he's a bartender." I knew which one he was, but he always looked angry so I'd never talked to him. Great spy, that no one talks to. He was new. He'd started work a few days after I did. "And Carla. She's a cashier. Part time."

"What's she look like?"

"Short, fat, green and black stripes."

I remembered her, barely. She was hardly ever around. If I were to believe him, Newt had less than a toehold at Blackjack. Well, names were names. I'd have to go with what I had.

"Thank you. I appreciate that. I'd also like to actually meet your soldiers, so maybe they won't attack me. Do they ever do any training? War games?"

"Every morning for an hour." They couldn't get much done in an hour. Run around a field. Punch each other a few times. Shoot targets.

"Where will they be tomorrow?"

"Look, I don't know if—" His protests were getting weaker and weaker. Time to attack full force.

"This is important, Newt. I can't keep operating in a vacuum. I'll end up being everyone's target. I'm not willing to do that. I just got badly wounded for you. As it is, I don't know why Hannah didn't shoot me. You said she wanted to."

"She had better targets."

Right. "She went for Samm. Was that on your orders or was it her own idea?"

"I didn't tell her not to," he muttered. Sounded like they both thought it was a good plan.

"Will she be at that practice tomorrow and is she still gunning for me?"

"No. She won't be there tomorrow. And I don't know if she's trying to kill you."

It was all I could do not to scream at him.

He had specifically said Hannah would not be there "tomorrow." That sounded like she was dashing in and out of town. Attack, run, hide—when would her next foray be? Where? Newt was trying to sound like he had no real control over her, like she did pretty much whatever she wanted whenever she wanted to, and kept her motives to herself. I didn't know how true that was. He had to be paying her. When he was angry at me, she was out to kill me. Now he wasn't so angry and she didn't seem to be out to kill me any more.

After a little more prodding, he told me where and when they'd be playing their stupid games the next morning. I'd do a one-hour show, get a long night's sleep, and drive out there early.

One more short call and I could finally nap.

"Yes, Rica?"

"Jo, I'm going to observe Newt's war games tomorrow."

"Good! Report to me the minute you get back."

"I will." I didn't have any choice. Medicine show indeed, and I was the juggler. For the next part, I had to clamp a hard hand down on my conscience. "I've got a couple more names for you. This may be all there is, but maybe not. Yulie. And Carla."

"Good thing you came through for us, Rica. Yulie's scheduled to help Samm tonight. I'll pull him off duty, keep him in the bar. Thanks."

Right before I went out on stage that night at nine, I noticed Drew arriving for the show, and Emmy was with him. They were holding hands. He had a girlfriend, or at least a date! That would take some of his attention off me. I was getting enough scrutiny from Colemans as it was. I waved to them, they waved back. What a cute pair they were. I hoped it would work out for them. It sometimes did, I thought with a pang.

The last time I'd seen Emmy she was searching my room. Had Drew told her I was really okay? They might be among the privileged few who knew I was now being given a once-in-a-lifetime chance to be a Coleman. Either that or Drew didn't know where else to go on a first date.

I'd gotten up from my last nap feeling stronger, but by the end of the hour I was ready to drop from my stool. The crowd wanted an encore, so I gave them one, but when they called out for yet one more, I pointed sadly to my sling and begged off. They seemed to understand. No one threw a drink at me.

After the show, Andy mentioned he had to relieve Quinn at Samm duty for a couple of hours. Despite my exhaustion, I stopped by with him. There was so much I needed to know about Samm and about his army if I was going to figure out what kind of threat and how much of a threat they represented to Redwood. Was there more to it than I knew? I needed answers for Gran's friends in Redwood, once I got them asking questions. Blackjack could be on the verge of recruiting hundreds of soldiers. They could be sending spies and maybe even recruiters into Redwood. Jo could be planning to send invaders into Rocky in a preemptive strike.

Andy checked to see if Samm was awake. He was; I could go in. His color was better. He gave me a sweet smile.

"How are you doing, Samm?"

"Good. How's your arm?"

"Still attached." We smiled at each other. I sat down. How to approach it? "I've been thinking a lot about that attack, Samm."

"Me too. What are you thinking?"

"I don't know what the point was. Do you think there was one?" I hoped that question would lead directly to his "educating" me. I thought he might enjoy doing that. "Were they just out to kill people? Especially you?"

"Could be. But I don't delude myself that I'm that indispensable, or that they think I am." I wasn't so sure. I thought he might be. He was a popular man, a stunningly attractive leader. "It's possible that they were trying to take the army down completely. Kill enough of us, enough of the top people, the loyal people, the strong fighters, and we'd be crippled. That would give Newt time to build himself up."

"A massacre?" Newt might think that way. But I couldn't get it out of my mind—that persistent vision of Hannah taking deliberate aim at Samm.

"Sure. Why not? We don't have a huge force." He grinned ruefully. A perfect opening.

"Well, what about that, Samm?" I stopped right there, open-ended. It wasn't hard to act like I was puzzled, at a loss, needing explanation. I was all of those things.

"What about what?" A little smile. He was pushing me to be more direct. Okay.

"How do we get bigger? Big enough get rid of the threat?"

"We're working on that, Rica. All our people are recruiting, all the time. I figure this time next year, we'll have hundreds." Hundreds? There probably weren't that many able-bodies in Tahoe. Which meant that they were going to go outside the town.

"And then what?"

"Then we protect ourselves. From Scorsi. From Rocky. If we're strong enough they won't attack at all."

I thought about it. I supposed there must have been more than one time in history when a country built a big military just to protect itself. In the Twentieth Century, there was a Cold War, everybody posturing. It wasn't as interesting as the World War; my knowledge of it was fuzzy. My memory was that one of the sides just collapsed after a while.

But really, I thought Samm's story was unlikely. You spend that much time, effort, money building an army, you're going to use it for more than parading back and forth at the border.

"Why not just get bigger, attack, and end the thing? Why sit around waiting to be attacked so you can defend yourself?" I wasn't having any trouble asking that question as if I meant it. If I'd been able to kill the merc before he had a chance to get close enough to me to bash my arm as he fell—the damned thing throbbed harder at the thought.

Samm shrugged. "Military aggression isn't always the most effective way." I wondered if he believed that. I thought the Colemans might.

"But Newt's got an army. And Rocky, what do they have? Do we know enough about them?"

"We always need to know more." An edge to his tone. He was looking tired, pale.

"I've talked Newt into letting me take a look at his training tomorrow morning."

His eyes got sharper again. "That's good! We've had some

intelligence, of course, but it's erratic, not sure how much we can trust—" He stopped and gave me a quick slider of a glance. He wasn't sure how much he could trust me, either, of course. "Let me know what you see."

"I will. I've promised to report to Jo, too." I wanted everything to be open, straightforward, so I could look and even feel somewhat honest.

Samm closed his eyes and sighed. He was worn out or trying to get rid of me. Either way, staying was not the best idea. I was pretty much done in, myself, and I had a date to visit the other side's war games the next morning.

The day was already warm, threatening to be hot and windy. The dust was blowing across the parking lot, swirling around the trees at the far end of the paving. I was stronger and in less pain than I'd been the night before but my body still had a few things to say about getting up so early.

There were new flyers on the fence this morning. Something about a political rally the next day.

I followed Newt's directions north and east until I came to a ruined log cabin flanked by tall firs, both of them blazed with an "S" about six feet up the trunk. For Scorsi, I guessed. Pulling behind the house, I parked near half a dozen other cars, none of them floaters, none of them Newt's, tarped and covered with branches.

No more than a couple of yards through the trees, I heard crashing, and a shout, and found myself wrapped in the painful hug of a huge merc. He was squeezing my wounded arm.

"Caught'cha, bitch! Hey, got a fucking spy!" He started dragging me through the trees toward a large clearing where a few other men stood peering at us.

"No! Newt knows I'm here. I work for him. Where is he?"

The grip on my elbow didn't loosen. It was all I could do to keep the tears back. He stank of stale sweat.

"On his way, Coleman bitch. But let's have some fun now." He was pressed against my back, rubbing himself on my rump. I could only be glad he didn't have a free hand.

The others were laughing, hard barking sounds, an excited giggle or two. One of them yelled, "Go, Ham!" I couldn't see the one who was holding me, but a few of the men looked familiar, faces I recalled from the raid on Blackjack and the attack on the Coleman training. Some mercs, some clearly bandits.

Ham was rubbing faster and beginning to grunt when Newt swaggered into the clearing. He stopped, stared, and grinned at me.

"Would you tell this toxbag to let go of me?" I screamed at him.

"Let her go, Ham." He sounded regretful.

Ham indeed. Hot dog, more like it. He gave me a couple more bumps, grunted louder, exhaled a blast of stinking breath, and let go. I spun around and swung at him, connecting with his left ear. He yowled and grabbed for me again.

"No, Ham." Newt sounded like he was talking to a half-trained dog. "Let her go." Ham stopped, glared at me, turned, and marched away to lean against a tree, sulking and petting his ear.

Right about then another half-dozen men arrived. More bandits. Ragged. Uncombed hair tied in various imaginative constructions. One of them had one arm and half a left ear. Several had visible scars that looked like the wounds had never seen a suture. I didn't recall seeing any of them before. New recruits?

Newt took me by the good arm and led me to a stump.

"Here. You can sit here and watch." He was still grinning.

Within ten minutes, the clearing was alive with a mixed bag of "soldiers." A few women, some of whom looked more like camp followers than fighters, soft, sullen, and slow-moving. A range of men from bandit-scum to hard, polished-looking mercs in leather and big boots, heads shaved or hair tied back neatly in pony tails. I had just counted three dozen when Newt ordered them into ranks, lined them up like he was going to march them all the way to Blackjack.

"Okay, you guys! Take a look at Rica over there on the stump." Their heads turned. "No matter where you see her or who she's with, leave her be. She's ours." Then he yelled over to me: "There, satisfied?" I nodded.

From that point on, he simply ignored me.

Samm's war games had looked pretty casual at the start, but had resolved into a capture-the-flag exercise that seemed to be heading in a reasonably war-like direction. Nobody had looked or acted like a rapist or a thug. But Newt's troops were just plain disorganized, and even more plainly a brutal bunch of dick-waving killers. Newt wouldn't have to pay them much. If they actually got a chance to do battle, they'd take their wages in loot, living and inanimate. I could smell their meanness and feel their eyes crawling around on my body. The raid on Blackjack had involved only a few of the mercs. The attack on Samm's war games had been sudden and over quickly. This was my first really good look at Newt's troops, in large numbers.

Once Newt cut them loose from their opening lineup, he strutted around looking thoughtful, occasionally yelling, posturing, while mercs clobbered bandits and bandits tripped over their own feet. A target-practice episode with old guns and a couple of laser pistols held together for a few minutes, and he had some impressive marksmen in the group, but when Newt strolled away to talk to a pair of mercs who were wrestling in the dirt, the target practice deteriorated into a wildly violent capture-the-pistol game. One bandit waded into the target practice waving a club and roaring, and effectively ended it.

Nothing but hand-to-hand from then on.

When the hour was over, Newt lined them up in their ranks again, a dusty crowd made up of equal numbers of bruised and bleeding bandits and chortling mercs.

Their mindless violence, along with their sheer incompetence and blundering aggression made them an incomprehensible and terrifying force. They could and would do a lot of damage. If they grew in number, and if they ever got to Redwood, they'd overrun it like the barbarian horde they were.

And I didn't think Newt's introduction would protect me even in the near future.

As wary as I was of the Colemans, I would do everything I could to help them stop this bunch and worry about the next step later.

Jo heard two quick taps on her office door. Rica strode in.

"I've been observing Newt's army. I'm ready to report."

Good. She looked stronger than she had the day before, but her injured arm was still in a sling and her eyes showed pain. Vulnerable. Appealing. Jo leaned back in her chair.

"Numbers?"

"Somewhere around forty. But Newt's not being fussy about his recruits. It could grow fast. I think you should stop them while you still can."

That didn't sound good. But the Colemans were recruiting faster, now, too. Newt wouldn't get ahead of them. And once the elections were won, she'd have power enough to stop anyone.

"I think we can keep up with them, Rica. We're working on it. What do you mean by 'not fussy?' "

Rica barely suppressed a shudder. "I won't insult animals by calling them brutes. A lot of them are just filthy bandits. I don't think any of them would hesitate to use babies as human shields."

An army of criminals. That was good to know. They'd be impulsive, ignore strategic orders, stop to rape someone when they should be cutting through the enemy's flank. She nodded, pleased. She was also pleased that a good look at Newt's army might have solidified Rica's loyalty to Blackjack.

"Thank you, Rica. Was Newt there?"

"Yes." She laughed. "He told them not to kill me, I was one of them. I don't know if they even heard him."

"Hannah?"

"No. She doesn't seem to be around."

"Okay. By the way, we've got a rally planned for tomorrow at the Lucky Buck Motel. In the afternoon, around noon."

Rica nodded. "I saw some flyers this morning, but I didn't take the time to read them."

"Political candidates. The ones we support. And Judith and I. We're both going to be running for the Sierra Council."

Rica looked surprised. Jo laughed to herself. I'm surprised too, Rica.

With only the slightest stab of guilt, Jo slid the *Sierra Star* across her desk.

"Did you get a chance to read this yesterday?"

"Yes," Rica said. "Godders, military, and breeders—they're all together now."

"Yes." At least that part was true, or true of the one group, anyway.

"Do you think Rocky really is planning to invade Sierra? They actually said that?"

A blip of conscience. "Yes. And Redwood too."

Rica nodded, silent.

"Will you come to the rally, Rica?" Jo wanted her to. She forced the lies to the back of her mind and looked into Rica's eyes. "I'd like it if you would."

Rica gazed back for a moment, smiling slightly. "I'll be there."

A few minutes later, someone knocked.

"Come in." Carla the cashier, one of the people Rica had identified as a Scorsi spy, walked hesitantly into the office, her eyes shifting above, below, and to both sides of Jo. She was holding a sack in her chubby hand.

"What can I do for you, Carla?" Besides put you out of your misery.

"Someone dropped this off and told me to deliver it to you." She dropped the bag on Jo's desk.

"Thank you. You can go now."

Carla fled. Jo sniffed at the bag. No offensive odors. She examined it for signs of blood. None. Probably not full of severed fingers. She opened it, carefully, and looked inside. Shredded paper. She dumped it out and looked at the biggest piece: "agrees to return to negotiations about the Gold Bug." She laughed out loud. The treaty. Newt had kept it a lot longer than she'd thought he would.

CHAPTER 33
SOME OF MY PEOPLE, WHO WERE HAVING A PICNIC

The courtyard at the Lucky Buck was already crowded when I got there. Must have been a hundred or more. They'd erected a stage at the far end, with a dais at the front and several chairs at the back. Some candidates were already seated—Judith, Doc, Andy, Timmy. Jo and Zack were standing to one side, talking, Drew and Emmy at the other. I had no idea what any of them were running for, except for Judith and Jo, and that was just because Jo had told me the day before.

I worked my way toward the stage, stopping next to Sheriff Frank, who nodded happily at me.

"Look back there," he said, jerking a thumb toward the entrance I'd just come through. I looked. In the time it had taken me to get up to Frank, the crowd had grown and was now spilling out into the street. "They're all real pissed off about Samm being hurt and Monte getting killed. Monte was a good guy, and Samm, everybody loves him. He's like a celebrity. He walks down the street . . ." Frank stopped, apparently overcome with the image of Samm's stardom.

Judith stood, walking slowly and majestically to the microphone at the dais. A solid burst of applause.

"First of all," she said. "I want to say a few words about Monte Accurso." There were a lot of rumbling murmurs and head shakes. "He was a good man, a good friend. We'll miss him. And everyone here knows why he died!" She chopped the top of the dais as if her hand were an ax. "He died because our neighbors, the Scorsis, ambushed a peaceful party of Blackjack employees and killed and wounded a dozen people." Boos. Hisses. "Does anyone think we'll let that stand?" She held up her arms, as if she were calling for her audience to rise and take revenge. The crowd began to yell, whistle, stamp their feet. The heat was building. Interesting that she called them neighbors, not rivals. And that she didn't say anything about anyone's army.

"We'll remember Monte. And my sister, Jo Coleman, will run for council in his place and in his name! Come up here, Jo."

Jo joined her sister at the dais. She got a lot of applause and cheers, overlap from the crowd's feelings about the murdered Monte. Nicely done.

"I'm going to let Jo tell you about some of the other candidates the All-Sierra party is running this year. Thanks for listening to me." The applause had dropped down a few notches toward enthusiasm and warmth now, as Judith strode back to her chair. The All-Sierra party, eh? Not a bad name.

Jo waited for the applause to die completely before she spoke. She didn't raise her hands or tell them to be quiet; she just stood, arms at her sides, looking out at them until they stopped. It worked really well.

"Let's start with what most of you already know. Zack Holmgren is running for mayor of Tahoe. Come on up, Zack!"

The crowd erupted again, cheers, whistles, shouts. I didn't know whether it was because they liked Zack, because they'd been so well warmed up, or because he was running for the big local office, but he was getting a great reception. He stood beside Jo.

"For cabinet," Jo said, "you all know Doc Mandell." Doc stood and waved his arms, marched up and stood next to Jo and Zack. Lots of applause. Everyone knew the town doctor. "Andy Caruso, bartender and piano man!" Same routine. Stand, wave the arms, join those at the dais. "Drew Coleman!" Drew forgot to wave his arms. "And Tim Shea, everyone's favorite waiter!" Tim trotted up, waving one hand, and took his place beside Drew, who clapped him on the shoulder

Zack took over. He introduced the council candidates—Judith, Jo, and Emmy. All of them waved at least one hand, and they all got a roar of approval. I noticed that Timmy moved over and gave Emmy the spot next to Drew.

Just at that moment, before the crowd had stopped hooting and yelling names, there was a dustup of some kind just beyond the entrance; Newt pushed his way through, point man in a group that included several of his mercs; a dozen or so ordinary-looking people, probably employees at Scorsi's Luck; and a guy who looked a little like Newt.

"Just a minute, there!" He was yelling. "I hear I've been accused of something and I want to set the record straight!" Oh, perfect. This was turning into quite a show. I had to stifle a smile.

Jo spoke into the mike. Sincere, calm, friendly. "Come on up, Newt. Everyone—let them through."

"That little twit better not start anything!" Frank was huffing and puffing. He pulled out his sys and started to head up toward the dais but Jo noticed him and waved him back. He practically screeched to a halt. "What the hell?" he muttered.

I'd placed myself next to Frank to make pals and do what mercs do—find out what people know and where they stand. Here was a good opportunity. "I think the Colemans can handle this, Frank. I know if they think there's going to be real trouble they'll call on you. They're smart and they trust you. Newt doesn't have a chance of convincing anyone he's innocent, and this little scene is just going to make the Colemans more popular. They can't lose." I wasn't so sure of that, but Jo and the rest of the All-Sierras seemed very calm. Zack was laughing.

Frank's scowl cleared and he looked at me gratefully. "Well, they know I'm here."

The crowd was shifting, some more reluctantly than others, letting Newt and his party work their way up to the stage. Jo stepped aside, letting Newt lean on the dais.

"I got some introductions to make here, too."

Jo nodded and stepped even farther back. She was smiling, acting like she'd planned the whole thing. At the very least, like she'd expected it. Or hoped for it. An actor to the core. A politician.

"I'm Newt Scorsi and I'm running for mayor of Tahoe!"

Applause, mostly from the people Newt had arrived with. A whistle or two. A "Yeah!"

"And this—" He reached down a hand and helped one of the men up beside him, the one that looked like Newt. Same big head and skinny neck. "This is my brother Larry Scorsi. He's running for the council. Some of you might know his son, Billy. He's a big hitter for the school ball team." Billy? He was more likely to use the bat on someone's head. "And this other guy here"—the merc I'd seen at the raid on Blackjack and on the posters jumped up beside Newt and Larry, making a loud thud when he hit the stage—"he's Abbo Swift, and he's running for council, too." More applause. "And I've got more good people coming along to be on the cabinet. Including"—he pointed at a fat bald man standing just below the dais and hauled him up—"including my older brother Carl. Some of you probably know his son Ky." They really were a lovely family. I sneaked a glance at Frank. He was fuming. Almost gritting his teeth.

Newt continued ranting. "The Scorsi party's got big plans for Tahoe, and for Sierra. We're the only ones who can protect this country from Rocky, The only ones strong enough and resolute and clear-seeing. And I resent what these Colemans here are saying about some ambush. I don't know what happened to

Monte, or Samm, or anyone else. I do know that a bunch of hoodlums from Blackjack attacked some of my people, who were having a picnic"—loud boos from the audience at that; I didn't know who they were booing, though—"and my people fought back. They got hurt, too, a lot of them. We lost some, too. But they started it!"

More boos, and some shouts of "You're lying, Newt."

"I don't like this," Frank said. "I got volunteers all through this audience and I can stop Newt and his garbage any time I want to. Run all their asses in."

"What will the Sierra law think about that? I mean . . ."

"You talking about Chief Graybel?" He laughed. "Not a factor."

The chief seemed to be disappearing, fading entirely out of relevance.

Jo stepped up to the mike now, forcing Newt to shift to the side. "Were you there, Newt?" she asked.

"No! I'm a busy man, don't go to picnics."

"Larry, were you there? Carl?"

Larry just stared at her. Same response from Carl.

"Abbo?"

"Bet your ass I was there! I saw her"—he pointed at me—"kill a man." Frank stepped closer to my side. "And he wasn't doing nothing!"

A rumble of doubt, until Emmy leaned into the dais, grabbed hold of the mike and yelled, "Nothing? He was trying to kill me! I was there. We were in a clearing and they came through the trees and attacked. I saw them kill Monte! I saw them wound Samm, laser-burn him in the leg, and I saw him fall. They invaded that clearing just like they've invaded this rally." Emmy had come a long way in the past two days. I'd never seen a grin that broad on Drew's face.

"Frank," Jo said. "Come on up here." He brightened. He was

needed. He hauled himself up on the stage.

"Tell this audience who attacked who, and who called you to report the violence. And who told you the Rockies were in town threatening people and causing problems."

Frank Holstein knew who his friends were. "Newt Scorsi's people attacked the Blackjack people. No question about it. And you, Jo, you called me to report it, just like you called to warn me that those Rockies were in town causing trouble." Had she? I doubted it. The town was small and the Rockies were obvious enough for even this sheriff to spot on the street.

Zack stepped up to the mike again. He glared at Newt and Larry, and pointed an accusing finger at Abbo, standing nearby.

"Yes, this man was in that clearing that day. I saw him there. I saw him waving a club and I saw the blood he spilled. Do you really want people like Newt Scorsi, and his brothers, and his mercenaries, and his toxie bandits protecting us from invasion by Rocky?" Newt's eyes were wide. He opened his mouth and shut it again. Larry tensed like he wanted to jump off the stage and run home. Abbo just scowled, looking confused and angry. He lunged at Zack and grabbed him by the throat, growling. Frank pulled his pistol and jabbed it into Abbo's neck. Emmy kicked his legs out from under him and he let go of Zack. Between the two of them, they got manacles around the merc's thick wrists. Frank's deputy showed up with a couple of volunteers and they took Abbo away.

Zack watched, a look of disgust on his face, rubbing his throat. He tried to speak but coughed instead. Jo shoved Newt entirely out of the way and took over, with Drew at her side.

Newt yelled at the crowd. "See that? They just arrested a man who was trying to defend—" The crowd began jeering and booing. They knew what they were seeing.

The people who had come with Newt were yelling, "Let him

speak!" but the hoots and hisses of all the others drowned them out.

"Get outta here, Newt!" Someone yelled. The crowd took up the chant.

Jo moved in fast and loud, Andy and Drew flanking her, shoving Newt and Larry and Carl toward the edge of the stage, where they teetered for a moment and jumped to the ground.

"First of all," she yelled, "what Tahoe needs is someone who can protect this town from Newt and his thugs!" Wow. This was exciting. The crowd screamed with joy. She was so good at this. "And while we're doing that, we'll protect Sierra from Rocky—"

Judith stepped up beside her and continued the oration. "And from their spies, and their terrorist godders, and their soldiers, and their breeders, all united now, all allied in a plot and a plan to invade our country, kill our people, destroy and conquer us. Newt Scorsi and his thugs can't protect our people. The All-Sierra party can and will!" Jo whispered something to Frank, who dropped down into the crowd beside me and glared at the little band of Newt supporters who had begun to work their way back toward the entrance. Then he swung on Newt and his brothers and gave them the same look. They stomped off after their friends.

I smiled at Frank. He looked smug and happy.

Jo picked up the speech again. "We all know the truth about Rocky now. We know we have to get strong and defend our borders. You've all read it in the *Sierra Star*." The crowd agreed noisily that they had, indeed, seen the story in the paper. "Those Rockies confessed. We know what they're up to."

Frank chuckled. "That sure worked. It was a great move, wasn't it? I tell you, we're unbeatable."

What did he mean? Move? I said it out loud.

"Which move are you talking about?" I smiled, going along with the joke, whatever it was.

"Making up that confession and putting it in the paper." He laughed. "That Jo, she's really something."

She'd lied to me. I'd barely had time to take that in when I heard Jo say, "We have a plan. Part of that plan is to build a strong alliance with our old friends in Redwood. Together, we can turn back the Rocky threat."

Alliance? Or conquest. What was she lying about now?

Rocky might not be planning to attack, but there was a nasty smell around its stronger presence. Newt's toxie army was growing, and there was an important election coming up. The Colemans looked like the only shield between Newt and Redwood, between Rocky and Redwood. What was I supposed to do when all the choices were bad?

Create another option that's all my own. If I could only figure out what that might be.

CHAPTER 34
WHAT'S GOING ON
DOWN THERE?

I stayed for the rest of it, long after I'd stopped listening to "This is a great candidate" and "Do you trust Newt Scorsi to protect us from Rockymountain?" I was busy obsessing about two things: Jo had lied to me; the Rockies never confessed, never said anything about a Rocky invasion. And the Colemans were campaigning for an "alliance" with Redwood that I was afraid was meant to be something more. Maybe the whole point of the Rocky lie was to grab Redwood. It was a rich country, rich in natural resources and in talent of every kind.

On the other hand, and there always seemed to be another hand in Tahoe, there was the nature of Rocky and its self-righteous intrusions.

So I waited, and thought about what to do next. First, I was going to challenge Jo on her lie. How she responded, how she acted, that would tell me a lot. I was supposed to be working with the Colemans. I had a right to ask some questions. Straightforward, honest, distressed, nothing to hide, unwilling to suspect her. A worried friend. I could do that. I was already partway there.

It took another hour for the rally to finally wind down, the crowd to drift away, the backslapping and jokes and earnest little chats to subside. The minute I saw Jo heading for her car, I fell in beside her.

"We need to talk," I said. She raised that damned eyebrow at me. "You lied to me. Outright lied. You said the Rockies confessed, said there was an invasion plan. There was no confession." Would she lie again, tell me the sheriff lied to her, she really believed it had happened?

She nodded, sighed. "Yeah. I did." She pointed to a bench behind the motel. We sat. "But it wasn't because I was lying specifically to you, Rica."

"What's that mean?" I kept the hurt-friend look on my face.

She chuckled. "It means, that's our story."

"And you didn't trust me enough to tell me the truth?"

She shook her pretty head. "Sweetie, no. I don't. Not yet. How'd you find out?" I wished she wouldn't talk to me that way. Sweetie indeed.

I stayed silent.

"Probably that moron Frank. Well, never mind. Now you know." She reached over and laid her hand on mine. It felt warm. I didn't pull away. "Look, Rica, it doesn't matter whether they actually said it or not. You know it's true. It's an invasion waiting to happen. As soon as they got their factions working together, in any way at all, the danger jumped tenfold. People need to be ready for that. We need to be prepared for it."

"So you made it all up, just so people would prepare?" How much more would she admit?

"And so we had a clear, strong issue for this election. We want our candidates to win. We want to protect Sierra, make it strong. Newt can't do that. Newt can't keep a spy on his side or control the people who stay with him."

She made it all sound so plausible, but I wished she hadn't used that word. Control. Was she controlling me?

"Did you kill them? The paper says they were taken to the border, but is that true? Why would you do that? Why turn them loose to cause more trouble?"

She frowned. "Kill them? No. We did kill one of them, on the street, before they were arrested, but he didn't leave us a choice.

351

We did take them to the border. We might regret doing it, but it was an opportunity to send them back with a message we wanted them to carry. We filled their little heads with exaggerations of our strength and warnings not to mess with us. They went back to Rocky thinking we have a real and ready army. They think Blackjack is in control and the citizens are behind us and any attempt to invade will be turned back and war will be carried right into the heart of Rocky."

"Maybe they just think you were bullshitting them."

"It's possible." She shrugged.

"I think it's more than possible."

"Even so, there's a difference between willingness to wage war and willingness to commit convenience killings. There are lines I don't want to cross."

I liked what I was hearing but she was a politician and she'd already lied to me once.

"Why didn't you just keep them locked up if you didn't want to kill them?"

She relaxed visibly. She seemed to feel as if she were on more solid ground. "We couldn't just keep them locked up without a trial. Word would get out. People wouldn't like it. It would make the citizens nervous to see candidates abusing people's rights. And we couldn't have a trial because we didn't want to give them a chance to defend themselves. We didn't want them convincing anyone they were just causie tourists. We didn't want doubt. Doubt is destructive. The slightest taste of it can destroy a political campaign."

"That sounds like another reason to avoid killing them. Besides reluctance to kill." I kept my tone neutral. Not just reluctance, on principle, to kill. Also reluctance to look bad in an election year if word of the murders got out.

She didn't deny it. She smiled. "Not a good time to take that kind of chance."

I stood up. "Thanks, Jo. Now I understand. I appreciate your honesty."

She gave me one of those soft smoldering looks she was so good at. "I'm sorry I didn't tell you sooner. I should have known a smart spy like you would find out." Flattery? Not a worthy move. It cleared my head again.

"One more thing, Jo."

Still sitting on the bench, she crossed her legs and cocked her head, waiting.

"When the chief and Newt first hired me to come here and spy on you, she said one of the crimes you were suspected of was skimming tax money."

"That kind of thing is hard to find out."

"People talk, sometimes." No one had to me, but that was beside the point. I tried to look like I knew more than I did. Maybe there was something here I could hold over her head. "You do seem to have a large supply of ready money."

"Not so large. You saw our weapons." True, but good guns weren't easy to find even with money.

"You're playing with me, Jo." She grinned and I could feel my face and neck flushing. "Are you skimming? Because that's okay with me."

"That's nice. But even if I were, I wouldn't admit it." She stood now, too. "Is that all you need?"

It was, for now.

I didn't stumble over the broken concrete on my way to my car, but it took all my concentration not to.

I drove to a side street, punched my sys alive, and called Gran. She answered.

"How are things, Rica?"

"Confusing, Gran. Here's what's going on. Those Rockies I told you confessed they were planning an invasion? They didn't confess. The whole story was a political maneuver by the Colemans."

"Those rascals." She laughed.

Rascals? She needed to take them more seriously than that. "To say the least, Gran. But the fact is, Rocky's got its people together and they are getting more aggressive. They are probably a danger, and a growing one. So lie or no lie, Redwood needs to be alert. And there's more."

"More?"

"Jo is talking about forming an alliance with Redwood to fight off Rocky."

"What kind of alliance?"

"That would be the question, wouldn't it? And another thing: I saw Scorsi's little army playing games yesterday. They're terrifying, they're growing, if they get loose, well, they're not going to stop at the border. I think the Colemans have to beat him down. Which means I'll have to help them. So it's a one-two-three Redwood has to worry about. A band of barbarians crossing the border from Sierra, the Colemans trying to get a wedge into Redwood, and Rocky aggression."

She whistled. "Damnedest thing. Well. Okay. I'll talk to my friends. It won't be easy getting them to listen, but I'll sure try."

"Tell them they need to put aside their wineglasses, step out of their hot tubs, and start thinking about covering the border and watching for Coleman-friendly politicians."

"Funny."

" 'Bye, Gran."

"I think," Jo said, "that Newt made enough of an ass of himself today to bring quite a few undecided votes to our side." She was very pleased with the way things had gone.

Zack grinned. "Judith says the next issue of the *Star* will have a front-page piece on the rally and Newt's party-crash."

"And his quick exit." They both laughed. Jo had made sure Iggy sent a Blackjack employee who also moonlighted as a reporter to cover the event. All it took was changing one of the full-page ads she'd already signed for into a double.

Jo and Zack were sitting up late in her office. Judith had already gone to bed; she rarely lasted much past midnight. They were talking about the rally and weighing the performances of the various candidates. They agreed that both Emmy and Tim had been charming, and attractive to the crowd, and that Emmy had been a powerful voice.

"Seems like a lot of people know Drew," Jo said.

Zach shrugged. "He's been all over this casino since he learned to walk. Sure they know him. And people trust him. He's a good kid."

"He's careful, he thinks before he acts, and they can tell. And he's not a kid any more, either."

They sat quietly for a moment, Jo congratulating herself on the way things were going, Zack scribbling ideas for campaign posters in a notepad resting on the arm of the couch. They were comfortable together. Jo was as sure of his loyalty as she was of Samm's. He'd been with the family for a dozen years. He worshiped Samm and his emotional attachment to the Colemans was very strong. Once, briefly, she'd wondered about his deep attachment to Samm, but he seemed to be working his way through a succession of women, just like Samm was.

The sys on her desk buzzed. The call was from a spy she'd all but lost track of, an elderly man who lived near the Rocky border.

"Yes?"

"Jo, bad news." He was an irritating man who had to lead up to everything dramatically; he couldn't seem to just spit it out.

"What is it, Fiedler?" She rolled her eyes at Zack, who grinned back at her. It was pretty late at night for one of his

"I've been thinking" calls.

"A gang of Rockies—big gang, several dozen, they took the border guard. They were all dressed like soldiers, in that brown color." Zack's eyes widened. He'd stopped scribbling and was focused entirely on the words coming out of the sys.

"What do you mean 'took' the border guard?"

"Not sure. Took her away or killed her, I got two different stories on that. But I think the guy who said they killed her is more reliable."

Shit. "Then what happened?"

"Then they just marched right into Sierra. Some of 'em had cars. Last they were seen they were heading due west."

Hardly a big enough group for an invading army. But they could do some damage.

"Are you sure?"

"Absolutely sure. I know something bad happened to the border guard and I know more than one person has seen them on the road."

"Anything else you know?"

"The ones who were walking, they were singing some kinda hallelujah song."

Double shit. Soldiers in vehicles, militant godders marching on the road to Tahoe. Well, they'd have to be dealt with. Idiots.

"Any possibility this is the lead bunch in a larger force?"

"Not that anyone's seen. No one else came through. That anyone saw, that is."

Zack interjected quickly: "Are they sticking to the road?"

"Up to an hour ago, that's where they were. Route 50. There could be more . . ."

Zack was on his feet.

"Anything else you can tell us?" Jo asked abruptly.

"I did hear that some of them took control of Colby, but I'm not sure. Maybe I'll hear more . . ." Colby was a tiny town, a half-dozen families, right near the border. Some victory. Was Rocky planning on conquering Sierra one village at a time? Just as likely this was one group of fools who decided to take expansion into their own hands and saw an easy victim.

Jo was standing, now, too. "Whatever you hear, even if you think it's meaningless, let me know immediately. Got that?"

"Yes, Jo."

The end light double-flashed.

"I'll report to Samm," Zack said. "Let him know we're mobilizing. I think we can at least double the army by everyone calling on some volunteers. Just in case there's more Rockies than we know about. People won't stand for this."

"No. Don't stop to report. Just get on it. Get out there, get everyone together, roll through the streets collecting volunteers. Find a way to commandeer every floater in Tahoe and anything else that runs. Head for Colby. Concentrate on Route 50 but look behind every tree, too. Tell Frank he has to stay in town; he might try to go.

"Meanwhile, I'll talk to Samm. I'll get his ideas, pass them on to you. And I'll send word through the casino that you need everyone who can fight." She had another thought. "Don't take anyone who was wounded badly enough in the Scorsi raid to be a drag on the others."

He nodded, already on his way through the door.

She followed him out and down the stairs. He ran for the back doors, she for the elevators.

Quinn the cashier was standing at the end of the hallway, looking out the window, when she got to Samm's room. It occurred to her to send him downstairs to find Zack and sign up, but Samm might need something. He was still weak and still too eager to do more than he should. And Quinn was a skinny little guy. Which made her think of Tim. Send Quinn and let Timmy take over at Samm's bedside? She brushed the thought away. By the time Timmy got himself up and got to the casino . . . Just let things stand for now. No time for this. What was wrong with her, anyway? She couldn't let herself get rattled by a raiding party. Why did she have such a bad feeling about this night?

Quinn hurried to her. "What's going on down there? Looks like a lot of people gathering. Zack's—"

"Some Rockies crossed the border, maybe killed the guard, maybe took a village. We don't know for sure, don't know how many, but we're sending the army and anyone else who'll go. Is Samm awake?"

Quinn flushed, his white eyebrows standing out like fuzzy chalk marks. "I should go!"

"Sorry. Need you here." He started to object. "Consider it an order from Zack," she barked. Enough of this crap. She pushed the door open. If Samm wasn't awake he soon would be. The noise coming from the parking lot would penetrate a more heavily drugged sleep than he was likely to be enjoying.

Sure enough, he was trying to get out of bed.

"Lie down, Samm."

"What's . . ." he waved a hand toward the window.

"That's what I'm here to tell you." She repeated what she'd just told Quinn, and emphasized that only a few dozen raiders had actually been seen.

Samm's face reddened with anger.

"Quinn!" he screamed.

Quinn came running in.

"Go down there and tell Zack I'm on my way. Then go get me some fucking crutches!"

"No, Samm!" Jo's voice rose to match his. "None of the wounded are going. Certainly not a man who can't walk."

He glared at her. "Then I'll walk! Quinn, forget the fucking crutches."

"You'll only slow them down. They'll be so busy taking care of you they won't be fighting. Use your damned head."

He shifted toward the edge of the bed, trying to stand, his face pale and shiny with sweat. "I'm fine. Much better. I'm in charge of this army, Jo, not you."

"Yeah. You are. And you're going to run it by sys. Open link to Zack." She retrieved his sys from the nightstand and dropped it in his lap. "I will not let you be a liability."

He tilted his head back and roared a string of curses they must have heard down in the parking lot. Then he fell against his pillows, tears running down his cheeks, and punched his sys.

"Zack?"

"I'm here, Samm."

"Keep it open. I'm going to be there, with you, by sys. Every minute!"

CHAPTER 35
WHAT ARE YOU DOING OUT HERE IN YOUR UNDERWEAR?

I was having trouble sleeping.

I knew a lot; I didn't know enough. I wanted to stay. I wanted to dash back to Redwood and actively, in person, rally its defenders.

Defenders? I had to laugh at the thought. Political dreamers like Macris and Petra and Gran? The social workers who tried so hard to get vax-dregs to the poor, and often failed? The cops who talked about bandit-bashing but managed to bash one out of twenty, if that? The collection of corrupt and silly and mostly harmless sheriffs who strutted around their territories and held meetings from time to time in San Francisco to talk about how good they were at keeping the peace and to eat a lot of sushi and pasta and dim sum? The chiefs who got drunk with the sheriffs or built moats around their own little castles? The council who had been talking for five years about creating some sort of guard that would protect the borders if they needed protecting?

What would happen to beautiful, incompetent, wonderfully disorganized Redwood if Rocky overran the West? The Colemans, attitude and all, were the only buffer I could hope for, and someone had to stop Newt's army of scum.

I didn't want to join a cause. Not the Colemans', not anyone's. It was all bullshit and I was a merc.

So were those tox-bags in Newt's army, but I'd always had some sense of decency even when I was working for thieves and petty tyrants. Hadn't I? Of course. I was not an indiscriminate killer, not just a merc, not even just a spy. There were too many things I cared about. Some of them even cared about me.

I hurled myself out of bed, jostling my punctured elbow. Even though Doc had told me to wear the sling for five days, I didn't need the stupid thing to pace around my room.

As I paced, I realized there seemed to be a hum of voices and vehicles coming from somewhere down below. Before I could get to the window, though—What was that? Horrible noises coming from the second floor?

Grabbing my pistol, I threw open the door. Someone shouting. Below and down the hall. The sound was coming up through the open window. Samm. Yelling. Something about fucking crutches?

I ran to the elevator, faster than the stairs, I reasoned, if it came soon enough. The doors opened instantly and I punched the button for the second floor. As I did that, I realized that I hadn't gotten dressed and was wearing nothing but a thin halter and skimpy pretty-much transparent underpants.

Quinn was sitting on a chair outside Samm's door. His eyes widened just a bit at the sight of me.

"Quinn? Is he okay?"

Quinn grimaced. "Yeah, just really burned because he can't go. Because of his leg."

"Go where?" As I said the words I remembered that before Samm had drowned everything else out, there had seemed to be activity down in the parking lot. I strode to the hall window and looked out.

There must have been fifty people down there, and more arriving. Even in the dim light of the lamps I could see that Zack stood in the middle of the crowd, and that Drew was handing out weapons.

I swung around. "Quinn, what's going on?"

"Border raid. Rockies. Sounds kind of bad."

I had to go. Why hadn't anyone told me? I was in their stupid army, too, after all. I was about to turn and go back to my room for my clothes when Jo marched out of Samm's apartment, scowling. The scowl turned to a flush. She took in my pistol, and then the rest of me.

"Rica? What are you doing out here in your underwear?" I was delighted, for once, that she was the one blushing.

"Why didn't anyone let me know?" I waved toward the window with my good arm.

"Because you can't go. You're wounded. You'll be a burden. Like Samm."

I stared at her. "Burden? That's ridiculous. It's just a little . . ."

"Major wound in the elbow. Just a little one of those. The only one-armed soldiers going are the ones who've been one-armed for years. Go back to bed. That's an order."

An order? An order? She must have noticed I wasn't taking that well.

"I said it's an order, soldier."

She was right. I was a soldier. In Samm's army. The army that was leaving without him. And, or so she thought, without me.

The business down in the parking lot was getting louder. I raised my voice. "How can I be kept informed?"

"If there's anything you need to know, Rica, I promise to tell you."

Suddenly, under her hot glare, I felt self-conscious and naked. I threw her a sarcastic salute and marched to the stairs. I didn't want to be standing there waiting for the elevator while she watched.

When I got to my room, I closed the door behind me and went directly to the windows overlooking the lot.

The crowd that was assembling was bigger than the one that

had shown up at the rally. Looked like close to a hundred people already and I could see a lot more coming on foot and by car, quite a few with floaters. Some were straining to hear Zack, who was yelling instructions through a bullhorn. Just as many were milling, talking or waving to each other, or trying to use a sys. Some of them never got out of their cars at all, which made sense to me. Someone must have heard Zack's orders, because they began consolidating, those without cars joining those who had them. At around two a.m., Zack handed the bullhorn to a woman with a noticeably crooked leg who supported herself with a single crutch. He climbed into a floater and pulled to the head of the line. They began to move out of the lot.

Stragglers continued to show up and I saw what the woman's job was. After the cavalcade had moved out of sight, she pointed to the road, explaining where the main group had gone, and telling them they could catch up if they hurried. I could hear some of her bullhorn-amplified instructions.

Before all the uproar, I had been considering taking one of the milder pain pills Doc had given me and getting some sleep. But that was out of the question now.

So was sitting around in my room waiting to hear about the battle.

The last of the would-be soldiers seemed to have gone. No one new had showed up for a while. The woman with the crooked leg stumped off to her very-old-model car, bullhorn tucked under her arm, and everything was quiet again.

I would wait another half hour, just to be safe. Then I'd set off in pursuit of the army pursuing the invaders. I might not be much use as a fighter, but I could still be a spy if I stayed out of sight and out of the way.

At just after three a.m., I threw on some pants and a shirt, tucked my laser pistol into my waistband, slid my arm into its sling, and headed for the elevator again. This time, though, the elevator button stayed dark when I punched it. I punched it again. Still dark. What the hell? No little lit-up arrows, either. The stupid thing was broken again. So Hannah was a lousy fixer, on top of everything else. I took the stairs. As I passed the second-floor landing and headed down toward one, a short, sharp cry of pain or fear, followed by a doggy whine, came through the landing door.

What now? I sprinted back up to the door, holding my bad arm close to my body, and shouldered through into the hallway.

Quinn was lying twisted on the floor, eyes wide, a laser burn through his forehead, blood trickling red into his white eyebrows. A few feet down the hall, Lizzie was standing over Owen the barker with the dog, Soldier.

She was waving a bloody fist, growling, "Did you kill him? Did you kill him?"

Owen was sitting on the floor, his back against the wall. His nose was bleeding; he was crying, tears flowing from his blind eyes, and moaning, "I'm sorry . . . I'm sorry . . ." Lizzie grabbed his shirt collar and shook him, demanding his gun. She had a knife in her hand now. I moved toward them and she glanced at me.

"Soldier," she said. "Soldier barked and we came out in the hall, and . . ." She swung back to Owen, clutching his collar tighter, choking him. He didn't struggle or argue, just moaned about how sorry he was. What was he sorry about? No weapon was anywhere in sight, and how could a blind man shoot a pistol, anyway?

But then I noticed that the door of Samm's apartment was open.

"Liz!" She turned toward me and saw where I was pointing.

"Samm!" she howled, letting go of Owen's collar. I dashed for the door and collided just inside with three bodies on their way back out. Billy Scorsi, Hannah, and cousin Ky. I grabbed for Billy. I was too late but Lizzie, right behind me, moved fast. He was down, blood spraying from his throat. Lizzie had used her knife.

I managed to catch hold of Hannah's gun hand with my one good one, saw her pistol skitter into the hall, and jerked her halfway to the floor before she chopped me away, aimed a kick at my sling and caught me in the hip, and bounced upright again. Lizzie jumped Ky, the dog hopping around them barking hysterically, snapping at Ky. Lizzie was roaring. Was she hurt? Hannah raised a short dagger. I kicked her in the head, hard, watched her drop and turned for a quick glance toward Liz, who'd been battling with Ky near the bedroom door. Ky was lying on the living room carpet, a bloodstain spreading on his chest; he looked stunned. Lizzie could have finished him off easily but she was ignoring him, keening, staring into the bedroom. I left Hannah on the floor, unconscious or dead, and dashed past Liz.

Samm was lying in his bed, a laser burn through his right eye, half a dozen knife wounds reddening the sheets. Lying in his own blood. Gone. In his own blood. I felt Lizzie grab me, clutching my shoulders so hard it hurt, the tremors of her body coursing into me through her hands.

I turned to hold her, as if I could still her shuddering, and saw Ky trying to stand up. Red rage all but blinding me, I hurled myself back through the door, tackled him, and aimed my pistol at his nose. Lizzie wrenched him away from me and began banging his head on the living room floor, over and over again. I pulled him back and began to hit him, hot tears running down my face, screaming with rage that burned my throat. I hit him until my fist gave out and my wounded arm dripped blood through its bandages. He was out again; another inert mass lying a few feet from Hannah.

It had all moved so quickly. Employees roused by the noise of the fight were showing up, half-dressed, running through the apartment door. First to arrive were Willa, the elderly cashier I'd met my first day at Blackjack, and one of the restaurant's day people, a new guy I'd never spoken to.

Lizzie took a sys from her pocket. "Jo . . ." she was saying.

But Jo was already there, racing past the bodies down and standing, heading for the door of Samm's room, the dog sticking close. I followed, all the way to the bed. She stood crouched unsteadily over him, reaching toward him but afraid, I thought, that she would hurt that wounded body, knowing he was dead but not knowing it, too. She reached out for Lizzie's hand and pulled her close. After a moment, Lizzie backed away.

In that same instant, I felt the pain of a dozen unhealed wounds, including a couple of new ones. The sling had been lost somewhere. My arm dropped to my side, a lump of agony.

I came up beside Jo, put my good arm around her, holding her up. She leaned into me, crying. We both were. I held her tight.

Then I heard that full, warm voice behind us, a roar of pain. "Oh god! Oh no!"

Judith had arrived. Willa reached for her, standing in the bedroom door, and tried to lead her to a chair. Judith wouldn't move. She was crying, too, but what I saw in her face wasn't just grief, it was an anger that twisted her soft features into a devil's rage.

Jo and Judith reached for each other and I reluctantly let my arm slide away from Jo.

The waiter was feeling for Samm's pulse. He shook his head and closed Samm's eyes. That was as near to a declaration of death as we'd get that night; I was sure that Doc was on his way to the border with the troops.

Jo had dropped into a bedside chair, speaking urgently into a sys, her voice hoarse and raw. Judith stood with her hand on

Jo's shoulder. No more crying for now. Action had to be taken.

It occurred to me then: the elevator. Hannah had disabled it. In the time between my first trip to the family floor, to see what Samm was yelling about, and my second, when I'd heard Lizzie's cry and the dog's whine.

Hannah had unfixed the elevator so that no pursuers could beat her to the first floor.

If Hannah wasn't dead she needed to be.

I heard a groan in the living room.

I stepped out again to see Ky holding his head, drooling blood and crying. But Hannah was gone.

CHAPTER 36
HOW MUCH COULD ELECTRA TAKE?

I left the Colemans to care for the Colemans. I didn't stop to tell Jo where I was going. Once she looked into the living room and saw that Hannah was missing, too, she'd figure it out.

My sling was lying crumpled near the door. I grabbed it up and stuck it in my pocket. Owen was still slumped in the hallway, only now one of the elderly janitors was standing over him with a gun that must have been as old as he was. Quinn's body was gone. I knew that unlike Hannah, he hadn't walked away.

I ran for the stairs and headed for my car.

That floater Newt had promised me—fat chance I'd ever see it—would have been faster than Electra, but maybe I could still catch Hannah. I had some idea of where she might be going.

My eyes were focused on the road but I couldn't get the Colemans out of my mind.

Their strongest people either dead or gone on the road to the border to fight Rockies.

Judith, a sister, almost a mother to Samm, her eyes covered by wide ring-laden hands, sobs shaking her big solid body. Tears I never expected to see on that strong, round face,

Jo, a sister, crumpled in a chair, talking into her sys, unable to move away from the bedside but struggling to organize, order, move her people where she needed them to be.

Lizzie, screaming, beating and kicking an unconscious killer.

Zack, a comrade. Hearing from a distance that his friend and commander was dead, driving toward a battle with troops that were now all his.

Drew. When and how would he hear about it? I'd seen the adulation in his eyes when he looked at Samm. He might not rage like Lizzie, but this would hurt him for the rest of his life.

And then there was me. I was just getting to know Samm. He had a wild edge I liked, a sweet smile, a ferocity and strength I admired. A secretiveness I wondered about sometimes. A touch of humor that made me think we could be friends. I pictured him laughing, dealing poker, and my eyes blurred. I squeezed them clear again. I was driving much too fast for tears.

The airport was easier to find a second time. Straight out of town on Stateline, northeast five miles. I followed the line of trees to the unmarked entrance, wondering how hard it would be to take off on the cracked and rubble-strewn tarmac I'd noticed that first time. Hannah was just learning to fly. Maybe she'd crash into a hangar or fail to clear the trees. That would be a shame. Side windows down, I pulled my laser out of my waistband, hoisted my wounded left arm up, stuck my hand out the window, and aimed straight ahead, ready for the first good shot. I knew I could shoot left-handed. I'd done it before. But every bump in the road sent pain screaming into my elbow. Doc had been right about five days in the sling, but almost-four would have to do.

I was going so fast I nearly ran over a foot-thick branch that had fallen across the entrance road. Zigzagging around it, tires spitting dirt and rock, I raced for the near runway. Because I could hear something, an engine starting up, behind the nearer of the two intact hangars. I kicked my speed up another three notches, flying down that runway so fast I almost expected to take off myself. There it was, the white Gullwing, swinging around, finding its position, pulling onto the bumpy tarmac dead ahead of me.

I heard the hiss of a laser; it melted a two-inch hole in my windshield and smoke puffed from Electra's passenger seat.

My turn, bitch. I steadied my arm and took aim. Zapped a wing, but not enough damage to stop her, I was sure. Fired again, missed. She was rolling fast now, the plane's engine humming. I kept after her, falling in behind, speeding up even more—how much could Electra take?—and firing again.

The plane jolted and jerked as the right wheel hit a big rock, shooting sparks. The wheel wobbled for a second but seemed to straighten itself. I fired at the open cockpit, but I couldn't see Hannah clearly. She was hunched down. I could only aim and hope for the best: a dead Hannah. Second best, a disabled Hannah. Third best, a disabled plane. But despite that wobble I thought I'd seen she was having no trouble keeping the Gullwing on a straight course; it started to lift. There was one more thing I could try, one more way to do some damage. Where was that storage niche again? I aimed for the fuselage behind the cockpit, fired again and kept firing until—got it! The safety parachute bay flapped open, the fabric lifting and snagging on a tree and ripping away from the plane. If she had trouble landing for any reason, the Gullwing wouldn't be able to float gently to earth.

As the plane rose into the air, banking and heading west, my car speeding behind and now below it, I took a couple more shots, one at the cockpit and one at her landing gear. Just as she rose out of laser range something dropped from the underside. I watched it come down, marking it with my eyes, and drove to the end of the runway. There it was, in the grass. That right landing-gear wheel.

I wondered if Hannah could set the plane down without it, and without the parachute. I hoped she couldn't. I hoped she flew until her fuel ran out, tried a belly flop into the ocean, split the Gullwing apart, and drowned. Better yet, got torn apart by sharks.

Chapter 37
Samm Would Be a Viking

Where was Lizzie?

Jo had seen her going into the living room a few minutes ago. She hadn't come back.

She wasn't there. Billy, dead eyes staring, lay in a wide puddle of blood that was leaching into the carpet. There couldn't have been any left inside him. Ky was bruised and bloodied, unconscious but alive. She yanked the curtain cords down and tied his hands and feet, tight, then pulled down a curtain and tied him to the couch. He needed a doctor but there wasn't one and the hell with him anyway.

Where was Hannah? Hadn't she been lying there, dead, just a few minutes ago? And what had happened to Rica? Where had Rica run off to? Was she with Hannah? Following Hannah? Running away? When would she be back? Would she be back? Jo hoped so.

Something caught in her throat. She coughed. Gagged. Oh, shit. She ran for the bathroom and knelt, losing her dinner, her lunch; would tomorrow's breakfast stay down? Who cared? She rinsed her mouth and wondered again where Rica had gone. And Lizzie. Where was Lizzie?

Jo thought about what she had to do next. She'd already rounded up the employees who were too lame or old to go with Zack and stationed an armed guard of sorts at the casino doors, in case Newt had more in mind than killing Samm. One of the guards was holding Owen until she could get to him and learn what he was moaning about.

Oh, yes. She should call Frank. Let him do his job.

He answered right away.

"Frank. Samm's dead." Her throat constricted on the word. He started babbling. "Shut up and listen. He was killed by Hannah and Ky Scorsi and Billy. They killed Quinn, too. Billy's dead. Hannah's missing. Ky's unconscious."

He said he'd be right there. Jo wandered back into the bedroom. She couldn't look at Samm this time. Judith was sitting in the chair next to the bed.

"Did Lizzie say where she was going?" Judith asked.

Jo shook her head. She needed to go look for her. Where? Maybe she'd just gone to her room, too flayed by grief to do anything else. But she doubted that. She buzzed the girl's sys. No answer.

She walked out into the hall again, thinking Lizzie might have magically reappeared. Quinn's body had been taken away. Owen raised his head and looked at her. She approached him. The man guarding him stepped back to give her room.

"Jo. I'm sorry. I'm sorry."

"Why? Sorry for what?" He couldn't have killed Quinn or anyone else.

He was sobbing. "I was afraid." She waited, lost. "Afraid that you and Samm would bring back the bad times. Newt said you would." Oh. Newt said she would. Did she have to know any more? "They picked me to help because I've been here so long, long enough to know when the halls are quiet. And to know where everybody's room is, pace by pace." He looked almost hopefully at Jo, as if his long-time status might save him. "There was only me to show them. And everybody left, so I told them it was quiet."

Show them. The blind man had diagrammed the second floor in his mind and guided them to Samm's room. Owen was a

Scorsi spy. She looked at him, his blind eyes raised toward her, begging.

"I'm so sorry. I was so afraid. Billy would have killed me, too."

He was a Scorsi spy and Rica hadn't named him. Had she not known, or was this all part of the plan? A man they didn't suspect led the killers to Samm's bedroom, and now Rica had run.

Jo stared down at him. She touched the pistol at her side. She pulled it out, aimed it at his head, right between those foggy, chemical-burned eyes. Of course he was afraid. The old days had done this to him.

It was the wrong thing to do, she knew. She might always regret it. There was no reason to spare him just because he'd been scarred inside and out a long time ago.

"Get out."

"Out?"

"Go away. Don't ever let me see you again."

He stumbled to his feet, hand reaching back to touch the wall, and felt his way to the stairway. She heard him fall once on the way down, scramble upright, and start down the stairs again.

The janitor who'd been his guard looked to Jo for instructions.

"Go down to the front doors and stand where you're needed."

Frank showed up with his deputy. Jo was glad Marty was with him. She had a lot more common sense than he did.

"You looked out the window, Jo?"

"Window?" What was he jabbering about now?

"Looks like a fire over at Scorsi's. I saw the smoke on my way here."

A fire at Scorsi's?

"Well. Guess we better clean things up, Marty," he told her, jerking his thumb toward Billy's body. "I'll help you get Ky into the car. You call Doc's nurse, take him over to the clinic, get him patched enough to go to jail."

Reluctantly, Jo objected. "Maybe he shouldn't be moved until the nurse sees him."

"You really want to keep him here?" She didn't. "He's okay. First the nurse, then we stick him in jail and keep him there until Doc can get a better look at him."

Without stopping to argue further, Frank and Marty hauled the now-conscious and sobbing Ky to the stairs. He didn't look so bad after all.

Frank came back, alone, a few minutes later.

"Where's Quinn?"

"We moved him downstairs and called his family."

Frank nodded. "Okay, then." He hoisted Billy's corpse onto his shoulder, smearing his pressed sky blue uniform with drying blood. "I tried to call Larry about his kid. Tried Newt and Carl and some of the others, too. Couldn't raise anyone over there. Guess they're busy. I'll go by and check on it."

"Good." Why was he bothering her with this?

"I suppose you want Samm to stay here, not go to the morgue or anything?"

"Of course!" she snapped.

She and Judith would talk about Samm. They would plan the cremation. A funeral pyre, like a Viking warrior. That was what he'd always said he wanted. Samm with his Asian eyes and dark hair. More like a samurai. What were samurai funerals like? She had no idea, and it didn't matter. Samm would be a Viking.

Her sys buzzed. It was Drew. His voice was hoarse.

"Zack told me about Samm."

"Yes."

He sniffed. Sighed. "I just wanted you to know that I know.

Is Mom okay?"

"She's okay."

"Lizzie?"

She hesitated. She had no idea about Lizzie. "She's okay."

"Oh, shit! Got to go!"

"Be careful." She didn't know whether he'd heard that or not.

Somehow they hadn't been paying enough attention to who came along for the battle. If anyone had noticed a dozen of Newt's finest driving toward the border, they'd ignored it.

Andy saw them first, while Drew was talking to Jo.

"Drew!" He pointed down the hill. A Rocky khaki-clad was on his knees, his head resting on a stump, and a big merc—oh, my god, it was the one Newt was running for council!—was standing over him, a couple of his buddies alongside, with a heavy sword in one hand and a laser pistol in the other. One of the buddies was Yulie, the bartender they'd just learned was a spy. He seemed very friendly with the other two. The lead merc raised his sword. No! Drew cut Jo off, pocketed his sys, and started running, screaming at them to stop.

The merc brought the sword down at the side of the Rocky's neck, a fountain of blood shot into the air, and his head tumbled to the ground. The killers, sprayed red by the murder, laughed, turned toward Drew, and began to run at him. In an instant, Andy was at his side shooting. They stood together and fired. The three mercs dropped. But before he and Andy could climb the hill again, shots from above crackled past them and they had to take cover behind a tumble of rocks.

Zack needed to know. They'd been trading information back and forth for hours. Drew punched his sys and Zack's voice, strained and half drowned out by screams and shouts, came through.

"Newt's mercs are here!" Drew yelled, thinking his own hoarse voice might be hard to hear in the melee. It had turned out that there were more than four dozen Rockies; they still didn't know how many, really. Zack's large force was spread thin, trying to push them back to the border, fighting to hold every hill, pursuing the ones who broke through and headed west, cutting their way through woods and down mountains, in twos and threes, to kill or capture them. A dozen Rockies and thirty defenders were shooting at each other across the top of this hill, the one that he and Andy were charged with holding onto. "And we've got a hard fight going."

His throat hurt from crying and screaming. When Zack had broken the news about Samm, he'd wanted to smash his sys and kill all the prisoners and race home to his family. But he couldn't do any of that. And he couldn't let Newt's toxies kill prisoners, either.

"Got it!" Zack responded. "I've already cut loose a dozen fighters to help you tie things down there. They should be five minutes away. I'm on the road right behind a carload of Newties heading for the border. We killed some, took some prisoner. Sending a few of them back toward you, too. They hit Colby. One rape, one murder, that's all I know."

Sport. Newt's men had joined the defensive army for the sport of it and for whatever they could steal, whoever they could rape along the way.

Zack finished with an order Drew was glad to hear. "As soon as you can, pull a couple dozen people away, leave someone else to deal with the prisoners, and head back to Blackjack."

Zack's dozen fighters arrived in two trucks and within forty-five minutes Drew's hill was secure, with only a few wounds suffered on his side. A half hour after that, a bus pulled up and three more of Zack's men, waving guns and yelling, tumbled four prisoners out the door. Not khakis. Drew recognized a couple of the scarred, hulking mercs who'd attacked Samm's soldiers during the war games and invaded Blackjack days before that.

They herded the new arrivals with the survivors of the battle and tied them all together in a small clearing. Growling mercs bound and linked to scared-looking khakis. They now had thirty-three prisoners. What the hell were they going to do with them? Zack didn't seem to be worrying about that, so maybe he shouldn't either.

Three cars came, carrying more soldiers. One of them jumped out and ran to Drew. "Zack says we're to go to Blackjack." Things were going well, obviously. They must be pretty close to mopping up if Zack could spare so many.

The troops were waiting. He put in his second call to Jo.

She sounded strong, ready for whatever news he had.

"Jo, we're heading back to help out there."

"Already?"

"The main group of Rockies was all clumped together. And Newt's mercs, quite a lot of them, they showed up and they're causing trouble." That was putting it mildly. "But we're doing fine. Still fighting in Colby, lost a few, got some wounded. Zack's leading a group all the way to the border, chasing some of Newt's trash and just to be sure nothing else is going on. He's already got people scavenging for Rockies and Newties in the woods and on the trails. He's going to round back this way and re-collect his main force as he goes. We've got prisoners here. Three dozen. I don't know if there are more somewhere else. Zack says we need to interrogate them. He'll be bringing them back to town later. Andy and I'll be sending our cars back with just a driver to help transport them."

"The jail won't hold them!"

"He said we'd make do. He said not to worry about it."

"Okay." Jo sounded doubtful.

"Expect us within two hours. I'm bringing twenty or thirty or so, depending on how many we need to watch the prisoners here and finish up the fighting if there's some on the way."

"Great work, Drew. We'll watch out for things here in the meantime."

"Jo—" he gulped back the tears, wanting to be as strong as she sounded. "You just hang on."

"You too, love."

It was probably good news that so many of Newt's people had run off for the border, hard as that made it for the forces there. It left fewer of them in town to attack Blackjack. Maybe he'd only wanted to kill Samm, cut off the Coleman's strong arms. But maybe he'd planned more and his plans hadn't worked out.

Judith had gone to lie down. Jo was sitting in her favorite chair, in her own living room. Her sys buzzed again. Frank.

"I've got Lizzie. I'm bringing her home."

"Lizzie? Where was she?"

"Scorsi's Luck. She torched it. She yelled 'fire' in the front door, people started running out, and then she ran back and lit the fire she'd laid along the rear wall. I found her hiding nearby with a gun in her hand watching the folks at Scorsi's go nuts." He chuckled.

Well, at least the kid had warned the patrons. She wasn't completely spots.

Frank went on. "Everybody over there has been pretty busy trying to put out that fire." He laughed. "I still got Billy's body in the car."

Gruesome. He was just a kid. A murdering bastard of a kid, but . . .

If Newt had been planning to attack Blackjack, he must have gone apoplectic when he discovered that not only did he have no troops, he had a fire to deal with. She loved the idea of Lizzie's fire diverting a raid, even if it was no more than possibility.

She was feeling calmer, now. Less likely to burst into tears, or start trembling, or vomiting, or kill someone. Maybe it was Lizzie's insane—brave?—act of vengeance that was settling her down. Or Drew's message of victory on the battlefield.

"Bring Lizzie right to my apartment, Frank."

"Will do."

"How long do you think it will take you to investigate Samm's murder?"

"Investigate?"

"Question Ky. Question Newt, Larry, the whole bunch. Find someone alive and present who was behind it. You don't think those two boys and Hannah did it on their own, do you? Don't you think Newt was planning to do something more when the casino went up in flames?" Was she going to have to write him the whole story?

"Oh, right. Of course."

"And then there's that information we got for you about who killed Madera. Roll it all up into a nice ball, Frank. A plot to murder Samm and attack Blackjack. Lizzie, a hero. See what you can do." Yes, her mind was definitely working again. She would spin this thing all the way out the door and down the street and up Newt Scorsi's ass.

By the time they'd finished their message, he was bringing Liz in the door of Jo's apartment. The kid looked defiant.

"Thanks, Frank, now go deliver your body. Lizzie, let's talk." Frank left; Lizzie sat down on the edge of the couch.

"They deserved it, Jo. I wanted them gone. No more Scorsis. Just gone!"

"You could have gotten killed. Arrested for arson."

"Frank wouldn't hold me. And sometimes you just don't think about getting killed. All I could think about was Samm."

True.

"You shouldn't have done it, Lizzie, but the fact is, you may have kept us from more attacks, more killings."

Lizzie's face brightened.

"I said may."

She smiled.

"What I'd really like you to do now is go to your mother. See how she is. Then go to your room. Some of the troops are coming back to protect Blackjack. You can join them when they get here."

Lizzie jumped up, ran to Jo, wrapped her arms around her, and squeezed so hard Jo thought her ribs would crack. Then she ran out the door.

No, the girl wasn't completely spotty. She'd be all right. Jo walked to the living room window of her corner suite. She watched smoke drifting away from Scorsi's Luck and looked out on the scattered lights of the strip, dimmed by the first pink light of dawn.

A dark green Electra was rolling slowly into the west driveway. Jo moved back to the bedroom to watch it pull into the parking lot.

Rica stepped out of the car. There, passing under a light. The auburn hair. She was walking so slowly, her head down. Where had she been? But she was back. Jo felt relieved and wasn't sure why. She needed to ask her about Owen in a while.

CHAPTER 38
I THINK YOU'RE NOT THERE

Well, I'd tried, but Hannah was gone and I couldn't be sure she would die. Funny, wasn't it, how thinking "I'd tried" never made anything better. Not for me, anyway. Samm dead. Was Jo broken? I didn't think that was possible. Judith? No. They'd recover. They'd all recover and Zack would be the new general.

Lizzie would either be part of the army or running it, someday, when she got things a little more under control. Or she'd be a really dangerous merc. And Drew would be running the country and worrying about his sister. A long time from now. What would I be doing then?

Drained, sick, my insides numb, I felt tears starting and stopping and drying and impossible to call up again.

There were employees watching the locked doors of the casino, several with weapons. Pistols. Knives. The janitor who'd been guarding Owen let me in.

"The army's coming back, soon," he said. "They won. I heard they're bringing prisoners."

One battle down, how many to go?

"I saw smoke at Scorsi's. Do you know what that was about?"

He laughed. "Young Lizzie. She set the place on fire."

Scary kid. I felt myself smile. I wanted to get to know Lizzie better.

"Owen?"

The man looked at the ground. "He brought the killers to Samm. He was a spy."

Oh, god. Newt must have planned to use him, kept him as a deadly secret from me. Jo would want to talk to me about that, I was sure. Would she blame me for being part of Samm's death? I didn't think I could stand that.

Leaving one light on like a signal to Samm ascending to a heaven I didn't believe in, I threw myself down on my bed. Stood. Fumbled in the drawer for my sys. I needed to talk to someone. Not Gran. I wanted to talk to Sylvia.

I began the message, watching the words float in the air.

"I'm surrounded by grief tonight. A good soldier is dead. A killer got away. One of them, anyway. The grief of his family, and I grieve for him, too, brings up all the loss I've ever had, the deaths and disappearances and the blunders and the cruelties and the defections.

"Is there really nothing missing from your life, as you once said? Such an odd, cold way to say it. As if it were some facile lesson you learned from him, from The Simpleton. The Guy of Glib and Brainless Words. The Cock of Conventional Wisdom. He said it, didn't he. And I'll bet he also said, 'Don't answer her. It's better that way.' Or maybe you said it all by yourself. It's better that way. Better than what? How can there be nothing missing from your life when you're missing from mine? Is that just my lunatic ego talking or is there some natural balance you're defying?

"Are you lying or do you actually discard bleeding pieces of your life? Are you lying? Or are you really just not there?

"I go to you, sometimes, at night, when I look at the sky and imagine East. I can see you lying in your bed and I touch you. Do you feel it? I think you do.

"So are you lying? Or am I making it all up and you're just not there?

"Why am I sending messages to a woman who isn't there?

"I think you're lying.

"I think you're not there."

I stopped, staring at the last words, "not there," as they formed and hung in the air, bright against the one-lamp dimness of the room.

I opened my mouth again and said, "Send to . . ."

And stopped.

Why am I sending a message to a woman who isn't there?

I think you're lying.

I think you're not there.

"Send to . . .

"Delete."

I must have fallen asleep. When I looked at the clock three hours had passed. What woke me?

Sounds in the street below. I went to the window. Soldiers returning from the front. Cars dropping people off in the lot, then driving away again. I thought I saw Drew. Doc. Someone being taken out of a car on a litter, a bloody bandage wrapped around his middle. Two men in khaki being marched off with a pistol pointed at them. Prisoners. Rockies. Where were they taking them? Jo was there, talking to Drew. Andy. Jo nodded, turned, and walked back to the casino. Her body stiff, held upright by strength alone, I guessed.

I watched for a while. This wasn't everyone, not yet. But things looked under control.

A sound behind me. The door. Someone was at the door. Did they want me to do something, help the soldiers somehow?

Irrational wisps—it was Hannah, coming back to kill me. Newt, enraged because he'd lost his Gullwing. My elbow hurt. My eyes felt crusty, the lids sore. I grabbed my pistol.

"Who's there?"

Another knock, a light rap. Had there been an answer? I hadn't heard one.

"Just a minute."

Would the chain on the door hold? I slid it into the slot and opened the door a crack, feeling like some paranoid old woman from a Twentieth Century movie.

Jo. She stood straight, shoulders back, but the posture was strained. It was an effort for her not to slump. I unhooked the chain, opened the door wide.

She marched in, standing just inside the door, glaring at me. "Owen," she said.

"I heard."

"Did you know?"

I felt heat crawl up my neck, acid and ice in my stomach. "Of course I didn't know! What the hell are you talking about? I told you Newt wasn't telling me everything. Do you honestly think I'd—he kept the important one, the one he was using to—he kept that from me!" I began to cry. I hadn't dried up, after all.

"You should have found out!"

"Yes, I should have."

She watched me for a minute, then she nodded, tears in her own eyes.

"I needed to—I don't know." She didn't hate me, didn't blame me. I felt the ice in my gut melt. She walked the rest of the way in, her body still rigid. I raised my good arm, touching her shoulder. There was no give to it. I stroked it, ran my fingers down her arm. She leaned forward and touched my lips with a tentative kiss. I pulled her closer, she rested her forehead on my shoulder. I rubbed her back for a second and kissed the top of her head. I think I moved toward the bed first.

CHAPTER 39
SPLASHED DOWN, THEY SAY, AND FLOATED FOR A LITTLE WHILE

The sys on the nightstand next to my head was buzzing. How? I hadn't left mine there. It was still in the pocket of my pants. On the floor. Bright sunlight was coming in the window. Something else was buzzing, too, humming, really. Outside somewhere far away.

Next to me, Jo shot upright and reached across me.

The voice coming from her sys was Zack's. The static behind his voice was a much louder and more distinct version of the muffled hum I was hearing through my window. Angry voices. Shouts.

". . . Frank's in there now. Newt won't come out. And I'm not going to hold them much longer. They're really burned. They came back . . ." I couldn't make out his next few words. ". . . and they want more blood." Now I could make out a word, a chant, really, loud and close to Zack.

"Samm! Samm! Samm!"

"I'm going to give the order because they'll do it without one . . ."

His voice stopped.

Jo was out of bed, searching for her clothes.

"I have to go, Rica."

I wasn't sure what was going on, but it sounded like something I'd want to take a look at, too.

We took Jo's floater for the sake of speed, even though Newt's casino was no more than half a mile away. The closer we got the more the sounds took shape: "Samm! Samm! Samm!" We were two blocks away when we saw the smoke. Again?

"Is Lizzie . . . ?"

"I'm sure she's there. But it seems a few other people thought it was a good idea, too."

The crowd was huge, biggest I'd ever seen. There must have been a couple hundred people cheering on the fifty or so who were actively and methodically destroying Scorsi's Luck, fighting their way through a few of Newt's people to do it. Mercs and employees. I didn't see any of the good-for-nothing bandits he thought he was turning into soldiers. I did see Waldo and his girlfriend. Watching the fire, smiling, holding hands. Ugh.

A fire was blazing at the back again. Men and women were hacking away at the windows and doors with clubs and pieces of debris, shooting ancient bullets into the walls, and lasering the carpets and machines and tables.

I spotted Drew, Emmy, and Liz together, and Zack, at his sys, standing next to Frank's sheriff car. Deputy Marty was sitting in the passenger seat. Just sitting. Drew was helping his sister break a big front window. Stupid kids, they could slice an artery that way. A merc was heading their way; I pulled my laser, stuck it through the open car window, and winged him. He wheeled around and ran down the street, screaming. It was like a signal. The mercs still standing took off, too. I didn't think I deserved all the credit for that; they were badly outnumbered.

"Nice shot, Rica!" Jo was grinning at me. It was, too. We jumped out of the car. I didn't know what to do; I wasn't sure what the plan was or if there was a plan at all. I followed Jo, who ran to Zack.

"Frank's on his way out with Newt," he shouted. We were right next to him but I could hardly hear him even so over the sound of crashing glass and crumbling walls and a crowd both gleeful and enraged. "He's the last one in there. Larry and Carl ran fifteen minutes ago. The fire finally did it. Newt's not willing to burn for his casino."

"Where's the rest of his army?" I asked.

Jo answered. "They decided to go to war. Some are dead. Some are prisoners."

I could just see that bunch "going to war." I could only hope they hadn't had a chance to do too much damage. Even more, I hoped none of them were still loose in the countryside.

The fire was moving fast. People were stepping back from the building, now, watching it burn. I was amazed at how many were just standing there in total silence, staring at it. Shocked by their own success? Stunned by their own violence and craziness?

And there was Frank, pushing a handcuffed Newt ahead of him to the car. The close-in crowd cheered and pressed in even closer.

"I didn't do it, you fucking idiot!" Newt was purple in the face, drooling with rage and panic.

"Sure you did," Frank chortled.

"Did what?" I asked.

"Quite a lot of things," Frank answered. "He's being charged with the murder of Mayor Madera and conspiracy to kill Samm and we'll see where it goes from there."

"Kill the bastard!" someone yelled. "He killed Samm!" The crowd surged toward the car. Frank pulled the back door open and shoved Newt in. He didn't have to shove very hard. It was Newt's only haven.

As Frank moved around to the driver's seat, Newt noticed me standing there next to Jo. His mouth dropped open.

I gave him a shrug. What else could I do? Even if I wanted him to think I was still on his side, I couldn't do much to help him. He glared back at me.

"I didn't kill anyone!" he yelled through the closed window. "I didn't kill Madera. I didn't kill Samm! It was those boys! And Hannah!"

I shrugged again. So much for that new float-car he'd promised me.

"Did Ky implicate Newt?" I asked Frank.

Frank sneered. "Ky can't talk yet. His mouth's all mashed up."

It didn't matter. It wasn't like Newt would ever have discouraged anyone from doing what had been done to Samm. Even if Newt hadn't ordered the killings, the boys had murdered Madera because they knew damned well that Newt wanted him gone. All Hannah'd had to do was look like she was working with the Colemans and the boys started to go after her. And Samm? Easy to imagine what Newt said about him at the family dinner table. If they ate at one. I could see Billy kneeling at a dish on the floor. But Billy was dead now.

And then there was Owen. The one he hadn't told me was a spy. No question, Newt was behind the deaths one way or another, as surely as if he'd done it himself. And the chief. For just a second I wondered if I should message her about any of this. A ridiculous thought. Old habit and nothing more. She was no longer involved. She was just sitting in Hangtown and, well, hanging onto her job until the Colemans decided to take it away from her.

I looked at Jo's profile. She was glaring at Newt; the softness of the night before was gone. I wanted to bring it back. I was afraid of how much I wanted that. There was too much power in it. Power that might make me—do what? Not do what?

Newt wasn't the only killer in Tahoe. I liked Zack. I more than liked Jo and her family. But it seemed to me they were getting increasingly casual about the deaths of their enemies, not to mention the niceties of truth and justice. They didn't hesitate to lie or at least push the truth to get support for their growing power. They didn't hesitate to kill if they decided someone deserved it or had to be killed. Sure, this was war. That was what was bothering me. This was war. Kill or be killed. Just as I'd had to kill the sheriff back in Iowa before he killed me. He wasn't the first and wouldn't be the last. And sometimes, it's not so easy to see the difference between really having to do it or doing it because it's a safer bet. Fine lines. Everywhere.

Did I want to be swept up in this? Was any of it right? Was Newt really enough of a threat to the Colemans to justify his destruction and the death of Billy Scorsi? Was Rocky really enough of a threat to justify an alliance that could make something of Redwood I didn't want it to be?

Did I want to even be worrying about fine moral distinctions and wondering where I belonged and who I belonged with? Did I want to be feeling anything for anyone but Gran and the ghost of Sylvia?

No, I did not. Was that my spine stiffening, along with my upper lip, or was I just going rigid with fear at the thought of how much I could get hurt?

A volunteer fire brigade finally showed up, but there wasn't much they could do except protect other buildings near Newt's casino.

A lot of the people who'd destroyed it continued to stand around watching, but a good many of the crowd who'd come to see the violence were bored by the last stages of firefighting and began to drift off toward home.

At some point, as I'd watched Newt get driven away and worn myself out struggling with issues of right and wrong and lust and power, Judith had arrived and Drew and Lizzie had moved in close, Emmy still with them. Drew looked worn, dirty, and angry. Emmy looked distressed. Lizzie looked peaceful, for some reason. Sad. Spent. Maybe the ugly complexity of it all was finally registering. Tim and Fredo arrived. They looked stunned. They nodded to me, I nodded back.

Judith stood gazing at the ruined casino. Somehow, she managed, on that ash- and debris-strewn street, in a royal purple dress, blue shawl drawn against the light breeze, to look like a monarch. And Jo, she had no trouble looking like Judith's in-charge minister of everything.

I didn't want to look at any of it any more. I sketched a little wave toward Jo, got a puzzled glance in response, and turned in the direction of Blackjack. I wanted to walk. Then I wanted to sleep for another hour or two.

It was mid-afternoon when I woke again. My chest felt heavy; guess I'd breathed in too much casino smoke. Jo had not come knocking on my door again.

Gran and her friends in Redwood needed to know what had been going on. The raid by Rocky, and the possibility that some of them had slipped through. The destruction of the Scorsis and what that meant about Coleman power. I had second thoughts about the chief. I decided to give her a quick last report, along with a bill for the time she hadn't paid for yet.

First the chief, and her bill.

"How are you doing, Rica?"

"Just great." Alive, no thanks to her. I told her everything I knew, everything I'd seen. I said nothing about her failure to pass on the information that Jo knew all about me. What good would that have done? She knew that I knew. Maybe she'd decide she owed me for it. "Is there anything you'd still like me to do here?" Like finish investigating the Colemans? "I never did find out if they were skimming." I couldn't help it. There was a sarcastic edge to my voice. We both knew she didn't care.

"No. Never mind."

"Okay. Well, you owe me a balance of eight-hundred fifty re-als."

"Let's make it a thousand reals."

I'd earned it. "Send it to the Redwood address. That's where I'm heading soon."

The conversation with Gran took a little longer. She wanted Macris and Petra to hook into it. I left out the part about Hannah escaping; it was too depressing.

"We'll pass it on."

Macris spoke up. "An alliance with Sierra could offer some interesting possibilities if they didn't swallow us up."

"They probably would," I said.

Everyone was silent for a moment. Then Gran chirped, "Could be interesting. Oh! By the way, something really strange happened, don't know if it has any connection to what's been going on in Sierra."

"Something strange?" What else could happen?

"A plane went down in the Pacific, a white Gullwing. Just offshore at Stinson Beach. Splashed down, they say, and floated for a little while. The pilot swam ashore with help from some residents. A woman. Skinny, tall. Said her landing gear was broken and her plane chute gone."

"Long scar on her face?"

"Nobody mentioned that."

CHAPTER 40
A WAY TO GO HOME

The *Sierra Star* did something the next day I suspected it had never done before: published a one-page extra. Samm's death and Newt's arrest was the main story, the border-war victory number two, and the burning of Scorsi's Luck and Newt's squeals of innocence, a pathetic bottom-of-the-page third.

Iggy Santos couldn't have done better for the Colemans if they paid in advance for ten years of full-page ads. He didn't exactly say the fire was an accident, but he put it this way:

"Soldiers celebrating the victory over Rocky invaders merged yesterday at Scorsi's Luck with an angry crowd protesting the murder of popular Blackjack dealer Samm Bakkar. The demonstrators, demanding the arrest of Newt Scorsi, attacked the casino and somehow, in the melee, a fire started at the back of the building. Firefighters were unable to save it."

That was it, the whole story in a dice cup. Somehow. Demonstrators.

What I'd seen was a defensive army turned into a mob of aggressors. Zack had given his soldiers leave to "celebrate" without the tedious restrictions of law. And Sheriff Frank had done his job.

When the cars had come back with the prisoners, Frank and the army had set up a kind of camp at the Lucky Buck. Tents in the courtyard. I wondered how long they'd be able to keep the Rockies there without some kind of riot erupting. But that wasn't going to be my problem.

Sitting in my room, I shot the screen on my sys and opened the line to channel one. A male face resolved shakily. Fading in and out. He was playing a flute. I muted the sound and sat thinking about my options. Was I compromised as a merc? Probably, at least here on the western end of the continent. I hadn't exactly kept a low profile in Tahoe. Things were happening, armies were moving. People would talk, and talk from Tahoe would spread. Too many people knew too much about me now. Even I knew more about me than I wanted to.

I could still work the back roads of Middle or shadow-of-the dunes villages in Desert, or goad Electra through the snowdrifts in New England. I could take the job in New Orleans.

All so far away. Endless miles away.

Webber Doe's pretty face showed. I punched sound.

". . . turned the invaders back at the border." Fade out. ". . . got a little out of hand in Tahoe when the returning army burned down a casino belonging to a man they said had murdered their general. He's been arrested. Some people think maybe the troops went overboard. Here at home, a sheriff's meeting . . ." Dead air. ". . . long way from the Rocky border, but we'll meet with the Redwood Council and see if there's anything we think we need to do. Next Data from Webber Doe—" I lost it entirely.

A long way from Rocky indeed. What a gang of fools. But at least "some people" back there, whatever that meant, thought the mob action wasn't just a fun party for the troops. Even if Redwood did agree to some kind of alliance with Sierra, eventually, they might remember that and be wary.

Lake Tahoe was hardly a sea, and a raft carrying Samm's floater was hardly a dragon-headed Viking ship, but Jo said that once, when they were kids, Samm had told her that he planned to die as a warrior, and when that happened he wanted a

Viking funeral. So that was what she would give him.

It was dusk, the light waning, pink touching the sky. I watched while Zack drove the floater onto the raft of bound fir logs and set it down on its park pads. Drew said they were afraid the floater, on its own, would sink into the water too fast once the fire hit the hover-set. They wanted it to burn completely.

Lizzie, Drew, Zack, Jo, and Emmy packed the kindling around Samm's shrouded body. Drew had begged for the honor of lighting the pyre. He towed the raft out to the middle of the lake, driving Judith's floater. He was to fire the pitch on a flaming arrow and shoot it back into Samm's car, where the windshield had been broken away, make sure the flames were well started, cut his line, and come back to shore where a crowd had gathered, family at the water's edge, friends at their sides, several hundred citizens behind us. I stood next to Jo. The spectacle was too far away to follow easily, but we saw the arrow arc, saw the kindling catch, saw Drew hover for a moment before he cut back toward shore.

The flames rose to three times the height of the floater. A few of the people cried out, wailed, wept; one woman screamed and fell to the ground. But most of us stood there silent in the dimming daylight, staring at the fire on the water. It took nearly an hour for the raft, the floater, and Samm to sink to the deepest part of the lake.

My sys buzzed. Jo.

"Rica, could you come to my office, please?"

We hadn't talked since earlier that evening, and then only a few words at the funeral. I wondered what she wanted. If she'd simply wanted me, I thought she'd come to my room, or she would have asked me to go to her apartment. I wondered why she hadn't. I wondered why I hadn't made it happen. Her voice stirred me, but from a distance, like a memory. Murder and fire and grief sat between us like a black moat. And lawlessness. I didn't want that kind of lawlessness used against Redwood. I needed to go home.

On the way to her office I passed the poker tables. Emmy was dealing at Samm's table two. We nodded at each other.

Jo was sitting behind her desk. She rose when I walked in, circled it, and gave me a tender kiss on the cheek. I kissed her on the mouth and won a tiny smile.

"Sit down, Rica."

"This sounds serious." We both sat on the couch, a yard apart, facing each other.

She laughed softly. "Everything seems serious. Let me get right to it. I don't think I'll really have time to take a council seat. Zack's going to need help, now that Samm's gone." Her voice broke. "The casino needs running. The campaigns and the policies need work. That's really where I belong. I want you to be the candidate."

That was the last thing I wanted.

"I'm sorry, Jo. I can't do that. I need to go home and see to things there."

Her eyes flickered. "You're leaving?"

"At least for a while." I thought it would be longer than a while. What was that noise out in the parking lot? Sounded like a lot of cars.

"I don't want to lose you, Rica." Her eyes dropped to her folded hands. "I mean I don't want Sierra to lose you. Either." I laughed; she smiled back at me. "So I have another proposal. We need to negotiate an alliance with Redwood. You're the perfect person to serve as our ambassador to San Francisco. Work with us, and with your own people. Make it good for everyone."

I didn't know what to say. Was she really offering me a job in Redwood? How much would I have to say about the relationship between Redwood and Sierra? Could I work for her and still keep the Colemans from setting themselves up as our royal family? A dozen clichés ran through my head. A light at the end of the tunnel. Beware of Colemans bearing gifts. For just a moment, I felt ambivalent about giving up the merc life, the merc freedom. But that feeling passed very quickly.

"I won't just take orders, you know." Even working independently, could I really affect what the Colemans ultimately decided, and were able to do?

She laughed again. "Would it help if I told you another raiding party came across from Rocky this morning?"

"It might help if it was true."

She had the grace to look slightly embarrassed. "It's true. Zack's on his way to the border in about an hour." So that was what was going on outside. The army was gathering again.

"You're going to have to keep troops closer to Rocky."

She nodded. "We're interrogating the prisoners to see if we can find out about crossing points, plans. So far, half of them are singing religious songs and the other half are trying to beat each other up."

"What are you going to do with them when you've finished asking them questions?"

She shrugged. "Try to absorb the ones who are willing to be absorbed. The others?" She shrugged again.

"And you didn't address my last point—I won't just take orders."

"I'm hoping you'll find my orders reasonable. If not, we'll talk about it."

"Or maybe you'll just arrest me?"

"Rica, Rica, Rica." She shook her head.

"Are you going to execute Newt?"

"I doubt it. Maybe we should just send him to Rocky and let him mess things up for them."

She was incorrigible. Adorable. I didn't really care about Newt.

"I'll have to think about it, Jo. And I want to see your proposals for the alliance. You screw with Redwood, I'll make sure they get off their butts and organize to defend themselves."

"I don't think you'll have any trouble supporting us."

I was not at all sure of that. But it was a way to go home, get off the road, do what I could for my country, and earn a living too. Although we hadn't yet talked about how much the job would pay.

"What if I decide to work against you?"

"You won't."

"I'm not sure I want to give up being a merc, you know."

She laughed. "I think you wouldn't mind. A merc, a spy— you're just a hired gun. You can do more. You can do a lot for Redwood. You can be a hero in Redwood's history."

I shot her a sardonic look. "There are no heroes."

She shrugged. "Spoken like a merc."

Restless, unable to sit still on that couch, too close to Jo, I stood and walked to the window. Andy. Zack. Drew. Emmy. As I was watching, Lizzie marched up to stand beside her brother. She had a pistol strapped to her hip. I was glad she wasn't taking Soldier, despite the dog's name.

I turned back around. "You're letting Lizzie fight?"

Jo sighed. "There's no stopping her. She said she'd follow the troops on her own if we didn't let her go with them. Judith's upset. I'm not happy. But I guess she's safer this way."

I leaned back against the sill, arms folded across my chest. I knew I looked defensive but I didn't care.

"I'll visit you, Rica. In Redwood."

"I doubt that. You're going to be pretty busy."

"I'll manage."

"I hope you do. I expect I'll be coming here from time to

time, as well." I'd certainly keep in touch with Tim and Fredo.

We looked at each other. We had a long way to go before we even thought about any alliances other than the one between our countries, and we both knew that.

"You still haven't given me your answer, Rica."

I turned back and looked out the window again. Some of the cars were pulling out of the lot.

"How big is this new raiding party?"

"About the same as the last one. Maybe a little bigger. They seem to be making a slow start. But I've heard fairly reliably that there's real organizing going on and these little forays are just diversions to keep us busy while they build for a real invasion."

"Fairly reliably."

"Fairly. But I don't doubt it."

Neither did I.

I faced her. She stood, walked to her desk, sat down.

"I need your answer, Rica."

She was a busy woman. So was Judith and I was betting she was waiting for my answer, too.

I sat in the guest chair, across the desk, and laid my hands on the polished wooden surface.

"Okay, Jo. How much does the job pay?"

ABOUT THE AUTHOR

Lee Singer lives in Petaluma, California, with her family, which includes people, dogs, and cats. She began her writing career as a reporter in Chicago, where she met many famous people, at least two of whom were murdered. Writing, teaching writing, and consulting about writing take a lot of time, but she plans to get her easel and paints out again sometime soon.

C014334901